What the Clocks Know

Rumer Haven

CROOKED
CAT

*Tweet a photo of yourself holding
this book to @crookedcatbooks
and something nice will happen.*

To London and the Expats

Acknowledgements

Time is a fickle mistress, yet she's been good to me and this story. So, cheers to the years and what the clocks knew that I didn't. I do know now to whom else I'm grateful.

Crooked Cat Publishing, for dusting off this book to show it the light of day! Thank you, Laurence and Stephanie, for welcoming me into the cat's cradle, and Miriam, for your editing expertise. You and this community of authors are truly the cat's meow.

My husband, who initiated the London move that inspired this story. Who'd have guessed when I started scribbling this manuscript as a floundering American expat that it would be published the year we became British citizens. Thank you, Ryan, for giving me the time and space I needed to become what our journey encouraged me to be.

Mom, Dad, and the rest of our family, who made it so damn difficult to leave US soil and keep me crying at O'Hare Departures to this day. It is tremendous to love and be loved that much. Not everyone is blessed with a strong sense of home, but I know where my compass points.

The London expats to whom I dedicate this story, especially (in the order we met) Emily, Jessica, Wendy, Christine, and Kat. You get it, and I'm grateful for all the hours of free therapy.

Bev, Shani, Elizabeth, and Lisa, whose insights helped shape this story at various stages. Gillian, Wendy, and Avril, whose Room to Write workshop in Durham offered warm guidance and support. Thanks as well to those I've never even met: Penelope Farmer and Rumer Godden, whose hauntingly lovely tales gave inspiration; Wordsworth, Whitman, and Yeats, too, for their words and philosophies.

And Charlotte Pidgeon, whose name lives on while she rests in peace.

The Author

Rumer Haven is probably the most social recluse you could ever meet. When she's not babbling her fool head off among friends and family, she's pacified with a good story that she's reading, writing, or revising – or binge-watching something on Netflix. A former teacher hailing from Chicago, she presently lives in London with her husband and probably a ghost or two.

Rumer has always had a penchant for the past and paranormal, which inspires her writing to explore dimensions of time, love, and the soul.

Find Rumer at:
www.rumerhaven.com
@RumerHaven

What the Clocks Know

I

The Soul that rises with us, our life's Star,
Hath had elsewhere its setting,
And cometh from afar:
Not in entire forgetfulness.

from "Ode: Intimations of Immortality in Recollections of
Early Childhood"
~ William Wordsworth (1815)

Prelude

19th-Century London

Though I ought not to mourn, I do.

The weeks shall pass and still shall I wear my bombazine silks. I should hope the dye creeps into the very pigmentation of my skin; oh, that it did count arsenic amongst its ingredients as well! I am already warned to maintain this black grief in privacy, though it is a needless caution; I refuse to quit my apartments after the death of my dear.

How is it that love can harden the most delicate and purest of hearts even when the vice of the streets does not? Love did harden us, and I, yes, I hated whom I loved.

Yet such mourning in its persistence shall be perceived as unnatural. Yes, I should have hardened my heart whilst beating it more tenderly for another far earlier than I had actually allowed; if I had done so, my dear might yet breathe.

Ah! It could have been my hands that closed that fine throat to the air. Algae might well rot beneath my fingernails as blackened green ropes of weed drape from my forearms and drip regret into a hopeless puddle at my feet.

I still see you, dear, as you were, before the reeds and filth tangled in your curls. I yet feel the course texture of your palm against my cheek, across my mouth. Life had roughened you so on the outside, and yet you had remained so fragile, as soft within as your pale skin in the moonlight. The price we could have paid.

The price we *did* pay.

Chapter One

An Old Soul

21st-Century Chicago

"You were born old."

At the familiar words, Margot snapped into the present. "What?"

"I mean, maybe travel back in time and use these pennies to buy yourself a clue, huh?" Sylvie held up a pair of penny loafers.

"That would be awesome, very Marty McFly," Derek chimed in as he sifted through photographs in a shoebox.

It was one of those sick-humored weeks in April that buried Chicagoland in snow, one last time to kill everyone's spirits before they dared pack their winter clothes away. For lack of anything better to do outside that weekend, Margot's fellow single friends sat with her on the floor of her childhood bedroom. Derek had been Margot's buddy since high school, and Sylvie wore the crown as Last Sorority Friend Standing. Together, they'd been helping to clear out Margot's old pack-rat closet so she could have some storage space as a successful twenty-something already on the brink of unemployment and moving back in with her parents.

"She actually put pennies in them," Sylvie murmured out the side of her mouth. She held the shiny, penny-filled burgundy shoes up for Derek before lowering them to give the black pair in her other hand center stage. Silver glinted through slits in the onyx leather like waking evil eyes.

"No," he said, and Margot winced, knowing he'd seen them, too.

"Yes," Sylvie said with brows raised. "Dimes."

Margot shrugged. "The silver matched better."

"Matched what, your tiara for the Enchantment Under the Sea dance?" A second later, Derek *oof*ed from a well-aimed combat boot to his groin. "Okay, these redeem you. Though I'm not sure how the same person rocked both looks. You're the most Goth preppie I've ever met."

With a grunt, Margot fished the other boot out from the bottom of a plastic crate and assessed its condition.

"The one thing about *Back to the Future* that never sat well with me," said Sylvie, "was that Marty McFly only gives himself five extra minutes to rescue Doc from the Libyans. I mean, you have a time machine at your disposal, you just went back thirty years, why be frugal with time now?"

"Good point," Derek said. "But is that really the *one* thing that bothers you? Not that Marty makes out with his mom or so obviously lip-syncs to 'Johnny Be Good' at the dance? Or that his girlfriend Jennifer is an entirely different actress in the sequel?"

Margot nodded without humor as she smoothed her thumb over a scuff in the boot's oiled leather. A few eye floaters glided in front of it, and she zoned out again as her ears crackled like her altitude had changed.

"If you need to talk about it, Margot," she heard Sylvie say.

"Yeah," Derek said. "We're better at listening than making any order of this shit. Sorry, sentimental shit."

Margot exhaled and tossed the heavy boot next to her loafers. "I wasn't thinking about him. But now that you bring it up…" She faked a quivering lip.

Sylvie cocked her head at Margot's little performance. "Really, though. You okay?"

"I think so. Still feel like I'm going through the motions, though, when inside I feel so…like…" She looked off as if she could see a dimension her friends couldn't. "Erratic."

"To this day I can't believe you threw a drink in his face," Derek said as he flipped through a middle school

8

yearbook. "Classic."

It *was* classic. Something right out of those smoky late-night film noirs that Margot loved. She'd always wanted to do that to someone. Only when she had, though, did she realize how much it sucked to have a good excuse to.

"I just couldn't take it anymore. Ever since we graduated, James has been like a puppy chasing after anything shiny." She chucked a cracked CD case into the designated 'Discard' pile. "I mean, Zurich? Why the hell was he all of a sudden interviewing in *Switzerland* and informing me after the fact? Shouldn't I be clued in on these decisions if it means packing up my life, too? Or not, and then having to fly ten freaking hours to see him? As if the two to New York hadn't already been an issue."

"It was a lot to ask without more of a commitment," Sylvie said. "At a point when he *should've* been committing. You're better off."

Margot stared at the old sorority T-shirts stacked on Sylvie's lap. "Knew I never should've dated a frat guy." She deepened her voice to dumb-jock tone to quote her college sweetheart: "*I've got to do this while I'm young, you know? We've got the rest of our lives to settle down.*"

Sylvie shook her head as she folded the cotton shirts. "Shame how the word *settle* holds such different ideas of contentment for different people." She tapped a hand on Margot's knee. "But it seems like you're getting to a much better place, lady."

"Aw, thanks, love." With joking sentiment, Margot signed their sorority symbol with her fingers – something that could've been considered vulgar out of context, which both women vindictively adored. To her further relief, Derek changed the subject.

"Do you want to store this one with your childhood stuff?" He held up a hardcover copy of *Charlotte Sometimes*.

"Oh, that's actually new. My crap from the condo must be getting mixed in with this mess."

"Never read it," he said. "Have anything to do with the

9

Cure song?"

"Must. A lot of those lyrics sound straight from it." Much as she loved The Cure, though, and their haunting musical rendering of "Charlotte Sometimes," Margot had bought the book the other day because, scanning the store shelves out of the sheer luxury of searching for nothing in particular, this one had tripped her eyes up cold.

Charlotte. The name held tip-of-the-tongue recognition for her, something both so obvious and so evasive that she'd bought the book assuming it was only a matter of time when she'd make the connection. She still hadn't.

"I remember reading it for one of my YA lit classes," Sylvie said. "The two British boarding school girls, right?"

"Yeah, Charlotte and Clare." For Derek's benefit, Margot added, "They're the same age and attend the same school, but one is there forty years after the other. Somehow they time-travel and swap lives overnight, and keep switching identities back and forth like that."

"And they write in a notebook that exists in *both* times," Sylvie said, "to keep each other informed on what's happening in their real lives. Or have you not gotten to that part yet?"

"I have, but what drives me batty is how objectively they keep it to day-to-day updates. Wouldn't it be more like, 'What the bloody fuck is happening? I piss my knickers each time I wake up here!'" Her friends laughed. "But who am I to criticize a classic when I've only written copy for local business ads. Must remember to shine my Pulitzer tomorrow."

Even Margot had to admit her work hadn't been enough of an excuse to not relocate with James to Zurich; she just resented his presumption of that fact. Quitting her job had to be on her own terms. Which it had been as of a few weeks ago, as soon as she'd received her acceptance into a London business school program.

"Speaking of," Derek said, "how'd they take your news at the office?"

"Surprisingly well. Doesn't put them into that huge a

bind. I mean, I gave plenty of notice and am tying up all my current projects. Someone new can easily take on whatever's in the pipeline."

"Don't talk like you're so dispensable," Sylvie said.

"It's not that. I just think they respect my decision."

She'd never been passionate about her day job at the advertising agency but still worked hard as any good girl with a good work ethic ought to. Yet these days she just couldn't muster the concentration; ever since the breakup a few months ago, she'd been phoning it in, still excusing herself most days from lunch with the group to eat alone in the stairwell. She didn't feel like herself, and her art director's sarcasm no longer rolled off her shoulder.

"I may be mistaken," she said, "but my director has been a little slower turning around the wise-ass commentary on my pitches."

"Bastard," Derek and Sylvie both said.

"Nah, he means well. I have faith that deep down he's not such a tool. Maybe he's realized he's going to miss me and is melancholy."

"Maybe he's realized you're exporting yourself out of the country and is ecstatic."

"Bastard!" Sylvie repeated.

"No, he *should* be excited about having someone with a fresh outlook on the team. I've been complacent. But the travel and coursework will hopefully revive me, and our boss got all schmaltzy, putting her hand on my shoulder and reminiscing over some year she 'thought about' studying abroad, too. So she's considering it a leave of absence for professional development and giving me my job back afterward if I want it."

"No shit, really," Derek said. "That's awesome. And rare, you do realize." His last words embodied all the cynicism of an aspiring musician who temped by day and struggled to find gigs by night.

"Not that I want to come full circle like that, but, hell yeah, I know. Oh, and I recently scored another nice safety net in London, actually. An old work buddy's letting me crash with him. Rand."

Sylvie frowned. "Is that his last name? Doesn't ring a bell."

Margot shook her head. "Short for Randolph. He's a Brit who worked with me a couple years before moving back to the UK. He was senior to me and sort of a mentor. I only emailed to let him know I'd be in town for a little while, figuring we could grab a drink sometime at his favorite haunt, and he ended up insisting I stay the entire summer at his place for super-cheap. Actually, he offered it up for free, but I refuse to take advantage."

"Oh, now you're just makin' this stuff up."

"Someone's hot for Margot," Sylvie sang.

"Hey, maybe it's just some of the good karma I've sent into the world finally coming back. Everything happens for a reason, right?"

When her friends only shrugged in response, she glanced at the next relic to surface in the closet. A smirk slowly spread across one side of her face, and she reached for the old box.

"Ouija, anyone?"

"You're shitting me," Derek said, though his eyes betrayed a childlike awe.

"Back off, Captain Condescending. It was George's, and I've never even played it. As a kid, I just claimed anything Big Brother abandoned as treasure."

Sylvie nodded with eyes squinted as though seeing the universe with clarity. "That would explain the Chinese stars and nunchucks."

"Yeah, in case you thought I nurtured sadomasochistic tendencies at an early age." Pause. "At *any* age."

"Thanks for qualifying that." Sylvie looked at Derek. "I've never played with a spirit board either. Have you?"

"I might have attempted it…once." He pinched at the raven tattoo on his bicep. "Remember?" he asked Margot, but she knit her brow. "That one night at Ian's during the teachers' strike junior year? No, wait, you'd left already because you weren't interested in getting shitfaced like the awesome rest of us. But do you remember how his subdivision backed up to that cemetery?"

"The one that had that sign, *Drive Carefully. We Can Wait?*"

"Terrible," Sylvie said despite her wicked smile.

"Well, we tried playing that night, on one of the graves. Just a stranger's, don't look at me that way! We didn't even do it. Just left and played Corn Tag in those fields up the road. But I remember how we were all paranoid over every sound we heard in Ian's basement afterward. Although, in retrospect, that was probably the pot talkin'."

"You smoked pot in high school?"

His raised brow screamed, *Duh!*

Okay, Margot should've figured that. Still, she slouched. "Why didn't you ever invite me?"

Dropping his gaze to the floor, he shrugged and picked at his thumb. "You were a righteous babe I always wanted to impress. Not to mention a *self*-righteous one." He looked to Sylvie. "Sandra Dee passed on grass. And a lotta things, apparently."

"It's not like I was the only one who didn't substance-abuse."

"That, or..."

"What? Put out?"

"How about *go* out. Like on a single date."

"Not true."

"Fine. But if the one with Ian is anything to go by, at the end of that night, you jumped out the door like a stunt double before he could even stop his car in your driveway, let alone walk you to your front porch for a goodnight kiss." He choked on a laugh.

"Yeah, it happened exactly like that." Margot snapped a pink, penguin-shaped rubber band at him from the rainbow-colored menagerie she'd just dumped from an old backpack. "So, what, everyone thought I was this big prude? I mean, 'self-righteous'? You think I acted like I was better than everyone else?"

"No, but..."

Fine ice cracked underfoot, and Margot squared her shoulders a degree.

"I think I know what he means," Sylvie hesitantly offered, then cowered when Margot shot her a look. "Just hear me out. It's not that you're prude or arrogant or anything, just that you've always set high expectations for yourself." In a slurring flurry, she added, "Whichisagoodthing!"

Nodding, Derek said, "She aced all her honors classes and talked about getting her MBA before she even had a high school diploma."

Margot straightened her spine, suddenly feeling like a microbe flattened between two glass slides. *"You were born old."* Her Grandma Grace had always told her that, too. But until now, Margot hadn't really thought about what it meant, only hoped she hadn't started life out with one foot already in the grave.

"Yep, forever studious," Sylvie said. "We'd give her such a hard time in college when she wouldn't come out to exchanges with us because she thought they were obnoxious and boring and welcomed the quiet time alone to read. And you *know* you still do that."

"Blow off frat parties?" Margot asked flatly.

"No, but us girls whenever we try to get you out, especially since you moved back out here to the 'burbs. And for the flakiest reasons."

"Who wants to drink high-fructose cocktails in a strip-mall?"

"Okay, *James*," Sylvie said.

Margot dropped her shoulders. "Fine, so maybe I'm antisocial."

"No, you can absolutely be the center of attention when you want to. Like when we got back from those parties and you'd ambush us with the squirty bird in the house foyer, yelling, 'Sober up, sluts!'"

Both girls slumped in laughter.

"Holy shit, I forgot about that thing!"

"Think it's in the closet?"

"Likely!"

Derek didn't ask for backstory, just expressed hope it was only water that made this bird 'squirty' should he ever find himself in its crosshairs.

Sylvie fanned her wet eyes. "You're such a dork, Margot."

"Which is why her homecoming-court ass ever gave the time o' day to the likes of me in the first place," Derek said.

Margot pished at the blatant ass-covering, ass-*kissing* going on, especially when her friends kept speaking in the past tense as if she were dead, and high school and college had been her only glory days. It begged the question what she'd achieved since then, what she had going for her now.

"You're like the whole Breakfast Club rolled into one," Derek continued. "That makes for popularity."

"Or multiple personality disorder."

"Huh." Sylvie summarized as she counted on her fingers: "The honors student who made homecoming court. The sorority girl who hated frat guys. And now the yuppie who renounces job and possessions."

"Does that make me an oxymoron or just a moron?"

"Stop," Sylvie said. "This change you're undertaking is surprisingly spontaneous of you, and *that* is good. Just know you don't have to do everything on your own." After a pause, she added with a smile, "And if all goes to pot, there's always the vintage shop."

"What vintage shop?" Derek asked.

But Sylvie didn't explain, and Margot only smiled. "Right." She slapped her lap. "Enough tangents. You've given me quite the love fest, kids, but don't try so hard. I'm fine."

They looked half-convinced but didn't put up a fight as she started unpacking the game board.

"Are we playing this, or what?"

The Ouija session began straightforwardly enough. Derek initiated the séance by questioning whether there was indeed a spirit present that would like to communicate with three mortals. None were surprised to see the plastic indicator skid toward the calligraphic *Yes*, and a ghostly "Wooo!" or two infused their chuckles.

The game was on.

Straight away, the trio learned that, *Yes*, it was a good spirit, *No*, it wasn't a male, and, for good measure, *Yes*, it was female.

Warming up to the ritual, Sylvie clapped. "My turn!" Her toothy smile radiated rainbows and kittens; no wonder children gravitated toward her Story Hour in throngs at the public library. She boldly asked how the specter had passed away.

The planchette didn't budge.

Again, Sylvie prompted, "How did you die?" Nothing. She pouted. "I'm not good at this."

"C'mon, neither of you can come up with a reason?" Margot accused, and the game's typical argument ensued, with each of the three blaming the indicator's movement on the other two. And every one of them denying it.

They opted for a less open-ended question – "How old are you?" – so that someone could think up a quick answer. The triangular plastic nudged to the lower-left quadrant of the board until *2* was visible through its circular window. Then, with some friction, the device tugged their limbs toward the right in a non-linear path; it reached a point where it faltered and subtly wavered around the *6*. After dawdling there for a few seconds, the energy lost strength and stopped.

Margot shifted, unnerved that she'd just celebrated that same birthday. "Huh. When did you die, then?"

Nothing happened.

"You guys wanna skirt around that topic, don't ya?" she asked, trying to lighten the mood in a literally darkening environment, to which Sylvie replied they might say the same of her.

"Fine, we'll sidestep the D word, Miss Eggshells," Derek sassed at the ghost, "and do the math ourselves. When were you born?"

1.

Then, zigzagging to the right with less conviction, the plastic planchette ultimately settled on *8* and powered out.

"Eighteen," Sylvie contemplated. "That could mean the eighteen hundreds. Or the *last* two digits of the year, which could be in any century."

"Or just one and eight," Margot said, "as in any of the four digits in the year."

"Or it's a month and date: January eighth or August first," Derek offered. "Or the eighteenth of some month. If we really stretch, it could be the eighteenth hour in military time, too. So, like, six p.m."

"Let's get some clarification." Clearing her throat, Margot asked, "Is that your time of birth?"

No.

"Your date of birth?"

No.

"Your time of death?"

Nothing.

The pause lasted nearly half a minute, and Margot assumed their session had ended. But she followed the others' cue and resisted talking, just in case.

Their darting glances still carried suspicion, though. Who was moving the planchette, and would they do it again, one last time for some closure? Margot knew they were all curious how at least one of them would continue weaving this fictitious life story. It was the death story, though, that she wanted *someone* to tell, be who or what it may.

Casting a wary eye at her companions, she noticed how the shadows of trees genuflected across Derek's features. Sylvie kneeled across from him with her back to the window, her head crowned with a dull halo of sunlight from behind. Sitting adjacent to both, Margot had knotted her legs into a lotus position and could feel the contrast in her face's temperature between illuminated and shadowed halves.

There was a small intake of breath, which drew her eyes back to the board.

The planchette had twitched back to life.

It circled an etching of the moon twice before settling back on *No*, where it gained momentum and vacillated so fervently it might have scraped away the board's surface had it continued more than a few seconds. Instead, it drifted down to *I*, then *L*, back to *I*, then sank a centimeter, where the tops of both the *U* and *V* sprouted into view through the clear lens.

During a pause, Sylvie twisted and reached an arm behind her for the pen and paper she'd used earlier to itemize the storage boxes. Margot nodded her kudos as Sylvie recorded letter for letter with her free hand, labeling the *U* and *V* with a question mark and using a slash to mark the pause.

In the meantime, the planchette had made its way back to the crescent moon, resting there for a while until slowly dragging to the far left, dwelling around that side of the alphabet.

BOO, Sylvie wrote with a heavy exhale and eye roll at this predictable reply from a ghost, and Margot half-expected a white cotton sheet with eyeholes to materialize at any moment to reinforce the corny image. Yet the plastic hadn't stopped moving beneath their fingertips.

I, N, G. Pause. *P, A, L, E, R.* Pause. *O, R, C, H, I, D.* Finally, it stopped spelling but dragged back up to the moon.

In the quiet, Margot stared at the little etching of the moon nesting in a puff of dark clouds. Her chest tightened with a keen sense of familiarity, and, trying to place it, her mind wandered its way back to her Grandma Grace and this gaudy yet amazing brooch she'd given Margot years ago – a large pearl set in a cluster of sapphire and turquoise stones that she always thought looked like the night sky. She wondered if maybe she'd find that brooch somewhere in her closet. In her nostalgia, her muscles relaxed and allowed the pads of her fingers to lie more passively on the planchette.

The activity picked up in intensity after that, leaving Sylvie with three more words to add to her notes as the grand finale:

I M / O P E N D I G / H E A R T C L O T

Derek shattered the stillness by flicking the plastic indicator off the board, which he then clapped shut with a "See ya!" Sylvie exaggeratedly trembled like she had the heebie-jeebies and bolted straight for the light switch. Margot sat in serenity.

Returning to her spot on the floor, Sylvie twiddled the pen between her fingers. "Why don't we debrief here."

"Well," Derek started, "we apparently dealt with a self-proclaimed benevolent female spirit, who is stubbornly tight-lipped when it comes to the details of her death yet has no qualms talking about her age. Which makes me doubt the truth of her gender, by the way, being so open with *that* info. But anyway, she's twenty-six—"

"Or sixty-two," Margot said. "In case it was transmitted out of sequence."

"Fine. She's twenty-six or sixty-two, but we don't know if the eighteen could be eighty-one or if it's the century, year, month, day, or hour – or minutes or seconds, for all we know – as far as when she was born."

"Aw, we never asked for her name!" Sylvie lamented, personable to the last.

"She might've given it to us in all that mumbo-jumbo at the end," Margot said. "Read that back to us, Sylvie. I stopped keeping track."

"Well, first of all, before I started writing anything down, there was that weird thing with the moon and the *No*. What's with that?"

"No kidding," Margot said. "What's the deal almost ruining the board? Have some respect for my brother's old crap."

"For the last damn time," Derek said, "*it wasn't me.*"

"*Me neither!*" the women groaned.

"I don't know," Sylvie said, "but when it was doing that back-and-forth, back-and-forth, it kind of reminded me of the kids at the library who'll launch into these raging tantrums. Like if their mom is making them check out a different book than what they want or making them leave without anything because they're being such brats. They'll just sit there and scream, 'No, no, no, *no*, *NO!*'" Her effective impression convinced Margot that Little Girl Sylvie had surely brought down her parents' roof with similar theatrics. "You know what I mean?"

"Yeah, you're right," Margot said. "It actually *felt* that way, too. Very insistent. But about what? We hadn't asked anything, had we?"

Derek looked up as if to find the memory in his eyebrows. "We'd asked about her death again, so it could've been a delayed answer to that."

Sylvie bit the tip of her pen cap. "Maaaybe, just maybe she doesn't *know* she's dead. Couldn't that be why she was here in the first place? If she really was."

"Ahh," Derek and Margot both mused.

"All right," Margot said, "I'm satisfied with that. Now back to the notes."

Sylvie sucked at her pen as she read off her paper. "Okay. There was that one time it got stuck between the U and V. But…if we assume it was V, then it almost spells out *I live*. Ha! Validation!"

"Creeeepy," was all Derek offered up.

Margot leaned closer to Sylvie to read ahead on the page.

"Then there was *boo*." Sylvie's voice rose as though her statement were a question. "But then I, N, G, so maybe it's the action of boo*ing*. That's a weird thing to say. So is *paler orchid*."

This opened much speculation:

"Maybe pale-colored orchids were her favorite flower."

"Maybe pale orchids were on her grave."

"Maybe she was im*pale*d by an orchid, and that's how she died."

"Unfortunate accident?"

"Nope. Murder."

"Interesting coroner's report."

"I suspect: Colonel Mustard. In the Conservatory. With the Orchid."

"All right, all right," Sylvie interjected. "Back to our very serious and professional paranormal investigation here. We're truth seekers! Lest we forget!" She punched a fist into the air, then laughed at herself. "Okay, so the last stuff I got was this…" and she just let them read for themselves to make of it what they could.

"I-M? What, was she text-messaging us?"

"The Victorians chose not to clutter the talking board with punctuation marks, dear Derek," Margot said. "If the majority of modern mankind can't give a rat's ass for correct grammar either, why should the supernatural be burdened? I say we let Vanna grant her a free apostrophe up on the board or let her buy a vowel to solve this one as *I am* to win the Acapulco vacation and advance to the Bonus Round."

"No freebies, not even for the deceased."

"Guys, two more words here. Can you just concentrate so we can wrap this up?" Sylvie pleaded in the waning light.

The sleuths recommenced their powers of deduction:

"Looks like they can be broken up into *open dig* and *heart clot*."

"Ew. Maybe *open dig* refers to her grave."

"She was dug up."

"Or dug her*self* out."

"And *heart clot* is cause of death."

"That trumps your orchid theory, Derek," Sylvie said.

"Not if it's the orchid that clogged the artery."

"I'm thinking even if it were possible for a plant stem to stab through your heart, a 'clot' would hardly be the way to describe it."

"Like when they say it's lack of oxygen to the brain that really kills you," Margot added, "but 'cause of death' is classified as what stopped the supply in the first place."

"The chicken and the egg."

Derek furrowed his brow at Sylvie. "Do you get how analogies work? You're a gatekeeper to literacy, for fuck's sake."

"Do *you* want your autopsy to read, 'Cause of death:

21

Strangulation after Ouija?'"

"Hey, it'd be documented that you participated, too, so you'd be the one *living* in humiliation. After your arrest, that is."

"Don't worry, Derek. When she's tried for your murder, she can just blame the evil powers we invited in. Maybe get off on temporary insanity."

"Oh, I don't want to think about evil after we've already played it!" Sylvie said. "It's dusk, for cripes sake. The undead love this time of day."

"That's right," Margot said, "and that's why Santa – an anagram of *Satan*, mind you – gave it to my brother, so our family could be damned and wreaking of feces our entire mortal lives. Haven't you noticed?"

"I just figured it's your natural musk," Derek said.

Sylvie reached for the box cover, then tilted her head and raised a finger to her chin. "Amazing how they can mass-produce paranormal portals to the dead."

Derek snorted. "Yeah, makes you wonder what could've crept into the Monopoly boards at the warehouse. Maybe all the little green plastic houses are haunted."

"I have no *Clue*. But that's the *Risk* one takes, I suppose. Ho-ho," Margot guffawed.

"What, do you script this stuff in advance?" he asked.

"The Ouija compels me, mwahaha!"

"Anyway, your plea in court won't hold, Sylvie. The spirit said she was good, and we made our peaceful goodbyes. As long as you do that, no ghosts can haunt or possess you."

"Hardy-har."

Margot glanced out the paneled window to see the sun shimmering through blackened branches; its low angle cast a faded film on the screen that made a sepia photograph of the deadened yard outside. A chill gripped her spine, and she sat upright, rigid. "I don't remember saying goodbye, though, do you?"

"Well, do we have to actually say it?" Derek asked. "Shouldn't the ghost bear the burden of responsibility?"

Sylvie huffed. "Do you invite guests over for a party just to let them see themselves out as you sit on your inhospitable ass?"

"Absolutely. Here's your hat, what's your hurry?"

"Host with the Most."

"Thank you, and she's Ghost with the Most for understanding."

Margot leaned over to snatch the brittle playing instructions from the Ouija box. "How pathetic that paper printed in our generation is already yellowing." She murmured a stream of directions, skimming for something relevant. "Doesn't say anything about ending the game, just protocol for asking questions."

"Guess we have nothing to worry about, then." Sylvie shrugged and, packing up the game as they'd found it, checked with Margot for her final sorting task. "So where does this belong?"

"Eh, the Discard pile."

Chapter Two

Dear Diary

Left alone in the center of closet clutter, Margot continued enforcing method on the madness lingering in her friends' wake. Still no sign of Grandma Grace's brooch, though. As she heaved a sigh, her bedroom door opened with a creak.

"Hel-lo," she sang with high-low inflection.

"Hel-lo," a disembodied voice replied, but with an intonation that asked, *How ya doin'?*

Without looking up from where her cheek rested in her palm, Margot said, "I'm o-kay."

"Yup, sounds like it."

A pair of black cotton slacks passed her peripheral vision before she felt a hand caress up and down her back.

"Oh, honey," her mom said. "This, too, shall pass."

The tears Margot had been trying to hold in slid down into her hand. She sniffed back liquid snot.

"Margot, what is it?"

Digging her voice out from the lump containing it like a raging fist, she sputtered in an octave higher than normal, "Everything!"

"James? Your job? Or is it leaving home for a while?"

"All of it. I don't know!"

"Honey." Her mother's strokes became firmer as if kneading all the pain of the world out of Margot's back. "I think it's just a lot of change at once. You'll get adjusted, wait and see. And you never know, you might end up finding something that makes you happy in London and stay there."

At this, her mom's face broke into a trembling struggle to

maintain composure, which looked comical and heartachingly sweet at once. Margot knew the woman was maternal to the end for both her children, just as her dad was their great protector. They were each other's biggest fans, and not one member of their family of four (or six, including George's wife and daughter) was about to apologize for that.

"Just remember when you're over there this summer," her mom said, sniffing as she glanced out the darkened window, "that when you look at the moon, I'll be looking at it, too."

Margot didn't have the heart to point out the six-hour time difference that would narrow the odds on that. She just wiped her nose on the dishtowel her mom had carried in and grappled with the full weight of the breakup as it finally hit her.

Her weekend with James had otherwise been going so well. Every Chicago-to-New York visit had been one more for Margot to count down toward ending their cycle of honeymoon hellos and grieving goodbyes. Seated at a tapas restaurant near James's Tribeca apartment on that frigid yet fun January night, she'd hoped, as always, that her smiling interest in his work stories would reinforce her devotion to him. Perhaps inspire him to reciprocate, to understand the consequences his decisions had for her, too, and be willing to sacrifice in kind. Soon.

And she'd felt certain he was closer to breakthrough until he'd opened his mouth.

"I won't work like this the rest of my life. The idea is to suck it up now and retire early, you know?"

In lieu of answering, Margot just stared at the wedge of Spanish omelet on his plate and almost hoped it would food-poison him.

"All our friends've settled into their typical lives," he chattered on, "just waiting to die on the same spot they were born. Those guys're still hangin' out with the same people at the same bars, pickin' up the same kind of chicks,

25

or getting married, and then when can they get away once they have kids? Their big night out'll be all-you-can-eat breadsticks and free pop refills. While we're eating tapas like this in Spain or," he raised his wine glass, "drinking Pinot Noir in France."

Margot set her jaw as he signaled her to toast that fine projection of European life with him. Clenched her teeth as she stopped mutilating her patatas bravas with her fork and pinched the stem of her glass instead. As she lifted it from the ivory tablecloth that would be rouged in a vintage 2006 ricocheting off James's handsome features seconds later.

That shut him up at least. He sat motionless and wide-eyed, other than blinking away the alcohol that surely stung as the red streaked down his face. The mouths of other patrons gaped open, and an older gentleman called for a waiter's assistance while his young trophy date giggled. A bit frozen herself as time seemed to stand still, Margot then did the first thing she could think of.

She ran.

Tick-tick tap-tap-tick *went her stilettos on the subway-steamed pavement as she stomped away from that SoHo restaurant. She couldn't hear over the tapping if James was following her at first, just tried to pace her breathing as her shoes* tap-tap-tick*ed with the same clockwork monotony as his thumbs on his smartphone keypad – the usual rhythm of his deals moving forward while the gears of her inner mechanism rusted to a stop. Clutching the lapels of her wool coat around her neck, she wanted to keep going until she reached the very tip of that neurotic little island.*

But there really was no other sound of footfall, no one calling her name in pursuit. Only the ghoulish wisps of her cold breath trailed behind, chastising her for striking off into the night alone with no game plan.

At least running away meant she wasn't following. And she would've had to follow him this time. No more sucking on her pride like a sour sweet instead of swallowing it. No more refusing like two years before when James had already foregone her and Chicago for Manhattan's greener pastures, fertilized in bullshit.

Rounding the corner, Margot had *tick-tick-tick*ed her way through the first revolving door she'd found before booking a room for that night and a flight the next morning. When she'd wheeled her suitcase back into her Chicago condo for the last time, though, she still felt his presence within its walls. They owned the Lincoln Park property together, so there would always be that daily connection with him. But what could've once been their love nest had only ever been his nest *egg* – a home for Margot, an investment for him. And while she'd covered the monthly mortgage on her own, with James annually paying down the principal and property taxes, she'd still felt like the Kept Woman – and that was as his girlfriend. As his ex, she just felt like a tenant.

Parting ways with James had made it clear Margot needed to live life on different terms. In a different place. So she'd chosen England as a safely adventurous place to start. She spoke the language, after all, and a student visa seemed easy enough to obtain to test the international waters with a summer study program.

In the meantime, she'd cleanly broken ties by moving out of the condo and back in with her parents, at least until she found her footing again. And now after signing a tenant to take her place, asking James to buy out her share, and officially vacating the premises to re-inhabit her childhood home, the reality of her chosen path closed in on her.

"You have to know that your father and I are proud of you no matter what," her mom said. "This pressure you always put on yourself, it doesn't come from us."

"I know. And I promise, I'm coming back. I am."

"And you're sure you can trust this Randy character?"

"Rand. And of course."

"He's an older man, isn't he?"

"By like five years, Mom. And he's serious with someone."

"Well…"

Margot turned to hug the padded frame that adjusted so

readily to her contours like an orthopedic mattress. The two women sniffed and snorted their faces to dryness, then set to work, seated there on the floor boxing items that told the story of a life, Margot's life. So far. The myopic vision of what would happen next seemed to blur the corners of the room beyond that closet.

All Margot knew was that she didn't want to jump into a relationship with someone else for a while. She didn't want to belong to anyone, just wanted to be herself and live with purpose. But who *was* she, exactly? And was she doing anything purposeful, really?

What, by saving lives one low-budget ad at a time?

She snapped herself out of it by reaching into her closet for a notebook that caught her eye. Oversized and loopy handwriting decorated its creased front, along with a dozen smiley-faces blurred by a grape juice stain. *My 6th Grade Journal*, the cover read.

"Oh, for gosh sakes. You kept that?" her mom asked as she hoisted herself up. "Always a writer."

"Always a dreamer. Geez." Staying on the floor with the notebook, Margot propped her knee up to use as a chin-rest. Ever since she was a kid, she'd found solace sitting this way, assuming it was how she'd been positioned in the womb.

"What're you talking about? It's great you keep writing life down."

"Yeah, well, doubt my memoirs will be published anytime soon." In fact, rather than bother with personal anecdotes anymore, she mainly recorded random thoughts and dreams these days, in case they'd inspire ad ideas.

Her mom swatted the air. "You've led a plenty interesting life, and it's only beginning." She was about to leave the room when she instead fixed an eye on her daughter and a hand on her hip, fisting the dishtowel like a weapon she wasn't afraid to use. "But I think this week we should get goin' on those cooking lessons, little missy."

Margot frowned. "Bah."

"I mean it. Even a modern woman should know how to

make a pot roast. You can't expect Rand to feed you, and I don't want you eating fish and chips at the pubs every night."

"Yeah, as if that's all the British eat. And even if I had the desire to cook, I wouldn't make pot roast. Or meat loaf." Margot shuddered with a mock dry heave. "What a gross word pairing: a *loaf* of *meat*."

"I'm just saying. You don't have to reinvent the wheel. I'll give you easy recipes. I find that if I leave a thawed chicken…"

The rest may well have been the trumpeted *wah-wah-wahs* of Charlie Brown's schoolteacher for as much as Margot took in the culinary-speak. She nodded and made eye contact frequently enough to pass for paying attention until showing her own savvy.

"*I* find that if I take a steak knife and pierce the plastic film of a frozen dinner two, maybe three times and set the microwave to four minutes…" She trailed off as the point was taken and her mom finally walked away to finish preparing dinner.

"Wisenheimer," she called back without turning around.

Margot supposed she was a product of her generation. One that didn't have to follow traditional gender roles or win any little league games to still get a trophy. Granted, the Credit Crunch had taught the new dogs some old tricks in austerity and work ethic. Margot had been among the lucky to still score employment right out of college and buckled down when others had bided their time with grad school, travel, or part-time jobs. Yet the easy money and opportunity of the Dot-Com bubble before them had left its legacy – the desire to hop off the corporate ladder and climb the rungs of Maslow's hierarchy instead, to reach the pinnacle of self-actualization whether anyone could afford to anymore or not.

People like James might stay married to their jobs, put in the hours and let their careers define them, but Margot was through with doing what she thought she was *supposed* to. She knew she was young, but she'd already worked hard and wanted what was due: life, independence…to run forward and not let anyone hold her back.

It's payday, she declared.

As if to prove to herself what a long way she'd come, she looked back at her sixth grade journal. Of all the items she and her friends had packed, stored, or discarded, this one was definitely a keeper. She flipped through its pages and grinned at how she'd written in a different color of ink each day. Tucking herself into the comforting blanket of the past, she read from the beginning.

August 26

My teacher Mrs. Nelson is really nice. I'm going to have a great year! My class is okay. Mrs. McGregor is our lunchlady. She's pretty cool. The F.B. Timer has to time the fruit break for ten minutes. Then he has to yell, "Fruit Break is over!!" And we get nemos. Nemo stands for NElson MOney. With nemos, you can buy permision to do certain things. If you do something bad you have to pay some nemos for punishment.

Well that's all the interesting stuff, so this ends my journal for today.

She snorted at her misspellings, the clumsy cursive, and what she'd once considered 'interesting stuff. If only everyday life still held such fascination. As it was, she preferred to skip over the next few entries to get to the bottom of a pre-adolescent's heart.

September 10

I chose Kenny today for square dancing. O-o-o-h!!!! ♥ ♥ ♥

The other boys I had to dance with were: Greg, Dennis, David, and Kyle. I don't like them at all. It was pretty sickning, but I still had fun.

I got 3 nemos stolen!! I brought in some auction items and got a 10 nemo bill! I was supposed to have 33 nemos, but I only counted 30. 3 nemos makes a difference. I can get a piece of cunstruction paper and a library pass. But tomorrow is Show-And-Tell. I am so-o-o-o excited. You get 5 nemos for bringing something in. I earn my lost nemos back. I'm bringing the pin that was Grandma's. The girls in my class are all going to feel jealous of my pin. This ends my journal for today.

Margot's heady amusement over her childhood crush and Ebenezer Scrooge-esque affinity for fake money plummeted to a sick weight in her gut when she saw where this was going. Of *course* she was never going to find Grandma Grace's brooch in that closet – she hadn't seen it in over a decade for a reason.

Before turning the page, she wondered if the next entry would describe the brooch incident in detail or if her eleven-year-old self had already been equipped with the keen mechanism of denial she'd refined to an art by now. She peeked and, sure enough, spied a huge paragraph. With held breath, she flipped the purple-inked page to behold the pink writing on the wall…

September 12

Yesterday was the worst day of my life!!! At first it was the best day. I brought my pin for Show-And-Tell. Julie and Brenda were jealous. They fake acted they wern't, but they were. Trisha asked if she could wear it. I told her no. She begged please please please. It was so annoying I told her yes. I told her she could wear it after recess til the bell rang. The bell rang and she asked to wear it in the hall til we got to the coat racks. I met her at the coat racks and I asked for it back. She LIED and told me she put it in my backpack! I looked, but it was not there!!!! I asked her for it again, but she said she gave it back. What a lier!!!! I hate Trisha's guts!!!!!! Today she blames Julie and Brenda.

I am SO ANGRY. Angry and sad. I thought my mom would be angry and sad too when I told her, but she was okay. She said she doesn't remember the pin. She's mad at Trisha still. She doesn't like her at all. She is calling

Trisha's mom. If I keep writing I'll cry. This ends my journal for today.

Margot laughed at the drama but resisted calling down the hall to share it with her mom. Better to keep this little discovery to herself; even if her mom didn't remember *her* mother's keepsake, Margot preferred not to implicate Trisha anew in The Affair of the Brooch. For as loving and forgiving as Margot's mom was, she could hold a grudge.

Margot could too, and almost wanted to stalk Trisha down on social media to give her a piece of her mind, see if she still happened to have what she'd surely stolen. Margot loved that brooch and could still picture it down to its last detail – more clearly, even, than she could remember her grandma. So young when the only grandparent she'd ever known had passed on, Margot recollected little other than the tropical-patterned muumuus Grace would wear, how she'd sneak candies to spite the diabetes that in turn sneaked away with her life.

Grace's costume jewelry being too kitschy for her mother's taste, Margot had delighted in an after-school treasure chest of rhinestones and clip-on earrings all to herself. What she presumed was a faux-pearl and blue rhinestone brooch, though, that had been the pièce de résistance. It used to pierce through the collar of her kelly-green blouse, which had matched all too well with her cousin's bubble-gum pink pumps and the bath towel supposed to be a mink stole. When not admiring the pin in the mirror, she'd stroke it while watching cartoons, finding it always cool to the touch.

Though the brooch's value could only be of the sentimental variety, Margot always fantasized it had been a gift from some secret lover other than her grandfather – some humble man who'd deemed Grace worthy of gems even if he hadn't been able to afford the real thing. Perhaps Margot was off entirely, but somehow she knew that brooch had a story of great, against-all-odds love behind it. Or maybe she just wished it did, until she could emotionally cash in on one of her own.

She continued reading.

September 13
Today Trisha, Julie, Brenda, and me are all still mad at each other. I don't know who to believe. I don't trust any of them. Even if Trisha's telling the truth, she should of been more careful. I told her she should of given it back to ME, not my backpack. She cried. I'm going to be nice to Trisha because it's the worst having her against you. But in secret she's not my BFF any more.

One good thing that happened is I got an A on my report on birds. This ends my journal for today.

September 14
We maybe solved the mystery today. I talked to Esther from Miss Monroe's class at lunch. She is so-o-o weird. SHE came up to ME, not the other way around. I was afraid she was going to ask me to play after school. She said she heard all us girls fighting at recess. She said she was at the coat racks before me and Trisha, because her class is right there. She said Charlotte has my pin.

"Well, serendipity-doo-da," Margot murmured. But who was Charlotte? She couldn't remember for the life of her.

I told her I don't know Charlotte. She said she doesn't either, but she's the one that has it. I asked Charlotte who? She said her last name was some kind of bird. That does not help. I know lots of birds, thanks to my report. I don't know if I can believe Esther. She needs a bath – she smells like garbage. But what if she is right?? I'm too embaressed to ask other students. I don't want them to know how I know. If somebody does know Charlotte, I might have to talk to their teacher to find her. But I'm not a tattletale.

I guess I have to except its gone. I shouldn't of let Trisha wear it. It's all my fault. This ends my journal for today.

"Hmm." Margot's curiosity about the brooch subsided as

disappointment in herself burned her cheeks.

Esther had been that token classmate whose few outfits were worn too often and laundered too little. She'd lived outside the subdivisions populating most of the school. While not an operating farm, the home had stood alone for acres just off a dirt road, fostering nasty speculations of what went on there (mass cat sacrifice was a popular theory). The kids on the school bus had also hated how bumpy the route was, bouncing off their green vinyl seats as the wheels went round and round, kicking up stones in their tracks. By high school, Esther's face had evaporated into the crowded hallways, and the last Margot had ever heard about her was an 'accidental' overdose of prescription medication some time in college, as reported in the obituaries shoved between the county newsletter's auto dealership ads and police blotter.

Sure, there'd been something a little off about Esther and she'd talk to herself, but Margot regretted not having stuck up for the poor girl more often. She'd always cared too much about what others would think of her. Even to this day. Otherwise, she wouldn't have balked so much under Derek and Sylvie's scrutiny earlier.

Clapping the notebook shut, she warded off a growing glumness by joining the din of pots and pans in the kitchen for an impromptu cooking lesson.

Tick-tick-tick.

With a sudden intake of breath and tickle down her spine, Margot woke to the light of her bedside lamp. The digital alarm clock flashed twelve o'clock.

A power outage? And had she left the light on?

Sweeping a hand across her face and rubbing her eyes, she sat up. She feared for her mind at times like these, those inconsequential moments like blow-drying her hair and questioning whether she'd even shampooed it in the shower. But aside from why she hadn't turned the lamp off, she wondered what in hell she'd just been dreaming about.

Twisted faces, disturbing cries, her dream-self's slow-motion attempts to run free… It all tapped into her childhood fears of the dark and what lurked under the bed. But with a brave click, Margot switched off the light and tried to fall back asleep to the lullaby of her heavy breathing.

It didn't work. Not even close to rapid eye movement.

A chill infused her skin with a feverish flush, and her heart hummed. Entangled in the sheets, she thrust a leg into the open air and curled it above the duvet for climate control but couldn't slip back to sleep.

Tick-tick-tick.

She sat up again and leaned toward the window to draw back the blinds. The sound was only a branch rhythmically blowing against the windowpane by the light of a full moon. Silvery white, the orb hovered weightlessly above a wispy, periwinkle terrain of clouds glowing against the sapphire night sky. A vague sense of déjà-vu washed over her with an icy prickle, and, tucking her leg back under the sheet, she clutched the comforter to her waist.

The brooch. In a tingling stupor, Margot wondered if her deceased grandmother knew she'd been thinking about it and sent this vision from above. A sign to comfort her, maybe, to tell her to just let go and allow the hands of something divine to carry her along.

Nodding to the elusive Jeweler in the sky, she fastened the moon's image onto her heart and vowed to try.

In the meantime, her eyes stung with sleep, but her mind was too restless. She turned the light back on. Wriggling herself into a cozy position, she cracked *Charlotte Sometimes* open to its dog-eared page. Annoying eye floaters swam in front of the text, but Margot ignored them to reenter Charlotte's world, traveling with the girl back in time…until the years and words began to swerve into and sidestep each other…

Tick-tick-tick.

Margot jolted awake mid-snore with her book on her chest. Breathing deeply, she went to close the novel and put it back on the nightstand when she realized it wasn't

Charlotte Sometimes in her hands but a hardcover book with a black linen cover. Margot's 'dream diary', which she'd kept in easy reach on the nightstand along with a pen. But though she knew she'd just been dreaming again, Margot stared at the new entry in her little black book as though someone else had written it.

Tear tears of anguish suffering tearing at my heart open wounds wounds wounds do not know where to go with this all of this my god what have I gotten myself into blood sweat tears they claw at my arms suck at my artery I cannot stop them the pain what do they want from me is not there something better something better about them about me for me somewhere I can go and do such as this without fear tears insecurity inscrutable squeezing trying to breathe the fresh peace air

"Say what?" Gnawing at the inside of her mouth, she felt within a private episode of *CSI: Margot*, but this paragraph went beyond her forensics. The anxiety of it matched her recent soul-searching, yet the spattered words *anguish, suffering, wounds,* and *pain* made her uneasy.

And who, she wondered, were 'they'?

II

I wandered lonely as a cloud
That floats on high o'er vales and hills,
When all at once I saw a crowd,
A host, of golden daffodils;
Beside the lake, beneath the trees,
Fluttering and dancing in the breeze.

Continuous as the stars that shine
And twinkle on the milky way,
They stretched in never-ending line
Along the margin of a bay:
Ten thousand saw I at a glance,
Tossing their heads in sprightly dance.

The waves beside them danced; but they
Out-did the sparkling waves in glee:
A poet could not but be gay,
In such a jocund company:
I gazed—and gazed—but little thought
What wealth the show to me had brought:

For oft, when on my couch I lie
In vacant or in pensive mood,
They flash upon that inward eye
Which is the bliss of solitude;
And then my heart with pleasure fills,
And dances with the daffodils.

~ William Wordsworth (1804)

Interlude

Lonely as a Cloud

19th-Century London

Who are we? Who *were* we? Who am I still?

I fear I hardly know myself in the void of the other. Yet we must all begin somewhere if we are to endeavor to understand our existence above the soil, and so I shall look back to the then that began the now…

My tale preceding the day she entered my life is not a complicated one. My family was of modest means. Papa was an ironmonger whose finances might have afforded us more if not for wretched Inheritance: Papa poured what little we had into legal disputes surrounding ancestral effects on which distant relations lay claim. He nevertheless managed to install us in a fine enough home upon the fringes of streets blighted by poverty, but not amongst them.

And still I knew enough of them. Dreadfully uncomfortable in my day clothes, I remember on occasion, whenever Mama was out calling, I would run about in my brother's old cap and knickerbockers that buttoned at the knee, my disguise awarding me the privilege of interfering in the mischief of street arabs. Returning home ruddy and dirtied, our maid-of-all-work would be too fatigued with her daily tasks to mind my tomfoolery – just enough to refrain from revealing my antics to Mama.

With the exception, of course, of that one instance, the very last of its sort. That particular evening, I was charged with violating the Fifth Commandment and made to sit in the cupboard. My shallow breathing and heartbeats thundering in my ears, I perhaps suffered more from boredom than fear in its dank darkness – though ever since then, I confess I am reluctant to extinguish the light when falling asleep at night. It is a wonder the fancies that invade one's mind at those times when one is deprived of sight.

It was also from that night onwards that Mama was all the more determined to make a lady of me yet.

Whilst I considered it distasteful even then as a child, she once consulted a chiromancer with whom she had become acquainted in the parlor of one of her garish friends – she had employed him to trace along the lines of my palm and speak of my future. Instead, he spoke of my past. Greedily eyeing the additional sixpence Mama withdrew from her pouch, it is a wonder he found opportunity to look away and read what he did on my hand. Nonetheless, what he revealed was that, in a former life, I had, in fact, been male.

"Of peasant stock," he said. "Eighteenth-century France." I had evidently rejoiced in the jubilation to follow the storming of the Bastille prison and partaken in evil revelry, debauching myself on wine and whores, only for the 'toffer' I would covet one day to cost me my head.

I snatched my tiny palm away at once; I was astounded Mama had allowed him to utter such vile words in our presence. How indeed was that intended to advance my instruction on becoming a lady?

Needless to say, Mama sent me away directly for my insolence and thereafter strove that much harder to overcome an unruly, masculine, and impoverished 'past' and groom me into something more feminine and genteel. As my formative years slipped by, she ran a hairbrush through every errant fiber of my being, smoothing and glossing my curious, innocently wicked ways into straighter posture, whiter gloves, quieter words (lest they be spoken at all), then plaited them into the web-work of her grand designs for my 'future'.

I suppose I ought to be grateful for the careful attention she paid my education. Her father had been a learned man and read with her in candlelit hours after her mother's lessons concluded. It was when Mama spied me clutching an oiled scrap of newspaper with my nose almost certainly imprinting itself with its ink – so buried it was in this unexpected treasure – that she did perceive in part what shifted my gears from within. The scrap, you see, had been wrapped around butter newly purchased at market, and on peeling it off, I had liberated poetry into the light.

From then on I was mesmerized and nourished soulfully by my maternal grandfather's little library, bestowed unto Mama on his passing prior to my birth. Mama had, alas, lost her use for such beauty as means of ascending to higher social ground. So it was that I, in delving through these dusty archives, found my heart in earlier voices, most notably that of Wordsworth.

Ah! How Wordsworth has allowed me to dance with the daffodils, if only in mind amidst those low-tides of emotion that otherwise dry my spirit in their ebb, and leave me barren, unfruitful.

Unworthy. A specter in my own home, flitting listlessly to scarcely rustle the curtains, let alone anyone's notice.

But to return my tale to its proper chronology, my training under Mama compensated just enough for my lack of breeding so as to make myself presentable amongst society. At one particular fancy dress occasion, I managed to capture the eye of a certain gentleman of means; indeed, he was the son of a judge and had himself studied to become a barrister only to pursue business in the law's stead. Always diligent and apt with regard to whatever he pursued, he possessed in his heart, although few realized it, a suppressed penchant for the visual arts – a proclivity that attracted him to the notion of one day becoming a patron. Whatever vision I supposed I was to his eye, so he was to my heart when during the quadrille I heard him speak the poetry of my mind through strokes and shading, colors that swirled in my fancies like the champagne tickling my thoughts. His waltz sent me reeling in a heady whirl.

Our wedding was an intimate occasion, as I had not so

many to attend on my side, and he – well, his side had not so many to attend the nuptials of one condescending to marry beneath him, or so I was put upon to understand. Yet Mama was in raptures, naturally, and Papa… Papa bestowed his blessings from above, God rest his soul, having lost to the cholera so long ago.

My being provided for relieved an immense burden from Mama's breast, yet a lingering regret gnawed at her intestines – a frustration that she had not procured from Papa the precise whereabouts of the inheritance she was so certain he *did* acquire through his legal tribulations, and likely kept hidden away in order to keep us meek.

Indeed, Mama deceived no one but herself in this, but still she participated in séances whenever she could in order to divine the truth, dragging me along into my twentieth year and beyond under the assumption that my precocious, sometimes nervous temperament would attract Papa's spirit to our table.

Ah, but I shall speak more on this presently.

Chapter Three

Old World, New World

21st-Century London

It was late May when Margot first set foot on United Kingdom soil. Her program didn't start until the first week of June, but she wanted to acclimate and explore before studies took up her days. Rand would be leaving on an extended business trip to the Continent, so she could enjoy the place to herself the first couple of weeks. *Enjoy* being the operative word, as she was determined to snap out of her funk once and for all.

After trudging through Immigration, she spotted her new flatmate among the crowd holding up signs with passenger names. Sight of all others fell away as pressure mounted on her chest.

The long-talked-about situation was finally coming to pass, and, fact was, they hadn't seen each other in well over two years and had only worked together. For as casually as Margot had played it off around her friends and family, bunking up with Rand would definitely be weird, at least at first. And she had to brace herself for the fact that his girlfriend Gwen might not be so cool about the living arrangement after all.

Margot dropped her eyes and bit her lip with a nervous giggle as she gripped her suitcase handle tighter. Her steps faltered, but on locking eyes on Rand's again, she felt a chord in her stomach pull her toward him as fast as those suitcase wheels would roll.

"'Allo, guvna!"

"Greetings and salutations, miss," he said with a graceful bow. Rand had always been a gentleman. With no prompting, he'd stated his plans to meet Margot at Heathrow as though a matter of course and not the generous, out-of-the-way favor it really was.

Her nerves melted away at his familiar lean frame and dancing eyes. He'd always had that good-humored magnetism about him, yet he was even more handsome than she remembered. His full, wavy chestnut hair had grown out, and he looked dashing in a well-tailored purple dress shirt and the striped multicolor socks that peeked from beneath his fitted trouser legs – a look few corn-fed Chicago dudes could pull off. And there was no contest against his smile. It wasn't the bleached-white and capped American grin of false promises, but a slightly tea-stained and asymmetrical one that seemed to earnestly believe in keeping calm and carrying on.

Once she set her bags down, Margot beamed at him with arms outspread. "It's been so long! I could hug the dickens out of ya!"

"The *Charles* Dickens, mind. You're in London now, Yankee." He grinned. "And you damn well shall hug me."

Margot could have stood in the welcome comfort of his arms for ages, feeling silly for her nerves just moments ago, but she made herself break away.

"This is surreal. I haven't seen you in almost three years, and here I am shacking up with you."

"Don't let Gwen hear you put it that way." He laughed.

Ah. Just what she'd thought. "Seriously, though, Rand. You're so nice to do this." She widened her eyes in full puppy-dog adoration of her old mentor.

"Well, it's about bloody time you finally took me up on my offer to visit." It was his turn to play the puppy, the one expression that actually made those polar-blue eyes look sad.

"Sugar, I could never stay away from my pale little bit-o-stuff."

The Englishman didn't have a prayer of hiding his blush.

Margot just stood exchanging smiles with him, elated to be reunited and wondering why she'd ever let life and its busyness keep them apart until now. She *was* going to enjoy herself here; she just knew it.

"Let me take your cases," he said. "I've hired a car, as the Tube's novelty will wear off soon enough."

A half-hour commute delivered them to his door. The Victorian building was one of a cluster of identical terraced houses forming the perimeter of a square. Spherical topiary bushes and flowers bloomed from nearly every sill, boasting the local penchant for nature. An old Anglican church stood just right of center, and across from that was a gated garden.

Chicago would never allot such prime urban property to parks like that, Margot mused. She'd barely been in the country an hour, and it was already so true to what she'd expected from countless film versions of *A Christmas Carol*, right down to the charming period banister that held her hand up the stairs to Rand's flat. From the moment she felt its polished wood, a new energy surged through her, and she felt at home.

"Some of these old stairwells have been retrofitted for lifts," Rand said as they rounded their way up the flights, "but hopefully you don't mind some old-fashioned exercise." With a smile, he opened the door to his unit and gestured, *After you.*

The grand tour took all of two minutes. The flat wasn't so small by London standards, but she was daunted by the little armoire in her new bedroom, where Rand first ushered her to park her luggage. It would accommodate the few bags she'd packed fine enough, but she couldn't fathom actually living here with all of her clothes. There was no built-in closet, and the room barely fit the bed, let alone the wardrobe and desk. Rand explained that this was probably a dressing room originally, given that the Victorian master bedroom would have occupied his entire living room and open-plan kitchen. So what he now deemed the master bedroom – his room – would've been only a secondary one. The flat upstairs would've been the children's or servants'

45

quarters, and the two flats below were once the drawing, morning, and dining rooms, with the kitchen being all the way down in what was now the garden flat.

Though Rand's unit was only one floor of what used to be a multi-story house, he had his own little set of stairs at the end of his hall, leading to the flat's only bathroom.

"I suspect it was once part of a servant's stairwell," he said, with the original 'bathroom' probably just a hipbath in one of the bedrooms before there was plumbing. That was the best explanation, anyway, for the bathroom's sunken layout and spaciousness.

Margot glimpsed out the large window above the bathtub and saw a group of backyards. Fenced off by low brick walls, they opened up to the overcast sky. "So *that's* why they're called garden flats," she *aha*-ed. "In Chicago, *garden apartment* just means 'dark subterranean bunker with no patio or sign of life beyond rodents'."

Suddenly desperate to use the bathroom for its modern purpose, she politely excused Rand's presence. Once she'd figured out how to flush with one of the two buttons mounted on the wall, she then stared down two separate taps at the sink. After scalding her hands with one while the other froze them, she swiftly alternated from one to the other to get the (almost) right temperature. Finally sorted, she glanced out a smaller window next to the sink. All she saw at first was a brick wall where the back rooms of the house next door jutted out in the same way, probably also a former stairwell. But stepping closer to examine the recessed wall between these rear extensions, she noticed an upstairs window…

…just as the grayish outline of a profile came into view. A woman, seemingly. She appeared distressed, raising her hands to her face to sob into them.

Margot looked away, ashamed of catching such a private moment.

In this short time, a pressure also began to weigh on her eye, and a glowing in her sight intensified. She sensed the stress of travel, dehydration, and sleep deprivation was probably bringing on a migraine, which loved to announce its arrival with a squiggle warping her perception like a private Hall of Mirrors. Locating a bottle of ibuprofen tablets beneath the counter, she popped a couple to avoid the nauseating headache that would follow.

Back upstairs, she found Rand standing in his kitchen at the sink. "Hey, fella. I think I'm gonna unpack and lie down for a bit, if that's okay."

"Certainly, my dear. My home is now yours, so do whatever, whenever."

His warm grin liquefied her heart with such a reassuring sense of home. "You're the best. I promise not to get in your way."

"You needn't worry about that." His eyes softened as he added almost shyly, "Please do get in my way."

Margot returned his sweet smile until her vision blurred it away. Time to rest.

Moving her biggest suitcase from the bed to the floor with a *whump*, she hopped onto the mattress and sighed at the church roof spanning her room's view. Even though she had to squint and move her line of sight around the migraine squiggle, she gasped at the mammoth steeple looming just outside. Then, grinding the sash upward in its slanted frame ("The old place is a bit wonky," Rand had said), she poked her head out to look across the square. The mansard rooftops with their dormer windows and chimneystacks brought childhood fancies to mind, and Margot half-expected Dick Van Dyke and his troop of chimney sweeps to leap and twirl atop them all.

But a gust of cool air made her yawn, so she crept back inside and swung her bedroom door shut. Losing momentum just before catching in the lock, it slowly creaked back open.

Wonky is right.

Giving the door a firmer push, she got it to lock in place, then returned to the bed. She crawled beneath the duvet and relished those initial seconds of shivers before her body heat warmed the covers. Her eyelids lowered over the steeple

47

and Mary Poppins roofs behind it.

I can't believe I'm really here. England. Europe. Not-United States. And with the street traffic out of sight, it could easily be the 1800s. The people who lived in this house over a hundred years ago would've seen exactly the same view. Unreal.

With a dull eyebrow headache, she drifted off.

May 25

Having a hard time getting started here. Dear Diary-ing my merry way through Jolly Old England has got to be more interesting than my usual day to day, but so far I'm still adjusting to jet-lag and sleeping in a lot, feeling guilty I'm the only loser in London without a real reason to get up, showered, and dressed by a respectable hour. Especially when I should be taking advantage of these free days. Thank God Rand's not here to see my sloth. The rainy weather doesn't help either.

His location is awesome, though. It's near the Tube, pubs, and cafés galore, which should raise my spirits before long. I'm also attending a religious debate tonight at St. Paul's Cathedral – the topic is the nature of the soul in relation to our identity. That deep thought being said, gotta go so my arse can get a seat.

May 27

The St. Paul's debate the other night was great. The panel spoke from both theological and scientific perspectives. Amazing to listen to while gawking at that massive dome overhead and all the intricate mosaics, sculptures, and paintings. A surreal kind of solitude even in a room filled with people. The intellectual, the faithful, the curious.

Yesterday, I pretty much just wandered around the local neighborhoods and got lost. First stumbled on a cool old cemetery – Brompton, one of London's 'Magnificent Seven'. It's huge and so serene, definitely my fave place so far. Then I cut through streets and squares that all looked like Rand's until I happened upon Kensington Gardens, where I sat and watched kids play football (soccer) and amazingly disciplined British dogs run around without leads (leashes) or even barking. From there, I found myself among the shops of a few high (main) streets that all looked alike and didn't help me find my way. I walked in circles past sundown, which here is pretty late, but in the black, rainy night, the Daunt Books store glowed orange like a beacon, so I warmed and dried there for a bit before making a thank-you purchase – ye olde ghost story! – and meandering back to the flat. I _did_ find it.

Today, I ventured further central via the Underground (subway) and crossed Westminster Bridge to walk along the South Bank. Perfect views of Parliament, Big Ben, Globe Theatre, and Tower Bridge (which, FYI, is _not_ London Bridge!). After a pub lunch, I crossed the Thames again to get a closer view of the Tower of London. From there, I successfully lost myself in the business district but looked to St. Paul's dome as my guide.

[Dream Entry – May 30]
I laid in paralysis so long, senses dulled as I treaded below the water's surface, looking up to see the pool of light above – was there a woman who wept at its center?? The one from the window? – but I kept sinking toward what was cool and black, warping my vision and clogging my ears a water-logged cadaver tangled in weeds where no one could see or hear me. That's what it felt like, not what happened, nothing really happened, just isolation and smothering stillness.

June 2
Just been lying around the last couple of days, not motivated whatsoever. For all my efforts to keep busy before, never realized how not having a schedule could throw me so off. I'd hoped new scenery would ward off old baggage, but now I'm afraid that for all this supposedly good change, I might've detoured myself into a dead end.

For the first time, being alone is making me lonely. Can't wait for Rand to return. In the meantime, nothing a little wine doesn't fix.

A few days ago, I did make a couple side-trips outside of the city. First, Stratford-Upon-Avon, which is darling. I saw Shakespeare's home and where he's buried at Trinity Church, then walked along the River Avon and back around to a museum on Sheep Street, with wax figures recreating S-u-A's morbid history of plague, civil war, and murder. Ended up buying an evening ticket, too, that entitled me to a ghost tour (mwahahaha!), which I'd assumed would be out and about town but was actually in the museum itself. Our group was led by lantern light into pitch-black darkness, so thank God I'd already toured the exhibits during the day or those wax people would have made me shit my pants in the shadows.

Anyway, we learned about specific deaths that happened in that very space: suicide at the noose of a rope, murder on the stairs, death from war wounds on a makeshift hospital bed, decay from contagious disease, etc., and of course everyone's spirits have remained behind. Granted, there's a lot of power of suggestion behind what visitors supposedly experience, but just as I was mentally bidding the tortured souls farewell, my eardrum seemed to blow in (mwahahahaaa! Not that my overactive sinuses would've had anything to do with that, of course... My ears keep popping as if I'm underwater all the time lately. Different climate here. Very damp.).

Afterwards returned to Sheep Street for a bite to eat (could it have been the ghosts that drew me back there? Mwaha—oh, all right, I'll give it up) and settled into a cozy restaurant for dinner. As I walked back there, I noticed that more skanks emerge at night than spirits, stumbling in their platform pumps and miniskirts to whatever club scene must exist. Shakespeare would've loved this. I have renamed the village Slutford-Upon-Avon, pending board approval.

Not as far away from London was Hampton Court Palace, where Henry VIII lived after basically booting

Cardinal Wolsey out for not supporting the king's divorce with Catherine of Aragon. The oval above the altar in the Chapel Royal is supposedly the only one of its kind in a Christian church, representing an egg (as opposed to a cross) as the symbol for resurrection and rebirth. And buried beneath the altar are the organs of one of Henry's wives, Jane Seymour (who died soon after giving birth to a male heir) because it was believed the soul resides in our innards. This inscription was written for her:

Here lieth a Phoenix, by whose death
Another Phoenix life gave breath:
It is to be lamented much
The world at once ne'er knew two such.

Then there was the Haunted Gallery. Henry's lesser-loved wife, Catherine Howard, was accused of adultery and locked in her rooms – apparently she tried to escape once and was dragged back kicking and screaming by the guards. She's now known as the Screaming Lady that haunts the corridor. Speaking of hauntings, it was only after my visit when I looked up the palace online to learn more about it that I found the video of a man's ghost dressed in period clothing that was caught on camera opening and closing a couple fire doors. I don't know if I walked that way or not, but I'm glad I didn't know about it at the time... Creeeepy, as Derek would say.

Anyways, I got there too late in the day to tour the gardens and maze, but I covered the palace and even did a twice-over in some parts. Instead of following an audioguide or reading every information plaque I passed, I just soaked in the general atmosphere, not bogging my mind down with facts but trying to experience it as an occupant might have. Since I was there so close to closing time, my departure was especially atmospheric in the sunset and empty corridors. Other than the staff waiting around to close up shop, it seemed to be just me and my high heels echoing off the walls as they clacked on the wood and *cobbles.*

This is silly, but I felt like it was my own home as I looked at myself in tarnishing mirrors that once reflected back images of nobility and the servants scurrying in their service. I found myself straightening my back, folding my hands at waist-height, and trying to walk like a proper lady in a corset, hoops, and painfully pinching little lady shoes (that last part not so much imagined as literally felt – the storyline in my head just helped me suck up my dumbass impractical choice of footwear for that kind of outing). I stopped gawking around like a tourist and looked straight-on as though all the décor was everyday familiar, with the occasional glance side to side to nod in acknowledgement of those milling about to pay me honor and attention as the next to bear a male heir. I felt important and inadequate all at once. So random...

Chapter Four

Fact & Fiction

Rand was finally due home the next day. Margot had already attended some seminars on *Cultural Considerations in Mass Communications* and *The Art of Persuasion*. Nothing too intensive assigned just yet, only a few chapters of dry reading to prepare for small-group discussion. It hadn't been easy getting herself up and going again, but she welcomed the routine and made a concentrated effort to stick to it.

She was feeling unfocused this evening, though. To get blood rushing back to her brain, she got up to walk laps with what range of motion the flat allowed.

When that wasn't enough to quell her restless spirit, she ventured out of the unit but not the building. She stuck to the stairwell, feeling the smooth wood of the banister glide across her palm with every step down. All the while, she imagined what it must've been like having to take the stairs in a long Victorian gown and not her yoga pants, how tricky it would've been to walk down or up without tripping on the skirts. She wondered if anyone had ever fallen to her death because of that and instinctively firmed her grip on the banister.

She made it all the way down to the foyer and was on her way back up when her pace slowed on reaching the next floor. The entrance to the unit below Rand's was actually a double door, looking like it could lead into a small ballroom or some kind of entertainment space. Having rounded onto the landing in front of it, Margot stopped to look at the doorway and imagine what soirées might've gone on behind it back in the day. Was it where the woman of the house would've received callers?

The more she stared at the deep mahogany stain on the doors, the more her imagination could see through them, just barely discerning a mustachioed man seated in there by the window and beside a lamp with a fringed shade. The man in her mind sat with his legs crossed and a newspaper on his lap, his expression grave as he appeared to study the periodical in his hands.

The image grew clearer until the man suddenly looked up and Margot heard a shuffle from within, breaking her spell. She tiptoed the rest of her way up the stairs and back into Rand's flat before the neighbors could catch her spying.

Once inside, she heard the thud of footsteps overhead as well. She always heard people above, below, and on either side of her, through the shared walls and floors, and she'd watch them walk outside, too, with their places to go and people to see. While here she was, alone on only one floor of what probably used to be a full and active house. Circling the living area that had once been part of the master bedroom, Margot imagined a Victorian husband and wife lying in each other's arms, pillow-talking of the future and filling their home with children. Her distance from a situation like that seemed to coat her in cotton, muffling her ears and dulling her senses.

Screw studying. She flicked on the TV and walked into the kitchen to open a bottle of Malbec. Entire-bottle-of-wine-unto-oneself nights had become her new thing with Rand out of town, so she filled herself a glass, gave it a swirl, and contemplated the scrawny legs streaking down its sides.

Liquid happy.

A dramatic flourish of orchestral music brought her attention to the television, just in time to see the film *Enchantment* begin on a movie channel. At the sight of David Niven, she raised her glass to toast the Last Generation of Gentlemen to Roam the Earth, then took a swill as she walked to the sofa to enjoy the flick. For all that she'd endured James's teasing for it, Margot was an unashamed sucker for classics like this, valuing dialogue over action, romance over sex, gradual over rapid. She possessed a nurturing patience for the slow-going in her need-that-done-yesterday world. Tried to find herself in such stories by losing herself in them.

The bottle of Malbec was three-quarters empty and Margot slumped three-quarters down on the sofa by the time Pax, a World War II pilot, departed Ninety-Nine Wiltshire Crescent. The home's owner, Rollo (played by Niven), asked his niece Grizel about the young man. He went on to stress the importance of being loved, but she insisted her heart had been broken before, so she wouldn't risk that again with Pax.

Knowing the feeling too well, Margot closed her eyes to lose her personal heartache to the darkness behind them. She drifted away a bit but brought her awareness back to see that Grizel had left and Rollo crossed the room to an armchair. Settling there, he heart-wrenchingly whispered into the air to his long-lost lover, Lark, asking if she'd heard Grizel's foolish words. Chastised, Margot felt warm tears stream down her face. She clenched her eyes shut again to quell their burning.

And then she passed out to sweet, black oblivion...

Until a blast jolted her back. She woke to the sounds of the London Blitz – the humming of fighter jets, the wailing of sirens. The tremendous burst of a bomb. Opening a bleary eye, Margot saw Rollo lying in the debris of Ninety-Nine Wiltshire Crescent. The house itself narrated the film's ending, about how the young would occupy it again with a new lease on life.

My name wasn't even on the lease to that condo, she thought before opening her other eye to see her wine glass hanging from her fingers. It pointed down to what looked like a violent crime scene, minus the chalk-outlined figure.

"Oh, shit! Fuck!"

She stumbled to the kitchen and yanked a dishtowel from the oven door.

"Fuck! Shit! Fucking shit!" She scrubbed to prevent permanent stains on Rand's pale carpeting. "Fucking cream carpeting!" she spewed while wearing the small dishtowel down to a fuzzy red nub.

Head spinning, Margot rose from her little puddle and ambled down to the bathroom to grab a bigger – and darker – towel. Grabbing one out of the cabinet, she stood and couldn't help but look in the mirror. Seeing her frizzy hair and the deep red stains on her teeth and lips, she strongly suspected she'd always live alone. Maybe with the exception of cats. A dozen of them. And knitting; she would knit afghans without end. But that would be fine so long as it was by her own choice. Right?

Wandering out of the bathroom and clicking off the light switch situated just outside its door, she soon wandered back in without turning it back on. In the absence of anyone else to acknowledge her, she needed to see in the large mirror that she was flesh and blood and interacting with the world, that she was here, in your face, and she mattered.

In the dim natural light still coming through the windows, she stared into the black circular voids of her eye sockets. Opened her mouth to see a larger cavity gape ghoulishly beneath them. She shut and opened and shut it again to the acute sound of her clamping teeth. The movement confirmed the reflection was hers, that she had control of it.

But the longer she looked at her skull-like image, it appeared to pulse and crawl like so many maggots, brightening every second with a throbbing glow. Freaked out, Margot hastily ran to flick the bathroom light on again before returning to the mirror.

Reassured by her brightly lit reflection, she decided to practice a conversation she'd started in her mind a while back, the tough-girl monologue she'd deliver if she ever ran into James again. As she fine-tuned the script, her reflection served as an acting coach, giving Margot feedback on body language.

I don't belong to you or anybody. I'm me. My—

"Self. Yeah? 'Sright."

Propped on her elbows with her hands hanging limply into the sink, she stared at the mirror until the image of her two hazel eyes merged into one. She wasn't certain whom she saw in the reflection, only that she didn't recognize herself anywhere in it.

Hugging the bath towel tightly, she lumbered over to the tub to turn on the faucet. When the water ran hot, she stoppered the drain, added some salts, and began to undress as she walked to her bedroom to fetch her little black journal.

[Dream Entry – June 5]
spinning and spinning my center cannot hold much longer it will flail apart from the centrifugal force that dizzies me takes my breath makes me vomit rips me open inside out again and again like a changeling child born to torment with premature death only to be reborn cycle after cycle a bittersweet reincarnation

She'd lost track of time in the tub, had just laid her head back on a towel and closed her eyes to their blurry vision. Whether she'd actually fallen asleep or simply slipped into some waking, wine-induced nightmare, she'd abruptly splashed forward with a gasp and reached for her diary and pen to scribble her fantasies before they escaped her.

Once finished recording and overwhelmed by the rapid beat of her heart in the heat and humidity of the bathroom, Margot finally stepped her pruned feet out of the tub. Disoriented but relatively sober again, she wrapped herself in the towel and walked a few more laps around the flat to find her breath. She eventually found her hand on the doorknob to Rand's bedroom. And then, oddly enough, she found herself turning it and opening the door.

Whoops, wasn't me. No witnesses.

She punched the light switch on as she entered the bedroom. Though bigger, the room was just like hers in architectural detail, from the decorative moldings to the crystal ceiling chandelier to the pale pine bedroom set. The sparse beige walls were true to bachelor-pad form, along with the orange rack on one of them for his road bike. But Rand compensated with an eclectic hodgepodge of framed photos on his dresser, the subjects ranging between anything from the exotic landscapes of his travels to family gatherings in what looked like a New England fishing village but that Margot guessed from her guidebooks was Cornwall.

The sentimental fool. She smiled.

In a few different photos, she saw Rand standing beside two equally tall and similar-looking men that she figured were his brothers. And in some way or another, he was always in affectionate physical contact with a petite and pale young woman; Margot couldn't tell if it was a sister or Gwen. In a couple of photos, he had an arm thrown around the woman's shoulders or both arms wrapped around her from behind, while in another he kissed the top of her head. The woman was attractive despite her down-turned little mouth. There was one photo she wasn't in, though, which looked like it could be more recent if Rand's hairstyle was anything to go by. Maybe it was a trip Gwen couldn't make that time.

Margot looked over at the rumpled sheets on Rand's bed and felt a hollow in her stomach. Walking to it, she sat at its edge and almost leaned down into his pillow to seek traces of perfume or cologne.

Okay, stalker. She sat up straighter and instead looked around at how he really made the most of tight quarters with coordinating containers stacked above his wardrobe and beneath his bed. *Why does he always keep the door to this room closed? It's not like it's that messy. Maybe he doesn't trust me.* Looking at herself sitting on the man's bed in nothing but a bath towel after she'd nearly sniffed his linens, she couldn't say she blamed him.

Before she left, though, she raised the roman shade to peer at the gardens out back beneath the dusky sky and smiled at their enchanting foliage. It was just like the bathroom's view through its big window by the tub, except the bedroom was set back by two or three yards, so the building's rear extension to the right – the old stairwell and the current bathroom itself – blocked part of the panorama. Margot looked down at an illuminated side window in this brick wall, the top of its frame situated just a foot or two below the bottom of Rand's bedroom window. Though the glass was fogged, she could make out some of the downstairs flat, which was such a voyeurish thing to do – again – yet somehow had the odd, cozy charm of peeking into one of the miniature rooms on exhibit at the Art Institute of Chicago.

The first thing she spied down there was a hairbrush, then a black and khaki floral cosmetic bag sitting on a counter near the edge of a sink.

Margot gripped the ledge beneath her, breathing shallower as her muscles stiffened.

Those were her toiletries. Hers.

That was Rand's bathroom. His.

The window was foggy from her own bath.

Paralyzed for a moment, she eventually turned with trepidation, knowing what she must do: She must walk out of this room and turn left at the hall. She must follow this hall to the stairs. She must go down those stairs and stand beside the smaller bathroom window. She must then look out that window towards the upstairs unit. She must confirm the upstairs window she'd looked through before was *not* the one where she just stood.

But that was impossible. Not because she couldn't follow this plan of action, but because, when she did, what she saw was without question Rand's bedroom window. Having left the light on upstairs, she could clearly distinguish a few crystals dangling from the familiar chandelier.

Maybe all the units have these as part of the same house, she reasoned until she saw, propped on an orange metal pole, a cyclist helmet and, just below that, the white-taped handlebars of Rand's bike.

On her first day in London, she hadn't registered how

much lower the bathroom was from the rest of his flat. She'd automatically assumed she was looking up into the unit above Rand's. Realizing now that it was *his* unit, Margot had only one question to ask:

Who was she?

On the verge of a bona fide panic attack, she forced herself to focus on the practical. She returned upstairs to Rand's room, shut the light off, and closed the door, even wiping fingerprints from the knob in all her paranoia.

And then a figurative light bulb beamed on her: Derek. She would call Derek. It would be late enough in the afternoon for him, and he didn't take his day job seriously anyway.

So she brewed up some coffee in Rand's French press, got dressed in her PJs, and settled at the desk in her bedroom. She chose not to dwell on what she *thought* she *might* have seen and vowed to hold a casual conversation with her friend. After signing into her online chat account, she opened the music playlist on Rand's computer, point-and-clicked on The Cure's *Staring at the Sea* album for some background noise, then propped her foot up on the desk chair and held her knee close to her chest for a sense of security, false or not. Her brain on overload, she spoke out loud as she audio-called Derek's cell phone.

"Okay, so I'm not going to talk or even think about what must not be talked or thought about. Just get a grip."

Fuck, I wish Rand were here.

Margot listened to the ring tone as she drummed her fingers to the beat of "10:15 Saturday Night." Unsure of what the actual time was, she flicked a glance at the screen's upper corner in time to see its clock switch from twenty-two fourteen to twenty-two fifteen. Margot was still adjusting to the military time used in Europe, so had to do mental math and subtract twelve from the hour to arrive at 10:15 p.m., just like in the song that had just begun playing.

I should start journaling these coincidences to see if there's a pattern.

"Good thing it's not Saturday or I'd really freak out," she

muttered.

"Huh?"

"Derek?"

"Yeah. Margot?"

"Yeah."

"Who're you talking to?"

"Who do you think?

"If I had to guess, probably your neurotic self."

"Bingo."

"Everything all right?"

"Sure."

"Yeah, right. Spill it."

I'm not getting into it. Ask him how his day is going.

"I think I saw a ghost." *So much for that.*

"What? Did you say a ghost or a goat?"

"Yes, a *goat*, Derek. I was strolling through the pastures today in my good bonnet." Calmed by joking around, she rode the wave and affected a falsetto British accent. "Dear, dear, I would have caught my death of influenza if the gentle-hearted goat had not so kindly carted me back upon its coarse hide."

"You're psycho. Or drunk."

"Mm, both."

"So wait, then, did you say you saw a ghost?"

Crap. "Eh. Well. Yeah. I thought so." She brought her other knee up to her chest.

"Where? What did you see?" Derek's voice sounded more fascinated than incredulous – desperate for a diversion from his bland administrative tasks, likely – so Margot ran with it and explained what she could have sworn she'd seen in the window of Rand's bedroom the first day she'd arrived.

"Whoa, wait a minute, so you're not talking a shadow out the corner of your eye. You saw an actual person? Distinctly?"

"Distinctly enough that I saw a face." She heard an odd bravado in her voice as she asserted this. *Am I so hell-bent on proving it to be true?*

"Are you sure you weren't looking at the window above?"

"Yes, I'm sure." Now that she thought about it, though, a tinge of second-guessing flapped in her memory.

"Were you the only one there?"

"Rand was here, too."

"Was he with you when you saw it?"

"No, I made him leave because I had to use the bathroom."

"So maybe he went to his bedroom and it was him you saw."

"I guess, but he was in the kitchen when I came out. And it looked more like a woman's figure."

"Maybe it was the maid."

"I don't know if he has that kind of service, and wouldn't I have seen her? Or at least heard her if she was busy cleaning?"

"I guess. But doesn't he have a girlfriend? Maybe she'd spent the night and was still over?"

That hadn't occurred to her.

"No, I didn't see anyone else all day." *Who's to say, though, that she hadn't been here? Rand's door was closed. Probably Gwen does sleep here, or did before I came into the picture. Maybe she was pissed he left her to pick me up from the airport. Maybe she loitered around to check me out and piss on her territory. But why didn't she come out and stare me down? Maybe she's antisocial. Maybe she hadn't showered yet and didn't want to meet me with the lower-hand like that. Why wouldn't I have seen her the whole rest of the day, though? Oh, right. She could have left when I was napping.*

But these thoughts were all too Mr. Rochester's-crazy-wife-in-the-attic for Margot to speculate aloud.

"And you could see clearly enough through the window," Derek said. "No reflections."

"Well, it was daylight, so I guess there was a glare from outside."

"Could anything have been outside to reflect in the

window?"

"Trees, maybe, and birds, but…"

"Were the lights on inside?"

"No."

"It's tough to see inside during the day, you know, especially if no lights are on."

"Yes, I *know*."

"But you saw actual movement?"

"Um, I thought so, like she was crying, or maybe it was more the posture that implied something like that. But still."

"That could've been a reflection of another building or trees. Or objects in his room."

Hmm, that bike rack. "But the curves looked womanly, like boobs and hips. Although…these windows are a little distorted. I don't know if it's their size or age or what, but they're slightly rippled."

"So the windows could have twisted a reflection into what you saw."

"Possibly, yeah. But I can't check now 'cause it's dark." Sinking in her chair with a frown, Margot replayed her memory over and over before brightening and sitting up. "Hold up. There *was* a movement. I thought I saw the woman raise her hands to her face!"

"A branch blowing in the wind? A bird swooping up?"

"True."

The computer monitor switched to screen-saver mode. Tapping the keyboard to return to the chat window and blue desktop background, she watched an eye floater drift through Rand's file icons.

"You know, my floaters are getting worse."

"I get those, too. I pretend they're sea monkeys."

Margot laughed. "Thanks. So much cuter to think I have parasites infesting my eyes."

"So you think maybe that's what you saw move? Your floaters?"

Pause. "Damn, I bet you're right."

Longer pause. "You almost sound disappointed."

"No, just concerned my own eyes could trick me like

63

that. But I did feel a migraine come on right after. God, do you think I'm batty?"

Derek sighed. "Of course not, darlin'. I think yer paranoid, but you've also had a lot on your mind." He chuckled. "That game of Ouija probably didn't help with putting ideas in your head."

"Seriously! Neither does being in this country where everything's haunted!"

Margot went on to describe her excursions outside the city. This included the ghost tour in Stratford-Upon-Avon, which reconfirmed the newly developed theory that her fright was fed by frequent exposure to all-things-haunted lately. Derek, for one, was settled on the case once they'd tried to change the subject to their latest book and film recs, and Margot described her current reading: Gregory Maguire's *Lost*, the story of an American woman who visits her male British friend in London and suspects his flat is haunted. She felt incredibly stupid as she heard the words leave her mouth.

"Oh, Christ, Margot! Duh?"

"Okay, I know."

"Since when are you this impressionable?"

"Shut up, I *know*."

"I mean, life might not be recognizable right now, but it doesn't mean you're in an alternate universe."

"Yes, I get it. It is a novel. A novel is fiction by definition. I am real, living a real life."

"You sure about that? I picture you lying on a chaise-longue eating bon-bons and getting totally absorbed in bad British soaps all day."

"Yep, you're right. That's *all* I do, *all* day."

"Oh, c'mon, I'm kidding…"

"No, really, I get it. I'm the neurotic loser without a job, so I have nothing better to do than make shit up with my idle mind."

"Damn, I was only saying—"

"Yeah, if only I could embrace life like you, apply myself by smoking pot and filing papers and brewing crappy coffee for crappy companies that pay me hourly."

"Right. Because we can't all be so worldly and attend summer school again in our twenties."

"It's *professional development*. It's not like I'm making up for a failed class."

"Just a failed career?"

"Hardy-har."

"That's right, because you don't stick with anything long enough to fail at it. You just quit while you're ahead so no one can see that even *you* are capable of failing, Margot."

"Don't sound so sure of it."

"I guess the world will never know, will it?"

"Oh, because you have it so figured out, Derek. I hope you and Sylvie can have a good laugh about this later, when you continue comparing notes on what an arrogant, overachieving, antisocial, tight-ass prude I am."

"Easy. Look, I'm sorry. I didn't mean anything I said."

Margot caged her next words behind clenched teeth. Breathing deeply through her nose, she maintained an uncomfortable silence until her spite passed as quickly as it had come on. Maybe she *was* still pretty drunk.

"I'll let you go, all right?" he said. "I know it's late there, and I have some very important filing to do and crappy coffee to brew anyway."

Ouch. Time to reboot. "God, Derek, I am *so*—"

"Ah-ah-ah," he *tsk*ed. "Love means never having to say it. Not another word. Just let it go and have a good night."

With those parting words, Margot of course knew there'd be nothing good about her night. She dragged her feet down the hallway and back into the bathroom to draw another hot bath.

Dipping into the steaming water and curling her knees into her chest, she slipped down against the slick porcelain until her chin met the bathwater. In over ten years, she and Derek had never spoken to each other that way, not even as hormonally imbalanced adolescents. And *she'd* been the one to provoke it, poking at her friend with a stick until he bit back. Why? When good friends started to feel like enemies, it left her with such a strong feeling of distrust in…who, exactly, she didn't know.

Mostly herself.

Chapter Five

Une Nouvelle Amie

The university computer lab droned with research as grad students met in small groups to kick-start their first projects.

Cranky after Monday classes, Margot was brisk with her assigned partners, contributing her ideas and delegating tasks so she could quickly dismiss herself until their next meeting. Not the best improvement in social graces to follow her call with Derek, but Rand hadn't returned until late the night before, and she'd wanted to wait up for him. They had stayed up for a while chatting – and trying to do something about that awful wine stain on the carpet – so neither had gotten very much sleep.

Margot yawned as she paid half attention to her two classmates. Chloé was a sprightly, doe-eyed Frenchwoman in her late twenties, while Londoner Viv looked at least thirty and rather tougher around the edges. The dark burgundy chipping off her chewed-to-the-quick nails seemed to taunt Chloé's buff manicure of their own volition. They'd quickly agreed on Margot's suggested topic, pertaining to how twenty-first-century women were portrayed in advertising; so, soon enough, as one primly snapped a leather tote shut, the other stuffed a backpack to capacity, and Chloé and Viv departed the lab.

Contentedly sitting alone, Margot zoned into her email. Sylvie had finally replied to her message.

OMG, Derek did tell me about that. I wouldn't take it personally, though. He's hurt, but feels bad about what he said, too. Am sure he's always been a little jealous of your achievements and let it get the better of him, but he'll come around soon. You know he loves to push buttons and will eat crow when we run the vintage shop :)

Both embarrassed and relieved by the kind absolution, Margot decided to let the matter drop as Derek had asked. She'd just give him the time he needed, which was easier to do half a world apart.

But she couldn't shake off Sylvie's last comment as easily. The vintage shop was their secret – and imaginary – escape route whenever real life got annoying. It was a game Margot had started, in which they assumed the alter egos of old-lady shop owners 'Marge' and 'Sylvia'. More and more, though, Sylvie had been talking about it as something they would actually own someday, and Margot hoped she was still kidding. Optimism was one thing, delusion quite another. Margot considered playing along in her response but didn't see the point in taunting her friend or herself with pipe dreams. She replied with a thumbs-up emoticon and left it at that.

Slowly gathering her things with growing fatigue, she stood to leave. But a flash of dusty pink pranced into her peripheral vision as she reached the main exit, and she felt a touch on her arm that sent a shock through its muscle.

Catching her breath, she turned to see translucent fingers resting there, then looked into Chloé's intent gaze. The Frenchwoman's chocolate irises were sweetly framed by a sandy blond pixie cut. Her cardigan of tea rose, thin as tissue, softened her visage with a dreamlike, almost halo effect.

"Margot, I wanted to see if you'd like to join me *pour un café*?"

Tongue-tied, Margot held Chloé's stare and fought off a sudden vertigo. "Uh, yeah, sure. When were you thinking?" she finally stammered, feeling tall and gawky beside the petite figure. She was also self-conscious of her harsh Chicagoan accent that must have sounded like nails on a chalkboard to Chloé's fine, elfin ears.

"*Maintenant*? Now, if possible? I thought perhaps we could take the Tube to a neighborhood convenient for us both."

Margot longed to go home and hole up in her bedroom so badly she could have cried. Yet, "Um, sure," was her reply when she felt her cheeks burn in a moment of hesitation gone on too long. A hesitation that also had something to do with the feel of Chloé's hand still on her arm.

"Please don't feel obligated." Chloé shook her head. "We can do another time that is best for you. Or not, too."

"No. I mean yes, yes, I can join you now. I'm totally free and would enjoy that. Sorry if I'm a little out of it."

Margot's recovery appeared a success when Chloé squeezed her arm with an excited "*C'est bon! Allons-y.*"

Dusk was falling as they walked toward the nearest Underground station. Chloé's meekness evaporated with the raindrops that had briefly showered the glistening pavement; she twittered how glad she was to be in Margot's assigned group and researching their topic. Margot asked her if she'd likewise invited Viv, but Chloé wrinkled her brow with a brisk huff.

"*Elle est incorrigible.*"

Margot had mentioned earlier that she spoke *un peu* French from high school, but she didn't want to give Chloé the impression she knew more than she did by attempting to reply in kind. "How do you mean?" she asked to keep things in English.

"Well, I've tried to engage her in conversation before, but she's evidently not interested in having any friends at university, because I couldn't get a response from her longer than two words."

"Shocking," Margot said with an eye roll.

"I think she could be a very interesting person and would like to know her, but I can only try so hard, no?"

Margot bobbed her head. "Pretty much."

"Anyway, I thought, '*Mon Dieu!*' when she was chosen to work on this project with me, so was very relieved when you were as well."

"Aw, thank you. Likewise."

"You have a casual kind of chic. You look almost European, so I was surprised when I first heard your accent."

"Thanks? I guess?"

"Trust me, it's a compliment. American tourists I see everywhere are dressed as though they're going for a run when they are actually at a museum. They *should* be running when they look like they eat six meals a day."

Margot got a kick out of how oblivious Chloé was that her stereotypical comments could offend her present company. That she was, on the other hand, fully aware was another possibility.

Chloé continued. "You at least know to wear a scarf. I can teach you new ways to tie it."

"Thank you. Though I confess I first bought this one here on a high street."

"Some UK fashion is acceptable, but so repressed. The English are such a mournful people, would you agree?

Margot sniggered. "I blame the weather. But that mournfulness has inspired most of the music I listen to, so I can't completely knock it."

"Oh, please do not sing The Beatles," Chloé implored rather seriously.

"Thanks to my older brother's influence, my favorite bands hail from Crawley and Manchester, not Liverpool. The eighties British Invasion, not the sixties one."

The exchange of tastes in music and fashion continued on the train ride, flowing naturally if not for the frequent jostling of commuters given that rush hour was underway; feeling like sardines, they were lucky to even have room to stand. Twenty minutes later, they pulled into Earl's Court Station, where Chloé said it would only be a few minutes' walk to the Troubadour.

Margot's inner social butterfly suddenly rared to unfurl its wings. She still felt like an inadequate ogre around Chloé, though, so was grateful to sit down once they entered the café. She just needed to mind how she moved her long limbs beneath the table to not kick her companion, a frequent hazard with scaled-down European furniture for an American used to grazing in the wide-open spaces of freestanding franchise restaurants.

A lanky waiter in a plaid cap brought them laminated menus of the evening's cocktail specials.

"*Salut*, Hal," Chloé said to him with a smile before suggesting to Margot, "Perhaps an *apéritif* would be nice instead."

"Twist my arm. Coffee would keep me awake all night anyway. I think I'll go with wine, though."

"*C'est bien bon. Moi aussi*," she agreed and, getting the okay from Margot to try a dry white, she turned to Hal and ordered a bottle of Sauvignon Blanc. "A proper French wine, not Napa Valley." This time the teasing was plainly intentional.

"Ever hear of the nineteen seventy-six wine-tasting in Paris?" Margot couldn't help asking. Chloé seemed keen on enlightening the Ugly American on all ways European, so Margot reckoned she could teach a thing or two herself. "The blind taste-test that included Californian wines? Guess who came out on top?"

Chloé maintained a poker face. "I have a cousin named Margot. It is a very pretty French name."

The abrupt change in subject took Margot aback, but she granted that maybe conversational esteem-boosters like smiling and nodding, with a sprinkling of *uh-huh?* here and there, were a distinctly American trait. "Thanks, I like yours, too. Also French?"

"Greek, but *merci*. I was named for Ravel's ballet, *Daphnis et Chloé*. My mother, such a romantic like me."

Margot smiled but didn't wish to indulge starry-eyed fancies or end up having to confess her own romantic sob story. She veered clear by asking, "Do you like ballet?"

"Not particularly, though I did train as a young girl. My mother always dreamed of becoming a prima ballerina. She hoped to live vicariously through me." She shrugged. "But, I didn't enjoy it, and she was good to know her dreams are not mine to fulfill. I have other talents, and I content her by accompanying her to ballets, though I prefer other types of performances."

"Like Moulin Rouge?"

Her incredulous expression made it apparent Margot's American sarcasm was lost on French humor.

"I was just kidding, Chloé. That was my perverse way of asking what types of performances you do like. Plays, musicals, concerts…" *Mimes…*

The conversation had become work. From that point, Margot divided her concentration between listening to her classmate's replies and thinking up new questions to stockpile as ammo. She dreaded awkward silences as much as having to tiptoe around cultural misunderstandings.

Spying Hal rounding the corner with wine in hand, she thought, Gee, if only there were some sort of serum that could make this feel less awkward… *Oh, what have we here?*

Once he arrived at their table, she wished she could speed up his flaunted pouring process. The initial tasting step always seemed superfluous, as if she'd ever be pretentious enough to send back a bottle opened on her behalf. Not even James pulled that crap, even when the wine was obviously corked. With Chloé, though, she supposed she couldn't be so sure what to expect, and, with trepidation, she watched her new friend sniff then swill the wine.

"Yes, very good. Thank you."

Once her glass was filled, Margot gulped the Sauvignon Blanc too quickly to appreciate its bouquet and flavor, but it did what she needed it to after four full sips.

Feeling the burn in her belly, she settled back more comfortably in her seat with her fingers intertwined on her stomach, finally taking in the atmosphere. This was a cozy place with its dark wooden fixtures, art mingling with antique instruments, and miscellaneous teapots along the walls. In a period of silence that she felt increasingly at ease in, she snatched a flyer from between the condiments and read a blurb on the establishment's history, impressed to find that its downstairs club had hosted the likes of Bob Dylan and Elvis Costello. A bohemian spirit was alive and well here, and she felt contentedly displaced in time.

"You like it here, yes?"

"Yes." Margot smiled. "Very much."

"I thought you might."

"It reminds me of my favorite café in Chicago."

"An Al Capone hideout?" Chloé smugly offered.

Margot found it amusing that all her home city was ever associated with was gangsters, Michael Jordan, and wind.

"No. Although," she figured she could indulge her, "it was only a few blocks away from where the St. Valentine's Day Massacre occurred, right in Lincoln Park."

Chloé's eyes widened, clearly under the widespread misapprehension that every American carried a gun.

"The place I'm talking about, though, was a coffee shop kind of like this. Similar vintage scheme there. Didn't serve alcohol, but had shelf upon shelf of these huge jars of tea, and amazing sandwiches, all named for something literary. I composed more ads than I could count there, usually on the second floor – sorry, to you, the first floor. I would camp out at this one window up there with my little pot of jasmine tea. I loved to stick my nose right above my cup and smell spring blossoms, even if it was negative ten degrees outside. Sorry, I don't know what that is in Celsius. Let's just say pretty effing cold."

Chloé listened without interruption as Margot's focus departed the café to stare off into the past.

"I loved being there at an off-time in the afternoon, when hardly anyone else would be upstairs. I'd pretend it was my house, but back when it was more recently built – probably the early nineteen hundreds – and that those same chandeliers and bookcases were there when I invited guests into the parlor and gentlemen came to court me."

Returning attention to her friend, Margot thought Chloé looked entranced. Or maybe she was zoning out, bored from Margot's boozy babble.

73

She decided to open the conversation back to two-way. "Have you ever done that before? Been inside an old place and used your imagination to peel away exit signs and outlets, replace electric light with candles and just try to sense the activity that occurred there in another time? Envision the people who walked where you walk and stood where you stand, in that very same space, seeing some of the very same things, wondering if maybe they felt the same things you feel?"

Chloé didn't speak readily, but held her eye contact. After a moment, she pinched the stem of her wine glass and twisted it clockwise then counter-clockwise a few times before raising it to her pale, glossed lips. Margot second-guessed whether Chloé understood that it wasn't a rhetorical question until her classmate swallowed, exhaled at length, and caught up her breath as if to speak. A hesitation followed, though, and Margot detected a change of mind in that space.

What Chloé was originally going to say would remain unknown. With that impassive expression on her face, she instead replied, "No, I have not done that." She squinted her eyes. "How unusual."

Margot shrugged. "Just one of my quirks, I guess." She emptied her glass to cue Chloé to pour another.

"Well, your country is so new. When you grow up anywhere else, the old is just a part of everyday life." Without another word, Chloé looked down and started unbuttoning her cardigan.

Finding these responses so absurdly dismissive, Margot decided where to slot Chloé in her life: Study Partner. *Maybe* Drinking Buddy if no intimate conversation was involved. With her boundaries thus established, she regained some sense of control to put her at ease again.

Until Chloé arched her back to slip off her cardigan, revealing a tight white T-shirt with no bra beneath. Unable to help noticing the pert nipples straining against the sheer fabric, Margot might've taken a second too long to look up and meet Chloé's eyes. The Frenchwoman leveled an intense stare as one corner of her lips twitched upward.

Margot coughed into her hand and said she had to use the toilet.

When she returned to the table, she let Chloé lead conversation for their remaining hour there. Uneager to venture out on a limb again just to be left hanging, she was also concentrating too hard on keeping her gaze eye-level.

Once outside the café's carved wooden door, Chloé paused to light a cigarette. Margot lingered a minute, then excused herself under the pretense that the wine had made her drowsy and she'd better fill her stomach with some leftovers she had back at the flat.

Chloé pursed her lips to the air and blew a stream of smoke above Margot's head. Then she grinned. "The 'doggy-bag', as you say."

Margot forced a corny chuckle. "Yep. You know us Yankees."

She was debating whether to give a departing hug or handshake when Chloé stepped up to plant two nicotine-incensed kisses to each of her cheeks – which caught Margot off guard, so she fell out of sync and almost kissed Chloé on the lips.

On that inelegant note, the women parted ways with promises to meet again in time.

III

She was a Phantom of delight
When first she gleamed upon my sight;
A lovely Apparition, sent
To be a moment's ornament;
Her eyes as stars of Twilight fair;
Like Twilight's, too, her dusky hair;
But all things else about her drawn
From May-time and the cheerful Dawn;
A dancing Shape, an Image gay,
To haunt, to startle, and way-lay.

I saw her upon nearer view,
A Spirit, yet a Woman too!
Her household motions light and free,
And steps of virgin-liberty;
A countenance in which did meet
Sweet records, promises as sweet;
A Creature not too bright or good
For human nature's daily food;
For transient sorrows, simple wiles,
Praise, blame, love, kisses, tears, and smiles.

And now I see with eye serene
The very pulse of the machine;
A Being breathing thoughtful breath,
A Traveller between life and death;
The reason firm, the temperate will,

Endurance, foresight, strength, and skill;
A perfect Woman, nobly planned,
To warn, to comfort, and command;
And yet a Spirit still, and bright
With something of angelic light.

~ William Wordsworth (1807)

Interlude

Phantom of Delight

19th-Century London

My first years as Victor's bride were peaceful, happy.

Heartbreaking. Indeed, whenever I found myself with child, I was soon after absent of child. My personal sadness was beyond measure, and Victor shared in this, encouraging his pretty bride that we only needed tend to additional practice. When 'practice' failed to bring about an heir yet another time, I was humiliated beyond repair. All ladies in our circle of similar age to mine had successfully begotten their offspring, their insurance of fertility and worthiness as Lady of the House; and yet, there was I, sitting about my well-appointed home amongst our crystal chandeliers and exotic carpets with nothing to busy myself "that the servants should not do to earn their pence," trifling about with my "silly poetry and watercolors," as Victor said. The watercolors had been a sympathetic gift from Victor himself on the first occasion I had not delivered a living child, intended to help release my mind from the more immediate woes at hand, yet after the third occasion, what I produced with my natural yet uncultivated gift began to meet with ridicule over my 'artless eye'.

"Why do you not receive Mrs— for tea?" Victor would ask to break the silence of our torturously long dinners together.

"How could I possibly do so when I have not called upon her first?" would come my reply, the same response to the same question in which the only variable of alteration was the particular lady's name – the constant being that she be of upstanding reputation and outrageous arrogance, the sort who always feel it necessary to impress upon one that their very presence is a favor.

When prompted as to why I no longer initiated calling on anyone else, here I would speak nothing and thus reconcile our dinner sounds to the clinking of silver on china. It was then only a matter of time when Victor would consult his silver pocket watch, muttering some obligation that required him to leave the table. His silver watch, the one of his bachelorhood. No longer did he wear the golden one I had given him on our wedding day.

As I increasingly felt less of a woman, I did little to help Victor feel more of a man. And so it came about that I dismissed my second lady's maid. The first servant had resigned to be married, you perceive. This second, alternatively, had been so careless as to mistake my husband's bed for her own when she sleepwalked down the stairs (Victor had since taken to occupying the smaller bedroom on our second floor, understand). She had even blamed a ghost for those wails I would hear behind the wall.

Ghost, indeed.

My third lady's maid arrived at our doorstep the subsequent afternoon. Mama desired that I waste no time restoring our household to domestic equilibrium, and so that day she had brought help in tow, accompanied by a lecture as to how I might make myself more attractive and available to my husband, as respectable lady's maids were so difficult to come by. She had discovered this one whilst hat-shopping in Leicester Square, and so charmed by the clever little 'hat girl' was she that she brashly enquired into her earnings and promised this advancement in station. The poor girl could provide nary a character reference from previous employers of relevance to this role (outside a proficiency in sewing and quilling, which is admittedly quite exemplary), though I presume due diligence is a significantly lesser priority when the thought of having to dress myself and fashion my own hair was too dreadful for Mama to bear.

"Please, address me by my Christian name," I heard myself say to my new maid upon Victor quitting the house the following morning. "I shall not suffer to hear myself addressed as 'Madam' a minute longer."

If you will allow an inadequate explanation for this audacity, there was something in her eyes upon that first encounter that struck lightning through my veins. I understood her, somehow, and, more surprisingly, she understood me. In view of my upbringing, it is not so unusual that I should relate to all of our servants to some degree; their economic hardship was not so foreign to me as they must have imagined, yet any empathy I was willing to offer for some warm civility among them was shunned. Indeed, one would have thought our roles reversed in the pompous disdain their faces expressed towards me whenever I attempted to traverse social boundaries. Such terrible snobs the serving class can be.

In view of this, imagine my perplexed astonishment when, pursuant to my entreaty, she replied, "If you desire it." She then articulated my name so naturally, so sweetly, my initial shock – even though I had been the one to request it – had dissipated into familiarity. I could have embraced her forthwith.

Propriety, however, bid me show her promptly to her apartments on the third floor and acquaint her with my bedroom, in particular the wardrobe of which I expected her to maintain consistent inventory. If I were pleased with her service I should be glad to offer her those garments I wished to discard.

Her manifestation could not have been more aptly timed. Feeling dried, inadequate, I found fresh breath in her that I could no longer reap from Wordsworth and his yellow daffodils alone. It was not by virtue of her youth – we were nearly equals in age, which I feel left me all the more eager to overcome any disparities in position at once.

She was already a grown woman, thus, except that she in so many ways resembled a child. I do not say it condescendingly. Aside from a petite stature, there was something readily alive about her, something raw and untamed despite the manners she worked diligently to affect at the outset. It was not me she needed to impress then, but, even so, she respected Victor and our domestic staff of which she humbly accepted to be a part.

In the beginning, it was so.

Chapter Six

Cemetery Gates

21st-Century London

Rand's appearance was priceless first thing in the a.m. No better a morning person than Margot, it wasn't until after he showered that he would snap out of sleep and assume his usual zest and vigor. Until then, with eyelids droopier than normal and the disheveled hair of a cowlick-covered guinea pig, he looked like he'd just crawled in from the pub.

The two of them stood before the large bathroom mirror, scrubbing their teeth as Margot mused at his reflection and how one blow of air – maybe from one of the hurricanes spiraling all over his scalp – might truly tip him over. Taking turns spitting and rinsing in the sink, he stooped over the counter as Margot toweled off her mouth.

"So," spit "it was a friend from uni, was it, that you were out with last night?"

"Yeah, this French girl in my group."

"Bloody French," he said with mock vengeance, then spat again. "No doubt she *surrendered* to your charms, my dear." He walked to the towel rack to take his turn wiping toothpaste off his lips.

She shook her head, then her gaze fell on the electric toothbrush he'd replaced in its stand. Pointing to it, she asked, "Why does that blink?"

"Means it's charging." As he watched Margot set her manual toothbrush down on the counter, he added, "Ah! I have something for you."

"Is that right."

He scratched his head with an uninhibited yawn as he fumbled through his toiletries in the lower cabinet.

"Yes. I'm sorry I didn't think of it before. Here you are." He presented Margot with an unused brush head. A band of pink wrapped around its base, distinguishing it from Rand's blue.

"Well, isn't that just the cutest thing in the world. For me?"

"I cannot watch you brush another day with that primitive tool. Once I went electric, I couldn't go back."

She was tempted to make a jab at British dentistry – he'd made it too easy, really – but curbed herself with sarcasm of a different tack.

"Hmm, among your other toys in the nightstand, I'm sure." She made a show of eyeing him up and down like so much meat, the svelte muscularity of his physique not going unnoticed in the process since he was wearing only pajama bottoms.

"Cheeky."

Margot had happily stored away her brush head when she checked her enthusiasm. "Wait a minute. What would Gwen think of this? You aren't using the pink one up on *me*, are you?"

Rand spoke as he yawned again. "No. Hers is the yellow one."

"But still, isn't this kind of imposing on her girlfriend benefits? Haven't I crossed the line enough?"

"Don't be silly."

"I'm serious. I am a female, remember."

Rand's gaze fell to just below her tank top's deep neckline. "I'm well aware of that."

She elbowed him. "I mean that I understand my kind, and the kittens have claws when need be."

"I'm aware of that as well. But Gwen isn't like that."

"Then why do I never see her? She isn't ever here, and you don't spend many nights at her place."

"I'm allergic to her cat. And she works a lot of evenings and weekends to show properties around people's work schedules."

"Shejules? *Parlez anglais, s'il vous plaît.*"

Rand shook his head. "Divided by a common language," he muttered, then rubbed his eyes. "You might see Gwen round during the day, by the way. But I gave her your timetable, if that's all right, so she knows to give you privacy."

Prih-vacy, he'd pronounced it. *Like vih-tamins*. She was loving this.

"Tell her that I was almost engaged," she said, "the break-up was horrible, and I'm not looking to throw myself at anyone for a long time, especially not another girl's guy, and—"

"She *knows*. Don't obsess."

"Sorry. I love my new toothbrush and promise to give you a big smooch on the cheek right after I've first used it. And before I've rinsed."

"I look forward to *that*." He reached an arm around her waist and bumped hips with her. "Now, you saucy wench, will I be joining you in the tub or are you joining me in the shower?"

"Yeah, ya see? I would've stabbed James's nut sack with my toothbrush if he carried on a morning ritual like this with another chick while we dated."

Rand raised his hands as if at gunpoint. "Fair enough. Though I don't trust you with that electric toothbrush now. Don't force my hand to issue you an ASBO."

"*Azbo?*"

"An order against antisocial behavior."

Mimicking his pronunciation, she said, "I am not an-tee-social! I was just out last night!"

Rand smiled and laid his hands on her tense shoulders. "It also means disruptive or threatening behavior. *Anti-society*. And I was joking."

Margot slumped but grinned, reassured that he didn't know what a crazy hermit she was without him around. And liking the feel of hands on her. Maybe what Gwen didn't know…

She wouldn't complete that thought. "Are we finished with the English lesson, Professah 'Iggins?" she said in a bad Cockney accent before turning and starting up the steps. When he called after her, she readily backtracked with a smile.

"Mind turning the light on?" he asked as he plugged his shaver in beside the cord to the toothbrush charger.

Her smile fell a little. "Oh. Sure." She climbed back up and flicked the switch.

"Just so you know, that has to be switched on for this particular outlet to work."

"Oh. Okay, thanks." And with that unexciting service rendered, she closed the door behind her to give him some *prih-vacy* – and herself a reality check.

But now that she thought about it, with all the daylight let in by the windows – the sun was rising as early as five those days – she hadn't even noticed the bathroom light was off.

"Waaait a minute." She turned on the ball of her foot and hopped back down the stairs to knock at the door. "Hey, Rand?"

"Yeah?"

"If the light has to be on for the outlet to work, then how was the toothbrush blinking?"

Silence. The door opened, and his eyes were wide awake without the aid of his shower. "You're sure it was?"

"Well, yeah, that's why I asked you why it blinks. This was the first time I noticed it."

He looked from her to the toothbrush to her again. "Oh, brilliant. You know what this could mean."

She thought of how his computer monitor also had the tendency to come out of its hibernation in the middle of the night, interrupting her dreams with its blue glow as if something – someone? – had touched the mouse or keyboard. She held her breath.

"*More* faulty wiring. One more expense to deal with fixing up this place. Bloody hell, I already installed new fuses last year."

Smirking with a relieved exhale, Margot tried to cheer

him, suggesting it wasn't the charger but the toothbrush's battery gone awry.

And, sure enough, his high spirits returned once he was cleansed, shaven, and clothed. He gave Margot full clearance for the loo, bidding her *adieu* as he would likely be gone before she resurfaced.

Minutes later, she stood in the shower stall with her back to the head, looking through the glass door. It was dotted with lime scale like a giant snow globe in freeze-frame, with her as the attraction inside. The toothbrush on the counter flashed its light like a warning signal.

As her vision blurred the light into two menacing eyes, Margot blankly looked over at the small window. She caught herself about to overanalyze yet *again* what she thought she'd seen out of it, wondering why she dwelled on such stupid things while the rest of the world carried on with big-picture importance. Got things done. All her brain wanted to do anymore was roam and reflect, not assert and achieve.

What if I permanently fall out of the habit of nine-to-five? Of suiting up in business casual and charging at the world in proactive high-heeled fury?

As it was, she'd easily gravitated to her black Converse sneakers and skinny jeans with graphic tees and cardigans every day, reserving every *other* day for tucking her unstyled hair into a man's tweed cap. Makeup optional. It was glorious.

Tipping her head back into the water's stream, she whispered, "Free…"

But when she looked forward again, all she could see was the enclosing gray of fogged glass. The shampoo stung her eyes, so she jolted her head back to rinse her face. The water seemed to surge with greater pressure, and she sputtered as she accidentally swallowed some.

Trapped, she now thought as her chest tightened.

A wave of claustrophobia seized her lungs, and, wheezing, Margot twisted the faucet handle to turn the water off. Instead, a searing stream stabbed at her flesh. Her spine arched, rigid, as she frantically spun the handle around this way and that until she found the off position. UK faucets sometimes reversed the hot and cold from what she knew at home, so she cursed her force of habit and that she hadn't taken a bath instead. Touching a cool hand to her singed forearm, she whimpered as it left white fingerprints on the flushed skin.

Once toweled off and dressed in Rand's terrycloth robe, Margot shook off her shock and ran upstairs to boil water in a stovetop kettle – not that she felt kindly towards this liquid in its heated form at the moment, but she did fancy some tea. Jogging back down to the bathroom, she combed through her hair's wet tangles before moving on to her moisturizing regimen.

She was dabbing gel on the thin skin beneath her eyes when a shrill scream rang out from behind.

"Jesus!" She'd forgotten about the kettle. One of these days, she'd have to adapt to Rand's electric one that boiled water so much faster, so much more quietly.

Still circling the pads of her fingers around her eyes to rub in the moisturizer, she made a beeline for the stove range to turn off the gas flame. Clattering about the upper cabinet, she fished out a tea press and poured a healthy amount of Earl Grey into its infuser. Then she filled the pot and inserted a tea light into the warmer underneath.

Leaving her caffeine fix to steep on the counter, she gave herself permission to lazily lie down on the sofa for a few minutes as she waited. Feet propped on the couch arm closest to the windows, she knew she should resume getting ready for that morning's lecture, but she felt a headache coming on after that adrenaline rush in the shower. She was listless, and suddenly didn't care if she was late to her seminar.

Now that she thought about it, she didn't care if she attended at all. Like she'd said to Derek, she wasn't making up for a failed class *or* career. She'd called it professional development, but it was more for kicks and changing things up than anything. It was all by choice. Her choice. She didn't *have* to be here and doing this. She didn't *have* to do anything she didn't want to.

And I could give a flying fuck if I don't see Chloé or Viv, whom she was supposed to meet for their assignment again after class. Maybe it was just Chloé's Frenchly superior airs, but something soured Margot's stomach at the thought of seeing her classmates, twisting it until she could almost taste the bitterness of bile rising to the back of her tongue.

It seemed a shame to waste the first blue skies and sunshine London had seen in days, but her chest was still tight, and her temples felt pinched in a vise. She closed her dried, aching eyes and just seeped into the sofa's leather.

Falling gradually to sleep, poetic lines glided into her thoughts like ripples on the waves of her subconscious.

For oft, when on my couch I lie
In vacant or in pensive mood,
They flash upon that inward eye
Which is the bliss of solitude;
And then my heart with pleasure fills,
And dances with the daffodils.

The sound of traffic outdoors rustled Margot awake, shattering the meadow of yellow she'd been reclining in. After a deep breath, she whispered the poem out loud again before sinking back to sleep.

Before long, though, she heard someone enter the room. Had Rand come back? Without opening her eyes, she sensed the presence approach the sofa and hover over her. Standing still, inspecting. While it didn't touch her, Margot felt its energy softly press on her in three areas down the length of her body: her arm, her hip, her thigh.

She couldn't move in her panic over who or what may have just let itself into Rand's flat when the door should've been locked. She was terrified to be so vulnerable, lying prostrate in nothing but a bathrobe. But she had to open her eyes. She needed to confront the invader.

Her brain signaled to her eyelids to rise, but paralysis

overtook her senses as if she were in rigor mortis. The eerie childhood chant, *Light as a feather, stiff as a board, light as a feather, stiff as a board*, whispered through her ears as her mind struggled to take command over her body.

Open your eyes, open your eyes, open your eyes.

She channeled her desire into a singular focus.

Just move, move.

The effort was tremendous, but Margot fought her growing dread and urged herself on.

Move, move.

She became aware of her head, aware of her neck.

Move.

Her arms materialized, if only phantom limbs. She wanted to lift outside of herself, to reach out and grasp her own shoulders where they were pinned to the cushion and shake them.

Her chest expanded, swelling with energy. With a sharp inhale, she lurched, and the morning sun ignited her eyelids. They fluttered, then opened, and just as she processed that she'd been dreaming and there was no one standing next to her, a crisp snap sounded in her right ear. She swiveled her face toward the kitchen – just in time to catch a cloudy white movement swoop the other way in the corner of her eye, toward the windows.

It had happened so fast. Steaming in sweat, Margot now saw nothing but the wall with its two gaping windows and her feet still propped on the sofa's arm. Slowly, she boosted herself up and swung around to a seated position, staring at the empty space between the couch and coffee table that she was so certain had been occupied less than a minute before.

To her right was the vacant kitchen and hall. She leaned forward to see more of the entryway. The unit door was closed. She then looked back at the kitchen where she thought she'd heard the snapping sound and remembered the tea. The flame inside the warmer flickered spastically beneath the teapot.

It was probably the wick that crackled and gave off that puff of smoke. It's probably almost burned down. God, how long had I been sleeping?

She sank her face to her fingers to rub away the sleep and salty moisture, breathing deeply to open her chest. A look at the clock confirmed she was most definitely not making it to class on time that morning. Assuming her project partners would call to reschedule if she didn't show up, she turned the ringer off on her pay-as-you-go mobile phone to let them go straight to voicemail.

Or hell, for all I care.

Margot lay back down and curled into fetal position for a few minutes. With her elbows tucked in and her fists pressed to her lips, she wondered what was with this nasty mood and what she should do about it. Her gaze traveled to Rand's bookshelf, and, after a few minutes, she finally stood to idle about in front of it.

Stroking her fingertips across the rows of spines, glossing over travel guides and narratives, biographies, and business guides, she found a slim paperback of poetry wedged between an atlas and art book. Slapped askew on its front cover was a neon-green sticky note.

Found it for 2 quid.
A sound investment in
your cultural literacy,
tho I know you already
luv your WW – and I don't
mean Walter White ;)
–G

An impulsive gift from Gwen, it seemed.

Wonder if she makes him laugh.

Ignoring the little pang reverberating in her stomach, she questioned if 'WW' was Walt Whitman and flipped through the book to read aloud at random.

"*She was a Phantom of delight*
When first she gleamed upon my sight;
A lovely Apparition sent

To be a moment's ornament."

Margot made theatrical motions with her free hand as she read the next few lines of not Walt Whitman but William Wordsworth. After praising the eyes and hair of whoever 'She' was, Margot went on:

"A dancing Shape, an Image gay,
To haunt, to startle, and way-lay."

She read the rest silently as the female specter evolved into a flesh-and-blood woman.

A Being breathing thoughtful breath,
a Traveller between life and death.

Even Margot's romantic pessimism gave in to the words' sentiment – the exceptional love they described, that didn't falter once the rose-colored glasses were snatched off. She wondered if a man could really love like that, if Rand could or already did for Gwen. Could Margot, for that matter?

Appropriately enough, the poem on the next page jabbed at her single status: "I Wandered Lonely as a Cloud." She begrudgingly began to read it but soon lost herself in the reverie of a simple moment gazing at daffodils. The final stanza repeated familiar lines.

For oft, when on my couch I lie
In vacant or in pensive mood...

The same lines she'd just recited in her sleep. But now that she was awake and staring at the poem itself, she didn't recognize it from anywhere but that dream. Where had she heard it before? And how had she come to memorize it? High school English assignment, probably, but could she recall that after all these years? Regardless, it was weird that she'd happened to open the book to that poem right after she'd just remembered it. She flagged the page with Gwen's note as a reminder to record the coincidence in her dream diary.

In the meantime, Wordsworth had painted his scene so vividly that Margot took it as an unequivocal sign of the cosmos to stop thinking about how beautiful it was outside and just get up to be part of it. It was for her own good. Though she ached for a relaxing bath despite having just showered, she got dressed before she could give in to the temptation and ventured out into the world.

She got as far as Brompton Cemetery.

Sunlight filtered through the leaves as if to bless the sacred ground. A stone angel veiled in ivy peered over the resting place of her eternal charge, while crows sitting on nearby obelisks sharpened their black beaks on the stone.

Margot sipped a chai latte from her takeaway cup as she sat on a bench of brittle wood. Her coffee-shop napkin was full of epitaphs, and she'd just finished writing, "lamented by one," all that was legible on the headstone in front of her. She wished she could read more and find out who'd been the "one." A spouse? Child? Sibling? Parent? And why only one person? This was a grand monument, but was the deceased's life so lonely that no one else grieved?

Mature trees canopied the graveyard in peaceful seclusion, but in the morning calm, the little demon flittering in Margot's mind had nowhere to hide. Among the daisy-like weeds growing from the graves, an image of James's face came before her, sunken into a striped bed pillow and smiling with soft words. An unexpected, gentle warmth pressed on her heart.

She did miss him. Of course she did; she had loved him, but had lost faith that she was ever *in* love. There was a difference, and Margot and James had tripped into the fissure between. He hadn't hurt her purposefully or in any concrete way, and he'd always been quick to apologize after any fight. But by this point Margot believed to her core that there was no least effective or meaningful word in the Standard English language than *sorry*.

If love means never having to say it, then how about loving someone enough to not do anything you'd have to apologize for in the first place?

Another specter of James materialized before her, and she remembered herself standing with him at an elevated rail station in Chicago on a bitter February evening last year. The temperature that night had been too low to even snow, so the moon and stars pierced the clear, navy sky more brightly than the cobwebby lanterns. James had held her close for warmth as their footing vibrated on the rumbling platform, and Margot recalled looking up at the stars, then releasing an arm to shake her hand in the air.

"Don't forget, we come from the stahz!" she said, affecting the voice of an exotic old woman.

James crinkled his nose. "What?"

"You know. My favorite movie?"

He shook his head with no recognition.

"Before Sunrise, with Ethan Hawke? American guy and French girl meet on a train and agree to spend the day together in Vienna? And a palm reader tells them we're all made from stardust?"

"Oh, I thought it was another of your moldy-oldie movies."

"Shut it. But it's true, you know."

"What is?"

"That people come from stars. Ashes to ashes, stardust to…just dust, I guess."

"Okay, Moby."

Shivering together, they looked northward for the El until turning their faces back to each other. Margot's stomach fluttered as James looked deeply into her eyes, searching, surely moved by what she'd said and overcome in the emotion he held for her.

And then he said, "Hold still a sec," and poked an indelicate finger at the corner of her eye, scraped, and grimaced in mild repulsion as he flicked the real object of his concentration away. "Eye snot."

No, Margot didn't quite regret breaking it off. Everything happens for a reason; she must have done the right thing. If she hadn't, would she be here now, experiencing life anew in a different hemisphere on her own steam? What was tugging at her, then? Making her feel less whole, more faceless each day?

When Rand wasn't at home, she couldn't shake that sensation of being strained through a sieve, dispersing her atoms to meld into the background as she soaked into the carpeting like her spilled wine – or evaporated with her bathwater, becoming more and more transparent. All she could do was look around the walls at someone else's books, someone else's photos, wanting to see herself somewhere in them. The closest she ever came was in the mirror.

Maybe that was why James, too, had always seemed to look right through her. But how closely had she really looked at him? Always so preoccupied with how she appeared in his eyes, she could no longer see his face as more than a smooth mask, couldn't recall whether he'd had any birthmarks or even the specific shade of his eyes.

In striving to see him, her gaze fell on the headstone in front of her again. She squinted at it while reaching into her purse to put her pen back inside.

Damn.

She just looked a squirrel right in its beady eyes, an unintentional invitation for food she didn't have. When it scampered over to get a closer look at what treats might lay within her bag, she stared at the animal blankly and held up her pen as all she had to offer. *"Useless human with your stick of uselessness,"* its wee rodent brain must've thought. "Next time," she promised, oddly flattered that the creature had at least noticed her.

She packed up and rose, accidentally knocking over her chai and anointing the dried weeds below with its milky spice.

"Meh. There," she said to her speckled-gray companions.

"Have yourselves a spot of tea, then."

The squirrels scattered, leaving Margot to walk until she found another epitaph to jot onto her napkin.

AFTER HAVING PAINFULLY ENDURED PROTRACTED AND INTENSELY ACUTE SUFFERING

That's, er, shockingly informative. Bet she was a huge whiner. And that it didn't cost so much to engrave by the letter back then. Hoping she herself would never suffer in a 'protracted' nor 'intensely acute' manner, Margot looked at another stone.

WRITE ME AS HAVING LOVED MY FELLOW MAN.

Sounded more selfless, yet she doubted it. *This guy asked to have these words penned for posterity?* Clearly he had a tremendous ego, or maybe he was hiding something, a string of mistakes that no well-intentioned epitaph could make up for. But why should Margot care? He was a stranger from another lifetime whom she would never meet. Yet here she was, wishing he'd lived his life better.

She flicked her pen back into her handbag like a dart and stood to walk toward the cemetery's rear gateway. And like every other time she visited, she felt an overwhelming need to pee by the time she reached this segment of the yard. Next time, she'd skip stopping at the café beforehand.

Fighting her sudden discomfort, she couldn't help wondering if maybe, instead of the tea, it was her body forcing her to remember that it was still alive, that she should assert that like the tall grass standing proudly and the wildflowers beaming yellow and fuchsia. She sucked the same air as these armies of perseverant life but related more to the disheveled tombstones, ruptured from their foundations to lean at awkward and inconsistent angles toward and away from each other. These monuments had surrendered to time, allowing the elements to file down their edges and render identities anonymous as, decade after decade, the dressed stone returned closer to its natural appearance. Gates of mausoleums rusted away and upper slabs of sarcophagi shifted and chipped, liberating the grass growing inside them.

Margot edged closer to a tomb that echoed loudly with buzzing insects; when she peered into its blackness, a cool, ancient scent wafted to her face. Continuing to idle along, she scanned the moss and vines that clung to and devoured the markers sprouting all throughout this garden of marble and granite, the Gothic juxtaposed with the Romanesque, Celtic crosses with Grecian urns.

Stopping at another grave, she saw Christmas décor rotting away by her feet. A depressing sight in summer, the winter wreath made her fancy how the cemetery's atmosphere must change with the seasons. She wouldn't be in London long enough to see it burn in rust and gold, the falling leaves mimicking the footfall of a pursuing stranger and the plucked trees revealing more of the sky and buildings beyond. Yet she could imagine how, on one chilled day that would paint the scene gray, someone would kneel again at a name of diminishing meaning to the present world and place another wreath of scarlet ribbon and silver baubles. Only for it to waste away during another sunny spring and rainy summer as the cycle continued: lather, rinse, repeat.

The effect of time would be noticeable enough, and somehow she felt she'd already seen it all before and would again, her grandest déjà-vu yet. To preserve its enchantment, she didn't analyze the reasons why this site had come to matter so much. She felt whole here. That was all to know.

But her bladder waited for no man, living or dead. Picking up her pace, Margot hightailed it to the cemetery's rear exit until a shiver clenched the muscles between her shoulder blades. Despite her urgency to get back home, she slowed to a full stop in front of a gabled gravestone. An ornate sprig of acacia crowned an inscription she hadn't seen yet.

READER, STAY.
UNDERNEATH THIS STONE DOTH LIE
AS MUCH BEAUTY AS COULD DIE;
WHICH IN LIFE DID HARBOR GIVE
TO MORE VIRTUE THAN DOTH LIVE.
IF AT ALL SHE HAD A FAULT,
LEAVE IT BURIED IN THIS VAULT.

Rather than grab her pen and napkin to write the poem down, Margot just stood there, rereading it. Contemplating it. If there was an afterlife, could people really leave their failings behind to putrefy in the dirt, safe from anyone's memory? She liked to think so.

Her gaze rose to the name chiseled in the stone.

CHARLOTTE PIDGEON

It so happened that Charlotte Pidgeon was born on the same day as Margot, but her year of birth was 1848 and year of death 1874. Despite all the other gravestones she'd recorded onto her napkin, copying anything down from this one somehow seemed blasphemous. So she just kept standing, with gravity fastening her in place. Gawking, until a weight on her breastbone made it more difficult to breathe.

The sensation was strange, no question. Margot had never felt anything like it. But she'd taken enough psychology courses as an advertising major to peg it for what it was: a psychosomatic response. The conditions were ideal for something like that. For one, the general creepy-factor of standing above hundreds of corpses as black birds crowed their 'Evermores' left and right. And now this moving inscription that kicked in her sympathies.

There was otherwise no meaning in it – even if, go figure, the given name should be Charlotte. A decent coincidence to add to her diary, but it wasn't surprising that such a popular Victorian name would find its way on an English grave or the spine of an English book. She must have seen a dozen Charlottes in that lot alone by now, along with all the Alices, Emmas, and Janes.

And so what if their birthdays were the same? The ratio of 365 days to the billions of people ever born on Earth was basically nil. She had to stop pandering to what the human brain did naturally: form correlations when it noted them. Only this and nothing more.

Exhausted with her overactive imagination and fantastically bored with herself, she didn't want to stand there anymore. But she didn't want to walk anywhere else either. Breathing heavily through her nose as a numbness dulled her, she didn't want to be anywhere in that moment, not even in her own skin. The effort and futility of life bore down on her as she considered all the bodies underground, all those who'd borne the burden of existence and thought it mattered until they didn't exist *or* matter anymore – just rotted in boxes under her feet.

She had to go back to Rand's. She didn't want to; she needed to. Not for the toilet any longer, but a bath sounded nice – something that could warm her against the nip of her fears, wash away the soil she felt falling over her. Drown the thuds each shovelful made on the lid of her inner casket. That sounded purposeful enough.

Forgive my intrusion, Miss Pidgeon. I will leave you to rest in peace.

Chapter Seven

Trespasses

Turns out, truancy was a tough habit to break. Seeing that her first absence from school hadn't brought the world to a screeching halt, Margot took it as free license to try it out again the next day. Then the next day, and then the next couple of weeks after that.

When she wasn't visiting the cemetery instead of the classroom, she'd while away her afternoons on indulgences like daytime lounging and soaks in the tub. Then in the evenings when Rand was home from work and not otherwise committed to Gwen, they'd go out to the pubs or dine in on takeaway curry or true Italian-style pizza that was a far cry from the Chicago deep dish Margot knew and loved.

This life as a Lady of Leisure was suiting her incredibly fine. Rather than fight her solitary moods out of some sense of guilt, she just gave in to them now. And just like that, her worries would disappear like the steam rising off her bathwater. Not even ghosts or death could scare her when she already felt halfway there, her brain and heart serving little more function than to keep her vaguely conscious of the mundaneness of day-in and day-out.

Not entirely true. There was something her heart beat for with increasing interest. Some*one*, whose friendship had been easy as breathing and was like the sun she so rarely got to see anymore. Who was also out of reach. Which was just as well; while she couldn't deny the attraction, even if availability were a factor, Margot still didn't want to become someone else's other half. Not until she felt whole on her own.

In dreams, at least, she could safely lose herself to the lips and caresses she yearned for. Not anyone's specifically, but palpable enough to satisfy the contact she missed. The phantasmic touches would glide down her spine and whisper over her breasts, nip at her lips and elicit sighs she hoped were only in her head and not audible to Rand. She'd written a couple of these dreams down in her diary but kept the rest safe from discovery.

And now, as her ethereal lover was once again on the verge of filling her where she felt most empty, she heard a mournful creak. Curled on her bed, Margot woke up to early evening sunlight slanting in through the shade – then shot an evil eye at the door's audacity to make her get up before she could get off.

"Rand! Your flat is broken!"

"Sorry?" He walked to the entryway.

She dragged herself to her bedroom door, smoothing her hair and adjusting her twisted leggings to look somewhat presentable. "This door never stays closed unless this thingy clicks into that thingy." Her index finger slinked toward the lock like an inchworm. "The slightest air pressure opens it."

"Right." He offered a thoughtful frown for a few seconds. "Well, I could fix that, but the ghost prefers it open."

"What?"

"Yes. She likes to walk around here now that she's eternally confined to the building and can't take a turn about the garden. You like whist, don't you? She's a devil at whist."

"You're joking."

"Obviously."

"What the hell?" She slapped his forearm.

Stroking his chin like a man in a razor commercial, Rand gave a weak laugh and was in the process of turning away when his raised brow seemed to yank his attention back to her. "Do…?" He cocked his head. "You're not…"

Margot readied for anything he might ask as her stomach

101

quavered with something like wishful thinking. Her mind and body still tingled from the dream, which hadn't fully released her from its spell given the door's abrupt cock-block.

"Really?" Rand's high-pitched giggle would have been effeminate if it didn't coincide so well with his boyish charisma, not to mention sound a bit forced. "Miss Margot…"

She gave a coy side-smile to tempt the question from him. "Ye-es?"

"Do *you* believe in ghosts?"

Crestfallen, and not a little rattled in view of her recent graveyard musings, she stammered like Shaggy from *Scooby-Doo*. "G-ghosts?"

"Yeah. Do you?"

"Methinks *you're* the one who too quickly concocted that story."

"Methinks thou dost protest too much."

"Methinks *methinks* is a ridiculous word from a ridiculous ghost-believing country!"

"Methinks…that you are quite right." It was one of those days when Rand relieved his corneas of contacts and wore spectacles of bronze wire, and his eyes twinkled the more for it. "Though I believe I saw that *Ghost Hunters* is on the telly in an hour, right after *Ghost Adventures*. Those would be American ghost-hunting programs, yes?"

Margot looked up at the ceiling and plugged her pursed lips with the tip of her finger. "Maaaybe?" She gave his arm a flirty nudge this time. "Hey, the US is old enough to be haunted, too, you know. Way before you people waltzed in like you owned the joint, Native Americans were living and dying there."

With arms crossed, he took a wider stance and shifted his weight slightly side to side outside her doorway. "So? Do you?"

Margot would have felt cornered if not for his playful grin. Shaking her head with an exhale that clicked in the back of her throat, she bristled a little but slapped on a smile. Just when she thought she'd exorcised them, ghosts were back to haunt her.

"Does it matter?" she asked.

"I don't know. I suppose the afterlife just makes for a stimulating if not inevitable talking point among friends, yeah?"

"Right, inevitable." *Friends*. "Like death and taxes." Margot crossed her arms for warmth against a draft, and she leaned on the doorframe to steady herself as her mind dizzied on an empty stomach. She shouldn't have napped through lunchtime.

Closing her eyes for a few seconds, she concentrated on her next words. "No, I do have those thoughts. I mean, I was raised to believe in an immortal spirit that survives our mortal body, so it wouldn't be that big a stretch to believe in ghosts, right?"

"Do you, then?"

She shrugged.

"Do you *want* to?"

What Margot wanted was an attorney present. *Did he tap my call to Derek?* She fidgeted, feeling lighter-headed by the second as though about to lift outside of herself.

"I…can't say that I do."

Rand narrowed his eyes. "Why not?"

"Well…sometimes I think I do," *because I thought I saw one in your bedroom*, "because there's comfort in the idea of living forever in some form, and still existing alongside loved ones. But it's terrifying, too. Like if a presence isn't familiar or wanted, or just takes you by surprise. As a kid, I would squeeze my eyelids shut at bedtime to block out anything that could be watching me. I definitely did *not* want to believe then."

Rand chuckled. "But don't you think in that fear *was* belief? Wouldn't that be proof of it?"

"I guess so. But at that St. Paul's debate I told you about, a scientist argued that the soul is really just misprints in our genes that give us unique personalities. And, like, imaging techniques show how the brain lights up when people feel

103

one way or another, so it's more or less something chemical than anything disembodied that survives after our body dies. You know, like…neurotransmitters, and…"

Though he'd laughed before, a light had visibly gone out in Rand, like when a child wakes too early on Christmas morning and sees Mom eating the cookies and stuffing the stockings. "But does studying a map explain the majesty of a mountain? Does reading sheet music capture the song you hear? Couldn't there be more to us than proteins, something that lingers?"

The guy's a consultant. He wears three-piece suits to work, not vestments or a toga, so what's with the Socratic seminar?

Margot remained silent a moment, picturing Rand's lean form in one of his well-fitted waistcoats. Her imagination decided to accessorize it with a silver pocket watch, too. As she grew more faint with her low blood sugar, she found distraction in the beguiling line of his jaw, envisioning him with well-groomed sideburns and a moustache.

I've read too much Dickens.

She broke her eye contact and demurely looked to the carpet, where her vision swam with the likelihood of an upcoming migraine.

"Well," she answered, "that's a fair argument, and an oddly poetic one at that, but…it *could* all be the stuff of fairies and witches, you know? Pixie dust. Mirage."

"Yes, I understand your point. You always did cater to redundancy in your ad copy."

He'd clearly meant it in jest, but the critique stung, echoing what Margot had read in her performance evaluations time and again. She gave a little huff as her ears crackled, and she was feeling so cold now, she half expected to see her breath come out in a frosty mist.

"But all right," he said. "You don't believe, and hopefully death *isn't* something you dwell on often." His eyes, locked on hers, appeared to pose this as a question. "I only ask because…well, I was just won—"

Bzzzzz! blared the door buzzer from just a meter away.

"Bloody hell!" Rand spun to grab its phone-like receiver. "Yeah, hi?"

"It's me." A female voice, as best as Margot could hear. And a haughty one, if she wasn't mistaken. As her head continued to swoon, a fierce territorialism swelled in her breast.

"Right, I'll come down straight away," Rand had barely said before Margot leaned toward the receiver and blurted out a peal of coquettish laughter. Shooting her a quizzical look, he rapidly said into the intercom, "Actually, come on up!" He stabbed the unlock button far longer than necessary as he stared back at her with an intensity that said their conversation wasn't over yet.

But Margot squared her shoulders and marched backwards into her bedroom, shoving the door into his next words – "It's Gwen" – to smash and send them wilting to the floor.

The door stayed shut.

[Dream Entry – June 30]
She rises aloft to meet her salvation, the mourners at her feet, shrouded in anonymity, but their pain is distinct... They sink, they slump, they writhe, they grind their fists to their teeth and convulse if not retch with her at the center...not prostrate with stiff hands arranged in artifice at her bosom, not her. She, wholly beneath cloth of ivory, lies on her side, revealing womanly hips and scandalously outlined thigh... A face, just barely perceptible where the fabric gathers at the nose and is pulled taut by gravity, but the fingers are flesh from where they peer... An arm that had slipped from her side... She looks slovenly, as though no care was tended to make her proper on Earth whereas the angels exalt her gracious divinity and cradle the infant in holy arms.

This was Margot's most vivid dream yet, and she took care to jot as much detail as fleeting memory would allow. Rereading the entry to the light of the computer monitor that had turned itself on and woken her again, she used a thumbnail to plow away crusty remnants of drool at the corner of her lips.

It was approaching ten o'clock, the sun only first giving in to its lengthened summer curfew so that the moon could step out. The blackbirds' erratic lullabies seemed to urge Margot to face the music of a mess she'd so foolishly strewn. First Derek, now this.

She started when a dull thud on the door sharpened into three knocks.

"Margot?"

The desk chair answered with a creak as she lifted her weight from it to open the door. Keeping her palm on the knob, she stepped into the threshold, hesitating several seconds before raising her meek eyes. Luckily, the face she met was not the scowling countenance of the Byronic hero she'd expected.

"Hi, you all right?" Rand's tone sounded like he hadn't analyzed the incident to remotely the same extreme as Margot had. He probably hadn't even given her behavior a second thought before going out on his planned evening with Gwen.

"Sure." She felt sickened by their resumed positions in the doorway and suggested relocating to the living room, where she sat timidly on Rand's club chair like a child sent to the principal's office.

"Gwen was here just briefly," he said, "then we went for dinner. Pizza, seventy-five centimeters of it. I have leftovers here for you if you like."

"That's nice of you. I'm fine, though."

"You did eat, then?"

No. "Yeah. But thanks." Not wanting his kind gesture to be thought in vain, she added, "Maybe tomorrow for lunch. Cold pizza's a national favorite."

"What were you up to tonight?"

"Oh, I just slept. Taking advantage of the fact I can."

"You *have* seemed knackered lately. I assume you've had some late nights studying. That takes its toll." His tone was light enough, but the words sounded strained.

"I haven't been to class in a while, to be honest. I never used to ditch, but I can, so I do. Just learning how to *be*."

Rand rubbed his chin slowly between thumb and forefinger as speculation shadowed his eyes. "Well, you're an adult. I suppose you know what you're doing."

Not likely, but she was grateful he didn't get didactic on her. Still, she tried to salvage her studious reputation to an extent.

"Well, I still meet with my project group, so they bring me up to speed. A lot of this stuff we get assigned is common sense or straight out of work experience, so I'm making good headway." That was half true; she'd sporadically returned phone calls and emailed bare-minimum contributions to at least not sabotage Chloé's and Viv's credits.

"Interesting projects? Challenging?"

"Not really."

Rand didn't probe further, even though it was an area of his own expertise. Among so many things, Margot appreciated this about him – that he knew where to draw lines and let her be. To a degree.

"What were you working on just now?" he asked.

"Huh?"

"I saw the notebook open on the desk. Were you writing? Chronicling your stay here?"

"Mm, sort of. Just a blurb about something on my mind."

"What *is* on your mind, may I ask?"

Shit, I handed him the perfect segue, garnished on a platter. She didn't know where to even begin explaining something she herself didn't understand, but she owed him a try.

"Not much. I don't know." She exhaled loudly to concede defeat. "Look, I'm…really, *really* sorry for my behavior before. I don't pretend to have a reason. I was tired and started to feel sick, but that doesn't excuse my rudeness. I'm sorry."

"Yeah, you were a bit of a prat, weren't you? Rather unexpected. What made you fancy laughing in hysterics like that? Only to slam the door in my face the next instant?"

So he did think about it. Just took some 'polite' passive-aggressive beating around the bush to get down to it. "I'm really embarrassed. I'm not sure. Did Gwen hear?"

His brows elevated. "Quite clearly, yes. I believe that was the point?"

Fuck. Blame hormones? "At the risk of making you uncomfortable, I think I'm approaching the end of my, you know…cycle. My estrogen levels are outta whack."

"Really now."

A prickling heat rushed to Margot's skin, washing over her entire body and tensing her muscles. Pressure seemed to shift in her brain as, provoked, she lifted the tail from between her legs and attacked – again.

"Why in hell are men incapable of understanding that? It would save your kind so much trouble if you'd just learn how to track a fucking calendar and know when to stay away."

Rand laughed through his teeth. "And what calendar is that? How am I supposed to know your menstrual cycle, pray tell?"

"You could ask." Even she knew this was an idiotic comeback.

"Oh, yes, quite right." Going from British Bloke to Valley Girl, he said, "So, like, Margot, when's, like, your next period? Need to borrow a sanitary towel?"

As funny as it was hearing *sanitary towel* articulated in an American accent, she was riled. "Well, hasn't Gwen trained you to follow hers by now? Or is she just a bitch all the time?"

"You're out of line."

"Sorry."

"No, you're not. And you don't know Gwen, so where do you get off insulting her, offending *me* in the process?"

"I was just making a joke. I apologize if the humor doesn't translate." Margot felt out of her body, like she was hovering above, looking down on the scene and helpless to stop herself from making it worse.

"What has come *over* you?"

She'd never heard Rand raise his voice before.

"This is getting all blown out of proportion," she said. "I don't even know where it started. All I know is, I'm sorry for whatever misunderstanding is occurring right now."

"*No*, you're *not*," he repeated. "Margot, in just a matter of weeks, you've become a completely different person."

"What? How so?"

"I realize you're only human and need your outlets for venting, but since when do you direct it at me? Or Gwen, for that matter? You're volatile."

The word launched across the room. She had no comeback this time, idiotic or otherwise.

He continued, "It isn't just tonight."

She may as well have had fifty Botox injections for as stiff and expressionless as she maintained her face.

He evidently interpreted the silence as permission to proceed. "Nothing that you've done against me personally. I've seen it before and just can't help but wonder if you're perhaps…"

Her manner didn't alter; she didn't move a hair's width other than to breathe.

"Well…perhaps at the early stages of…"

She wouldn't make this easier for him, just watched him press on to complete the sentence.

"…a clinical depression."

That roused her back to action. Rapidly nodding her head, she said, "Depression. Clinical. That's your diagnosis."

"It's a thought."

"Based on *what*, Doctor?"

"Well, this attitude for one. You swing from one extreme to the next. I'm not blaming you. You've been through some changes. What I'm not certain of is whether *you're* aware."

"Evidently not. I thought we've been having fun. I thought you enjoyed my company. I stand corrected."

"Honestly, Margot, this is only recent observation for me. I could sit round and wait for it to get worse, or I could address it now. I'm being a friend. I don't want you to undergo what my sister did."

Margot recalled the family photos on his bedroom dresser, how the recent-looking one was missing the woman she'd assumed was Gwen. She managed a reverent pause before responding, as calmly as she could, "How is she now?"

Rand inhaled, closing his eyes as he did so and then opening them to stare down at his lap. He licked his lower lip. "Not well." The way he said it communicated clearly enough that, if it was a topic to be pursued at all, it should be in the past tense.

A metallic clatter punctuated Margot's thoughts. She only just noticed that Rand must have loaded laundry into the washer-dryer situated in the adjoining kitchen.

"When?" she asked. "How old?"

Taking the last question first, "Twenty-four. Going on three years now."

Margot didn't desire the details any more than she figured Rand wanted to relive them. It sufficed that she could do the math and understand what had brought him back to England those years ago.

"And you think I'm capable of hurting myself."

The jostling laundry thudded in its spin with clockwork consistency.

"Not at present, no. But then, I hadn't thought *she* could either. That she would." Leather moaned as Rand sank further back in the sofa, knees spread and fingertips thrumming on the taut armrest. "Look. It's possible I'm the one overreacting now. It's clearly something I'm sensitive about, so maybe I'm misinterpreting—"

"What, exactly? I just don't see the evidence stacked against me to consider…" Margot couldn't say it, only hoped that he'd approach his next words just as sensitively.

"Well, to start, I'm tossing out more wine bottles with the recycling, aren't I? And if you're not in bed for the evening by eight o'clock most nights, you're there in the afternoon."

"What's wrong with that on a weekend?"

"Weekdays as well." Before the question could rise to Margot's mouth, he explained, "Gwen, as you know, doesn't spend a lot of time here. But she *is* here, Margot. She has her own keys. She pops in between viewings when in the neighborhood, uses it as a home base to freshen up or use the computer, or just... I don't know. As it were, she's been here when you've been, and she's related to me that in the last couple of weeks she's often seen you sleeping in bed or on the sofa. Or you're in the bath, talking to yoursel —"

"Whoa, whoa, whoa here." She pumped her palms at him. "No, no, you let me talk. Why have I never received warning that she might, time to time, 'pop in' unannounced? And why wouldn't she assume I was just talking on the phone? And how in *hell* would she know if I were taking a bath? I know this is your place, Rand, and she's your girl, but as much as I don't want to cramp your routine, as long as I *am* living here and paying to do so, I demand some respect for my privacy." She accentuated her Midwestern long-I sound in the last word.

The washer hummed with some more clangs as its contents tumbled in the drum.

Rand appeared mystified, his mouth hanging open. "You *have* received warning. I've told you."

"You have not!"

"I *have*. Although I question how much you actually hear me when you take on that absent stare of late. Listen. She wasn't spying on you, Margot. You're supposed to be away at class. You gave me your timetable, and we've observed that because we do respect your privacy. But it's a small flat. It's easy to determine when the bathroom is engaged. And when it's engaged for two hours. She second-guessed at first whether you were, in fact, in there, and out of concern listened at the door. Sometimes she heard you arguing, but other times it was just the sound of water lapping." He raised a hand that held Margot's attempted interjection at bay. "It's fair enough for her to surmise you're speaking to yourself when she also hears your

111

mobile ring in your bag upstairs, same time."

"Fine. I have a habit of talking to myself in the mirror when I'm alone. So what. A lot of people do that."

"I can see that, but what concerns us more are those silent afternoons in the bath. And those were just the hours she *was* here any given day. She's never heard running or draining water, so who knows how long those lasted. Could you say?"

A spin cycle began to vibrate the floor.

Margot became intensely interested in her torn cuticles as she spoke. "I enjoy baths once in a while. I get stressed, and, like wine, they relax me."

"For *over* two hours."

"Once in a while."

"At least twice this week."

She shrugged, still looking at her nails. "Americans care about their hygiene."

The floor trilled.

"Come now, do you need to resort to ethnocentric insults? It's not like you."

She looked him in the eye. "You wanna talk insult, I am *beyond* offended by all this. I'm an adult entitled to my personal habits and could care less if you find them strange. It's hardly grounds for this accusation."

An aggressive hum of acceleration from the kitchen swallowed the room.

"*Couldn't* care less," he said under his breath.

"What?"

"It's *couldn't* care less," he repeated. "Otherwise, it would mean you do care."

She could've leapt out of her chair. "Really?"

"Sorry." He held his palms to her. "What you've said is fair enough. But I'm not *accusing* you of anything, only intervening in the off-chance it isn't all rubbish. Is there damage in that? I do apologize if I'm crossing a boundary here, but you're my tenant, so I feel responsible for you and what may happen to you whilst here."

The propelling drum whirred with the force of a jet

engine, like the flat itself was ready to launch.

"Well then, Lord Randolph, as your *tenant* who pays her rent in full and on time," Margot spat, "respects the condition of your property, notifies you when shitty fixtures like your shitty door need attention, and keeps to herself, I'm fulfilling *my* end of the contract, so why don't you and Gwen fuck off!"

"I resent your tone."

"It's the best I can do."

"No, it isn't," Rand retorted sadly. He paused, then sighed, unable to look her in the eye. "Margot, there's more to my suspicion."

She tilted her head and affected a creepy clownish grin. "And what, pray tell, would *that* be?"

He matched her hostility as well as his temperament could. "Your diary."

"What?"

"Your *diary*. The one you were writing in just now. You'd left it open on the coffee table here, and Gwen couldn't help but see the large print." Guilt flittered behind his eyes. "It leapt right off the page, really, without even trying to read it."

"*What?*" The first time, she honestly hadn't heard him over the washing machine. This time, though, his message rang clearly.

One of his knees bobbed up and down like a piston as his thumbnail twitched against the underbelly of his middle finger. Margot clawed her armrests.

He slumped. "It was an accident. Honestly. The handwriting was so large and looked like it was intentionally placed there. Gwen thought it might have been a note from me, left for her."

The washer wound down like a rusted tin toy needing another twist of its key.

Margot's voice softened as the words caught in her throat. "What did… How much…"

Roses bloomed through Rand's pale cheeks, and he lowered his eyes. "I don't remember. Not word-for-word, just…the essence. Please, I didn't mean to make you cry."

Swallowing, she felt warm, wet streaks down her face. She closed her eyes and shook her head. "I'm sorry, but… there's no way I left that book out here. Never brought it out here in the first place, let alone left it wide open."

"There's no other explanation for it."

"Isn't there?"

Rand squinted. "She couldn't have done it. She wouldn't."

"Did you read it, too, or just hear it from her?"

"She told me what she read."

"And you believed what she told you."

"Of course I believed her!"

"Of course. It's just me you don't."

"There is nothing I'm disbelieving about anything you've said, only that you might have forgotten that you left it out here. I believe, though, that *you* believe you didn't."

"Gee, thanks for that much. That would only mean I'm crazy, then."

"That's not—"

"So, what was the 'essence' of what she told you?"

With a sigh, he recited a phrase that sounded even more bizarre coming from a mouth parenthesized by such friendly laugh lines. Margot blinked twice and screwed her face.

"I did *not* write that," she said, vaulting from her chair to get her diary and prove it.

She returned just as swiftly as she'd left, rapidly turning the pages as she perused her writing with both conviction and self-doubt.

"These entries are just random notes. Some travels, but mostly dreams, not real life." She licked her thumb to expedite the page turning. "I mean, some of these do sound disturbed, but aren't most dreams?"

She relaxed the more she flipped through the book. She'd scanned every entry she'd ever written, which renewed her confidence that Gwen was talking crap.

Until.

She felt the blood drain from her cheeks as a clammy

114

coolness washed over them. At least a dozen blank pages past her most recent entry revealed some scrawling in her same black ink, but she could hardly recognize the formal cursive. Rand's paraphrase had been alarming, but the exact words were a horror to actually see.

You have signed my death sentence
and I am to be my own executioner

"What is it? You found it, then? What does it say?"

Margot played it off weakly. "Oh, yeah. Now I remember. Crazy dream. I'd totally forgotten."

"It would seem it's all coming back to you now."

"Yeah." She cleared her throat, then swallowed. "Yes. It was…distressing."

She racked her brain for a storyline, using *executioner* as her springboard.

"I was…standing on a scaffold…taking the fall for a wrongful accusation. In the dream I was a man, and the last thing I saw was this woman in the crowd…the same woman I loved was the one to betray me." Almost as disturbing as the entry was how easily this improv came to her. "And this is what I, as this man, said…to her…still looking at her… just before the blade dropped."

When her eyes ceased searching the room at the same time she stopped lying, her steadier gaze met Rand's. He crossed the room to kneel at her feet, folding his hands on her knee like a Greek tragic hero in supplication of Athena. But he didn't say the S word.

That's how she knew he meant it.

He didn't say anything, just rested his chin on his knuckles and looked up at her from her lap. Margot didn't say anything either, only ran her fingers through his hair gently. After a few strokes, he closed his eyes.

For a minute, they remained frozen in this tableau of mutual apology and forgiveness. The sweetness of it almost vanquished the phantom entry from Margot's mind.

Almost.

IV

Thou, whose exterior semblance doth belie
Thy soul's immensity;
Thou best philosopher, who yet dost keep
Thy heritage, thou eye among the blind,
That, deaf and silent, read'st the eternal deep,
Haunted for ever by the eternal mind,—
Mighty prophet! Seer blest!
On whom those truths do rest,
Which we are toiling all our lives to find,
In darkness lost, the darkness of the grave;
Thou, over whom thy Immortality
Broods like the Day, a master o'er a slave,
A presence which is not to be put by;
To whom the grave
Is but a lonely bed without the sense or sight
Of day or the warm light,
A place of thought where we in waiting lie.

From "Ode: Intimations of Immortality from Recollections of
Early Childhood"
~ William Wordsworth (1815)

Interlude

A Lonely Bed

19th-Century London

I am amazed to find it is not all that long ago on which I look back when I envision myself seated at the dressing table with my lady's maid, my friend, standing attentively at my side.

The first few weeks had passed since our acquaintance, and so close already was our companionship that, when she consoled me after another wicked argument with Victor, I thought at once that evening – goodness, it was more accurately almost morning! – to consult my jewelry box and select for my friend a gift. I wished for something most fine to symbolize the mutual respect and adoration for one another we had developed, yet all my glistening strands of pearls and twinkling baubles bore the vestige of Victor, he who had first gifted them all to me. Nothing would do.

"If you will permit me," she whispered as she eased her fingers down into the crevice of her bosom and retrieved from it something small, concealed in her hand.

Having extinguished the wicks on the chiffonier, our sight was aided only by the candlestick on the dressing table, which I normally kept lit out of my nagging fear of darkness. But it, too, then flickered out, though I had already closed the sash to the breezes.

Having procured the mysterious item from its body-heated encasing, she now pressed it into the soft flesh of my palm as she drew me up by my same hand to lead towards the window. I had left the curtains drawn, so it was

119

by the cooling light of a piercingly white moon that I uncurled my fingers to reveal her treasure: a brooch of sapphire gems and turquoise, with a large, milky pearl nested within its center.

I gasped when I saw it. I know false gems when I spy them, with all the trinkets Mama would flash about. These, however, were not mere paste. Yet she did not snatch the jewels back with greedy misgiving as one might have expected from one of her station. No, she clasped my hand that held the brooch and raised it aloft such that we could both behold it glittering in the moonlight.

Looking from the pearl to the moon, she said, "I shall forever remember this night."

My eyes began to well then in tears of an entirely different variety than those I had grown so accustomed to shedding; these were tears of a renewed confidence in myself to carry on and accomplish anything to which I aspired from then on, and it would no longer be Victor who supported me but her, in all matters of the soul. If Wordsworth had inspired me to dance with the daffodils, this woman was his poetry in motion.

Perhaps the brooch was not hers to give, however. She, honest soul, granted that. And it was not for me to question how such a girl should come to possess such a fortune, yet she of her own willingness eventually related the tale of how she had acquired the ornament as a child.

I saw her redden as she spoke of her mother, who had served some of her days as a painter's model to scrape together what earnings she could to raise her child. My dear friend's father, a drunkard, would disappear days at a time, so she and her mother had grown to count on him for very little.

Too young to be left unsupervised, she had been made to attend her mother's sittings in the homes of less-than-respectable artists who offered less-than-respectable wages, thus obligating her mother to work with more frequency. There was one painter who described her mother as a 'stunner' and so requested her regularly. Whereas other women were sometimes chaperoned for propriety's sake, my friend's mother had no one, which was all the more suitable as this artist preferred to work with his models alone. He claimed his work was more inspired this way.

With little to entertain herself in the shadowy corners of his attic, she – my friend, the sole chaperone at an age hardly above five years – could not help but notice her mother's costume diminish in layers with every appointment. After a time, the child was asked to remove herself to the adjacent room where the models normally undressed.

She would while away the time there sifting through trunks of colorful costumes and accessories, pulling one out after another and trying them on before the dusty mirror, and humming quietly to drown the moans and cries of 'artistic inspiration' in the next room. Curiosity overtook sense when she craftily picked the lock to a wardrobe. Though limited experience prevented her recognition of the fabric found within, she knew at the touch these were of thread far finer than anything her mother had ever been asked to wear. Inside a little box resting in a bottom corner, she found even smaller cases containing a brilliant necklace, a bracelet, a pair of earrings, a ring, and…a brooch.

In retrospect, she understood these had been items on loan from the artist's wealthy benefactor, for use in portraits commissioned by privileged families. At the time of discovery, however, she had known only that this was something precious to the painter, and she would take it from him just as he had been taking something precious from her.

It was many weeks later – after he had already tired of her mother's features, which he had helped to fade – when he first arrived pounding at their door and demanding the brooch be returned. Her mother was understandably perplexed, but it was her father (who chanced to be home this day of them all) who knew precisely what had occurred beneath his nose and, after turning the artist out into the street in a rage of crass, violent threats, proceeded to inflict upon his wife the physical promise of those words.

The child never uttered a word, only willed that the brooch go far, far away from her for all the trouble it had caused.

Imagine her astonishment, then, when one day it did vanish! She had suspected theft or a poor memory, but either way was blissfully rid of it, never to be seen by her eyes again until it *did* return several years later.

Though not yet a woman by that time, she had taken to wandering the streets alone for long hours when, one night, a hand reached out to seize her arm. Although alarmed by the sudden motion, she breathed easily enough on perceiving an old woman crouched in the alleyway, illuminated only in part by a lantern of filthy glass.

"Do you see?" the ancient woman asked, her black eyes staring beyond the girl. "Do you see her?"

My friend stiffened only to reply that she did not.

"Ess," the stranger hissed, still clutching her arm. "Eehhss…or is it *est* as in the east? Yet she, she is in the west." With one widened, bulging eye, she inspected the girl's face and frame. "She is close to your age, you know. They both."

My friend could make no sense of this speech. "Sorry, ma'am. I must go."

The grip on her arm tightened.

"No, no. No fear."

The dark woman then raised the lantern to her face, which appeared gashed by the fine black shadows cast by its moles; she muttered nonsensical words until both females' attention was drawn to a metallic thud on the toe of my friend's shoe.

Grabbing the old woman's wrist to thrust the lantern towards the sound, she screamed at the sight of a brooch. Her brooch.

In the circular clasp of their arms, the girl and woman searched each other's eyes.

"She will get it back, child," had been the stranger's last words.

"From that day I have believed in fate," my dear friend now professed to me. "As mysteriously as this ornament absented my life when I requested it, it returned to me for a reason."

For what had remained of her childhood, to escape the voices reverberating through her house's walls, she would remove the brooch from her hiding place and rub it with her little thumbs, placing wishes upon it as on a magic lamp.

"I dared not pawn it, for it was the prettiest thing I had ever possessed or would likely. Until you, though I would not offend by claiming you as my possession. I only mean that I believe you are the reason this brooch returned to me. I do not understand how, yet I know *why* it brought me to you." Closing my hand around the brooch again, she curled her own fingers around mine and pressed them to my breast. "So to you it now belongs."

"I feel as though it has always belonged to me," I said, my chest heaving beneath our tender clasp. "And now I belong to you."

My sense of renewal ensued for the months to come. I felt in better equilibrium, with spirits and paintbrush uplifted again. I had neither the training nor the encouragement before to hone the craft, but my friend urged me on, and it transpired that she began to sit for me.

Despite the fact of our close relationship – or indeed *because* of it – for all outward appearances, we had to remain discreet. The lower servants were envious enough of the rank a lady's maid enjoyed; I could only imagine their ire had they known the hours I allowed her to be at her leisure with me in my bedroom! I daily hid the canvas behind the wardrobe and replaced it with one of a rather plain still life that did not betray the rapid development and application of my talent, now that it was inspired.

Sensations awakened deep within me, and so often I felt a certain heat lick its way to my surface. Perhaps my stimulated state had thus rendered me more outwardly attractive, and perhaps Victor did recognize such, for he came to me once, but only once in all of those first months when my dear friend was in our employment. In that one night, I saw the sheepish vulnerability of the man I had first met; he seemed almost shy to approach me and stroke his fingers down my back. I trilled at his touch, and welcomed him into our marital bed, yet only that once. Thereafter, he did not return.

Had my beauty fleeted so soon? No, not so soon as his emotion; not so quickly as the bitterness of resentment could seep back into his tongue. Victor's temperament had again run quite short with me, even when the thickening at my waist became perceptible to us both in the months to follow.

By springtime of this year, as yet among the deadened leaves of winter, woe was to befall me again.

I awoke to a familiar tacky clotting, then an alarming sight. I wailed in anguish and fainted once more.

When I returned to consciousness, I was perspiring, bound up in bed sheets. In a blurry haze, I saw my friend weeping in the corner at the sash window, which was already filling with gray-blue daylight; she had not been permitted to come any closer. The doctor, who had since arrived with all manner of tools to treat me, used the simplest of which to slice my wrist, jerking my left arm above a washbasin as I feverishly watched the blood drain out. Struggling to regain my focus, I wept and moaned my lamentations, looking about the room at the faces at my bedside that always frowned their disapproval in expecting so much from me. I searched for the one face that defied this pattern, now concealed behind her bony fingers.

My dear girl was permitted to nurse me back to health, but my strength was found wanting for a longer duration than ever before – before, in particular, such drastic and barbaric measures in healing had ever been attempted on my person, the same sort that had helped suck the life from our Princess Charlotte. When I think of the 'monument' to Her Highness's memory, indeed… To me, that edifice of marble is the gravestone of the Spirited Woman's defeat, tamed to Her undoing.

Ah, that I had *this* woman instead, of flesh and bone and the spirit that I required, to remain with me at my bedside when all others abandoned me to shadow.

Chapter Eight

Darkness of the Grave

21st-Century London

<u>*July 14*</u>
Last night Rand introduced me to the guilty pleasure that is the döner kebab (which is basically the after-bar burrito of the UK) to follow an impromptu drinking game I came up with for every time an 'advert' on the 'telly' involves an animal (drink once for domestic, twice for livestock). Those shenanigans aside, I've actually been making a conscious effort to cut down on my alcohol intake.

I'm finally getting myself back out and about, too – or at least Rand is. He and Gwen had a big fight – heh-heh-heh – so when she ditched him for her parents' house in the country the other weekend, he took me to Windsor Castle. It was a cool, spitting day, but we spent most of the time touring inside the castle and chapel anyway. The castle itself was impressive with its grand staircases and halls. St. George's Chapel, though, was the real point of interest for me. Henry VIII and the reigning Queen Elizabeth's parents are buried there.

I keep thinking about what Derek said, and, honestly, no wonder I've been such a mental case. In this city, you're constantly confronted with your mortality, be it the old buildings or tombs blatantly piled up in every cathedral. I saw Henry's armor and tried to picture his tubby body moving around inside it. I saw the ornately carved wooden balcony built for Catherine of Aragon over the altar and pictured her up there in silent prayer. I walk by and through

126

these places and see the people striding around on streets of dirt, not asphalt, or riding in carriages, not cars.

I get enchanted by this romantic past and wish to be a part of it, like it was somehow better. But was it? The pop culture of those past times wouldn't have held special charm or fascination for those people living then, right? So then what's the source of <u>our</u> fascination? Our stuff will outlive us one day, too, and will future generations gawk through glass at our smartphones and skinny jeans and revel in the mystery of them? We read and sigh over the literature of Victorians who were riddled with disease, drinking from putrid water and breathing polluted air. The stairs that I climb to the flat – imagine the servants having to haul basins of water up and down them constantly in lieu of indoor plumbing. I've seen massive gravestones at the cemetery with up to four or five names on them that are all children aged a matter of months, with the usual exception of that one lucky son who got to live to year ten or even eighteen. That must have been a harrowing time of stench and heartache, but retrospection coats it in a layer of stardust like a woman's corset would contain her fat and stretch marks.

In any case, that was the reality hitting me when I saw the monument to Princess Charlotte in the chapel. No need to describe it here. In fact, it looked <u>exactly</u> like what I saw in my dream the night Rand and I fought. The body beneath ivory cloth, mourners at her feet, her spirit rising and angels cradling "the infant in holy arms"... So I must have seen a photo of it somewhere before. Here was a woman who died in childbirth in the early 19th century, no less mortal in her royalty after the doctors treated her through bloodletting. Really? <u>That</u> was supposed to save her from another miscarriage – draining her of more blood?! So is the past something to be sentimentalized as so elevated, beyond our reach? They lived and died like we do and will.

At this point, what reminded Margot of her mortality was the pain shooting through her right hand and shoulder. Her fingertips were blotched with white and pink from gripping the pen so tightly, and her printing carved grooves into the paper.

Maybe I am *jealous of those past people, not having keyboard-induced carpal tunnel pain sabotaging their handwriting.*

Massaging the fine bones in her hand, she yawned and checked the time on the wall clock. She had five minutes until she had to go meet Chloé in Chelsea, so she chugged the rest of her tea and threw a tweed cap over her greasy hair. Grabbing her leather tote, she went to throw it over her right shoulder out of reflex when she thought better of it and instead shifted it to her left, then made her way out the door.

Though she wasn't ecstatic about seeing her classmate again, Rand had been motivating her to socialize more, and she was actually surprised, and maybe a little relieved, that Chloé still wanted anything to do with her after being alienated for the last month. Viv apparently thought nothing of it, if anything seeming to like Margot's attitude better, but Chloé's persistence was all too indicative of an impending *WTF?* – or at least *Quel est ton problème?* – just dying to be said. Margot had even intermittently started going to class again – just enough to not completely waste her tuition fee, yet not enough to waste her time. Interestingly, it was Chloé who'd ended up not being there a few of those days.

"Margot, here!" She waved from a small square table on the sidewalk. Her short golden tresses were swept back with a pair of tiny clips above her shallow forehead, and she looked like the ballerina her mother had wanted in a jagged mini-dress ruffling over leggings that defined her slim limbs down to a pair of flats.

Margot beamed one of her fake smiles and adjusted her sunglasses as she maneuvered in ninety-degree angles through the other tables. She bent to give Chloé a savvier cheek-to-cheek kiss than last time, then sat and adjusted for comfort on the chair's wooden slats. "*You* look darling."

"*Merci.*"

When Chloé didn't return the compliment, Margot

shuffled one now glaringly plain denim leg over the other and tried to sit up straighter than a slack-ass teenager.

A warm smile soon spread over her classmate's features. "Margot, I'm glad to spend time with you again. I consider you a friend and have missed you."

"That's sweet, Chloé. Thanks. Sorry I haven't really been…present. I hope you haven't taken it personally."

"No, no. *Pas du tout*. I wasn't surprised."

"How do you mean?"

"Do you want to go inside and order already?"

"Uh, sure."

The two ladies ordered ready-made baguette sandwiches and sparkling water at the counter and paid before returning to their outdoor table with trays in hand. Chloé delicately unwrapped the cellophane from her *jambon et fromage* and bit through the tough bread with grace. Margot, on the other hand, inexpertly writhed her jaw like a lion cub learning to rip meat from its prey.

Shielding her mouth as she still chewed, she asked, "So, um, you were saying before?"

Chloé looked at her with interest but showed no recollection of what Margot was talking about. She instead paid compliments to the sandwich. The sun shied away behind the clouds, making Margot's sunglasses redundant, so she reluctantly removed them.

"You look tired!" Chloé said.

"Yeah, I *feel* tired, though God knows I get more than enough sleep. Too little fresh air and exercise."

"You're just so dark under the eyes."

"Probably my sinuses."

She figured Chloé would prescribe some obscure foreign cream with placenta or foreskin or something to brighten the skin, but the lecture would've fallen on deaf ears. For all her bathing before, Margot hardly bothered with skincare anymore.

A tremor rippled within her ribs when instead her friend looked imploringly into her eyes and said, "Take care of yourself. Please."

Margot squinted and gave a sideways smile. "Chloé, that's nice of you. I do, and I'm fine."

To her relief, Chloé changed the subject. "Are you wearing contacts?"

"No. I get that a lot, though, since my eyes are hazel but one's more brown where the other's more gree—"

"I ask because you wear spectacles in class, so those are for reading only?"

"Oh. Yeah, I only wear them when I have to concentrate a long time. I can still read without them."

Margot felt that same strain of maintaining conversation with Chloé, who took another crisply flawless bite of her baguette and put the burden of filling the silence on Margot.

She thought hard, but only the mundane came to her. "Oh, um, speaking of glasses, I need to find an optometrist here. I have these, like, floaters? I don't know what you'd call them, but do you know what I mean? Those little squiggles that float around in your eyes sometimes?"

Chloé looked at her but only chewed.

"Well, I know everyone has them, but mine seem to have increased, to the point where I really notice them all the time, and it never used to be like that. And then as of maybe a week ago, I've been getting these little pinpricks of light. They flash into my vision every now and then."

Chloé took another silent bite.

"So, I looked it up online, and it said those could be symptoms of retinal detachment. I'm obviously not insured, but I don't want to wait and go blind before I return home. Do you know anything about eye exams here and what they might cost out-of-pocket?"

Swallowing and wiping her mouth, Chloé replied, "No. I have clear vision." She widened her eyes as though showing off that fact, then dropped them to her sandwich. "So I don't bother with them. I don't think many people, though, have a vision allowance outside the national healthcare, so it's probably very reasonable."

"Okay, good. I'm a little concerned I literally cried my eyes out."

She'd only meant it as a joke, but Chloé looked concerned again. "Cried?"

The small talk is too much work. To hell with it. "Yes, I've been crying a lot lately, and before you ask why, I really don't know." Margot picked up her baguette. "Anyways, I've been doing all the talking, so just shut me up."

"Oh, life has been dull. I need you to entertain me."

Margot stalled with a voracious bite of her sandwich, signaling Chloé to just continue feasting on her own. This bought a minute of silence as she shifted her attention to the motor and foot traffic on the Fulham Road.

Once ready to become the floorshow again, she spoke up with more daring. "So, before. You were saying you weren't surprised that I've been acting the way I have."

This time, the recollection took. "Yes. I could sense from the beginning that you were..." Chloé appeared to measure her next word carefully "...transitioning."

Margot nodded. "It's a tough adjustment coming to a new country alone. Although maybe not as difficult for you. Europeans seem more worldly in mindset."

"Yes, but I still understand how it's difficult."

She was a little disarmed by how the Frenchwoman chose the sympathetic versus snide route. "Yeah, but it's not just that. I'm not even here for that long, and students younger than me do this all the time. It's just..."

Chloé's eyes twinkled. "You're unhappy in love."

"Love? No."

Chloé raised her brow.

"I mean, I *was* in love and had a bad breakup, but that was months ago."

"Why should time matter?"

"Because I've had a while to get over it. And for all I know, he's found himself a new *fräulein* by now." Rather than an imagined Swiss Miss, however, the image of the woman in Rand's photographs flickered to mind. Still unsure who that was, she huffed a cynical laugh. "But I'm not pining for the guy. Not anyone right now. I honestly

131

don't see what value a relationship would bring into my life anymore. All the fun of it is in the beginning anyway. Once that's over, it becomes the reality of toenail clippings on the bathroom tile."

James's hygiene habits had made her skin crawl. Yet when she thought about the stray stubble that escaped Rand's razor to scatter on the countertop, remaining home with her when he wasn't there, her stomach stirred with a softer sensation. Which she indulged all of two seconds before conceding that only illustrated her point: how easy it was to suspend reality until it became long-term, everyday tolerance at best.

She channeled nervous energy into picking the fat off her prosciutto. One by one, she laid the white strings in a coil to the side of her plate.

Chloé frowned. "Is that really how you feel, then? About love? What about this man you're living with now?"

Margot inhaled a flake of bread crust into the wrong pipe, and she coughed spastically for a moment.

"We're not really *living* together. I'm staying with him. He's a friend. And taken."

"That doesn't mean anything until he's married. Even then, I don't know that it means anything."

Margot's head jolted as her eyes widened.

Chloé smiled. "I only mean that, when you have a soul mate, factors like that don't make much difference. What is meant to be *will* be."

"Right, *que sera sera,* as your people and Doris Day say. But sorry, Rand is a *flat*mate, not soul mate."

When Chloé cocked a brow in lieu of words, Margot dropped her eyes to her plate and began to arrange the thin strips of fat into straight lines. She found it easier to speak earnestly to Chloé when not looking her in the eye.

"You know, I did used to believe in that. I really did. But then I heard a theory that soul mates aren't necessarily the people we're meant to fall in love with and marry, but the ones who hold a mirror to us and make us see something we couldn't on our own." With a fingertip, she curled the greasy white strings into one big spiral on her plate. "So, working in that definition, maybe I *can* see how he could be mine. In even the short time I've been here, he's been there for me, to call me out on stuff."

"What sort of stuff?" Her appetite probably lost to Margot playing with the fat, Chloé had ceased eating and interlocked her arms, resting her elbows on the table.

"I don't know…stuff. My moods."

"You're temperamental?"

Margot snorted. "You could say that. Though I like to think of it as passionate."

She screwed her lips to bite at the skin inside her mouth as she studied her lap. She wasn't sure why she now felt eager to divulge everything to someone she'd been holding at arm's length, other than because it was just that: Chloé wasn't of consequence to Margot's life going forward, so what happened in London would stay in London. And maybe if Margot turned her off just enough, it would solve the problem of having to hang out together again. If that was what she still wanted.

"Really, though," she said, "he's been a good friend to me. I've always been moody, but…not like this." She jerked her right shoulder forward, then glanced around at other patrons before finally looking at Chloé directly to feel out whether this was safe territory to embark on with her in tow.

Bobbing her head with a readiness to listen, Chloé reached into her fraying satin clutch for a crushed pack of cigarettes without breaking eye contact.

She has the face of an angel, Margot thought out of nowhere, accepting the cigarette handed to her. As the rising smoke shrouded her face, she already felt calmer, and her limbs tingled.

Chloé had re-glossed her lips and now pursed them to blow wisps of smoke into the open air. She tipped her head.

On this cue, Margot let go and decided to relate everything that had led up to that horrible confrontation with Rand a couple of weeks back. She kept her voice low so others wouldn't hear, but once she unscrewed that rusted tap, everything poured out in the strange warmth of Chloé's undivided attention. After a time, Margot wasn't even sure how long she'd been talking, only that she couldn't stop babbling as she sensed Chloé's awareness silkily stroke every contour of every word and lap it all up like honeyed milk.

"I did just soak there," Margot said, "with the water up to my chin, looking down at how my body looked drowned." She zoned out on the bubbles inside her water bottle, which she twisted side to side. "Ophelia in her watery grave. Just lying there, feeling nothing and wondering what difference it would make if I died."

The tip of Chloé's cigarette smoldered into a fiery red in the corner of Margot's eye. Snapping out of her trance with another shoulder tic, she added, "Don't worry, I wasn't considering pulling a Virginia with rock-loaded pockets in the river or anything. I didn't want to die; it was more like…is still sometimes like…just a really strong *apathy* toward dying. You know? Like if it were to happen outside of my control. Crossing the street and getting hit by a car or having a heart attack or something like that. And when I feel that way, it's like I'm inside and outside of the experience at once."

Chloé's eyes twitched. "Why?"

Margot shook her head and stubbed out her cigarette. "*Je ne sais pas, ma petite fille.*" She heavily exhaled the last of her smoke. "And I don't think I really care either. I'm strictly taking showers now so that I don't freak Rand out, but I think I'm allowed to feel and *not* feel at my own discretion."

"One thing you feel is more comfortable with me," Chloé said as she reclined in her seat.

Margot nodded, knowing it was true without understanding why. Had she really just unloaded all this on someone she barely knew? She still hadn't even talked to anyone back home about it.

Chloé lit a new cigarette and stuffed the pack back in her clutch after Margot declined another one. "Have you discovered any more of these writings in your journal?"

"Nothing like that, where I can't remember writing it. I was so creeped out by that whole thing, honestly, that I don't even write my dreams down anymore. I don't want to remember them."

"Are they always about the same thing?"

Margot shook her head. "I don't know. If I don't write it down immediately, it's out of my head." She shrugged, and the motion made her grimace.

"Are you injured?"

"Huh?

"Your shoulder. You seem in pain."

Conscious of her fidgeting but hoping Chloé hadn't been, she felt her face warm. "Oh, right. I did inflict a bit of voluntary pain on myself recently."

"Are you hurting yourself?"

"No!" Her cheeks burned. *I must seem like a complete carnival sideshow*. "I'm not hurt, just healing. I did something sort of…impetuous the other day." She glanced around before hooking her left thumb beneath the neck of her T-shirt and bra strap. Twisting her back to Chloé, she delicately bared as much as she could of her right shoulder blade, wincing slightly. "It's still pretty tender."

From beneath a fine layer of scaly skin emerged a bird blazing in reds and oranges. The feathers of its outstretched wings and streaming tail resembled a peacock's, curling like fern fronds around eyes of sea green and violet as tongues of flame licked at each tip.

With rounded eyes, Chloé shook her head. "Why?"

Margot extinguished the image with her cotton tee. "Ow. It itches *so* badly, but I can't scratch it." She laughed. "My parents'll kill me. Which makes me sound fifteen." Meeting Chloé's stare, she answered, "But I don't know…. As tired as I've been, I also have this, like, restlessness. So for once I didn't think, just walked in and did it before I could change my mind."

"The artistry of it is beautiful. Does it mean something to you?"

Margot shrugged again despite the chaffing. "I was at Windsor and saw a similar image on the chapel's altar cloth. It was so striking and fiery, I guess it burnt its impression on me."

"A phoenix."

"Yeah." Margot twitched her shoulder again. "The chapel at Hampton Court also had an inscription about one, so I took it as a sign."

"It's intense yet whimsical. It suits you—"

"Thanks. I've always loved birds." In her excitement to share her newfound naughtiness, Margot realized she'd interrupted Chloé, talking over what sounded like "more than you realize." To cover the gaffe, she quickly said, "Oh, sorry! You were saying?"

Chloé merely shook her head with a cheery smile. "Oh, I was simply beginning to ask if you realized today is a national holiday in France."

"No, really?"

"*C'est le quartorze juillet.* As you would say, Bastille Day. Though in France, *la Fête Nationale* means so much more." She proceeded to explain how the holiday went beyond the French Revolution as a celebration of national pride, finishing with, "We must go to Paris. Have you been?"

"My ex and I always said we'd go during one of his work trips but never did."

"Ah, but I'm certain you would have spent all day in the Louvre and thought you'd experienced France. I can show you *my* Paris."

"That would actually be perfect to coordinate for when my friend Sylvie visits."

The corners of Chloé's lips tugged down, but she didn't say anything.

"Versaille's near there, right? Sylvie's fascinated with Marie Antoinette."

Chloé's forehead creased. "Eh, well, that's really for the tourists."

The cooling air of the clouds pressed on Margot's brow,

and as soon as her eagerness to talk and plot travels with Chloé had infused her, it fled. She felt tired. As usual. But trying to make an effort, as this was her new thing these days, she asked if there was anywhere else Chloé wanted to go after the café, making the excuse that she was feeling stiff from sitting for too long.

Drawing an ornate silver pocket watch from her clutch, Chloé declined. "I really must be somewhere. I had almost forgotten."

"No worries," Margot offered, not certain whether it was disappointment or relief that tickled at her ribs.

There was still something weighing about Chloé's presence, almost penetrating, that sucked a bit of Margot's life force from her, yet a new energy also streamed through their connection and had her almost craving more. She faintly panicked that she may have succeeded in putting her classmate off, and with the insecurity of a girl handing off a cocktail napkin with her phone number, Margot air-kissed Chloé's cheeks with an eager "Call me" in her ear.

Her friend nodded back, and Margot walked onward alone, feeling hollow. With no destination in mind, she let her inner divining rod guide her as she meandered for blocks, looking at people and places but not really seeing them.

The sun parted the clouds but left her in shadow. The wheat-like weeds were gilded with gold, yet she remained gray, shunned by the light.

Just out of the sun's reach, the stone woman was a pitiful sight. Margot had been watching her for the last half-hour, ever since wandering to the cemetery after lunch with Chloé. The spell broke when a black-and-white pigeon swooped to her feet.

After letting the bird peck near her toes for a while, she finally rose from the bench to stand eye-level with the statue. A vine spiraled down the lady's form like a fluttering green boa, and from that sorrowful stone face, Margot imagined tears cascading down the ivy, trickling leaf to leaf.

And then one did; an obsidian black drop crawled out from the corner of one frozen, downcast eye. It eased its way down a track of stem, and Margot squeezed her bag strap.

No. Just an insect. She relaxed.

But then the sunlight fell away from her, too. Pulling on the pilled gray cardigan that had practically become her uniform, she set off down the path. As she walked, her eyes ambled over the lumpy bed of ferns that smothered the headstones beneath them. Feeling a little short of breath herself, she stopped to turn around and nearly stepped on the pigeon. She sidestepped it to continue on her way.

After a few yards, the hairs at the back of her neck stood on end, and she had a strong feeling she was being followed. Still walking, she peeked behind her to see it was only the pigeon.

"I don't have food," she told it.

Ten yards or so further, though, she looked over her shoulder again. The pigeon was still in pursuit, so she stopped and flashed a pair of jazz hands so it would finally believe her about the food and go away.

It seemed to work as the bird diverted its search to the grass. But when Margot started up again, the pigeon circled back into the walkway, treading lightly in her wake.

Ookaay...

She turned onto a narrower, grown-over footpath. The pigeon rounded the corner as well. Twenty yards deeper into the cemetery, Margot stopped again, waiting for her feathered stalker to catch up, its sooty markings making it look like a white dove fallen from grace.

Again, the bird closed in on Margot, but once at her feet, it strutted off the path and then took flight. All view of it disintegrated into a blaze of sun.

Margot squinted and looked back down to the ground while circular afterimages of solar light reverberated against her retinas. Opening and closing her eyes a few times, she finally focused on where the bird had stood – right on the grave of none other than Charlotte Pidgeon.

Well, fancy meeting you here! What a coinc—

Her chest squeezed, and the hairs prickled at the back of her neck again. The bird was gone, but Margot still didn't feel alone. More than that, she sensed she was being watched. Stumbling back a pace, she spun to see a massive cross mounted on a pediment about a meter high. Behind that, something hid.

She held her breath, taking notice of the few curls of hair and slim sweep of a gown sticking out just to the right of the cross. Sprouting out from either side of the vertical beam were two immense slabs of feathers.

Angels would make poor spies. Wings are the dead giveaway, she joked to herself, but other strange, distorted thoughts appeared in her mind's eye as if she were writing them on the pages of her diary.

Yet this wasn't a dream, and it couldn't be real either. She prayed it was only the pulsation in her vision that now made the angel's wavy locks appear to draw up its rigid shoulder. Nauseated, Margot watched the granulated curls ease along and imagined the angel twisting around the cross to glare back at her.

A crow cawed from a branch directly overhead, and a woodpecker's drill rattled with the low growl of a jungle cat.

The acid in her stomach churned, prickling her face and arms, and her heart squeezed. She didn't understand what was happening but gulped dizzily and stepped backward off the pavement until her calves backed into a headstone.

Without taking her eyes off the angel, she gingerly stepped over the shallow marker and sank into the overgrowth behind it. Sitting, she then leaned her shoulders down to the earth. With the weeds tickling her ears and nose, she pushed her heels against the back of the stone. Her hair caught in the dry grasses as she eased her spine along the dirt, burrowing deeper within them until consumed from view.

The overhead bellow of airplanes faded into white noise behind the sounds of insects and Margot's breathing, lulling her to sleep as ferns caressed her cheeks and words whispered in her ears with delicate pops:

thou Eye among the blind…
Haunted for ever by the eternal mind…
we are toiling all our lives to find,
In darkness lost, the darkness of the grave…

A presence which is not to be put by
To whom the grave
Is but a lonely bed without the sense or sight
Of day or the warm light,
A place of thought where we in waiting lie.

I recite these words, and though they embody my heart's sorrow as I look upon the love lost, I cannot help but rejoice in the love found.

No, it is not the frivolous fabrication of artistic dispositions, suckled like a sweetmeat and reserved for those with the foolish propensity to devour it sooner than a climbing boy would his ration of bread; no, it exists, as real as my heart, could I cut it out for those palms to cup on this instant. Yet we are not alone here, and must practice caution.

With a start, Margot woke up to a rustling sound just a few feet away. She darted up from the weeds, remembering where she was.

Both groggy and alert, she looked over at the twitching grasses making all the racket – just in time for a small fox to step out of them and pad onto the moonlit pathway. For a second, it cocked its head up, ears stabbing upward and rotating to catch their radar signals. Margot stayed as still as possible; Rand had told her there was no rabies in the UK, but she still didn't want to attract a wild animal's attention. Before long, though, the fox lowered its head and trotted away.

Left in peace to find her bearings, she scanned the

graveyard from where she sat. What the dark had pillaged of the sun's gold, the moon had re-plated in platinum. The moon was full and bright enough, in fact, that she could see everything for what it was.

Her winged stalker was still there but looked not only disinterested but like…rock. Rock that had been chiseled by a person to look like something it wasn't.

And there was no woman crying because there was no woman. Just another rock carved by a living person to look like someone else who's living but isn't.

At dead of night when graveyards were supposed to be their most alive – it was not.

An eerie calm fell over her as she got practical and looked for her way out. The farthest she could see through the mercury-licked tendrils of grass was the black silhouette of catacombs at the cemetery's border. She gazed along the wall, her night-vision squiggling and squirming all the way, until the front gate came into view. And then she realized…

She was locked in.

Margot swallowed and thought through her options. There weren't any, really, unless she figured out a way to scale that wall. But even then, she could be trapped in a private garden and have to wake someone to let her out. Under any other circumstances, she'd have thought she'd choose embarrassment over shacking up with the dead, but somehow staying put felt better. Closed-circuit TV cameras would probably catch her, too, if she hopped out onto one of the roads at either end, and she'd get in as much trouble if she tried to find a night guard within the cemetery, so that settled it: she would have to remain interred out of sight until sunrise.

But this overgrown grave was getting itchy. She stood up and cut a diagonal across the grass toward a blackened mausoleum. She'd walked by the structure a few times before in the daylight, knowing it had an open doorway and no coffins inside. It was just an aging shell supported by scaffolding. A blend of calculated steps and contortions delivered Margot through the framework of pipes to the mausoleum's center, where she sank cross-legged on the gritty floor like a little girl in her backyard playhouse. She ran her palms against the ashy ground surface and, for company, tried to conjure Derek and Sylvie on either side of her, just like the last time all three had been together playing a silly board game.

A silent wind picked up. Though the dead leaves around her didn't stir, Margot felt the chill sharply, and she pulled her cardigan tighter. Drawing her knees up into her chest, she concentrated on happy thoughts to see her through the night.

Chapter Nine

Reckoning

She saw a swirl of colors, a flickering of light – then, with a rustle of muslin, she stepped around an easel to run her finger down an ivory neck. She caught her breath and exhaled in ecstasy.

And then she woke up to the door flying open.

"Margot!"

Uncurling and rolling over to lie on her back, she felt able to do little more than raise her eyelids to Rand's pallid face, lit by the daylight. He'd already crossed to the bed and sat at its edge with a fist jabbed into the duvet on her other side, pinning her.

She remained limp, like her muscles were in atrophy. *Easel?* she questioned, but her dream-thoughts were interrupted.

"When? Where?" Rand was too flustered to articulate, yet Margot, now fully awake, understood.

"Must've been eight or so, once the cemetery opened."

"Cemetery!"

She was too tired to be anything but frank. "I fell asleep there."

"Fell asleep!"

"I'm fine! Don't worry. It just got to be after hours, and I got locked in. But I'm fine!"

"What were you doing there so late? Were you alone?"

She answered his full line of questioning as rationally as she could. She owed him at least that, especially after learning he'd stayed awake all night waiting for her to return, had phoned the police to no avail, and must have only just nodded off in his armchair less than an hour ago.

"It was so stupid, I know, and I'm so sorry and embarrassed I worried you. I'm just tired, and you must be, too. Seriously, don't worry about me, just get some rest."

His fist had since softened into a flat palm, and then to an elbow, which lowered him inch-by-inch closer to her. His gaze zigzagged in all directions about her face; her own eyes followed, eventually rolling backward to trace where his had strayed upward on her head. He reached to pluck a few dried weeds from the oiled strands of her hair and flicked them to the floor to join the rest she'd tracked in.

"The thing is…" she began.

Finished preening the outdoors from her scalp, Rand occupied his fingers with stroking her tresses.

"The thing is," she repeated, "*I* am worried about me. I am now. And it scares me." She hiccupped with a sob, hating to undo her progress in one fell swoop. But as the corners of her eyes moistened, her face broke, and she poured out in a higher voice, "You were right!"

"About what?"

"I'm unbalanced."

His arms curled beneath her, hands cupping her shoulder blades as they raised her to an upright posture where he could embrace her more fully. He rocked her slightly until the worst of her fit ran its course. "Margot, try to breathe."

"I'm sorry!" Her voice rose again with a renewed outburst that Rand muffled by holding her tighter, rocking her harder. She knew he was scared, too. "I didn't write that entry, though. I mean…" She caught herself in her earlier lie and tried to backtrack in an honest way. "I mean, I didn't write it as a threat to myself. You have to know that."

Decelerating his sway, Rand nodded into her shoulder. "I know."

The dull remains of his musk mingled with the sweetness of his natural oils, aromatically soothing her mind as she inhaled. Together, they slowed to stillness.

She was the first to detach, though distanced herself only far enough to look at his face while her hands lay at his thighs. She noticed how his blue eyes were flecked with gray and committed this effect to memory, along with the lean muscle her fingers sensed through his softened denim.

Moving her gaze off to the side and out the window, she shrugged and shook her head with purpose. "It has nothing to do with my menstrual cycle, or stress, or whatever other lame-ass excuse I could make. You were right. You and Gwen. Both." She was nodding rapidly. "Right."

"I don't want to be. And maybe I'm not." Rand cupped her ear and ran a thumb over her wet cheek. "But you know I'm here for you, right?"

Nodding slower this time, she still stared outside.

"What are you thinking?" he asked.

She looked down and fingered a small hole forming in the denim at his knee. "You've been so great. I just…maybe I need…more support, like…" She let the silence drag out, as though saying *therapy* out loud would concede defeat.

He bobbed his head. "Possibly." Another pause. "If you think it would help." His tentative gaze appeared to wait for her to flare at his agreement.

Margot just bit her upper lip and looked back out the window. Then, deflating her shoulders, she looked him in the eye. "I think…yeah." She nodded with a new tear blazing a trail down her skin, then dropped her chin to her chest. A knot had loosened in her breast, though. There was now a goal, a plan. That was something more familiar to her.

Giving a quick tremble as if to shake the discussion and prior evening off her, she looked up and muttered that she probably ought to shower and rinse off the mausoleum dirt. To her surprise, Rand laughed.

"Amidst the dust and decay of bygone generations, you, Margot, *you* slept soundly." He pinched the inner corners of his eyes with his thumb and middle finger to wipe the sleepless crust from them as he continued to laugh merrily, shaking his head.

She caught his contagious smile. "Find that strange, do you?"

"Why, not at *all*," he puffed in a deep voice, sounding like an old-time broadcaster.

Margot broke down again, but this time in a giggling fit. She clasped her hands over her mouth and keeled over onto her side. The sensation felt so foreign, and, once started, she couldn't stop.

Rand exacerbated the situation by tickling her underarms and waving a hand before his nose. "Whew!"

Margot faked ladylike indignation before initiating a surprise attack that she'd mastered after years of George's noogies. She peeled back her T-shirt sleeve, lifted her arm, and buried his face into her armpit as she toppled him.

His turn to keel over. "Bloody hell! Fancy shaving that now and then? Pu—" He lost himself in laughter. "Putrid girl!"

Expending the last of her energy, she collapsed on top of him, panting. A few more chuckles bubbled out of his chest before he wrapped his arms snugly around her again for one last affirming hug. "Aw," he sighed, punctuating it with a peck on her head. "All right, milady. Time to change that oil."

She reluctantly sat up. "Oh, all *right*." She hadn't used a bathroom since the previous afternoon, anyway, so she stood to escort her full tank out of the bedroom. Yet once she stepped a leg past the threshold, she turned on the ball of her foot. "Hey. Really quick."

Still stretched on her bed with his head propped on his hand, Rand raised his brow. He looked so good there, relaxed at last, with his distressed tee bunched up a bit and revealing a toned swathe of skin. Margot bent one leg and pressed her thighs together, reckoning she'd be aroused if it weren't for the sudden pressure on her bladder.

"That time we were standing here," she said, staying the course, "talking about ghosts and the afterlife. You remember, *that* night."

He squinted an eye as he nodded with an expression of mock pain.

"What were you getting at?"

With a pout, he shrugged. "I was only teasing that a ghost had opened your door."

"*Nooo*. I'd forgotten, you twat, but before Gwen buzzed up, you were about to explain why you were asking." She looked at her hand resting on the doorframe, then back at him. "You had a reason and raised the subject on purpose. The sooner you tell me, the sooner I'll remove my stench from the room."

After some hesitation, Rand gave in to the bargain. Looking less relaxed now, he sat up. "Oh…it's not a massive issue. And I don't want you thinking her mad."

Margot didn't have to ask who 'her' was. Her own leap in logic had already tightened her jaw. "Of course not. Tell me."

He rolled his eyes and drew a preparatory breath. "You've brought it up before, how Gwen is never here. Well, now we both know she *is* here sometimes during the day, but never at night. She *never* comes here at night anymore. Even that night we're speaking of, she only came as far as the second landing to meet me."

Margot stood rigid. Besides her desperation to pee, the idea of someone frozen on the landing and refusing to climb any further ignited Victorian Gothic fancies in her imagination.

She cleared her throat. "Is she…afraid to meet me or something?"

Rand wetted his lower lip. "Well, she *is* afraid, but not of you. She's quite reasonable, really, almost skeptical to a fault." As if only to himself, he muttered, "Cool enough to preserve beef mince, actually."

"Stop stalling, Englishman. You're talking to an American. Be direct already."

"So, ah…" Cough. "It so happens that she doesn't, ah…" Sniff. "Well, she doesn't sleep here anymore, you see, because she…believes this flat to be, uh…"

"Oh, for God's sake! Just spill it!"

"She believes the flat to be haunted."

The one who spilled it was Margot, right onto the

carpeting between her bare feet.

Margot didn't poke fun at Gwen. Partly because 'taking the piss', as the Brits said, would have been outrageously hypocritical on both literal and figurative levels at the moment.

It was also out of respect for Rand. But mostly, it was because Margot believed Gwen's fears were true.

Rand had promptly scrubbed his carpet with only concern, not judgment, after Margot had fled to the bathroom to shower and hand wash her panties and leggings. Then when she'd rushed back to her bedroom in a bathrobe, he handed her a change of clothes through a small crack in the door – a purely chivalrous gesture, as she obviously had plenty of her own clean clothing on hand. He'd also offered to reschedule the rest of his day's meetings.

But as she started to get dressed, Margot insisted through the door that he finally start his day. She had an afternoon lecture anyway and wanted to look into both an optometrist and psychotherapist – she felt all the more pressed to not delay *that* appointment now that her mental debility was showing itself through mortifying bodily functions.

Nonetheless, as she heard Rand swing open the unit door, she wanted to rush out and make him stop, make him stay. But she didn't, and she didn't have to. All she did was open her bedroom door and lean on the molding, wearing nothing but fresh knickers and his Joy Division T-shirt. In her haste, the boxers she'd meant to put on, too, remained bunched in her hand.

Glancing over his shoulder at her as she posed in her doorway with one long leg bent, her knee swinging lightly, Rand ran his gaze up and down her height and stopped mid-step.

"Are you sure you want me to go?" he asked.

Margot grinned and nodded. "Go to work, Bread Winner. It's just…"

"Yeah?"

"Never mind."

She couldn't have said it more unconvincingly, and Rand was already backtracking into the foyer and closing the door.

"All right, *fine*," she said. "But it's going to delay you a few more minutes."

Shutting the door behind him, he guided her to the living room. She would've slipped on the boxers then, but his shirt hung low enough to cover her fanny in both the British and American senses of the word – front and back – and Rand hadn't exactly lodged any complaints of indecent exposure. So they sat together on the sofa, where Margot tucked both of her legs up on the cushion. Rand sat close, a hand at her bare knee and the other on her shoulder as she interrogated him for all the details.

He hesitated, but the long and short of it was that Gwen had seen a weeping woman in his bedroom.

"Your bedroom."

"Yes, my bedroom."

He continued to describe how Gwen had woken with a start on more than one occasion and, gathering the duvet to her chest, sat propped on her knees and pointing to his bedroom window.

"Your bedroom window," Margot whispered.

"*Yes*. Stop repeating everything I say." Rand offered a fleeting grin, then explained how Gwen had frozen in this way, just pointing. On the third night of the occurrence, she'd elaborated that it was a woman, standing right before the window and weeping. On the fifth night of the sighting, now that Gwen had grown used to the routine, she'd admitted there had been another presence, but not anything she could see.

Until the fourteenth night.

On the fourteenth night of her visions, Gwen had described the other being as less defined in form but tangibly present. It exuded a bluish, effervescent vapor that at times extended around what she'd come to name Lady Grey.

And from that night forward, Gwen had ceased staying at

Rand's flat at night.

She'd implored him, of course, to stay at her place until he could sell or rent his. She could quickly take some pictures and list it with the local branch of her lettings agency for no fee. At the rate property was moving, he could expect it to be snatched up by a tenant within a week's time, if that long.

And yet Rand hadn't seen anything. He didn't question Gwen's sanity, but he himself hadn't been bothered by a single inconvenience in the flat beyond ordinary home improvements, so he didn't see any point in renting it out and moving. As for selling the property altogether, that wasn't an option. He would hold on to his place as long as he could to build equity. On that stubborn point, Gwen grew resentful. As Rand saw it, he was retaining a long-term investment that would contribute stability to their future together. As Gwen saw it, he was clinging on to his single life, a bachelor pad at his disposal even if they did move in together.

This had become a bone of contention, and the 'ghost' was an all the more convenient excuse for Gwen to fall back on during every successive argument they'd had – tackling the wicked relationship question of "Where are we going?" that tortured any infatuation into bitter submission.

"So that's the real reason I never see her," Margot said. "I have to say, it's insane that I still haven't after almost two months. I mean, I get that she wouldn't go out of her way to meet me, but still. If I were your girlfriend, I'd want to."

"Well, true. But we've been going through a strained time. I suppose it's one of those situations where… What did you call it when you spoke of James? 'Make or break?'"

"Yeah. Or to put it technically, 'Shit or get off the pot.'"

He bobbed his head without humor.

"Ah, so nothing's lost in translation there," she said.

"It's a familiar theme."

Margot reasoned she ought to take one for the team and stand by her fellow woman looking for more commitment, but she found herself sympathizing with the opponent more this round. She stayed silent.

He, on the other hand, seemed to want to say more but faltered, and Margot perceived an inward struggle between his mind and heart. "The thing is," he eventually said, "there's more that ties me to this property."

She watched his eyes glass up.

"I'm doing all right on my own, financially, but in this city, I needed a little help. The money I put down on this place came from my sister's trust." He pressed his lips as he stared sideways at the window. "My parents decided that parceling out the fund between their living children would be an appropriate way to celebrate Sophie's memory. Her death left us grieving for such a long while, they thought this was one way to help each of us begin to breathe easier." He gazed up toward the molding that lined the walls near the ceiling. "This flat...it's something solid. Something visible. This house has stood for a hundred and fifty years, and I think it could stand for the next hundred if tended to properly, if given the attention it deserves. I wasn't there for her. But I can be *here*, can't I?"

He'd spoken so quietly that Margot had watched his lips to be sure she wouldn't miss one syllable. She wanted to console him, but all she could say with certainty was "It wasn't your fault."

Beyond that, she simply rose to her knees and lay forward onto him, wrapping her arms around his shoulders and not thinking twice if the gesture was inappropriate or bared her bottom beneath the T-shirt. More than anything, she wanted to communicate to him that she understood – everything. If not his tremendous loss, then his vulnerability, his need to hold on to the past, his relationship quagmire. And his ghost.

Though it was afternoon, the living room's shades were still drawn low, dimming the room. It had a sedating effect on them both, given neither had really slept the night before. For their best of intentions to get on with their respective days, they slumped into a mild stupor while enveloping each other. Dazing halfway into sleep, she slid down a little, feeling his heart thumping against her chin. For an unrecorded measure of time, they both drifted to sleep.

Margot became vaguely aware of her face nuzzling into soft fabric, pleased to pick up where her dream had left off. The warm body rising and falling with heavy breaths felt so real. She perspired with the acute sensation that had been building in her core, close to release.

Wrapped in her phantom lover's arms, she felt their grip loosen as hands slid down to the small of her back, holding fast there while lips buried into her hair. Grinning and tingling in a hazy limbo of half-sleep, she spread her knees and slid up until she could feel a pressure right where she wanted to, as palms skimmed over her bared cheeks to cup them and secure her hips in place.

Then Margot heard a rapid sniff and jolted up to meet Rand's equally bemused expression.

Oh, God. Tell me I was only dreaming.

Blinking twice, Rand ran his fingers through the waves of his hair as his cheeks flushed, possibly thinking the same thing.

"Ah, good kip," was all he said. But even at half-mast, his shifting eyes betrayed he was just as baffled if not embarrassed as she was. Hopefully it was just over the fact they'd fallen asleep hugging like that. Nothing more.

Careful to avoid more contact, Margot eased her leg over Rand's lap to dismount and liberate him of her warm, sweaty weight.

"Right," he grunted as he sat up. Appearing thoroughly disoriented, he stood to fetch his laptop bag and keys. But before he headed to the door, he backtracked to Margot and briskly kissed her on the forehead, suggested she put on some trousers, and then promptly left for work.

In the cooling effect of his absence, she walked into the kitchen to pour herself a glass of water. Sipping it meditatively, she was ashamed of what she may or may not have just done on top of her friend. It was bad enough she'd caused him so much worry and made him late for work. Yet niggling on the outside of this shame was guilt over Gwen. Not only because Margot was pretty sure she'd just half-consciously dry-humped the woman's boyfriend, but also for not validating Gwen's ghostly fears to Rand when she'd had the chance.

As she sucked a stream of water through her teeth, she looked at the shaded window's beige light. No, what had happened between her and Rand was just a fluke. Neither knew what he or she had been doing, so chalk it up to dormant hormones that will play while the conscious mind is away. *If* anything had even happened. But one thing she did know: she didn't want to restore his confidence in Gwen. Not yet.

The water ran right through her. Pounding the glass on the countertop, she strode to the bathroom and pushed the door shut out of habit, as though it mattered with no one else home. She relieved herself in a more civilized manner this time, and, rinsing her hands afterwards in pleasantly warm water, she ran them up and down her face, finally beginning to calm.

Until she heard the bathroom door push open.

She immediately looked at its reflection in the mirror to see it was still closed. But just as she exhaled, wondering what the sound could've been instead, she heard it a second time as she watched the door nudge open, scraping on the carpeting. It stopped for a second until a third shove swung it open. Margot instinctively bounded up the steps to slam the door back shut against a palpable force.

When she heard the door fasten in its lock, she realized she might not have fully closed it the first time because she didn't remember hearing the click then. Opening it, in that case, wouldn't have required turning the handle – just a push.

She turned to walk back down the steps, feeling a cool breeze caress her legs. The larger window above the bathtub was still cracked open a few inches – she'd raised it earlier to air out the steamy room after her shower. But a thought struck her now as she dried her hands. Tentatively, she made her way up the stairs to reopen the door. As she did so, she saw no one was in the hallway, and stray strands of her hair floated atop another chilly draft that blew from the front of the flat.

Of course.

Margot had also opened one of the living room windows earlier, where she'd positioned a drying rack to better aerate her hand-washed leggings.

Cross-ventilation. Only way to go when still without AC in the twenty-first century.

This calmed her a little.

The sound and vision replayed in her mind, though, and she couldn't shake how deliberate the door's motion had seemed – not like the swift force of airflow but a rhythmic heave-ho on the count of three.

With terror creeping back in, she treaded back to Rand's bedroom, needing to confront it again. The fact remained that he still slept there and she herself had to sleep just a matter of yards away, so she needed to get over it. She'd just spent the night in a cemetery, for God's sake. Daylight was no time to be a coward.

Rand still kept his door closed, and now she understood why the room was out of bounds – for Gwen's peace of mind if not Margot's protection, regardless of what *he* believed. Maybe he still questioned the phenomenon himself, keeping an open mind given his faith in Gwen. Which would also explain why he was so keenly interested in Margot's convictions on the afterlife. He hadn't been interrogating. He was searching.

How can he keep sleeping in here, though, she wondered as she entered the room for the first time in weeks. Feeling a prickle at the back of her neck, she braced herself to look over at the window. Her head swiveled first, her body trailing after.

Exhale. Nothing. Her eye floaters bobbed lazily against the white light of day.

Turning to leave, however, Margot's chest caved as she heard the bedroom window shudder in its frame. Though she wasn't looking at it, she knew the sound from past struggles trying to open the flat's tall Victorian sashes; their hidden weights helped counteract the heaviness of their oversized panes, but the uneven layers of paint on the frames often caused resistance. She retraced her steps to look for certain.

The shrunken, rotted wood of the bedroom's lower sash rattled in place.

Margot looked outside at the trees. Their leaves shook gently, commensurate with the breeze she'd just felt from the open windows, but nowhere near violent enough to match the pressure against this closed one.

It's tucked between the building's rear extensions, though, so maybe that creates a wind tun—

A pinprick of blue light stole her attention. It flashed once into her lower peripheral vision. Seconds later, it returned and held constant. She looked down toward the point of light and focused on it. Appearing at waist-height, it didn't maintain one position; instead, its movement was elliptical to small degrees, subtle but deliberate. A floater hovering just above and off to the side of it quickly levitated, and then the light vanished. Margot's eyes chased around for it desperately, but there was nothing. The window held still.

Drawing the door closed behind her, she went to get dressed, searched online for the name and address of the nearest vision-care center accepting walk-ins, and left for class.

Chapter Ten

Twenty / Twenty

"Well, Margot, your eyes appear to be healthy. You're long-sighted with a slight astigmatism that we can correct."

"Is long-sighted like farsighted?"

"Exactly. But your current lenses are actually too strong for you. It seems your vision is improving, so I'm going to give you a lighter prescription."

"Can eyes do that?" *How can I be seeing better?*

Chloé hadn't been at class that day, which left Margot deflated on her journey to the optometrist. Since their heart-to-heart at lunch yesterday, she'd retrieved her friend from the Drinking Buddy bin and lowered her gently into the Confidante basket. Granted, she was ready to pay a therapist to listen, yet had hoped to first fit in another session with Chloé, free of charge.

In the meantime, though, she was anxious to hear what the eye doctor could say about it from a scientific angle. A graying man with a mild manner, he stood darkly silhouetted against the illuminated X-ray of her eye, which burned golden in the dim room like a setting sun.

"They can improve for some lucky people, but probably only for a time. At some point, your sight will deteriorate again, so you might want to hold on to your old spectacles."

"Are my retinas okay?"

"Yes, they look good." He turned to the X-ray and motioned across key areas of the cross-section. "No signs of retinal detachment, glaucoma, or inflammation in the optic nerve. Have you been noticing anything abnormal in your vision?"

He was at the ready with his clipboard and pen, just in case.

"Yeah, I think. I see this pulsing glow, especially in the dark." As she said it, Margot splayed her two hands and motioned them to mimic what she saw. Instead, she felt like a pervert squeezing a woman's breasts, so quickly folded her hands and shoved them between her knees.

"Huh," was the doctor's unhelpful reply.

"There's this other type of light, too. And floaters, which are a lot more distracting than they used to be, so I've been afraid there's an issue."

"Huh. Those are symptoms of retinal detachment, but from your pictures and examination, everything does look healthy. Is it a flash of light that you see? As though someone's taking your picture?"

"No, not a big flash like that. Just this tiny dot that appears in my peripheral vision, but I can also look at it directly. Same with my floaters sometimes."

"Directly? No, you can't look at floaters directly." He set down his clipboard, evidently concluding there would be nothing of relevance to transcribe.

"But I've seen them stationary even when I roll my eyes."

"No, you might see them in your outer field of vision, or they might appear to drift in front of your cornea, but their nature is to dart away as soon as you move your eye to look at them. You can never truly focus on one."

"But I have."

"I'd suggest it could be an ocular migraine, but, just like the floaters, the impact on your vision wouldn't behave that way. You must be seeing some reflection of light, maybe sunlight glinting off your watch. At any rate, your eyes are healthy."

I don't wear a watch.

"But mind that you do try to count the floaters when they're noticeable. If you have five one day and a significant increase – say, twenty – the next, that could be a precursor to detachment, and you should go to hospital immediately. But unless that happens, you're healthy, Margot. Your eyes are in brilliant condition."

With a grin, he punctuated his diagnosis with a click of his pen and plunked it back into his jacket pocket as means of dismissing her.

"Actually, right now I think I see…"

"Pardon?"

"Um, I think I'm already beginning to see a little better with the dilation drops wearing off."

"Well, hopefully you don't have much planned for the next hour, as it'll take at least that long for your vision to fully return to normal."

Blindly, Margot selected a new pair of frames with great trust in the store associate's taste. She maintained a pleasant farce of trying on different ones, pretending she could see clearly and not the multitude of light and shapes swarming before and around her.

She'd been about to tell the doctor she could see the number of floaters dramatically increase in the time it had taken for the drops to take full effect, but decided against it when it became too obvious that what she saw was something different.

Graciously placing her lens order and smiling and nodding her way out the door, Margot tried to navigate her way safely through the throngs of blurry shoppers on the sidewalk. With her pupils enlarged, the glare of the overcast sky stabbed her eyes, so she wore sunglasses. Several times she stopped short before walking right into someone, and she flinched at motions coming at her from the side.

The high street is ridiculous today. Are all the shops on clearance?

She concentrated on the nearest people walking in and against her direction, yet the more she tried, the more people she saw, clustered against and intersecting each other, some fainter than others. Unable to stand it any longer, she ducked into the quiet alley of a residential mews building that once housed horses and servants yet could now, ironically, only be afforded by the more affluent.

158

Feeling her way along a cool brick exterior wall for a bench, Margot decided the cobblestones would serve just as well. She sank with her back against the wall and drew her knees to her chest, crushing her bag in her lap. Regulating her breathing with closed eyes, she imagined the empty corridor to which she would open them; it would contrast so sweetly with the street's bustle.

When she did, she froze.

From left to right, she scanned traces of colorless figures in motion around her, rhythmically rising and falling and distorting her vision like rippling water. She leaned now and again as though to lamely clear their paths, but if she was an obstruction she felt nothing.

This seemed to continue for several minutes. She shook nervously, and, after a time, she had the sensation of elevating. Digging her fingernails into loose gravel, she knew she wasn't lifting from the ground. Yet, looking straight ahead of her, she had the perspective of something translucent but discernible – horizontal lines within a tall, narrow trapezoidal form that conveyed jerkily downward in relation to her like a malfunctioning escalator.

Her vision dimmed somewhat before brightening back. This time, rectangular shapes in assorted lengths, widths, and heights emerged with vertical movement between and on top of them. With a sweeping feeling of motion, Margot, too, felt she moved among them. Though she shut her eyes, a negative imprint of what she saw continued to play out against the black screen of her inner lids. Her eardrums popped as though depressurizing, with tinny words echoing through them like a distant phonograph:

I saw her upon nearer view,
A Spirit, yet a Woman too!
Her household motions light and free,
And steps of virgin-liberty…

Margot vaulted back out into the busy high street, exalting in the physical sensation of bumping into and brushing against other pedestrians. She walked the rest of the way home as she waited for her sight to merge back into one, singular focus.

"Hey, Mom. How are you?"

"Oh, my goodness! Hey, Father! Phone call from overseas! Just a minute, your father's getting on the other line."

Margot had just enough credit left for another Internet call to her parents' landline from Rand's computer. She heard a click, then some static.

"Well, hello, Marty! Good to hear your voice!"

Sitting in her bedroom, Margot concentrated on holding her voice steady after hearing her dad use her old nickname, the identity she'd have been given had she been a boy. "Good to hear yours, too! Hope I'm not calling at a bad time."

Both parents spoke over each other in shared, emphatic assurances that it could never be a bad time for their little girl to call.

"So, what's up?" her mom said.

"Oh, nothing much." *Just losing my mind, is all.*

"Are you still working on that project?" her dad asked.

"Thank God, no. All done with that one and just waiting for the next – and last. Then I'm home!"

"Oh, we can't wait for that," Margot's mother chimed in as her father continued, "Good, good, Marty. So you're learning a lot there?"

"Yeah, on so many levels."

"Ah-hah. Good!"

"There's so much depth to this city, so many layers."

"Boy, I bet so."

"Well, your father and I've been talking about maybe planning a visit, but we don't want to interrupt your studies. We were thinking unless you had to go back to work right away we could come when classes are done, just a week or so. But not if you don't want two old codgers there."

"No!" Margot checked herself. "I mean, no problem,

that'd be awesome! I haven't asked because I didn't want you to feel pressured, but, yeah, that'd be so cool."

"Well, we can think about it. We don't want to keep you from getting back to work. But if it did work out, we'd stay at a hotel, you know. We wouldn't impose on Rand."

"It wouldn't be an imposition whatsoever. He's so laid-back like that. He'd probably offer to stay over at his girlfriend's, or if he's away for work, he's got a queen-sized bed you could...or, whatever, unless a hotel would be more comfortable and private for you." She couldn't believe how soon she'd forgotten such a critical detail: *Oh yeah, sure, there'll be plenty of room for the two of you and Lady Grey to three-way spoon.*

"Sure, a hotel would be easy enough," her dad insisted. "We don't want to take advantage."

"Either way. It's up to you," Margot played along, cringing at how insincere she sounded. "I could also take the couch."

"No, we wouldn't want that..."

There was an awkward silence for a few seconds.

"So what's been your fav—"

"I just got back from the eye—"

"Oh, sorry, go ahead."

"No, I'm sorry. You were saying?"

Margot's mom plowed through the polite banter of father and daughter with her own agenda.

"So, when *do* you think you'll be getting back? Have you talked to anyone at your office?"

"Uh, I actually haven't...yet. Other than those love notes I mail my dear director, sprayed with perfume."

"Well, it would be good, you know, to know where you stand. Just in case something else doesn't come up. It would be good to know you've got a job there."

"Yeah, I agree. I'll email them this week."

"Otherwise you know you can stay with us as long as you need to find something else here. It'll be so much easier than dealing with work permits and everything, you know. Working at home."

"Yes, Mumsy, you're a master of subtlety. I get the point. Don't worry, there's nothing keeping me here." Again, the conviction behind her words faltered, but this time she herself didn't understand why.

"Have you heard anything from James?" her mom asked.

"Where does that come from?"

"Well, I just thought maybe he'd be in contact with the two of you in Europe at the same time."

"But he doesn't know I'm here. Does he?" All she believed James had needed to know when she moved out of their condo was that she didn't want to exist in a space connected with him. That he could mail the check for her ownership percentage to her parents' address. "Has he called you?"

"No, not us, but wouldn't friends've told him?"

"I guess, but I haven't been in touch with our mutual ones in a while. I don't think any of them would even know." Margot thought for a moment. "You're not afraid we'll get back together and I'll stay in Europe, are you?"

Her mother's tone became aloof. "I'd be lying if I said the thought's never crossed my mind."

"*Mom*. I haven't talked to him in months, and there's no way he could just whisk me away now."

"I'm just saying. You never know. It's as they say, you know, 'Absence makes the heart grow fonder'."

"Yeah, well, they also say, 'Out of sight, out of mind'. Not to mention, 'Too little, too late' if he did try to make amends."

"But what about, 'Better late than *never*'?"

"I'm thinking if there's a cliché out there to contradict every other cliché, there isn't so much wisdom in those words after all." With her eyes still aching from the dilation drops, Margot really didn't desire a mother-daughter catfight. It was time to call in the referee. "So, Dad, what were you going to say before? When I interrupted you?"

"Huh?" He sounded surprised to be acknowledged, having grown so used to melting into the background during the women's squabbles – preferring it, as Margot well knew.

"Oh! Nothing much. I was just going to ask what's been the highlight so far."

She chewed her chapped lip. "Hm. It's difficult to pinpoint any one thing." *It's a toss-up between the depression and the paranormal presences.* "Probably the cemetery."

"Cemetery?" her mother sounded off in concern whereas her dad, ever encouraging of his little girl, gave an interested, "Oh! Ah-hah?"

Margot couldn't escape explanation. "It's a really pretty park, actually. It has a lot of flowers and trees and beautiful old Victorian gravestones, and just makes for a really solemn place to think."

If she hadn't felt so creeped out still by her hallucination there, that might have been a good place for her to go after her eye appointment, to sort through what she'd instead tried to escape with this phone call. Even as an adult, she still believed her parents had all the answers, but they'd done so much for her – always – that for once she wouldn't stand for making her problems theirs. Not before she'd tried solving it on her own. Not before she even knew the problem needing solving.

Her mom seemed convinced enough, though. "I bet that's really neat. Just don't get stuck there alone after dark, missy."

Margot bit her lip again to stifle a laugh. "Please, Mom. Like *that* would happen."

Making the excuse her online chat minutes needed topping up, she began to wind down the conversation with some benign suggestions of what they could do during their possible visit at summer's end. Margot knew her father would love the pubs and Churchill War Rooms, and her mother would need to see Kensington Gardens and the V&A.

"Aw, heck, we'll be happy with anything. I'm sure your father will like the museums, but I'm just curious to see where you buy your groceries!"

"Ah, Marks and Spencer will be at the top of our list,

then."

"Gosh, to think we'll actually *be* there. It doesn't seem real!"

So little does anymore.

"All right, we'll let you go, honey, so this call doesn't get expensive for you. Love you so much."

"Yes, it's good to hear your voice, Marty."

"Love you guys, too, and don't be silly, Internet calls are so cheap. I could video-call you for *free*, ya know, if you'd get an account and webcam."

"Eh," her mom grunted, like always, against all things technology. "We like the phone and will reimburse you for it. Love you, toots."

"You are not paying for this. But I love you, too, and enjoy the rest of your day."

"Yes. You, too. Is it night-time there?"

Oh boy, here comes the marathon goodbye... "Yeah, going on seven."

"Is it dark yet?" her dad asked.

"No, won't be for like another three hours."

"Gosh!"

"Boy!"

"Yeah, so I should probably get some work done and something to eat before bed."

"You haven't eaten yet? You'd better go, then, little missy."

"All right, I will. Take care."

"We will. Take care of yourself, too."

"Love you."

"Love you, too, Marty."

"Talk soon. And say hey to George and the fam."

"Okay, sounds good. Thanks for calling."

"Of course! I'll do it again soon."

"Sounds good. Love you."

"Love you, too. Bye."

"Bye. Or 'goodnight', I guess."

"Yeah, right. And 'good day' to you."

"Yep, we'll try. Love you."

"Love you."

"Bye."

"Bye."

"Bye."

Click.

Not in the mood for additional calls home, Margot started surfing the Internet as another sidetrack. Her spirit was certainly warmer since speaking to her parents; the familiarity of their voices had snapped her into place, and she felt more herself.

Riding that high, she'd composed emails to George and Sylvie and then, for good measure (or else her mother would never let her hear the end of it), a casual check-in with her boss.

Writing was so much easier than calling anyway. Writing gave control, the ability to pause, reread, and revise. Margot didn't trust herself with speaking any longer; the restraint in talking to her parents had been difficult enough, and they were even too innocent to pick up on vocal cues. Her not-as-innocent friends and brother, on the other hand, were risks she couldn't take. Not after she still hadn't heard word from Derek.

She'd been writing back and forth with Sylvie pretty regularly, though, to firm up plans for Sylvie's visit next month. Refreshing her screen, Margot was surprised to instantly receive a message back from her.

Hey! So I looked at tickets to Paris from London. That's doable. Think we'd be too rushed if I only come for 5 days in August? Turns out I need to be back to run the back-to-school workshop, too. Oaf Boy got himself fired. They won't disclose why, but I swear he's a sexual predator. Omigod, just waaay too friendly with the teens. Bummer to cut my trip short, but I'm excited about the workshop – Cinderella stories!"

In her mind, Margot could hear Sylvie clapping.

Did you know every culture has one? Egyptian, Native

American, Persian, etc. She goes by different names, and there's usually not a glass slipper, but the gist of it's the same even if some civilizations had no way to communicate it to others. Carl Jung called it 'collective unconscious'. Doing quick web research now to get some materials organized and thought it might relate to your ad studies :)

Anyway, chica, just let me know your thoughts on Paris and whatnot. Miss you, girlie. I want to put on muumuus and open that vintage shop with you in London.

Margot smiled, even at that damn remark about the vintage shop. Whatever her annoyance with it, this was good. This was distraction. Hoping to catch Sylvie still on the computer, she played along.

Sylvia! Where's my martini (squawked w/ menthol cigarette hanging out of mouth)?! And what are we chargin' for the ol' fox muffs?!

Sylvie instantly messaged back:

Fox muffs on special for 15, Marge! (hacks on self-rolled cigarette stuck to end of long, black, bedazzled cigarette holder) Christ Almighty…burned another hole in the kidskin!

Margot giggled out loud, happy to have returned the game to its original form – not a pretend plan for the future but an idea that filled her imagination *now* with musky, netted hats and old mink stoles with monogrammed linings. Just another way to touch the past, as if treasuring people's old stuff kept their experiences alive. Just as it had been with Grandma Grace's kitschy jewelry collection. Just as it was with the brooch.

Oh, btw, Sylvie wrote before Margot could reply, *hear from our ghost friend lately? LOL! Don't know why I just thought of that. :) k, bye!*

Whenever Sylvie abbreviated her words outside of a text message, Margot took the cue that her friend was in a rush and needed to go back to work. So she sent her off with *Miss you, too. Stupid ocean :(But see you soon!* and set the computer mode to standby.

Sylvie's shining presence would surely be welcome when she came to visit, and Margot did miss her. But only in this instant did she feel less enthused about it, as though it would throw off the balance she'd been trying so hard to find in her London life.

And why in hell did she have to bring up the Ouija? Seriously.

Out of curiosity, Margot stirred the computer from its brief nap to open a web browser and look up *collective unconscious*. From a cursory search, she gathered that its basic premise was that people innately have a shared awareness, across each other and over space and time.

Huh. She did remember something like that from college.

Margot then got serious and searched for *ocular migraine* to self-diagnose her warped vision. This led into related links that she clicked again and again to spelunk into a cyber-labyrinth of medical knowledge: *blurred vision, double vision, jumbled vision.*

Her next search string – *scrambled vision* – generated ads on the side for online vision tests and word scrambles. Looking at one of her books resting on the desk corner, she contemplated the rumpled sheet of paper tucked in its pages. Her packing list – or, when flipped over, the Ouija transcript – had been flippantly shoved into her copy of *Charlotte Sometimes* months ago as a riddle to reason out another day in the event the 'words' they'd received were actually anagrams. But her interest in deciphering the transcript had faded into the forgotten, and she'd only brought the book to London to appease the weird separation anxiety she'd felt when she had finished it and gone to stow it on her parents' bookshelf, only for a fierce sentimentality to snatch it back. She figured maybe she'd reread it in its country of origin.

But now she couldn't bypass the coincidence of reading *word scramble* on the same screen that Sylvie's ghost comment had just appeared. And to have that book with that transcript within arm's reach at the moment felt nothing less than providence.

Letting curiosity get the better of her, Margot plucked the notes from her novel. The paper gave a soft emulation of thunder as she unfolded it to see Sylvie's large capital letters. Wondering what clarity time might bring, she scanned the messages she, Sylvie, and Derek had 'divined'.

I L I UV (?) / B O O I N G / P A L E R / O R C H I D /
I M / O P E N D I G / H E A R T C L O T

She remembered Sylvie's idea that *ILIV* could've meant *I LIVE* and felt satisfied with that, but when she read the other 'words' over and over, she found it impossible to conclude anything other than the rubbish they already had.

Anagram theory it is, then. Grabbing a pencil from Rand's desk drawer, she jotted her brainstorm on the piece of paper.

BOOING
BOO GIN
BINGO [O]
BIG NO [O]
ION GOB
ION BOG
GOO NIB
OBI NOG

PALER
ALE [PR]
ALP [ER]
APE [LR]
LAP [ER]
LEAP [R]
PEA [LR]

PLEA [R]
PARE [L]
PEAR [L]
PEARL
EARL [P]
RAPE [L]
REAP [L]

ORCHID
OR HID [C]
CHOIR [D]
CHORD [I]
CORD HI
HI DOC [R]
HI COD [R]
HI ROD [C]
DO RICH

Few of her results used all the letters. Of those that did, the ones for *BOOING* and *ORCHID* seemed nonsense. *PEARL* used all the letters of *PALER* in a single word, which charmed her, but, otherwise unsatisfied with how any of these iterations could fit together, she gave another term a try.

OPENDIG
DIG NOPE
DOG PINE
GOD PINE
GO PINED
GONE DIP
DOPE GIN
PIG DONE
PIGEON [D]

Aw, I like that last one. Even though it doesn't use the D. And even though pigeons are dirty flying rats. But again, the message was meaningless.

Her last resort was to combine the words for a mass unscrambling. That being way beyond the scope of her pea brain, however, she typed *online descrambler* into her browser. She clicked on an appropriate link and started to input letters into its search field, only to discover she couldn't enter more than fifteen at a time. So she paired each of the first three words in the three possible ways: *BOOING* and *PALER*, *PALER* and *ORCHID*, and *BOOING* and *ORCHID*.

Starting with *BOOING* and *PALER*, Margot snickered at the results: *BOLOGNA PIER*, *GOBLIN OPERA*, *PIGEON LABOR*, and *POOR BELGIAN*, among others. She noted one, though, that was more serious: *GONE BIPOLAR*.

No shit I have…

The next combination, *PALER* and *ORCHID*, likewise produced a bunch of crap: *CHIRP ORDEAL*, *CHORAL PRIDE*, *CLIP HOARDER*, *HARDCORE LIP*, *RICH LEOPARD*, and so forth. There also seemed to be a lot of men's names: *ADOLPH CRIER*, *CHARLIE DROP*, *HAROLD PRICE*, and *RICHARD LOPE*.

If the spirit was supposed to be a woman, could this have been a husband, boyfriend, brother, father? Murderer?

Each result led her to speculate a larger storyline, much like she did with the gravestones at the cemetery.

Maybe the man in her life lost his temper and attacked her? she wondered on seeing *RAPID CHOLER* next. *Or her own rage drove her to suicide?*

The following result ushered in a more natural, yet no less horrible, cause of death: *CHOLERA DRIP*. With a gag reflex, Margot could almost hear bodily fluids dripping into a rusted bedpan, filtered through a saturated mattress from a death by dehydration.

Her next word groupings could have been clues to the setting where this death occurred: *ORCHARD PILE* or *RAILED PORCH*. Her imagination drifted to a rural house in need of a fresher coat of paint, its gray sides contrasting with the immaculate white railing of a wraparound porch. Two rockers and a swing bench swayed in the apple-scented wind swept off acres of branches bowing with the weight of their bulbous, ruby crop.

An inky black cloud bled over the tranquility of the scene, though, as she read the next iteration – *HORRID PLACE* – and tensed at what that could mean.

Horrid place. In life or afterlife? Is that where she is now? Horrid place.

"Oooh gawd, let's move awn, shall we?" she continued aloud in her worst fake British accent. She hoped to find some more silliness in the next search akin to her first results, something to send her to sleep with a smile. "Right. *Booing orchid*, let's have at it!"

But *BOOING ORCHID* only gave choices of either *BINGO CHOROID* or *BROOCH INDIGO*.

"Well, since I don't know what the bloody fuck a *choroid* is, let's go with *brooch indigo*. Indigo brooch."

As her eyes searched around for meaning, they fell on her paper and the third word she hadn't included in the search because of the letter limit: *PALER*. Going back to the unscrambling she'd performed manually, she spied the *one* complete anagram she'd written using all the letters: *PEARL*.

"Indigo brooch, pearl. Pearl, indigo—"

Margot smacked the paper off the desk and leapt to her feet, grabbing her hair at the roots.

"No-no-no-no-no," she repeated just above a whisper while shaking her head side to side. She gasped for air as she backed into the corner and crouched between the wall and wardrobe, rocking to soothe herself and regulate her diaphragm.

"She said Charlotte has my pin," was all that looped through her mind's eye.

Tears trapped in her lashes overhung her sight when she reopened her eyes. The sheet of paper lay within reach after air resistance had arced its flight path like a boomerang. What she desired to be so far away had instead come straight back to her.

She glanced at the transcript and scanned one of the last

batches of letters left to decipher: *HEARTCLOT*.
Concentrating, Margot saw in the letters what she had not
before and desperately wished she couldn't now. Her active
mind separated and sorted the letters, rearranging them on
the page to form another complete anagram:

C-H-A-R-L-O-T-T-E.

A low moan vibrated in her chest, and her heavy head
went limp and fell back against the plaster. Her face
screwed up again as she gently whimpered.

Chapter Eleven

Reflection

"It could just be coincidence."

"There is no such thing."

"Is that what you believe?"

"It's what I believe now."

Ill at ease sitting in a chair opposite Dr. Fitzgerald, Margot had asked if she could play it old-school and lie on the couch, facing away. The psychotherapist consented. And so Margot had kicked off her black pumps – she'd wanted to dress up for the appointment – and lay flat on her back with her hands properly folded on her stomach, playing out the scene exactly as she'd imagined it from movies and daring the good doctor to explain everything away.

Dr. Fitzgerald – or 'Fitz', as she'd invited Margot to call her – was Canadian-born but had attended university on the American east coast. She'd returned to Canada to pursue doctoral studies in psychology and began her career in Toronto, but had since run her own office in England for fifteen years. Her expat background eased Margot somehow, encouraging her to speak more freely in the laidback presence of another North American.

So, Margot had started by speaking freely about Lady Grey.

Fitz found the coincidence interesting, but had conjectured that Gwen had an active imagination she was either consciously or unconsciously using to persuade Rand to move in with her and take their relationship to the next level. And as far as what Margot thought she'd seen that first day in London, Fitz's conclusions went the way of

Derek's – blaming reflections, tricks of light, or Margot's jet-lagged migraine.

"Often we generate a false positive through pareidolia, which is like when we recognize images in the clouds or the craters of the moon. All it takes, really, is a circle and two dots to identify a human face."

"Like the Grilled Cheesus in *Glee*?"

"*Exactly* like the Grilled Cheesus in *Glee*. It's a type of apophenia, the perception of patterns and significance in otherwise random and meaningless data."

Fitz went so far as referencing recent studies that revealed a connection between caffeine consumption and seeing and hearing things. The time that had elapsed also contributed to an unreliable memory that Margot's subsequent experiences might now be reshaping to fit the mould.

Margot had then talked about seeing the orb in the spot where Lady Grey stood by the window, and how the eye examination yielded no explanation for it. How it even less so accounted for the movement and feeling of ascension she'd had while squatting in the mews afterwards.

Fitz repeated what the optometrist had said about eye floaters and migraines and suggested that the blurring effect of the eye drops had distorted her perception even further, displacing light and shadow and causing dizziness.

And now, on speaking about the Ouija game, Fitz showed the same skepticism over Margot's claims. "If it isn't coincidence, what do you think might be the meaning behind this?"

"Just what I've told you. My grandmother's brooch, Charlotte…"

"But what could be the connection?"

"I have no idea."

"Margot, I'm listening to everything you say with an open mind. Please do *not* take it personally or get defensive if I play devil's advocate for a while. It's not for me to declare what is wrong or right at this point, or at any point. I just want to explore all the possibilities. Is that all right?"

"You don't believe me. You can say it."

"It's not that whatsoever. I only mean that, generally, in order to distinguish truth from belief, we have to first evaluate evidence objectively. Proving a hypothesis to be true, after all, actually lies in the *disproving* of it."

"Okay."

"To go back to what you said about the message you decoded. Barring the fact that you found the letters stood for other words as well, let's get to the root of why those letters existed in the first place. Your friend who wrote them down – is she reliable?"

"Yes, very. And she wrote them as they appeared, not after the fact. Our other friend was there to witness it, too."

"All right, so we can reasonably strike flawed memory from the list. Now there is obviously the supernatural explanation for why those letters came about: that a ghost, perhaps by the name of Charlotte, was communicating directly to you through the board game. But belief in the supernatural is subjective. You and I both entered this room with our own belief systems, so we cannot allow this to bias our conclusions."

"Okay, so…should we go back and start from the beginning? Talk about my mother and figure out if I was traumatized as a kid or something? Because I had a *perfect* childhood. Nothing happened to warp me."

Fitz chuckled, a deep-throated *huh-huh-huh* that shook her chunky turquoise necklace like a maraca. "We can pursue a more chronological approach, if you prefer."

"Well, no, I just mean…you don't really know me yet, my background. I didn't mean to derail things with my randomness."

"Trust me, Margot, I'm holding the reins on this session. I wouldn't let our conversation deviate beyond what's relevant. The truth of the matter is, we might not follow a linear course, but wherever we meander, it *is* all related. And I *am* getting to know you by talking about this, in this organic way. I suppose I'm like you and tend to jump around as well. But if you've ever seen a scatter-plot diagram, you know how those plotted points still follow a general trend. It's like stepping away from a Monet to see the clear picture."

"Uh-huh. So, ruling out the supernatural, for our purposes now—"

"Yes. I want to take the skeptical point of view again and ask if you've ever heard of the ideomotor effect."

"Maybe. I forget."

"All right, let's begin with an example. You've mentioned your mood swings. So then when you're feeling sad, what does your body do in response?"

"I guess my heart feels heavy. I might cry."

"Yes, perfect. So sometimes when we have sad thoughts, our tear ducts automatically release a secreted liquid. This physical response is beyond our direct control, yet it *is* caused by our thoughts. Does this make sense?"

"Yeah."

"So, the ideomotor effect is your body's automatic, muscular reflex to an intellectual or emotional stimulus. So then it's possible, just possible, that *you* spelled those words on the game board."

"But I didn't even remember the brooch until after then. And regardless, I'm not genius enough to come up with anagrams on the spot like that."

"But that's just the point, Margot. It may have been subconscious. Whether or not you were aware of these thoughts at that particular moment in time, they were nonetheless there, stored in your mind, to be buried there forever, withdrawn on command, or to surface on their own in response to some event. You wrote that journal entry about the brooch, after all. Even if you were only a child and forgot it since, *everything* you do and think and hear and taste and smell and feel is transcribed in the record of your mind."

"I understand what you're saying. I just don't get why. It's so random."

"That's how the subconscious works. It may seem random to us when these thoughts decide to surface, but

176

they're a purposeful response to some trigger or other."

Margot lay silent, but Fitz seemed to wait for her to speak again.

"You know, I hadn't thought about that pin for years. Not until this spring when it randomly came to me during the game."

"You say 'random' a lot. Is this your belief – that these little events only occur autonomously and at no predetermined time?"

"No. I mean, I do believe in free will…"

"But…"

"But I guess I've always figured we only operate freely within a larger structure already put in place – by God, or whatever you might or might not believe in." This felt so oddly reminiscent of that conversation in the doorway with Rand. Margot wasn't used to getting confronted on her theology so often, but she did like the chance to talk it out. "I think we have an ultimate destiny, even if we mostly control the paths we take to get there. There might be those 'little events' planted here and there for a purpose, then, like occasional guideposts to keep us on track.

"I read a theory on déjà-vu once. That what we see that feels so familiar is actually a sign that we're on target. Like on some level we've already lived out our destiny, and what we see as déjà-vu is the playback, in brief clips, to show us that what we're doing, at that exact point in time, is exactly what we're supposed to be doing and where."

"That's an interesting philosophy."

"I thought so."

"Any thoughts as to what your destiny might be? What these little signs might be guiding you toward?"

"No, but what's been happening is way more than just coincidence and déjà-vu. And I'm starting to question whether it even has anything to do with *my* life. In the hypothetical case that I'm being haunted, this could be someone else's baggage I'm bearing."

"And what makes you think this? Assuming for our purposes that the clues you've decoded were transmitted by a supernatural being and not your own subconscious, they still have personal meaning to you. They're about *your* past."

Margot was mute for several seconds. Then she asked, "Can…can I show you something?"

"Of course."

"If you don't mind giving me a second, I have the transcript in my purse."

"If it would help for me to actually see it." Fitz affixed reading glasses on her nose that had been hanging from a gold chain around her neck.

Margot sat up and reached for her handbag. Unzipping its front compartment, she drew out the wrinkled sheet of paper and handed it to Fitz.

"I see," the doctor said. Her coral-beaded bracelets clacked as she twitched her upheld wrist to adjust them for comfort. "So this is the message from the board, and what you've added below is your initial attempt at decoding it?"

Margot nodded.

"I see nothing about the brooch or Charlotte here, so those were revealed at a later time when you checked on the computer?"

Margot nodded again.

"Okay. Well, I confess you'll need to help me out here. Maybe I'm overlooking something obvious, but I'm not quite sure what additional information I'm meant to pull from this."

Margot spun around and lay back on the sofa before speaking again. Bending her knees, she drew her feet closer to her bottom and scrunched her toes like fists.

"There's one more word there that I hadn't unscrambled online. After I saw *Charlotte*, I was too freaked out to play with it any more. But, before this appointment, when I retrieved the paper to put it in my purse, I did look at it again."

"All right. Which word is it?"

"*Opendig.*"

"Mm-hm."

"You can see where I tried to decode that one, too?"

"Mm-hm."

"Doesn't look like anything, right?"

"Not as far as I can see. Of course, your experience might inform you differently."

"No, I hadn't seen anything either at first, except maybe that it spelled *pigeon*, but without using the D."

"Mm-hm."

Margot propped herself up again. From her trouser pocket, she withdrew a crumpled napkin. Again, she handed it to Fitz and remained sitting up but fixed her gaze to the floor. She left it to the doctor to unfold the napkin and make of it what she would.

Fitz read it in silence. "Where is this from? Why didn't you mention it before?"

"Because I didn't want you to classify me as an outright loon from the get-go. There's this cemetery here that I like to walk through."

"Okay. Do you walk through it frequently? And this is from a gravestone there?"

"Yeah."

"When did you write this?"

"A couple days ago." Margot concealed the fact that it had followed her graveyard slumber party; before walking home that particular morning, she'd decided to cast off reverence and finally jot down the engraving. "But I'd seen her – the grave – before. A few weeks ago."

"And is there any particular reason you decided to copy this one down?"

"I liked the poem, and I've written down other epitaphs." Margot knew she was stalling and needed to come forward with some of the truth. "But I guess it's the way I came about this one. I was about to pass by it but stopped short, like gravity held me down. I just stopped, turned, and this was the first thing I saw."

"So the deceased's name was Charlotte Pidgeon."

"Yes. Pidgeon. With a D."

As Margot expected, Fitz didn't have an answer. Instead,

the doctor devoted the rest of the session to relaxation techniques to bring Margot down from near hysterics.

It had turned out that after she'd directed Fitz's attention to the name on the gravestone, Margot had only first noticed the numbers also inscribed there on the napkin. She'd looked from the *18* in Sylvie's writing on the transcript to the *1848* in her own writing on the napkin, then from the *26* on the transcript to the twenty-six years of difference between the birth and death years on the napkin. Side to side, her head had twisted back and forth between the two until Fitz had gently asked if she might take them away for the time being and if Margot would please lie back down.

Margot knew it had been premature to dive into the subject at their maiden session, but how else was she supposed to have answered the question, "What brings you here today?"

So that was it. If she was to spend a portion of each remaining week in England on the therapist's couch, she needed the doctor to know what she was getting into. Time was scarce, and she couldn't deal with the idea of beginning this process all over again at home with someone new. Fitz had also borne this in mind and asked if she thought it would be beneficial to schedule their sessions on a biweekly basis. Fortunately, cutting out the cost of her booze intake lately helped Margot justify the hourly fee.

And then there was Rand. Dear, sweet Rand, who greeted her with a kiss to the cheek outside the doctor's office building so they could have lunch together and discuss her first session. He steered her toward St. Paul's, and on entering a restaurant perched atop a nearby mall, they were seated by a window overlooking the cathedral's majestic dome.

"So," he inquired from above his menu, "how was it? You all right?"

Margot bobbed her head. "Fine." She noticed how closely he observed her from across the table. Though probably already caught red-eyed, she looked down at her own menu to conceal evidence of her crying jag.

"You look lovely."

"Thanks." She self-consciously fingered the high-neck collar buttons of her black silk blouse. Her cap sleeves were trimmed in a dainty band of dark lace, and she hoped her earlier tears hadn't accessorized her cheeks with any matching black mascara. "Trying to make more of an effort. But…"

Rand set his menu down and reached across the table, gesturing for her to take his hand. After only the slightest hesitation, she did, and he asked, "But?"

She raised her weary eyes and drew in a deep breath. "But…I feel like I'm acting the role of myself. Or at least who I used to think I should be."

"Margot, my darling, you are the same person as you ever were. And there's nothing false in that. Don't try so hard to change. You don't need to. You only need to feel better."

"I am, for the most part." She wanted to tell him how she'd been channeling her energies back into school to avoid dwelling on anything she couldn't readily explain. But in so doing, she'd have to explain what she *could*, the paranormal paranoia that had officially overtaken common sense. And while she was fine letting Gwen look ridiculous in Rand's eyes in that respect, she still wanted to enjoy some semblance of an upper hand.

"But?" he repeated as he ran his thumb over her knuckles.

"But…" She shifted her feet under the table, desperate to break with decorum and kick off her heels again. "Ever since we last talked about this, I feel like I've been going through the motions. Doing what I'm supposed to just because I'm supposed to, as always. It's like I have to make myself smile long enough to convince myself I'm happy."

"But *are* you any happier?"

"Right now I am." She held his hand tighter.

"Good." He grinned, returning her squeeze. "Then so am I."

A wordless moment passed as they held eye contact, but

their hands and eyes broke away when the waiter approached the table. Asking him for another minute, they silently perused the menu. Margot pinched the sides of hers as she tried to calm her rapid heartbeat and redirect her appetite to the savory items on the list.

Rand didn't speak again until she had flipped her menu to lay it facedown on the table. "So, how did it go? Do you think you would go back again? Does it seem helpful?"

"Well…yeah. Yeah, I think so. It's worth another shot, anyway." She tried to recap the session with Fitz as vaguely as she could, and Rand didn't press her for more beyond that, respecting her patient confidentiality. He simply encouraged her to talk to him as well whenever she needed to.

She twisted her hands in her lap, ready to change the subject. "What are your plans for the rest of week? You and Gwen got anything fun going on?"

He fumbled his warm grin for an instant before fixing a stiffer version of it back in place. "Oh, ah, not really, no." He scraped the corner of his eye with a fingernail. "She's spending the weekend with her family up in Yorkshire again. Helping her mum with the garden."

"That actually does sound fun. Unless they put you to work, too? Dress you in a sun hat and gardening gloves?" She grinned.

"Ah, no. Her dad and I would pop to the local while they potter around in the dirt. He has a hilarious band of mates that assembles there every day, without fail. They claim the same table each time and try to one-up each other, chuffed with their storytelling."

Margot laughed, picturing the scene of Rand encircled by a bunch of gabby old men, ruddy from their ale. "They sound adorable. And must love you." *Who wouldn't.*

"Yeah." Rand smiled as he looked down at the napkin he kept readjusting on the table. "Only I won't be joining them this time."

"So you *are* helping the ladies? With your silver bells and cockleshells?" She winked.

"No," he groaned out brusquely and, pressing his palms against the table's edge, pushed himself back in his seat until his arms were almost straight. Staring down at the table, he tapped his fingers against its surface. "I won't be leaving London at all."

"Because you can't or you don't want to?"

"Because once again I wasn't invited."

Ouch.

"But I also don't want to."

Huh. "What's going on with you guys? Have you decided if you're making or breaking?"

Rand leaned back in, resting on his forearms and watching himself fiddle with his napkin again. "Spending time apart, you could say."

Margot leaned in, too, inviting him to meet her eye. "'Apart' as in giving each other some space or *apart-apart*?"

"She wants to take a break for a while." He remained looking down with a frown. "I'm...otherwise inclined."

"Oh." She sat back again. *Her idea. Not his.* "I'm sorry."

His eyes did flicker up at her then. Then down, then up again. He held her gaze intently. "Well, it—"

The waiter chose just then to reappear.

By the time orders were taken and beverages served, the original conversation had lost its momentum. Rand resumed his smiling inquiries of Margot's days at school and exploring London, and she let him, asking in kind about his work and upcoming travels so that she didn't have to hear how much Gwen had broken his heart.

Lunch passed by pleasantly enough but too quickly, and after an hour, she reluctantly returned him to his workday and caught the Tube back to the flat. Once there, she fought the impulse to bathe or nap and tried to clear her mind instead with the frivolity of the Internet. On checking her email, she'd seen that her boss hadn't written back yet.

Damn.

And still hadn't by the next day.

Damn-damn.

Reckoning she could hear the ropes of that safety net snap one at a time, she felt the burn as they slipped from her grasp.

Fitz and Margot reconvened two days later.

"Nice to see you again, Margot. Are you feeling well?"

"Yeah, all right. I think even just that hour with you helped a lot, just talking about it."

"That's very good. Do you feel like you *haven't* been able to talk about this before? To others?"

Margot kicked off her pumps and swung her legs around to resume her position on the sofa. "I've talked to friends about bits and pieces, maybe not so much the ghost stuff. But it helps having someone objective listen. I worry that someone who knows me too well will try to fit the square peg of what I'm going through into the circular hole of my normal personality, maybe wanting to comfort me too much to face the truth with me."

"What is the truth?"

"That's why I'm here."

"Hm." Behind her head, Margot could hear the therapist's pen scratching notes on her pad. "So how do you think these friends would describe you? The ones you don't feel would be objective."

Margot gave a little laugh. "Well, the night of Ouija, I'm pretty sure *those* friends diagnosed me with a combo inferiority-superiority complex."

"What did you think of that?"

"Like I have a split-personality or something."

"I wouldn't diagnose you with dissociative identity disorder just yet." After a pause, Fitz added, "But I shouldn't joke."

Margot rolled her eyes sideways at the doctor's blurred figure with misgivings of what that hokey remark might mean for her sessions going forward. She wasn't sure what to say but decided to speak up before becoming another punch line.

"I don't know. They didn't actually say that in so many

words; it's just how I took it. But when I look back on it now… I don't even feel like the same person they were talking about. I don't know what motivates me anymore. But then… I don't know, maybe I *do* get what they were saying. I have such different sides that I feel like…like I'm constantly opposing myself. Like, in trying to cater to one side or another, they just cancel each other out. And I end up achieving nothing."

"We're all made of dichotomies, Margot. You needn't feel like you're functioning within an inconsistent identity that'll either blank you out or rupture you in two like Jekyll and Hyde. Individuals having multiple, if not conflicting, facets is typical."

"Like the id and ego?" *Look at you, Psych 101, coming in handy for something.*

"As a classic Freudian example, yes. The theory of the primal id and the rational ego, with the superego that steps in to reconcile them."

"Yeah. Okay."

"You sound confused. Or just disinterested."

"No, just preoccupied."

"Charlotte?"

"Yes."

Margot heard Fitz inhale deeply, as though bracing for episode two of *The Ghost Whisperer*. The woman's hanging spectacles clapped against the amber pendant she wore as Margot heard her readjust in her chair. "If you think it will help."

"I just need to make some meaning of it. And I'd rather obsess over it here than anywhere else. I'm sick of draining my friends' energy, like I'm this emotional vampire sucking their spirit away. It only makes me feel worse."

"All right, then let's talk about Charlotte."

Margot opened her mouth to speak, but only held her breath when the words didn't come.

Fitz took over. "That poem on Charlotte's grave. I actually looked it up online and found it's from the sixteenth or seventeenth century, written by Ben Jonson."

185

"He's the one buried standing up in Westminster Abbey, right?"

"Standing up? I didn't realize that, but prime burial property, I suppose. In any case, it's certainly a lovely poem that he wrote, but what moved *you* to write it down? Why write down any of these epitaphs?"

Margot paused a moment to articulate her thoughts in her head before she spoke. "I like to develop a storyline. Take the facts, then fill in the gaps to give the deceased some substance."

"What do you mean by that, exactly?"

"Make them three-dimensional, flesh and blood."

"Your stories bring them to life?"

"In my mind, at least."

"Why must they live in your mind?"

"I don't know. They don't *have* to. I just want to acknowledge that I noticed them. Let them know that *I* know they lived."

"Why should that matter to them now? Why does it matter to you?"

"I don't know."

"Well, if you don't mind me giving it a go, I would conjecture part of it is purely an outlet for your creativity. You're a copywriter by profession, and if you're a writer by instinct, you'll have that kind of keen observation. And reflecting on the deceased is a pretty common way of coming to terms with our own mortality. It's a means of giving life a purpose, that it isn't all in vain."

Fitz cleared her throat. "I would also venture to say that you might be an *empath*, Margot. Someone who is hypersensitive to the emotions of others. You used the term 'emotional vampire' before, but an empath is empathetic, meaning you take on the negative energies of others, not suck away the good ones. This results in *you* feeling the need to shoulder *their* burden, which, if I'm not mistaken, is similar to how you described your relationship with Charlotte last session. You follow?"

"I'm not sure I do."

"You feel an affinity for this Charlotte because your empathetic nature drives you to intuit the life experience of even a stranger like her. Those who believe they have psychic powers actually tend to be empaths. That's what helps them tell so-called fortunes with some degree of accuracy. Enough to convince people they're the real deal, anyway."

"I take it you don't believe in psychics."

"I believe in empathy for feelings, which can lead to logical conclusions of what *causes* those feelings. But only those feelings that are *present*, in both the temporal and spatial senses of the word. I don't know that I believe in foretelling the future so much as having an educated hunch. But this isn't about what I believe. What do *you*? Have you seen a psychic about this?"

"No, but what does they or me being empaths really explain anyway? I didn't know Charlotte Pidgeon from anyone when we played that game, and it doesn't account for why I stopped at her grave that day." *On both those days.*

"Granted. Though if that was only a simple coincidence, your empathy does explain that you internalized it because it's your sensitive nature to. The brooch weighing on your mind as well – even when you're not consciously thinking of it, you may be projecting it in other ways. In games of Ouija, for instance."

Margot could swear she heard the broken record of this conversation skip over the same scratch. "I understand your point, but it seems dismissive."

"You don't want to trade your belief in the ghost back for belief in coincidence, do you?"

"What do you mean?"

"Doing so might make life seem random again, which places more accountability on *you* in how your destiny plays out. The recent changes you've experienced this past year are all the result of *your* decisions, so maybe what you're going through is just coming to terms with how in control you indeed are, as opposed to being a victim."

"I'm not trying to throw myself a pity party here. I just thought we were going to leave no stone unturned." *And no headstone overlooked.*

"Fair enough. Then on one hand, we can believe these incidents have been signs, as you said yourself last time, that show you're heading in the right direction. And on the other, perhaps we can consider another classic theory of the psyche that you might know. Introduced by one of Freud's younger colleagues, Jung."

"Carl Jung?"

"So you have heard of him."

"Yeah." *And if I still believed in coincidences, this one would take the cake.* "Just his collective unconscious theory. A friend of mine told me about it."

"Brilliant. Like Freud, Jung broke the psyche into different parts, including the *personal* unconscious, where we store memories of our own experiences, and then the *collective* unconscious, which stores the combined experience of all humankind – like a joint bank account that we all deposit into and withdraw from. I was thinking of this when you brought up déjà-vu last time, in fact, because some believe the collective unconscious is what causes that 'already seen' sensation. A concurrence of our external and inner realities."

Silence.

"Have I lost you?"

"Yes."

Fitz's jewelry clicked against her glasses again with her deep-chested guffaw. "Forgive me. I lecture at university, but in this room, the patient should do most of the talking."

Margot indulged her with a weak giggle as she rubbed the gooseflesh that had just prickled up on her forearms. Even her nipples pinched a little from an apparent temperature drop.

So much for the patient doing the talking, as Fitz carried on. "Now, bear in mind there's a lot of theory out there, outdated and new, and it's often a mix that'll help you develop your sense of capital-T truth as life experience shapes your perceptions."

Margot curled her knees up to warm her hands between them. "But do you think that, no matter what happens to us, we're always the same person at our core?"

"Yes, I do. But to each her own. Which is why it's important you understand being dismissive is not my intention."

At this, Margot sat up to face her doctor in apology, her cheeks being the one part of her body to heat up and admonish her earlier lack of tact.

Fitz sat back and folded her cocktail-ringed hands in her lap. "The fact is, if you only suspected something supernatural to be at hand here, you could have consulted a parapsychologist or medium. But you came to *me*. So the best I can do is approach this within the realm of *my* expertise. This is what you want, isn't it?"

A flush of recognition washed over Margot, and one of her ears popped as though the room had depressurized as well as cooled. "Is this not what I wanted?"

"That's what I'm asking you."

"Sorry, I thought…it's happening. Right now, a déjà-vu."

"You and I here, asking this question?"

"Asking this question, yes, but the visual isn't synching up." Margot thought hard to recall the words, the vision, the feeling. "No, it's passed." She shook her head. "Weird."

"Mm."

Is this not what I wanted? The conviction trickles away to a puddle at my feet as, again, I am questioned.

"I do not know what I want," I reply, "nor indeed ever did."

It is evident my feeble response is found wanting, but I question how it is that I am to satisfy any further on this point. I move to close the door – how the sound carries through those corridors! – but my interrogator draws it back open, just slightly ajar, just enough.

"You did know, once. When it was convenient for you, when you had everything to gain and I nothing to lose. Well,

189

I have lost something, haven't I? I lost it to you, and now am I to lose you as well?"

"Contain your volume," I foolishly preach, and it is received in the ill manner I could have predicted.

"Contain myself, indeed! I am not the one with so much to conceal!"

"I lack the fortitude to address this now. You must know."

"Must I?"

My hand falls from my bosom, its opened palm now flat to my waist instead, and I plead, "I should hope, yes, that you do."

"I should think not," is spat through a hard-lipped scowl before the door swings with swift force upon its hinges.

Chapter Twelve

Refraction

Smoke spirals stratified the world with gray from where Margot stood. When these columns dissipated, the Portobello Market reemerged as a colorful, bountiful Land of Oz.

"Do you think I should do it?"

Chloé tapped her cigarette with her forefinger, watching the flecks of fire and ash dance to the pavement. "I'd be interested to hear. But be comfortable that this woman isn't playing with your mind."

Ever since last week's therapy sessions, Margot had wanted Chloé's opinion on Fitz's methodology. Even though she'd met Rand for lunch again directly afterwards, she wasn't sure to what extent he'd remain open-minded about the doctor's most recent suggestion, and somehow it seemed more in the realm of Chloé's savvy. But as far as either friend knew, Margot's sessions were strictly about her sanity, not the supernatural. Fitz's always-ready rationale was really helping her stay grounded in the physical world, so she didn't want to set her progress back by entertaining any further delusions outside that office.

Regardless, after the last session's déjà-vu, Margot had felt like her heart was squeezing, as it so often did. Fitz thought this sounded like a good case of anxiety so had proposed hypnotherapy for their next session, preferring to leave medication as a last resort. Chloé hadn't been to class until today, so Margot wasted no time asking if she'd join her afterwards and help sort out this latest advice.

"She said it'd be on the order of the relaxation technique

we used during my first session," she told Chloé. "Just more prolonged and deeper to 'focus my consciousness into alertness on a different level.' What do you think, does she sound like a quack?"

"Hypnosis isn't the hocus-pocus many people think. It's a meditative state for reaching higher planes of understanding. For some that is spiritual enlightenment, for others a transcendence of mind."

Margot's instinct had been spot-on; Chloé was definitely the right person to consult on this.

"It requires a high degree of trust, though, Margot, so if you don't trust her, you should not go through with it."

"No, I do. I guess I'm just surprised it's actually coming to this. I even said to her that I thought it only happened in movies. Like that one with Emma Thompson – *Dead Again.*"

Fitz hadn't seemed thrilled with that remark. The psychologist had merely nodded and said, "Aside from being a cliché plot device, past-life regression is a controversial tactic that skeptics like me have concluded really only constructs false memories from bits of the real ones. Empirically, the historical inaccuracies that have emerged from those run rampant."

At which point Margot had to concede that *she'd* been the one to cry ghost there, so really shouldn't judge.

"Just be careful," Chloé said. "I know people can sometimes wake to a distorted reality."

"Oh, God. Distorted like how?"

"Unable to distinguish past from present, seeing things that aren't real that the hypnotist only whispered in the ear."

"She's a professional, though. What would she have to gain by messing with me like that?"

"Sadistic pleasure." Chloé smirked, placing her lit cigarette between Margot's lips to replace the extinguished filter resting there. "A pin number for a more robust bank account."

Margot felt herself go as ashen as the snuffed tobacco flicked to the pavement. "And here I thought the worst-case scenario would be her making me tap dance and juggle whenever I heard the Canadian national anthem."

"Or flap your arms like angel wings every time a bell rings." Chloé smiled and lightly tapped the soft underbelly of Margot's chin. "I don't believe she will take advantage of our dear Margot. And when done properly, it can be like a window to the soul."

"Have you ever done it?"

"In a way, yes. Not in the company of anyone else."

"Well, I should hope she's not selling tickets!"

"I mean to say, I've done it entirely alone." She pointed at one of several mini-dresses hanging in a street stall. "You would look nice in that."

"Mm, maybe if we pass by it again on our way back. But" – getting back on topic – "is that possible? On your own? I can't even imagine how that would work."

"It requires some practice but is achievable."

"How'd you learn how?"

"Rather by accident. I was in an unusual, raw frame of mind when I experienced it for the first time. Grieving for my grandfather as a young girl. It made me feel close to him, as though he was right there holding me on his knee as he used to. Afterwards, I tried again and again to bring him back. But I had been trying too hard, and had to experiment for years with different ways." She fingered through the fraying satin interior of her clutch. When she retrieved her compact mirror, she clicked it open and fleetingly inspected her reflection, like a parent peeking in at the nursery door just to make sure the kids were still there. "By the time I was sixteen, I had refined it to a technique I could recreate whenever I wanted."

Margot blanched. "Did you feel him again?"

"Yes, as a girl I thought I did." She met Margot's eyes directly. "The experience was different, however, as a grown woman. It was not about him after all."

Margot interpreted this as an offer to help her achieve self-understanding. "Is it something I could do, too, then? You'll teach me?" Sensing reluctance, she added, "Maybe it

193

would be good for me to try on my own before I let the shrink do it. Just to see if my mind's receptive, and how I might respond. What, haven't you found it helpful?"

"What people find in such a thing will be different. Some windows are best left with the curtains closed." Chloé veered to the curb to contemplate a trove of raspberries.

"Now how could that be? How does anyone benefit from hiding? Chloé, please." Margot asserted her presence among the garnet fruit. "I'm hanging on by a thread here. What could be the harm in letting out stuff that's plaguing me?"

"It's what you could let *in* that may pose the problem. *Monsieur*, two batches, *s'il vous plaît*." Chloé turned her attention back to Margot as she waited for her goods, folding her bare forearms just as Margot had absently looked down at them. Thumbing a dark patch on the thin inner skin of her elbow, Chloé pressed further. "Margot, I must ask, if I teach you and you do this, let me be present. *Merci, Monsieur*." She dropped the exact change into the vendor's palm and claimed her bagged purchase.

"Oh." Margot fidgeted as they resumed walking down the road's center. "Well, the point of trying it on my own would be to, you know, try it *on my own*. I'd be embarrassed with you there and probably unable to relax the way I'm supposed to. Not to sound like an ingrate before you've even told me how to do it."

"Margot, please. I have shared this much with you. It will be my responsibility. The question becomes, do you trust me?"

Margot's inhibition disappeared into the brown eyes beseeching her, and she gravitated toward them headfirst, falling into Chloé heavily with their first hug. She heard Chloé's purse and bag of berries fall to the pavement at their feet.

"I do trust you," she breathed into the perfumed scarf knotted at Chloé's neck, then pulled away while still clasping her frail arms. "*Dites-moi?*"

Chloé's clothes-hanger posture slackened as her face twisted into an expression that Margot found inscrutable.

She slid her arms away through Margot's grasp until their palms met. Squeezing her hands in this warm clasp, she consented, "I will. When would you like?"

"*Ce soir?*"

"*Oui.* Well, no. You need more time to detoxify."

"I haven't had a drink in a while now."

"Not just alcohol. Caffeine, nicotine…" She snatched the cigarette from Margot's mouth and banished it with flourish before bending to retrieve her bags. "Even dairy. A diet of fruit and veg only."

"Meh. Fine. But for how long? I go back to Dr. Fitzgerald in a couple of days."

"I think if you start now, we can try it as soon as tomorrow evening."

They agreed on this timeframe and drifted uphill into the antiques strip of the road, falling silent as they scavenged vintage jewelry.

Margot pointed toward a cluster of pocket watches dangling from a display. "Like yours. Is this where you found it?"

Chloé's cheeks drained white before flushing red. "N-no. Those are reproductions. Mine is authentic."

"Oh, yeah? From France?"

A rapid nod as swift and nearly unseen as a hummingbird's wings.

"Cool. Is that what you swing in front of your face when you wanna see your grandpa?" Margot wasn't surprised when her irreverence wasn't dignified with a response. "Sorry. How old is it?"

Looking from jewelry case to jewelry case, Chloé muttered, "Eh, *je ne suis pas sûr. Quelle heure est-il?* What time is it?"

Margot shrugged. "You're the one with the watch."

"*Mais oui.*" Chloé cradled her purse in one arm to rummage inside and consult said pocket watch with the other. At this, Margot stole a glance at the rusty, dime-sized birthmark in the crease of Chloé's elbow, the distinct marking on otherwise unblemished skin that Chloé had

195

seemed self-conscious of before.

"Margot, this has been so fun, but I must go back toward the Ladbroke Grove station."

Sensing that she didn't desire company on her return journey, Margot made it easy on them both. "The District Line will be more direct for me, so I'll keep heading this way to Notting Hill Gate, but let's touch base after class tomorrow to arrange tomorrow night? You'll be there, right? I notice you're getting as sporadic as me."

This time the expression on Chloé's face was unmistakably relief. "Yes, I'll be there and will explain to you the process then. Remember, fruits and veg." She thrust one of her cartons of raspberries at Margot with a side-smile. "And no stimulants or depressants."

A swift kiss to each cheek sealed their abrupt separation.

With a gyrating wrist, Margot finished darkening the funnel-shaped spiral she'd sketched down the margin of her notebook page. As her mind swirled into the coil's vortex, she questioned why she'd bothered attending lectures again when their relevance became ever more distant from her. Aside from her current preoccupations, her boss still hadn't replied to her email, so who knew what job she'd be going back to, if any.

Her impatience for class to end was almost intolerable. She lifted her eyes from her pen tip to Chloé, who sat across the semicircular lecture hall and several rows further upfront. Margot had been late to class, so she'd sat in the back by the door to not stir up attention. It wasn't as though any of her classmates would save her a seat anyway, not even Chloé, who was always engrossed in her black notebook. Margot watched again that afternoon how feverishly Chloé recorded her notes, writing them by hand like Margot did and unlike all the others, who typed on laptops or tablets.

But it wasn't until then that she'd noticed the motions of Chloé's strokes were broader than one would make to handwrite – as well as flowing up, down, and all around rather than left to right. Drawing, it would seem.

Fair enough, for so was Margot. Yet as she paused to take in Chloé's sprite-like features, their symmetry and softness, something was off. Chloé sat upright and proper as usual, never being one to slouch, and her pale, fine-boned fingers conducted her pencil with sweeping grace across the page nonstop. Her face, however, remained lifted, stoic, and she stared with dull, vacant eyes directly in front of her – seemingly without ever looking down at her page. If Margot had ever had any experience with such a thing, she would have thought her friend was in a trance.

Maybe she's practicing the technique and jotting down the steps before she teaches it to me. But Chloé's expression gave Margot chills, so she broke her stare and brought it back to her own pen.

She has something to hide, she wrote automatically. It surprised her to read it back, and yet she couldn't deny this was what she felt. So she wrote more as she extracted memory after memory to reduce the clutter of her mind.

—She seemed nervous when I asked about the watch. And left abruptly for the second time like that.

—She's been skipping class lately.

—She was reluctant about teaching me self-hypnosis (cautioning me on what I could 'let in'??)

—But she was the one defending hypnosis and now insists on being there when I do it!

—The way she looks at me

Margot paused to consider this last item, how to phrase the rest of it adequately.

—The way she looks at me has an intensity that makes me feel naked. Vulnerable and vibrant at once. But I like it.

Her cheeks burned, and when she peeked up at Chloé, she met her full-on in the eye; Chloé was no longer drawing anything in her book. Neither woman smiled or looked away for several seconds, and it seemed they wouldn't have if it weren't for the students who stood up between them to gather materials into their book bags.

Margot waited until the room cleared out, only to see Chloé's empty seat.

"Margot, I am—ry I didn—you—after class," crackled through Margot's mobile phone. "Something—ame up—bliged me—leave. I al—ost didn't come—cause of it, but—ad promised you."

The broken voice carried over the airwaves softly, with intermittent zaps of frequency in between. Margot got the gist of it, however, and spoke back loudly into her mobile, as if volume would overcome a bad connection.

"It's okay, Chloé! I—what's that? I can't—no, I can't really hear you! You must be out of service! Huh? What? Can you hear me? Can you hear me? Look, I'll just try you later! *Later!*"

Click.

Exasperated, she sat at Rand's desk and stewed.

Though he'd required a hearty degree of convincing, her flatmate honored this week's business trip to Luxembourg, trusting enough in Margot's improvement. She missed him severely, having enjoyed the extra time with him while he and Gwen were 'apart', but it was good for her not to become too dependent. She'd been relying more and more on his unconditional encouragement, on him being there to give her a hug after every therapy session, but she needed to stand on her own inner strength. And this fortuitous timing allowed her to experiment in privacy.

If she could commence said experiment that night. She was losing faith in her friend's follow-through and didn't know how to proceed without it. Even if she researched other strategies, she had no idea what the outcome could be, only that Chloé's caution had been ominous. Maybe Margot did need a witness to testify on what happened if her consciousness drifted elsewhere. Maybe she needed someone there to cheer her in case the experience left her frightened and vulnerable. And maybe she needed someone there to intervene and bring her back if things turned unpleasant.

She was urgent to quiet her churning mind, to fight restlessness with rest. So she lay down on the bed on her back, feeling like she was on Fitz's couch.

Maybe I am crazy...but crazy people don't know that they're crazy. Me analyzing this so much must mean I'm not crazy. But me convincing myself that I'm not crazy must mean I believe I'm not crazy, in which case I could be crazy and just not know it.

She yelped and sat up, grabbing her phone to dial Chloé.

"*Allo?*"

"Chloé."

"Margot, yes."

"Can you hear me okay?"

"Yes, yes, I apologize. I was underground. Eh, I was heading down to *the* Underground, to the Tube."

"Oh, okay, fine. Um, so what's the story, then?"

"I'm sorry, but I can't make it tonight."

"Chloé! Come on!"

"No, I'm sorry, I cannot help you right now."

"But I'm supposed to see my shrink tomorrow. I really want to do this. Do you think I could just try on my own?" That wouldn't have been Margot's first choice at this point, but she was impatient. "You all right?"

Chloé had lapsed into a mild coughing fit, but when she spoke, her grittier voice sounded short of breath. "I wish you wouldn't, but I can't argue now."

Seeing an opening, Margot launched a whiny "Pleeease?"

"All right. I'll give basic steps that you can try as a test. Stick to them, and be careful."

The candle's flame flickered spastically after Margot set it down on one of the bathroom steps.

She'd moments earlier relaxed on her bed in the dark for several minutes, listening to The Cure's *Disintegration* album. As she used her tongue to pick a raspberry seed from between her teeth, the music lulled her to a calm state with its lush layers of lamentation, checking off the first item on Chloé's list.

The clock on the wall did not tick because she'd removed its batteries, and her mobile would not ring because she'd turned it off.

All lamps throughout the flat were out, including the bathroom's, so the flame now dancing on the wick was the only source of lighting. Trying to keep her nerves at bay, Margot, in her yoga pants and gray cardigan, perched herself on the stool she'd positioned in front of the large bathroom mirror and wrapped a quilt around her legs like a little nest of security.

Okay, candle behind me, and me in front of mirror. Check and check.

Chloé's next instructions dictated that she hold on to meaningful possessions, things that embodied who she was in order to tap into both her conscious and unconscious awareness. There were few things of great sentiment that Margot had lugged to England, so, by default, she'd grabbed her dream diary.

What she really wanted, though, was the brooch. Even with its spooky connotations now, it held personal significance, so she conjured a visual of Grandma Grace's ornament and imagined she could feel the weight of it resting at her clavicle.

Check.

The next step was to stare deeply into the dark depths of the mirror, without focusing. This was something Margot could ease into on command. It reminded her, actually, of those books she'd loved as a kid, with pages of three-dimensional images revealing themselves when looked at just right. She'd found entries about it in her sixth grade journal, in fact, where she'd written how, despite struggles at first, she eventually impressed all her friends with her ability to see dinosaurs and space shuttles in the same patterns where they saw nothing. And perhaps she'd gotten a little cocky when she claimed to see objects outside of the books, too – like the vases and mantelpieces that appeared to her within wallpaper prints and wood grains.

Wait… That sounded weird now that she thought about it, but it must have just been another case of that pareidolia Fitz had talked about.

Back to the task at hand, Margot regulated her breathing and visualized the brooch at her neck. Holding the closed diary firmly and staring into the mirror, she relaxed her vision.

With the candle behind her, she couldn't make out even an outline of her face, just the shimmering halo surrounding her silhouetted form, scrambled by her many eye floaters and pulsing with a glow as her vision adjusted. Deeper and deeper, she allowed her blurred sight to crawl further into the reflective surface, which, when looked at this way, no longer appeared as a solid pane. It seemed to elongate, tunnel-like, beyond the wall and past the gardens, into what Margot imagined were the infinite corridors of her mind.

Trying not to think too hard about anything, she couldn't help but wonder if she was *supposed* to see something, like a metaphorical hallway lined with doors that she could open and peer into. Chloé hadn't clarified whether the mirror served any purpose beyond simply providing a false perspective of depth to lose her sight into.

Either way, she did see something.

The glowing scribbles of her sight seemed to smooth over and grow dimmer and darker into an oval of black. Margot's heart rate slowed as her body slumped by incremental degrees, her arms feeling heavy and her fingertips tingling against the diary's linen cover. She succeeded in quieting her thoughts and letting go into the trance-like state, yet remained lucid as to everything she was seeing and hearing, including a barely audible, high-pitched tone.

From the center of the dark concentration, a milky cloudiness slowly emerged and congealed into an egg shape that teetered on top of a broader, misty pediment.

Margot numbly leaned forward, feeling drawn into the mirror just as the milky figure emerged out of it, the hum against her eardrums loudening to a mesmerizing ringing.

Just when she met the image face-to-face, felt them fusing into one another like conjoined twins, a pressure at her throat threatened to close off her air passage. Margot seized and choked.

Snatched from her trance, she started to her feet, entangled in her quilt as the diary clapped against the tile floor. She knelt at the toilet, feeling she might vomit. As soon as the sensation had come on, however, it passed, and she cautiously rose from her knees.

In the pitch-black, her ears crackled with heightened sensitivity, and she could smell the flinty smoke of the candle no longer in view; it had burnt out. As Margot rubbed the braille of her goose-bumped forearms, a pinpoint of light flashed into her periphery, and she willed herself to look over at it, expecting to see the blue orb from Rand's bedroom. But no – it was only the toothbrush again with its insistent sign of recharging even though the bathroom's main electric switch was off.

She concentrated on gathering her props to return them upstairs. When she bumped into the sink on picking up the stool, though, she realized that, sitting there, she couldn't have gotten much closer to the mirror than the countertop's edge. The sensation of passing into the mirror must have been a sheer trick of the mind, the choking a product of forgetting to breathe.

She put everything away and sat at the bedroom desk to write a new entry in her diary.

Starting with a brief description of what she'd just experienced, she then sketched the form she'd seen in the mirror. When she held the diary away from her to get an overall look, she noticed the striking resemblance the image bore to a bust statue. She hadn't noticed that at the time, though, and, hearing Fitz's voice in her head, she cautioned herself against retroactively painting in more human features than had actually been there.

Icy fingertips tickled down her back, and all she knew was that she needed to flip the pages and confront that ominous sentence again, the one that Gwen had allegedly 'found' and forced Margot to make up that ridiculous dream about being executed at the guillotine.

How would you like to bet that bitch wrote it herself.

But then she saw something else, newly penned.

I pray the Lord my soul to take

Every muscle – from the slabs braided at her thighs to the ribbons threaded through her finger joints – contracted so tightly that Margot stiffened like a corpse to the point of pain.

She read the sentence again. It was in the same handwriting as the one before. The only distinction was the ink. This ink was black but faded and appeared to bleed into the page's fibers with flecks of dark residue scattered beneath the letters. Grabbing her pen to test it, she drew sharp, defined strokes.

She got to her feet, first fishing through Rand's desk organizers to find only highlighters and pencils, then marching into the living room and kitchen to comb through every stack of envelopes and newspapers to be found on the table and countertops, searching for pens that might have been set aside there by her, Rand…*Or anyone else who would have any business being in this flat and fucking helping herself to our possessions.* But if Gwen and Rand were on a break, she shouldn't have been stopping in at the flat anymore during the day – unless she still did so out of convenience since Rand wouldn't be around anyway.

Margot found two writing utensils and knelt by the coffee table to test both on a blank diary page, but one was a blue ballpoint while the other turned out to be a mechanical pencil. Standing up and slapping them both down on the kitchen island, she was about to carry on her search-and-seizure in Rand's bedroom when she realized Gwen probably carried the crime weapon in her purse.

In frustration, she chewed her thumbnail, only then noticing that the fingertips of that hand – her left – were smudged in black. Margot was right-handed, though that didn't mean she couldn't have gotten her left hand dirty when removing the pen cap. Who knew.

More irritated than scared now, she returned to the bathroom to wash the ink off. A smattering of dark spots also dotted the sink's white surface, some larger than others and some smeared, which could've happened when she'd opened her mascara or liquid eyeliner that morning.

But when she looked up at her reflection, it reminded her that she wasn't wearing makeup that day. That she hadn't in a few days.

Chapter Thirteen

Research

"Morning, Margot. Lovely to see you again."

"Likewise, how are you?"

"Doing well. A slow week for the crazies."

Wow, that's inappropriate.

"But I shouldn't joke." Fitz's earrings, which looked like shellacked coffee beans, jangled. "So, have you given any further thought to what we discussed last time? I kept my next hour open just in case it's something you're inclined to do."

"Weeell, about that."

"Uh-oh," the doctor said with a kidding smile.

"I sort of did a little experiment on my own first."

"Uh-oh." The doctor frowned this time.

Sitting on the sofa, Margot rested her interlocked arms on her knees and studied the fibers in the rug as she summarized the self-hypnosis method Chloé had taught her.

"How long have you known this classmate?"

"Only since June."

"Yet you've become intimate?"

Margot hesitated. "What?"

"You've become good friends, close enough that you speak this candidly with one another?"

As her cheeks burned, she replied, "Oh! Yeah, we hang out outside of class. We're friends."

Fitz narrowed her eyes for a few seconds before following up on her own question. "I see. So have you told her about Charlotte?"

"No."

"Why not?"

"I hardly saw her after the real shit-show happened, and by the time I did, you'd helped me rule out most of it as anything…beyond natural explanation."

"I'm glad to hear that. So what was the outcome of this 'little experiment'?"

Margot pulled the dream diary out of her bag and read aloud about her session at the mirror. While she was at it, she showed Fitz the two cryptic entries also scribbled in the journal but not by Margot's hand.

Regarding both 'freaky-ass' passages, as Margot described them, Fitz referred back to the ideomotor effect and proposed that, as with the Ouija planchette, Margot had likely performed automatic writing. When Margot mentioned there'd been no pen present the second time, the doctor suspected maybe Gwen had indeed written it, as Margot had originally thought. Given Gwen's instability in her relationship with Rand, if she was willing to lie about a ghost, she could be willing to lie about Margot, who would serve as a reasonable object of jealousy. Or, Gwen might really believe in the things she'd seen without assuming accountability for their creation; in either case, the doctor believed Gwen sounded like a good candidate for therapy. She handed Margot another of her business cards.

But for as easy – and desirable – as it had been to blame Gwen for what she'd encountered last night, if it meant finding the connections that would piece everything together, Margot wanted to scatter all the possibilities out there again.

So, when Fitz asked her if she'd ever experienced anything similar to her hypnotic state before, she wasn't ashamed to finally talk about her other incident at the cemetery.

"You fell asleep? The entire night?"

"Yeah, I don't know why. But it was definitely some kind of trance. All I remember is a pigeon following me and somehow ending up back at Charlotte's grave. And then I was seized with an extreme feeling that I had to hide."

"Hide from what?"

"It felt like someone was watching me, but there was no one else around. Just statues and birds."

"So, when you hid, you…?"

"Laid down in the tall grass. On a grave."

"Were you frightened when you woke up?"

"Oddly, not as much as you'd think. It was still dark, so I just found shelter and waited for sunrise."

"Hm. To be frank, you're either very brave or very in denial."

"In denial? Of what?"

"Whatever it was you thought you were hiding from. Now, you don't seem to have a chronically paranoid personality. You distrust Gwen, that much is clear, but I don't see suspicion entering into your view of others. So where this paranoia is springing from…"

Fitz explained that Margot could have possibly allowed her conflicted thoughts and emotions to manifest into an external entity, one that had existed in her perception, not her reality.

"Or perhaps of the non-human bodies that *did* exist – the statues and birds – you anthropomorphized them into perceived threats by attributing human traits to them. You may have thought you saw someone spying on you at the cemetery through this sort of projection and, in your paranoia, even further projected onto it a distrust or dislike of you."

"Why would I do that?"

"Because *you* distrusted or disliked yourself. Your insecurities may have gotten the best of you that night. We never know how far our minds can take us, which is why so many phenomena are misinterpreted as having external causes. You've heard of poltergeist?"

Margot caught her breath, unnerved if Fitz was about to change her tune and subscribe to the spirit world after all. "Yeah?"

But Fitz continued in a medical tone. "It's German for 'noisy ghost', yet poltergeist is more likely connected to subconscious psychokinesis. That is, that the people experiencing the activity are the ones, in fact, causing it."

"What, through Jedi mind tricks or something?"

"Well, yes, in a way. It's transference of energy from one form to another. For whatever that's worth."

"Because you don't believe in ghosts anyway."

"What I believe is irrelevant. And I don't know that I believe in psychokinesis either; the research is conflicting. I only bring it up for sake of argument. Remember, no stone left unturned."

Margot expelled her breath in thought before asking, "You do believe in energy, though, right? That there *is* something we exchange as living beings, because that was your whole explanation of empaths."

"True."

"But then…if energy can't be created or destroyed, what happens to our energy when we die?"

"Hm."

"Because I can see that explaining a lot, actually. Our life force being displaced, leaving something non-corporeal behind." In re-visualizing her experience at the mirror, Margot saw the light of Rand's toothbrush blinking back at her in the dark. Recharging without electricity.

"Sure."

"But it would have to continue existing in some form. And I can only conceptualize that as something that could maybe be felt but is invisible or like a shadow or mist. Not something in human form and wearing clothes and everything, like so many people claim to see."

Fitz chuckled. "We're back to ghosts again?"

"You're the one who brought up poltergeist."

"Yes, but as I explained, that isn't associated with hauntings. I thought we'd moved on from this."

"But it's interesting to consider, isn't it? A scientific way to explain spirits."

"The Catholic needs scientific evidence?"

"Hardy-har. If energy can't be created, then where did it come from? Huh? I can believe in a God that created energy and put all systems into place to run more or less on their own. So I can still see miracles in photosynthesis and reproduction even though there's a biological reason for every step."

Fitz chuckled again but said nothing, probably curious as to what would come out of Margot's fool mouth next.

Fine, then she would deliver. "I searched some stuff online last night, just to see how people account for what they see, and it all does basically boil down to energy. We can leave imprints behind in the spaces we occupy, which could explain the human shape people see. Even actions can appear as residual images, repeating over and over again like a video loop."

"Hm."

"And sounds can be captured as EVP, uh, electronic voice phenomena. Then there's EMF, which is, um…"

"A one-hit-wonder Nineties band." Fitz laughed – alone. "Before your time, perhaps. Though you *are* 'Unbelievable'."

Margot shook her head at the lost reference and sat up to face her nutty professor in all seriousness. "No, electromagnetic field. Both that and EVP have to do with shifts in pressure and energy, which some people associate with paranormal activity. Some have also linked phenomena to solar flares and lunar cyc—les…"

Grandma Grace's brooch leapt to mind, as did that April night in Margot's childhood bedroom when she'd stared out the window at a full moon – the same night of her disturbing dream; the night after Ouija. Then the depression she sank into about a month later. And the full moon she'd woken up to in the cemetery about two lunar cycles after that.

"Uh-huh," Fitz said in the silence that had fallen. "That's very interesting."

"But, uh…" Margot took a second to get her thoughts back on track. "Even Thomas Edison ran experiments based on the belief our souls are made of tiny particles that can rearrange into other forms but still contain our personality.

An inventor he mentored, too, John Hammond, specialized in radio waves and created devices to facilitate telepathic communication." The scientific objectivity of it all was at once feeding Margot's momentum and bringing her to stillness. She sat back, satisfied she may have just dissected the mystery and stored it away in a jar of formaldehyde. Even the doctor had to give her credit for that.

But Fitz only said, "So," then paused, rolling her eyes around the room. "Is this your way of telling me you think you communicated with the dead last night?"

At that, the clinical safety of energy and particles disintegrated, abandoning Margot to the realization that, no matter how she attempted to explain it, someone was trying to reach her from the grave.

Corpulent raindrops splattered against the windowpane that Margot stared through into nothing. The dim shade of purple cloud-cover made it seem like night was falling when it was still early afternoon.

Without Rand around to offer company and consolation, she'd gone to gaze at St. Paul's dome, but the rain sent her inside a coffee shop for a warm drink. Now tucked into a corner on a stool, she alternated between reading and ruminating on where her therapy session had left her.

"All right, okay, but this 'research' is all very cursory, Margot," Fitz had said, adding insult to injury by actually making the air-quotations with her fingers. *"You can't trust just any source you find on the Internet."*

Feeling foolish, Margot had withdrawn into herself, reluctant to share more details. But she *had* shared them, including the sketch of what she'd seen in the mirror and how the candle had blown out with the windows closed.

She dismissed her thoughts to the present as she watched scurrying City commuters scatter like slickened rats on the pavement, producing umbrellas out of nowhere.

"Perhaps the form you saw in the mirror was your reflection, just a negative of your dark silhouette," Fitz had said. *"You've seen the perception game, haven't you, where*

if you stare at a white dot against a black background long enough, you then see a black dot when you look at a white background?"

And, of course, Margot's tingling fingers and feeling of strangulation (which Fitz had redefined as 'labored breathing') must have been symptoms of hyperventilation. Which, but of course, was a symptom of depression.

Margot drew in a shallow sip of hot chocolate to fight her chills. She watched a taxi speed through a puddle and splash a kid in the face. Stifling a laugh through her nose, she readjusted her reading glasses and refocused on the brittle pages of an early edition book she'd found at a local antiquarian bookseller – Rumer Godden's *Take Three Tenses: A Fugue in Time*, which the David Niven film *Enchantment* had been adapted from.

But she had to reread the same paragraph over a third time to concentrate on what it was saying and not what her memories screeched:

"But I say if you're really serious about this," Fitz said, "you should employ the services of someone who purports to have experience with the paranormal. Though I can't see how you could possibly vet their credentials."

Bitterness crept onto the back of Margot's tongue as she registered the betrayal. She'd trusted the doctor with her most embarrassing thoughts and couldn't understand why every single one had been treated like a clay pigeon to fire on and shatter. And yet she knew Fitz had a point there. For as much as the therapist had weakened her trust, Margot still had none for paranormal professionals. Or maybe she just didn't want them to confirm something she was helpless to do anything about. Much as she resented it, Fitz's skepticism had been a comfort.

The sky had darkened enough that Margot saw her reflection in the window; it seemed to mock her, so she clapped her book shut and stood.

Having foregone Chicago-style smiling-at-strangers for London avoiding-eye-contact-at-all-costs, she looked to the floor as she squeezed out from between the stools and adjacent tables, nearly running into a businessman at the exit. She timidly stared at his blue wool lapels as their mutual dodging of each other became an awkward doorway waltz.

"Margot?"

In confusion, she broke her tunneled vision and looked into the man's eyes.

"James, oh my God!"

Chapter Fourteen

Stardust

Fucking coincidence was all Margot could think as James held her.

He was in town on business. And for all the reunion speeches she'd practiced in front of the mirror, the reality of seeing him again in the flesh had rendered her, well, speechless. He, too, lost the composure that would've otherwise accessorized his three-piece suit.

Since she'd been on her way out, he didn't want to oblige her to stay at the café. Instead, he suggested an old pub down the road where some of his colleagues had gone for lunch, if she was available and hadn't eaten yet. The rain had lessened to a misty drizzle, so they could probably make it back inside before the sky opened up again.

On their walk down Ludgate Hill, Margot was no less surprised when James offered her a cigarette than he was when she accepted it. It seemed life since they'd last seen each other had granted both a new substance to abuse, and they exchanged shy smiles as James lit both cigarettes in his mouth before inserting one between Margot's ready lips. She appreciated how he exhaled smoke into the air behind her so that the wind couldn't blow it into her face.

"It really is amazing to see you here," she said as she straightened her posture and ignored her lack of makeup.

"Honestly." He seemed to want to say more, but didn't.

They walked on without words, the silence broken only by the whir of engines and splatter of tires in puddles.

Biting the inside of her mouth, she spoke up. "This is kinda weird, huh?"

"No. Well, yeah. I'm surprised to see you here. I wouldn't have expected it." The comment would have come across as a lame redundancy, but Margot knew James better, and she knew what that pinched expression on his face meant.

"Is something bothering you?"

"Mm-mm." He shook his head, but his pursed lips gave away there was definitely something. "Just a long workweek and looking forward to a midday pint."

Margot didn't press the issue. She looked forward to some coping in a cup as well; the circumstances seemed to call for lifting her ban, so it worked out well that he hadn't been committed to the café for lunch. Their silence resumed until James gestured toward a narrow alley leading off Fleet Street and into seventeenth-century London.

"*Re*built in sixteen sixty-seven?" Margot asked on reading the sign in the entryway.

"Yeah, one of my coworkers mentioned it burnt down in the Great Fire," he said as he followed her inside, "but the downstairs cellar supposedly dates back to the twelve hundreds."

"Incredible. And chauvinistic!" She pointed to the faded printing above a wooden doorway that indicated the room was only for gentlemen.

James laughed. "I doubt they still enforce that."

"Looks like drinks only." She peered across the way. "But that room looks like it's for dining." When James didn't show recognition of anyone seated in there, Margot scooted further down the wonky hallway to pop her head through yet another doorway, where she was confronted by a few staring businessmen drinking their lunch. "And that one looks like standing-room-only. Those might be your mates, though."

"Listen to you, Madonna. Talking like a local."

She leveled him with a flat stare.

"I'm just kidding," he said.

"Yeah, you always are, aren't you, with your truth in jest."

"Look, don't be mad. We haven't seen each other in a long time. Let's not start this way."

She inhaled an inward vow not to let James's knee-jerk condescension get to her. It didn't matter anymore. So playing innocent, she said, "I'm not mad. Don't be so sensitive. Let's just have fun."

That sentiment was still caught in her head when, one round of pints and meat pies later, she asked, "That was our problem, wasn't it? Having fun."

Nestled within a small alcove in the cellar, they had some privacy away from the tourists in the larger adjacent rooms. James had been gracious enough to shrug off his coworkers since he'd get to see them soon enough back at the office, so Margot had kindly fought back a laugh when he'd thumped his forehead (hard) on a low beam walking down the creaking stairs to where they presently sat.

With loosened tie and rolled shirtsleeves, James asked, "What are you talking about?" before finishing his amber ale with a double sip.

"You always complained that you wanted to have fun and that I was always preventing it."

"Well, you used to turn everything into an argument. I could never do anything right, and it *wasn't* fun anymore."

"But life *isn't* fun!" she asserted, like she had in countless quibbles before. "At least, it's obviously not going to be *all* the time. As a whole, it has to involve a lot of serious work, too."

"Yes, exactly. Enough of that comes from things outside our control, so I think as far as what *is* in our hands, we should make the most of it and not spend it arguing." He stared at his empty glass. "Like now, for example."

"I'm not turning this into an argument. I'm just saying I do want to have fun but don't understand why you made me feel like it was my fault whenever we didn't, never considering that it may have been something *you* did to upset me."

James kept staring at his pint glass as he twisted it on the aged wooden tabletop, pursing his lips again as he did so. "I know. I'm sorry for that." He paused. "I never knew how to make you happy."

Margot was next to look down at her glass, escaping into the inch of honey-colored ale that remained. "The thing is, James, it was never your or anyone else's responsibility to make me happy. We decide that for ourselves. I understand that now. And I'm wondering if maybe not all of us are meant to be happy. I might be biologically incapable of it."

When she lifted her eyes back up, they were caught in the intensity of his stare. Her contact faltered for a moment in mild self-consciousness, but she forced herself to look back at him.

"What are you doing here, Margot?"

"I'm finishing my brew," she replied to lighten the atmosphere, and gulped down the remnants of her glass.

"No, I mean what are you doing in London? I thought you never wanted to leave home."

"I don't, and I haven't. It's a summer thing."

"You don't think it's at all possible you'll stay and find work here?"

"The thought crossed my mind, yes. And I guess I should stay open to all my options, but—"

"It's just me you're closed to."

"What are you talking about?"

"You wouldn't move to Zurich even temporarily for me, just to see how it went. Not even New York when it was only a couple of hours away. I figured you were a closed-minded homebody and nothing would take you away from there, but it turns out it was just me."

That was the frank way she'd always wished he would speak, yet she didn't know how to handle it now that he was. "Time for one more pint? My treat."

"No, it's okay, I'll get it. Same thing?"

"Yeah. Thanks."

As she sat alone in the dim light, she looked at the other few tables tucked away in the nook. Given the confined space, it was mainly other couples speaking barely above whispers, with the bare surroundings offering no distraction from their companions.

How weird that James would choose to sit here, away from the activity and phone reception.

She pressed her palm against the bumpy white wall beside her, and its subterranean coolness traveled to her shoulders. Reading a little blurb on the pub's history to pass the time, she remarked, "Dickens and Voltaire used to drink here," when he returned with two glasses dripping down their sides.

"Oh, yeah? That's cool."

Do you even know who Voltaire is? It was so like James to pretend he understood what he didn't. "I guess we're in good company, then," she said.

"Well, maybe would've been. Somehow I suspect there's been a downgrade in this place's patronage."

"Snob."

"Cheers."

They clinked their glasses and swallowed a sip or two before speaking again. Margot felt emboldened.

"We might still be in good company, you know."

"I know, I was only kidding." James shook his head as he always had when conceding to one of her points, like a child acquiescing to his mom's discipline. Knowing he affected this demeanor when at his most agreeable and apologetic, she went for it.

"No, I mean the *dead* people."

"What?" James laughed.

"I'm serious. If souls were happy here when they were living, why not stay when they're dead? Seems a jolly place to spend eternity."

"No doubt. I'd be pretty happy." He cleared his throat with a hoarse *ahh* after another sip and shifted on his short wooden stool. "I read on a plaque that a hospital from the fifteen hundreds stood where my office is. Seems like that'd be fertile haunting grounds."

He'd taken the bait.

"It's everywhere. This central part is probably the most haunted, the old City. People take their smoking breaks in corporate gardens where there are still tombs and burial mounds from the plague. And think of all the executions between Tower Hill and the Old Bailey."

"Yeah, I saw where William Wallace was executed at Smithfield. Can't even walk to lunch without stumbling on something like that."

"It's everywhere," Margot repeated. "How could you have such mass death in one spot for centuries – hell, *millennia* – and not have a few resident ghosts?"

"You serious?" His smile faded, and Margot evaluated the expression when he continued to say, "I think there might be something to that stuff, too."

"No, you don't."

"I dunno. I just remember my great-aunt's old house as a kid. Her basement scared me shitless because my cousins had stories about it… I dunno. That stuff kinda stuck with me."

She appreciated the way time and alcohol had loosened his tongue.

"So I guess it's something I'm *open* to," he said, "just when that seems impossible." He reached for her hand.

Aw, shit. He's not talking ghosts anymore.

"James, don't…" She slid her hand out and grabbed her pint glass for another deep swig.

His hand thus unoccupied, he interlaced it with his other and leaned his elbows onto his knees. He looked dejected, but kept his tone light. "So I downloaded that Ethan Hawke movie a few months back."

"Oh, *that* one."

"I mean your favorite, the one you always quoted. *Before Sunrise*."

Her eyes widened. "Oh, yeah? How'd you like it?"

"I liked it a lot. I was surprised. The ending sucked, but I actually watched it over again a couple times."

"Really. So why didn't you like the ending?"

"I won't lie. I like a Hollywood ending that's all tied up and happy. That one was just too open-ended."

"But it leaves something to your imagination. It lets you

decide what happens later, like a litmus test of your optimism."

"It lets the writer off the hook, is what it does. So what do you think happens? Do they meet at the train station six months later?"

"Well, before I saw the sequel that tells us exactly what happened, I believed they didn't."

"Always negative."

"Always realistic. I presume you think they do meet up."

"Yeah, why wouldn't they?"

"Life happens. Things come up. And maybe what people think is love just fades given enough time apart."

She'd struck a blow; the impact appeared in his eyes, which even in low lighting she at last distinguished as a dark blue-green. She made note of every feature on his face.

With a smirk and huff of air out his nostrils, James sat up and took a long drink of his beer. He lowered the glass between his knees and held it in both hands, which assured Margot he wouldn't attempt further contact.

"So what does happen?" he asked. "In the sequel."

"Nope, no spoilers."

"What's it called, then?"

"*Before Sunset*."

"How clever."

"Shut it. Watch it before you judge."

"Maybe, if there's nothing better on TV."

Margot ignored the wounded insolence. "Never mind the ending of the first one. What did you like about the rest of it?"

"I dunno. That it took place in Vienna. I like that city. We have an office there."

"Uh-huh." *Should've figured.*

"And, you know, the conversations. They seemed really natural. They were like a real couple just hanging out. I saw the scene you talked about once with the woman telling their fortunes and how we come from stars. But Ethan kept —"

"Jesse."

219

"What?"

"The character, his name's—"

"So, *What's*-His-Face," James continued after shooting her a why-do-you-do-it look, "kept killing the romance with some smart-ass comment about that palm-reading stuff being a fraud."

"Well, it probably is."

"Yeah, you would say that. He reminded me a lot of you, actually."

"Oh, yeah? How so? The eternal pessimist?"

"No, more like how he'd reflect on stuff and develop little existential theories."

"Pretty annoying, huh?"

"No. Pretty interesting."

If you'd ever paid attention, that is.

"I did pay attention, you know."

"Huh?" *How did he do that?*

"I did listen to you. I just don't always know what to say. I can't express myself like you. If I tried, it would sound stupid."

"I wish you did try." If there was one thing James was, it wasn't stupid; he just always left his savvy at the office.

"Yeah, well…" He rolled the glass between his flattened palms. "There were some interesting things Jesse brought up. How if there's such a thing as reincarnation, for the world's population to increase like it has, souls would have to be split between more and more people."

When he didn't elaborate, Margot took the liberty. "So we'd just be scattered fragments of previous selves."

"Yeah. I thought that was interesting. Maybe it explains why things could get worse in the world as people become more disconnected. Or maybe it means we're more connected, I dunno."

"Uh-huh."

He had tried.

Walking along the Embankment after lunch with James, Margot wondered what meaning, if any, there was to their

220

chance encounter. She could've caught the Tube at a station near the pub but desired more of the cool summer air to think now that the rain had passed. As she languidly made her way to the Underground at Westminster, the London Eye floated off the water, watching her.

She practically pissed her pants again when she walked into Rand's flat to see the Man of the House himself sitting on the sofa watching television.

"No way!" She ran to plop down on the cushion next to him.

His meetings in Luxembourg had gone well, and he knew he could further conference remotely from London, so he'd decided to catch an earlier flight home.

"Disappointed to lose your alone-time?"

"Thrilled." She cozied beside him to watch a celebrity chef cook up some classic British fare with a modern twist – smiling in thought of her mother as he demonstrated onscreen how to make homemade beer-battered fish and chips. *Touché, Mum.* She even sinfully moaned over the sticky toffee pudding he started to prepare next.

"Ignorance is probably bliss there," Rand said in time for the chef to drop half a block of butter in a bowl of sugar to cream them together. "So, pudding at the pub tonight?" he teased.

Margot both laughed and groaned, but as she looked away from the TV and at his boyish grin instead, dread of ever saying goodbye to it soon overwhelmed her. The time was ticking nearer.

"Actually I should enjoy it while I still can." Before she could help it, she added, "I want to enjoy you as much as I can, too."

"Aw, come here." He reached his arm around her shoulders and pulled her close, then rested his cheek on her head. "I'm going to enjoy you as well, as much as I can."

She slid an arm around his waist and closed her eyes contentedly. For all her efforts to resist relying on him, being with Rand was like riding into a tunnel that blocked all wireless signals – even those transmitted from beyond

221

the grave. She couldn't help but sink into the remote peace of it.

"But, really, what are your plans for tonight?" he asked softly into her hair.

"Mm…" she murmured in drowsy thought. "No plans."

"Is that so? Because I haven't any either." He wrapped his other arm around her waist.

Margot's pulse quickened. Opportunity was practically crawling into her lap, and she wondered if she should just seize it. Take her chances now that he was technically available and deal with any awkwardness afterward.

To feel the situation out, she was about to make a few saucy suggestions for what they might do together – in jest – when she realized this gift of time with him should probably be used to own up to everything she'd experienced in his flat. For all that he knew, there was so much he didn't, and if Gwen had separated herself from Rand even remotely because he wouldn't believe in her ghost, Margot would bear the guilt if her own truth could've made the difference for them. If it could still, before a break became a breakup.

On an inhale, she opened her mouth to come clean when "Shit!" came out instead. She felt Rand start before holding her a little tighter.

"What is it?"

"I almost forgot. At six-thirty. I'm meeting a friend for dinner." Talk about denial; Fitz would've called her out on another massive case of it in already forgetting such recently made plans.

"Someone from school? The French hen?"

"No, someone from home. Well, someone I knew from home, a while ago."

"Well, she's free to stay here this weekend if she's visiting you."

"No, he's here on business. We only happened to run into each other."

Rand's arms slackened. "Oh, well if *he* wants to spend the weekend here with you, that's fine."

"No, we already had lunch together this afternoon, too,

so…"

He removed his hand from her waist to scratch his nose as his other relaxed its grip on her shoulder. "Well, it's up to you two."

Sobering from a sense of rejection she'd only brought on herself, she sat up to look at him. "*No*. And I need you to be my excuse in case he suggests that, too." With hesitation, she confessed, "It's James. We're having dinner tonight and nothing more. I need you to help me enforce that."

"Why do you need help? Think you won't resist him?" He stood to warm a kettle for tea, leaving Margot to feel cold in his absence.

"*Tuh*."

"Push a button, did I?"

James had needed to return to the office after lunch, but he wouldn't part ways with Margot until securing a dinner date. She'd suggested a Chelsea gastropub to stay within Rand's territory – and far from James's corporate housing – to keep temptation at bay. No need being in stumbling distance of a private apartment in case anything she drank to fortify herself ended up crumbling her defenses instead. It was a cool place anyway and would show James a different, more residential part of London, so it wasn't the most selfish suggestion she could've made.

"I'm going to shower," she said, reckoning their once-promising afternoon had officially been spoiled. The heavy, hoppy lunch would also make her sleep if she didn't get up and refresh. "I might pop into the bookshop before dinner, too."

"Hm, your disregard of my question just answered it, I think."

"Interested in joining me?" she offered.

"Fair enough," she heard Rand say under his breath. Then, with a grin, he answered, "That's charming of you, but I'll wait to shower after my run."

"I meant the bookstore, cheeky."

He winked. "You go on and have a good rest of the day. And night."

Margot sneered at his lack of help and was just lowering the TV volume against a blaring insurance ad when she heard a scream peal out from the square – and then the clopping of hooves, clear as anything.

She looked at Rand. "Hear that?"

"Huh?"

He was preoccupied with refilling his kettle as Margot made for a window to pull up the shade. "What the hell?"

"What?"

"Horses! Swear to God! I wonder if they bucked their bobbies off."

Rand abandoned the running faucet and jogged over to her, but the horses didn't reappear. "Must be off to violate traffic law elsewhere."

"Ever see that?"

"Christ, no. Did a wormhole just puncture through from Victorian London?"

"If so, dear Randolph, I needs must make myself decent!" Margot theatrically threw her hands to her cheeks. "Some dashing gentleman in a cravat and morning coat may come through next to reclaim his steeds."

She pulled the wide neck of her T-shirt down over her shoulder and pumped her phoenix tattoo flirtatiously, hoping it would make him reconsider the bookstore. Rand smiled with approval at first, appearing to trail his gaze from her bare shoulder to her clavicle, which renewed Margot's faith in wishful thinking. But then he grit his teeth and squinted, rubbing his fingers against his thumbs distractedly before fisting them as he turned back to the kitchen.

"Someone's reclaiming his mare, anyway," she thought she heard him murmur as he poured steaming water into his mug.

"What'd you say? Did you just equate me to an *equine*, sir?" She planted a fist on her hip in mock offense.

He toasted her with his mug. "If the horseshoe fits."

Her lips parted on a silent gasp, which would've been out loud in more fake indignity were it not for the way he'd said it with a straight face. Her breath halted a moment, and she could only press out a shallow huff before striding to the bathroom to shower and in other ways avoid her flatmate until she could leave.

Dinner conversation remained casual enough. Margot made sure to ask most of the questions, sticking to James's life in Zurich, mainly, and how the logistics of his relocation went, though also sharing a bit about her studies in London. Unless he was holding back, it didn't sound like a new lady friend had entered the picture yet, and Margot spoke of Rand as nothing more than a live-in landlord, which for all intents and purposes was true yet didn't keep her cheeks from burning whenever he came up.

James escorted her home afterwards, but with what expectations, Margot had no idea. When they rounded onto Rand's street, she simply pointed out his upstairs windows.

The closer they got to his address, the heavier the air around them became. It held the weight of awkward first-date goodbyes, the anxiety over whether there'd be a second-first kiss on the doorstep or if she could tactfully send him off without one. Jumping out of a moving car wasn't an option this time, much as she now pined for Derek to tease her about it if she did. Or would it be easier to just invite James up? Introduce him to Rand and let James see himself out once he saw they wouldn't be alone?

With Derek still in mind, she remembered how he'd likewise expected their Ouija spirit to dismiss herself from the game. If Margot's stomach weren't being such a contortionist, she might've laughed at the memory. But as it was, she couldn't pin down what exactly distressed her, only that, unequivocally, a threshold of no return was about to be crossed. Was *being* crossed. This very moment.

She distracted herself with windows again.

"The stained glass is so pretty when lit up at night, isn't it?" This time, she pointed at the church across from Rand's building. "It makes me think of those cute miniature Dickens villages at Christmastime."

James glanced over. "Would be even prettier if the panes were different colors."

"What are you talking about? They are."

"I'm sure they *were*. Probably had to replace them over the years with something more cost-effective. Or maybe it's because it's not all the way dark yet that they just look clear. I can't believe how long the days are here in summer. You can tell it's a higher latitude."

Margot wasn't to be sidetracked by daylight savings. "Clear? But can't you also see the colors? Blue and green? Yellow and red?"

He stopped to stare at the leaded glass straight on. "Am I looking at the right windows? You mean this large row here, right?"

She nodded fervently.

"Margot." James pinched his features as he looked from her to the church. "I'm not colorblind. Those are clear. Maybe you had too much to drink."

She stared at the windows directly across from them in silence. Her eyes trickled down the vivid fragments of multicolored glass, and she exhaled in short, measured huffs.

The sound of James's "You okay?" crackled in her ears.

Do not lie to me.

"Margot?"

"Take your hands from me."

"I-I'm not touching you."

The volume of her breathing rose, picking up in pace like her pumping heart. James did touch her now, only to steady her. He did so just in time for her to collapse into his arms.

"Take your hands from me."

Swift pursuit brings me to further ravages in the bedroom.

"Must we endure this again?" I ask.

"Ah, but there is nothing to fill you with trepidation, my dear. Why, you will never be alone for as long as you have her."

226

Her, her. The 'mysterious M'. From the banshee cries of the day's accident to this, my evening's nightmare. I can scarcely recognize whom I love and scarcely recognize in me the woman capable of such love.

"You ought to refine that laughter of yours. It would be most unpleasant if you betrayed your breeding whilst enjoying one of the multitude of soirées upon which you must be so certain you shall encroach. It would be a pity indeed for some gracious benefactor to spoil your champagne when he tosses a shilling into your glass as alms."

Moments later comes the final prick that leaves me on the floor in the spill of my overturned washbasin. My options are spent, I am certain, and I have nothing but expected decorum and acceptance of my lot as so generously bestowed by a spiteful, merciless Fate.

Chapter Fifteen

Le Bain

Margot raised her lids to see the ceiling glow dully from the church light below. Beside her, the computer screen cast its own blue illumination against the wall. Her bedroom door was closed, but through it, she heard the hum of deep voices. Shadows flickered in the slim gap beneath it.

She reached for the black linen journal on the desk and, sitting up in bed, removed the pen she'd clipped onto the first few pages. Flipping to an empty space, she wrote:

My companion...my lover? My friend? My companion betrayed me, left me – laughed and spat and smeared black, then kicked an easel, and it crashed at my feet. Something launched at me, something that burnt me with its ice and pricked before it and I both fell

"An easel," Margot said. When had she seen an easel before? She shut the book and tossed it back onto the desk.

The shadows beneath the door congealed into darkness just as she heard two soft thuds on its wood.

"Come in," she called out.

The door scraped a wide arc along the carpet to reveal a large two-headed silhouette.

"Margot?" She knew the voice.

"Did we wake you?" That one, too.

She shook her head. "No, I'm just getting up."

The black figure backed out of the door, where it divided into James and Rand. Squinting beneath the bright foyer light, she scuffed her way around to the dimmer living room to sit in the armchair, with the two men meekly following her. In her foggy state, seeing those two faces side by side on Rand's sofa was tough to comprehend. She'd never imagined a time when they'd coexist, and it made her claustrophobic.

But facing her expectant panel, she spoke. "I just had a dream where my life flashed before my eyes, and I thought I was going to die."

The menfolk dumbly shook their heads out of rhythm with each other. She didn't know what kind of response she'd expected, but no mincing words anymore. Shit or get off the pot.

"The thing is, it wasn't *my* life that I saw."

Rand cleared his throat. "Ah, that's... Whose life was it?"

"Charlotte's, I think."

"Who's Charlotte?" James asked.

"I don't know."

The men exchanged a look before Rand asked, "No one in your classes? Friend or family from home?"

"No."

"A character in a book or movie?"

"No."

Rand's voice faltered, but his gaze never left Margot's, which she found strangely unnerving. If he was withholding any apology in front of James for his comments earlier, it wasn't even reaching out to her through his eyes.

She looked away as he seemed to process his next question, but James filled the void first.

"I don't understand. Who are you talking about?"

"I told you. *I don't know*."

He licked his lips as he shook his head and turned to Rand.

Still, Rand didn't look away from her. "Is she someone you've spoken to, uh, Fitz about?"

"*Doctor* Fitzgerald, you mean?" Margot appreciated Rand's nondisclosure in using her counselor's familiar nickname, but she looked at James point-blank. "James,

I've been seeing a therapist here. Things have been happening that I don't understand, and I—" she looked at Rand accusingly "—*we* thought I needed outside help." She admitted that she'd just been to see the doctor, actually, right before running into James at the coffee shop.

"Okay," was all he said as he looked back and forth between her and Rand.

"And, yes," she looked to Rand again, "I've talked to Fitz about her." She watched his countenance deflate. "The cemetery, the journal… I think it all has something to do with her. And I've seen what Gwen has and think it does, too."

There it was. She felt remarkably better and dreadful at once.

Rand turned his head to look down the hall and, presumably, at his bedroom door. "You have, have you?" He seemed listless and didn't look back at her. "Why didn't you tell me?"

"Why do you think?" She turned to James, who still sat passively. "Why do *you* think I might not've said anything about seeing a ghost in this flat?"

"Shit. Are you serious?" James had clearly fallen out of his element. "Is this what that was about at lunch? 'Being in good company' and all that?"

Margot nodded once as she felt the world teeter underfoot. "'All that' and *you* saying you believed it, too." In her peripheral vision, she saw Rand's face swivel around to him as well.

James's pink cheeks deepened. "I just said I was open to it, not that I've had experiences myself. So, what, you're saying this place is haunted? Is that what you really think, Margot?"

Spasms twitched within her cheeks. Her throat constricted, and she had to inhale deeply to breathe. She just sat silently this way for a moment to get her air, and the men let her.

"It's either…" she finally began, her respiration quickening as it had before, and she caught her breath to try

230

again. "It's either that or I'm...I," she gasped and finished on each exhale, "am royally...fucked...up."

Both men were at their feet to support her before she could fall from the chair.

"I d-don't want to, to..." she managed to say in spurts as she hyperventilated, "go...th-through this any-mo-ho-ore..."

She felt James rub her back as Rand pried her fingers from the roots of her hair.

"Chloé? Hiya, this is Rand, Margot's flatmate. Yeah, hi."

He was following the instructions Margot had given once she'd calmed. As he stood speaking into her mobile, James comforted her in his arms on the floor, where she sat hugging her knees.

"Ah, yeah, well, she's asked for you, you see." The high pitch of Chloé's voice dotted the airwaves in response. "Ah, well, yes and no. If you're not busy, it might be—Oh. Mm-hm... Yeah, well, it's just her, a mate of hers, and myself... Right... Sure. Yes, that's correct. All right, cheers, bye." He clicked off the phone. "She's coming straight away. Is that what you want?"

Margot confirmed with an emphatic nod.

"A woman's touch, maybe." James shrugged.

Margot knit her brows. "I didn't hear you give the address."

"She knew it," Rand assured, rather curtly. "Have you invited her over before, to study?"

"No, I'd ask you first if that was okay," she groused, as his question sounded oddly territorial. "Maybe you should call back."

"No, she knew it. She recited it to me."

Margot huffed and shook her head.

She didn't speak for the next half hour, communicating only through shakes of the head and grunts when the men offered her tea, a blanket, pillow, and a multitude of unnecessary things to demonstrate their joint ineptness in a time of crisis.

James held her tighter when she lurched in surprise at the severe sound of the door buzzer.

"Hello?" Rand answered immediately. "Right, come inside. Second floor." He buzzed her in.

Chloé scraped her feet on the mat and shook her umbrella out at the entrance. Rand helped her remove her trench and lamely commented on how he hadn't realized it was raining again outside.

"Yes, it was sudden." Without waiting for invitation, she stepped into the living room. Ignoring James, she kneeled to Margot's level. "Are you all right?"

In answer, Margot's eyes welled up at the sight of her sodden friend, here at once on her account.

"Nice to meet you, I'm James." He freed an arm to extend to Chloé.

"*Enchanté*." She looked back at Margot while addressing him. "James, I hate to send you boys into the rain, but would you mind taking Rand to the pub? Have a little male bonding?"

"I get it. You want *female* bonding. Hey, Rand, whaddya think? That okay?" He sounded relieved to have a changing of the guards.

Rand watched Margot skeptically. "If that's all right with you."

Margot adjusted her posture to detach from James's lingering arm. Leaning closer to Chloé, she clasped her friend's hand in response.

"Right," Rand said. "Well, James, my local's just round the corner. Some brilliant craft beer on draft."

"Let's do it," James exhaled as he hoisted himself up. Grabbing his coat off the back of the kitchen stool, he offered Margot one last questioning glance while Rand looked at Chloé.

Margot closed her eyes. "It's fine. You boys have fun." She kept her lids down until she heard the door open and shut, then beseeched Chloé, "Tell me what is going on."

"What do you mean?"

"I know you know. I don't know how, but *I know you*

know, Chloé." She heard crumpling, then noticed Chloé's fist tighten around the neck of a brown lunch sack. The paper pulled tautly around a stout cylindrical form. "What's in there?"

"Herbs," Chloé said. "Bath salt."

"Is that for me?"

She nodded.

"Are you going to fix me a bath?"

Chloé nodded again.

Pause. "Are you going to join me?"

Another nod.

"Now?"

Nod.

"And then you'll explain?"

Chloé nodded once more.

The candle that had accompanied Margot's séance at the mirror found itself perched again in the bathroom, this time on the counter. Two additional tea lights stood watch at two corners of the tub. The triumvirate flickered disorienting shadows about the walls of the dark room.

Margot watched steam levitate off the rising water that Chloé drew for her. Removing a golf-ball-sized metal sphere and a plain mason jar from the paper bag, Chloé shook a quarter of the jar's contents into the stream and reached down to tickle the salts into the water.

Next, she picked up the mesh ball – a tea strainer – and dangled it by its thin chain so Margot could see its dried captives.

"Sage," Chloé said. "Most would bundle it into a smudge stick, but I like this way."

The two sat on the tub's edge in silence until the water filled it more than halfway. Twisting the tap off, Chloé looked at Margot and gave a nod.

Margot stood and untied her bathrobe. She stood paralyzed a moment with the ends of the waist tie dangling on either side of her robe's slim opening, which her hands clasped together at her chest and crotch. She looked at

233

Chloé, then up at the bathroom door.

"Come now, don't be so uncomfortable. We're both women. Try to be more French," Chloé kidded with a sly half-smile, rooted to where she sat.

Margot released her hands and, curling her fingers around the terrycloth lapels at her breast, she gradually peeled the robe from her shoulders and let it slip to the bath mat. Easing herself one foot at a time into the scalding water, she caught her breath and flinched until fully submersed.

Chloé dipped a washrag into the bathwater and swept it above Margot to let it dribble over her head, neck, and bent knees. She did this a few times before squeezing it out and wiping it over Margot's shoulders.

"Your tattoo has healed nicely. The phoenix is moving in the candlelight, as though it may take flight." Chloé grinned peacefully as she wiped Margot down her back and across her clavicle.

Margot stared straight ahead and concentrated on the sound of the trickling water as the drops anointed her.

Slapping the rag aside, Chloé again picked the tea ball up by its chain and carefully lowered it into the flame of one of the tea lights. With a sizzle and pop, the herbs' angry embers glowed. She raised it away from the candle and swung it gently to quell the fire and make it smolder into smoke. Then, like a priestess swinging incense down the aisles of a temple, she gracefully circled the sage above Margot's body.

Margot closed her eyes and inhaled what she expected to be a sweet essence but smelled more like pot. Feeling a bit dizzy after a while, she opened her eyes again to overcome it, wondering if Chloé might have mixed up her herbs.

Chloé narrowed her motions to a tighter circle about Margot's head and ultimately hung the ball in front of her face and let it oscillate there in place like a pendulum as she whispered soft French somethings. When the smoke dissipated, she plunged the ball into the water and set it aside with the rag.

"Relax," she cooed as she rolled a dry towel behind Margot's neck and bid her to recline lower in the tub. Margot obeyed.

"What is this all about, Chloé?" she asked once settled. "You promised."

Chloé lowered herself to the floor and rested an arm along the tub's edge. She laid her head there, with her chin angled toward Margot, and extended her other arm down to dip her fingers into the bath. She stroked the silkened water as she had done before.

"Tell me, do you derive any pleasure from this?"

Margot swallowed. "It's very relaxing."

"Does it offer you any stimulation?"

Margot's water-logged heel skidded against the bottom of the tub. "I feel a little light-headed. Tingling."

Chloé's finger stroked along Margot's thigh, just once, just subtle enough to have been an accident. "Good."

"Tell me," Margot said.

Chloé swallowed this time. "I want to know if my cleansing is working."

"I'm pretty sure I'm clean."

"Not from dirt. Entity contamination."

Margot's other heel gave, and her foot thumped against the end of the tub. She tensed, but didn't otherwise move.

Chloé tilted her head upwards to prop her chin on her forearm. "I have reason to believe you have something attached to you. Some*one*."

Margot's breathing came out in heavy huffs again. She let Chloé continue.

"I was not certain at first. I had drawn your image—"

"In class?"

"Yes."

"In that black notebook."

"Yes. My sketchbook. My grandfather instructed me on how to sketch caricatures. I had great fun with it as a child, drawing friends at festivals and classmates at school."

"I've seen you. It's a little intrusive, isn't it? When you do it without people's permission?"

"Perhaps. But I never meant anything by it until other things began to show up in my drawings."

"How do you mean?"

"Mind waiting here *un moment* while I fetch my purse?"

Margot tensed beneath the water, a captive audience but with someone to keep her company, apparently, in Chloé's absence. Little comfort that brought.

Chloé soon returned, agitating the candle flames with her swift motion. She dried her hand, and, drawing folded sheets of sketch paper from her purse, she detached one and explained, "This was the first time I drew you."

She held a candle to it so Margot could see a fair rendering of her features, other than a pronounced squiggle at the side of her face.

"What's that, my hair?"

"It's a profile."

"Of someone sitting behind me?"

"Within you."

"What?"

Chloé set the paper down and unfolded the next. "This was the second time I drew you, the day we were assigned as project partners."

Margot blinked in the dim, moving light, trying to make out what she saw. Bold black strokes once again depicted a strong resemblance of her, sitting with the same slackened posture from the same angle. A notable difference, though, was a fainter set of extra limbs extending out from her torso, giving her a Hindu god quality.

"What are those? Arms?"

Chloé nodded. "I suspect it is the essence of another presence occupying the same space as you. I see it around you all of the time." She paused for a few seconds. "I don't think it was coincidence that we were placed in the same study group. I needed a reasonable way to know you better, and fate delivered you to me."

Margot gagged on the pungent air. She sat up abruptly and stood to step out of the tub, not caring whether she splashed Chloé's sketches and hoping they'd disintegrate if so. Yanking on her bathrobe, she fastened it tightly around her as she ran up the stairs to flick the lights on.

"I've upset you." Chloé looked up at Margot from the bottom of the steps, appearing even more diminutive. "Please, don't be angry with me. I cannot help who I am."

"And who are you, Chloé? This is crazy!"

"Well, what did you think was happening?"

"Friendship! I trusted you!"

"You can still trust me. You can trust that I am helping you."

"How? I'm not relaxed anymore, that's for sure. I'm not 'tingling' anymore," she spat. "That hypnosis you had me do. Was that some way to speak to the dead? Is that what all this witchcraft has been about? Why can't you be honest with me?"

"I am *only* being honest with you! As though you didn't suspect all this yourself. Look in my eyes and tell me you didn't!"

Margot leveled her glare down the steps, taking full advantage of the domination her higher position granted her. "How did you know how to get here?"

"What?"

"You knew this address. How? I never told you."

For the first time, Margot felt she had the upper hand on her friend, who never looked more disconcerted. Chloé's mouth hovered open, but no voice issued forth.

"Chloé. How did you find me?"

The little woman's china composition gave way to that of a doll emptied of its stuffing. "I promised you I would explain." Her large eyes swept the floor. "But it's too much at once."

"What are you talking about? This is my life here!"

A jangle of keys at the door diverted her attention toward the other end of the hall. Chloé scrambled up the steps, purse in hand, and brushed past Margot.

"Hello, gentlemen!" she greeted with a skip toward her trench coat.

"Good evening, milady!" James bowed with exaggerated,

inebriated energy.

"Hiya." Rand poked his head around the corner into Margot's view as she ascended into the hallway. "Did we pop back too soon?"

"No, your timing's perfect. Chloé was just leaving."

"*Salut, à bientôt!*" Chloé chirped as she frolicked out the door, shutting it securely behind her.

Rand watched where she had breezed out, then looked past Margot to the bathroom door. She could smell burnt sage mingling with the humidity traveling into the hall, and when Rand finally looked at her, he eyed her down the length of her bathrobe to where she dripped water onto the carpet. "You're sure you're all right?" he asked, frowning.

"Yes," she said tersely. "I'm beat. Good night." She strode past both men and ducked into her bedroom. She'd hoped to leave it at that, but a lingering sense of etiquette brought her back to the door. "James?"

"Yeah?" Raising his brows, he smiled and stepped toward the door as if intending to join her.

"When do you leave town?"

He stopped in his tracks, his grin weaker. "Oh…not 'til Tuesday."

"Okay, then I'll catch you sometime before then, all right? Sorry, I'm just really tired. Thanks for everything, though."

He shoved his fists in his pockets and bobbed his head. "I'll see you in the morning."

"Will you?"

"Yeah, I'm crashing here."

Over James's shoulder, Margot saw Rand stare at the floor.

"Oh." She retreated back within her room. "Cool," she threw out politely before closing the door on him.

The church lights had since turned off, handing over total illumination to the pale moonlight. Margot squeezed her eyes tightly against it as she heard the sleeping computer hum to life on its own.

238

Chapter Sixteen

Empty Wells

Yellow bled against the egg whites of their English Breakfasts. The unlikely trio of Rand, Margot, and James had crawled out of the flat unshowered to enjoy an early afternoon brunch before James would head into the office to prepare his Monday presentation. A pint apiece helped loosen their tongues amidst a tangible awkwardness, but Margot still said nothing about what had transpired with Chloé in the bath.

Back out into the gray day, they reached the intersection where James could catch the Tube. He gave Margot a chummy hug.

"I'll call you, okay? I'll see you before I go?" His gaze penetrated hers, and for a moment she expected him to swoop in and remove another eye snot. But he didn't. For the first time, he looked at her the way she'd always wanted him to.

"Yeah." Margot felt the familiar lump in her throat. "James, thank you again. I'm sorry you had to see me like this."

"Never apologize. I feel responsible, at least in part."

"Don't give yourself so much credit," she chided with an elbow to his ribs.

He laughed. "Okay. Well, bye…honey." The hesitation sounded as if he'd thrown in the old endearment like an afterthought. Maybe because he was out of practice using it – and for her, specifically – but Margot could tell he wasn't sure if he was allowed to anymore. The corners of his lips still held up a smile but twitched slightly as his eyes wandered over her face and momentarily flickered to Rand. "I'll give you a call later. Before I leave. Bye, honey," he said again, with a sad sort of finality. With a tight grin, he glanced back and forth between her and Rand once more and nodded.

Margot knew not to expect her phone to ring that soon. That James would give her the space he had before so she'd have a fighting chance to move on. Putting on a brave face like his, she smiled and said as casually as she could, "Good luck getting your work done. See ya."

They went in for another hug, holding each other closely this time.

"Cheers, mate," Rand chimed in once they separated, and he shook James's hand. "Nice to finally meet you, and thanks for breakfast. Cheers."

"Yeah, thanks for the drinks last night and letting me crash, man."

As James started for the Tube entrance and glanced back with a departing smile, Margot flashed him one last wave before turning on her heel to walk the opposite way with Rand.

After rounding the block, he wrapped an arm around her shoulders. "He's a good man."

"He is," she said, accepting the unspoken apology. *And he'll make someone so happy*. She wanted someone to make him happy, too. *Just not me.*

Once on Rand's street, they passed the series of identical columned entrances until chancing on the only one with a Chloé planted on its doorstep.

"Ah, hello." Rand greeted her with a stiff cheek-to-cheek kiss when she stood.

"Hey," Margot managed, making no motion to greet in kind.

Chloé looked at Rand first. "I am so sorry if I'm interrupting your afternoon. I can leave."

"Well, we're just getting back. It was a short night for us all, so I thought I might rest. What say you, Margot?"

She appreciated his lifeline but said, "Um, I'm fine. I can

do whatever."

"I was thinking we could go for a walk?" Chloé asked.

"Maybe a short one. I could probably use a nap, too."

"Sure, a short walk. Then I leave you be."

Up at the door, Margot gave Rand a hug goodbye. While she held him, she leaned back to take in his concerned face, his eyes that seemed to study hers. Without overthinking it, she leaned back in to peck him softly right beside his lips. "Thank you," she whispered. "For everything."

"I'll see you *soon*," he murmured back, raising his brows on the last word. He then turned away from her to unlock the door, but not before throwing a quick, suppressed grin at Chloé.

He must realize she upset me last night, Margot thought as she watched him step inside and close the door after himself. She slumped back down the steps to the sidewalk. "Anywhere particular you want to go?"

"Wherever you wish."

Margot motioned in a direction.

After a minute of silent walking, Chloé spoke first. "Margot, I am so, so very sorry. I didn't mean to frighten you and would never want to insult you."

Dropping her head and shoulders, Margot exhaled heavily. "I would be ridiculous to accept that apology."

Chloé sighed. "I don't know what else to—"

"Because it's not necessary. You were only trying to help, doing exactly what I asked."

"Yes, but it's not easy confronting the truth. Even if it is what you believe, to have it confirmed is terrifying."

"True, but what have we confirmed?"

Eventually, she steered Chloé through an immense concrete archway. The women stuck to a main path that bisected the acreage of stone.

"There's someone I'd like you to meet," Margot said after a time.

A couple of minutes later, the two stood over a grave.

"Chloé, meet Charlotte. Charlotte, Chloé." Margot affected the grace of the perfect hostess.

"So this is her."

"I don't even have to explain it to you, do I?"

"Well, perhaps a little. But I feel the larger connection."

"Of course you do. You have 'clear vision', as I recall. Or as the French would say, '*clairvoyante*', *n'est-ce pas*?"

Chloé grinned toward the ground.

"Is that how you knew Rand's address?"

"Mm," Chloé grunted in what Margot took as a yes.

"So am I right about this?" Margot continued. "This is her?"

Chloé shook her head. "I do not know." With a modest laugh, she added, "My vision is perhaps not so perfectly clear."

"But you do see something, right?"

"With this place, yes. There's a link here that is binding you, and…" Chloé's eyes held transfixed in the way Margot had seen during class, except rather than zoning at nothing, she clearly stared at the tombstone.

"What is it?"

"Out of curiosity," Chloé said, still looking at the stone, "when is your birthday, Margot?"

"Funny you should ask. Same as *hers*, actually. Does that mean anything? Something you're seeing right now?"

Chloé nodded with her empty stare.

"Well?" Margot asked.

"Her death date."

"Yeah?"

"It is today."

Margot paid attention to it for the first time with an incredulous laugh. "Well, the anniversary of it is. Go fucking figure."

With no explanation, Chloé said, "I wonder if you might walk with me a little further."

Dizzy and tired, Margot sat mutely through most of the Tube ride. They had connected to the Northern Line several stops ago, and a nod from Chloé cued her to alight at the next one.

242

Once at street-level, Margot twitched her tattooed shoulder in camaraderie with the demographic swilling through a large marketplace, though she still felt a few piercings too shy to remove her eyes from the brick walkway.

"Here," Chloé motioned, and she ducked her head into a small entrance.

In unpopulated dimness, Margot couldn't determine into what sort of venue she'd just stepped, only that it reeked of marijuana and fruity shisha tobacco. Chloé exhibited familiarity with a low-purring silhouette that soon vanished in the shadows, and after which she beckoned Margot to follow.

Feeling her way down a confining stairwell, Margot heard the creaking in front of her eventually stop, and a series of clicks revealed an opening bathed in a beam of artificial light.

"*Merci*," she heard Chloé whisper before sounding two swift lip-smacks, presumably on the cheeks of the shadow – a being of flesh-and-blood that brushed Margot's arm on his way back upstairs as he bid her a raspy "Enjoy your exploration."

Chloé's cool hand eased into Margot's sweaty palm to guide her. Late-day sunlight filtered through iron grills overhead to supplement the flashlight.

"What is this place?"

"They call it the Catacombs," Chloé said, "though no one is buried here." A few carefully traversed yards later, she resumed, "We're now under the market, inside old stables for horses that once towed barges along the canal. Some above ground have been converted, but these down here are not for public access."

Margot didn't question the connection that granted Chloé this privilege; somehow the more she came to know about her, the less she wished she did.

In the dank crumble of the subterranean ruins, they wound their way down different passages, avoiding flooded ones. Passing beneath another gray brick archway off the corridor, Chloé stopped inside the musty, darkened nook. Though the intensity of the marijuana and tobacco lingered in Margot's nostrils, a sweet-and-sour scent tickled at their edges, too, and she noticed a couple of dusty wine bottles when Chloé clanked into them in setting down the flashlight.

"You're not going to booze me up on Amontillado and wall me up in here, are you?" Margot let out a nervous laugh when Chloé narrowed her eyes, apparently missing the Edgar Allan Poe reference as Margot felt ever more the Fortunado fool.

She half expected Chloé to pull a trowel from her purse when she made a move to unsnap the clutch. Instead, Chloé removed two smaller items from it and placed one in each of Margot's palms. Margot's left hand twitched automatically around the small form of its hard, cool treasure, and she squeezed it only to uncurl her fingers again, bracing to see Grandma Grace's brooch lying there.

But it was Chloé's pocket watch, the polished silver almost burning Margot's hand with its frost. She let it drop to the grainy floor.

"Sorry," she said as she quickly bent to retrieve it, then stood again to dust it off with her T-shirt. She held it there cushioned in the cotton fabric and glanced down to notice for the first time that the central flourishes of its engraved design formed a monogram: VPA. Popping open the cover to inspect the watch face, she saw the second hand wasn't ticking. "Oh no, did I break it?"

"It already was. Broken."

"Since when?"

"For some time, *je pense*. It has never operated as long as I've had it."

"But…" *Those occasions I saw her check it…wasn't it to tell the time?*

After a pregnant pause, Chloé said, "In your other hand is only my compact mirror, nothing special in itself. As you have learned, any reflective surface will do."

"For what?"

"For contacting the owner of that watch."

"Aren't you its owner?"

"In some way, yes. You must understand, Margot, that the original owner of that watch had been hurt, and in scarring himself, he gave me this." She pointed directly to the brown splotch on her arm that until now she'd seemed so intent not to showcase. "I don't remember feeling pain, but, you see, he has the same-shaped mark in the same place on his own arm when I see him in larger mirrors than that one."

Margot nearly dropped the compact this time, but she recovered and handed it back to Chloé for safety. Her stomach churned. "But weren't you born with that? Hence '*birth*mark'?"

"I have had this since I was young, yes, but, according to my parents, not when I was born." She proceeded to thumb the mark.

"So, what, can the dead do that to us? Hurt us, I mean?"

"Not intentionally."

Margot thought of the faint birthmark on her forehead, and extended her bare arms in the air to look them over as well. She scanned along to her inner left wrist, where she knew an elongated brown spot had recently appeared above her vein.

"They're age spots, Chloé."

"Age spots on a child?" She stared out toward the corridor. "The unusual thing is that when that man bounced me on his knee, the man whom I'd thought was my deceased grandfather... It was *his* father."

"You're grandfather's father?"

"No, the boy's. The future owner of the watch. And it was as though I was him, and I still wonder if he is me when I enter his life this way."

"Who?"

Chloé lifted her shoulders toward her ears then dropped them.

Margot believed the world above must have fragmented into tiny pixels and scattered away into oblivion for all she trusted in her own understanding of it anymore. "I've been looking to you this whole time for the answers, but you don't have them, do you?"

Adult laughter and children's cries echoed through the stagnant air along with the waterfall sound of cars in motion overhead, providing Margot small consolation that the world outside still remained intact.

"There are times I am so certain," Chloé said. "I can summon him whenever I open that compact – see him, feel him, be him. It is a possession unlike I've ever heard of before, no matter how much I've researched, and there is no one I know like me to ask for those answers."

Margot took a couple of shallow breaths. "Esther."

"Pardon?"

"I don't know how, but she might have known."

Alerted, Chloé stepped closer to lay a hand on Margot's forearm. Trivial as it sounded in this context, Margot explained her sixth grade experience – of the day her brooch had disappeared after Show-n-Tell and her classmate Esther told her Charlotte had it.

"I just assumed," Margot said, "that it was another kid at school who'd stolen the brooch off Trisha or out of my backpack. It obviously never dawned on me that Charlotte could be *dead*."

"And Esther actually said it was Charlotte? She said the name?"

"Yeah. And that her last name was some kind of bird. A *pigeon*, perhaps. You think she could do what you can?"

"It's possible."

"Then why wouldn't she have just told me?"

Chloé raised her eyebrow.

"Easier said than done, huh?" Margot said.

"Huh," Chloé repeated as she nodded, as if to say, *Ya think?* "Sometimes I can sense when a person will be readily receptive. But other times, so much skepticism is present, I would appear a lunatic. And second chances are not often given."

The way she hung her head filled Margot with heartache

246

over the loneliness that must accompany such a gift.

"Besides," Chloé said, "at such a young age, she might not have understood herself. Or perhaps in telling you that much, she did want you to know, but in her time and in yours. Is there a reason she might not have had that chance?"

Though limited in old memory, Margot shared how her classmates had made fun of Esther for having imaginary friends. The poor girl had already been alienated beyond repair in childhood and lost any chances beyond age twenty.

"But even if Esther really could communicate with spirits," she said, "how would that explain how Charlotte *had my pin*? How could she possibly steal it? Do you think maybe it was moved by a poltergeist-type energy? It couldn't have just vanished into thin air to wherever Charlotte was, could it? Is that how you got the watch?"

"There is much about space and time we don't understand. Though it's not for lack of trying." Chloé released her hand from Margot's arm to lean against the brick wall. Staring off into the shadows, she sank to sit on the rubble. "Imaginary friends," she whispered at first, then raised her voice to a soft yet more audible volume. "As though she interacted with them. Is this what would happen? When you would tease her?"

"Look, I'm not taking responsibility for the teasing. But, yes, we'd see her talking to herself sometimes."

"Did she talk to Charlotte in front of you?"

"No, but I guess I assumed she must have in order to learn her name. Maybe not."

Chloé fluttered off in a whispered monologue, most of which was unintelligible to Margot until she was eventually brought back into the fold.

"What I sometimes question is… It's only that I can't interact with them like this, you and me, you see. And I can accept that we're not meant to, although you hear of those who can, as if they have conversations, and—"

"Well, maybe there are different levels of sensitivity. Or maybe just like most of us aren't aware of spirits, some

247

spirits aren't aware of us." She thought back to the Ouija game and how Charlotte had refused to answer how or when she'd died. "Maybe they don't even know they're dead."

"Yes, and consider for a moment why someone would not be aware they're dead."

"Because it happened suddenly, traumatically maybe? They didn't have a chance to realize they were dying?"

Chloé appeared to mull this possibility over, yet her tone sounded less convinced. "Margot, this man that I see in the mirror—"

"I thought it was a boy." She narrowed her eyes.

"Yes, but he has grown as I have grown, into a man. I at first believed I could only see him as I would best understand him. I mean to say that, as a child, I could understand another child better, so that was, perhaps, the aspect of his nature – his past – that presented itself to me. But now I have to wonder if this is a dead spirit after all. What if he is alive? Aging as I age?"

"Alive! Well, you've got his initials and know what he looks like. Could you try to find him?"

"*C'est impossible*. It's still not enough to go on. And he is of this place, I feel, but not of this time."

Chloé's heavy, resolved silence after that made Margot uneasy. Without asking for explanation, she sat next to her before her legs gave out. Milky drips of melted wax bubbled into visibility on the stone ground, and the spiced sweetness of the interior wafted up her nostrils again.

"I have not been overly troubled by this before," Chloé finally said. "I have come to even accept it as a fact of my everyday life, thinking nothing more of the renderings I sketch because it is nothing new to me anymore. I have come to care less and less, have wanted so *badly* to care less." Chloé looked over at Margot and reached to touch her jaw with an extended index finger. "But with you…"

She shifted her body closer and slid her fingers up and beyond Margot's cheek to comb through her hair.

Margot blinked rapidly, her eyelids clicking through the

slide reel of her thoughts. "You actually see that someone is attached to me, too, right?"

"Yes." The stoicism of Chloé's face didn't break.

"But someone who has died."

"Or someone who is alive—" Chloé inhaled "—but is going to die. Today."

Margot's focus on Chloé's doe eyes crossed and blurred as it readjusted to diminishing distance from them. As the gentle caressing of her hair sent tickles over her breasts, she found her friend was nose to nose with her; their eyelashes nearly brushed against each other in a moment of humid hesitation.

"Try not to fear what you have not been able to see," Chloé said.

"I don't know what I'm supposed to see," Margot whispered back.

"Don't try to see, but feel." Chloé's voice trickled through Margot's consciousness like a syrupy nectar.

Margot swallowed as Chloé kept stroking her hair. "What am I supposed to feel?"

"Feel her. Feel him. Feel me."

Margot caught her breath in the still, close air. Her back clenched against the brick's cold damp. "What are you saying?"

"We are connected, you and me. We are because *they* are."

"They are? Are they here?"

Stroke. "Of course. They are here because we are."

"Why are *we* here?"

Stroke. "This is where I found the watch."

"So you didn't always have it?"

Stroke. "I didn't always have you."

"Why do you need me?" Margot asked breathlessly. "Why bring me here?"

Stillness. "Don't you feel a wholeness? I have missed class to spend afternoons here. With the watch but without you. Something draws me here, but something else has always been missing." Chloé breathed heavily, and she

249

passed her tongue across her lower lip. "You and I," she said, "we arrive here together, each empty wells. And now we fill each other."

Her hand traced down the track of Margot's spine, settling at the small of her back, where Chloé pressed the heat of her palm. Feeling a pulsation as her pelvis yearned to yawn open, Margot rolled her eyes to the side to refocus; as they adjusted to the shadows, she drew her face away from Chloé's slightly.

"But don't you feel it?" Chloé asked.

Margot could just barely discern cushions in the dark recesses of the niche, resting between stumps of burned-down candles. Golden embroidery glinted against deep red where light strained to reach.

"Don't you feel it?" Chloé repeated as she leaned to close their space again, the pillows of her breath warm against Margot's face.

With her eyes on the cushions, Margot imagined lying on them, layers of fabric peeled off until she and her friend were skin to skin. "What is this place?" she whispered. "What do you do here?"

"Nothing but seek answers, same as you." She raised her other hand to clasp Margot's face, rubbing her thumb across her cheekbone.

Still, Margot stared at the cushions. Their crimson bled over her sight, making something stir within. The oversized pillows were ripe as raspberries; she supposed she could suck the juice of sensuous delights from them in a haze freeing her of thought and expectation. Maybe that was how Chloé made more sense of her *sense*, how she tapped into it more lucidly, by just letting go of the reality right around her and yielding to pleasure in whatever form it came. Maybe Margot could do the same, then, if Chloé would show her how.

Yes…

So tired of thinking, Margot needed feeling…friction, connection…the feel of fact not fiction, something authentic and tangible that she could touch and taste and smell if only she'd finally and truly let go…

Margot's fingertips clawed the sandy stone beneath her. Her mind dizzied, verging on euphoria as she nearly winced with want – for Chloé's lips to press on hers…for her hand to slip from her face to slide over other curves. How she desired to succumb to that hand…

Until the sensuality searing through her turned to nausea on a dime. She broke from Chloé's hold.

Breathing heavily as she avoided her eyes, Margot said, "I don't know whose watch that is, or if he has anything to do with these stables or Charlotte. And I don't care."

Chloé's unoccupied hands slapped her thighs. "How can you possibly still doubt it? After all that has happened to you. All I have shared with you? How can you still run from what is so obvious?"

"It's not obvious. It's a series of coincidences strung up on a fraying thread."

Chloé snorted in incredulity.

"And even if there's something more," Margot said, "why do I need to solve it? I need to get my own shit together before delving into others' lives, who *aren't* living!" She was at her feet and laughing, exhaling bursts of air through her nose to expel the fusty scents from her lungs and almost wishing for the safety of a Suburban USA strip-mall appletini.

"No," she continued, "it's like you said with Esther, this is all stuff I have to deal with in my own time."

Chloé leaned back and folded her arms. "I do not know if you have that kind of time."

Chapter Seventeen

Charlotte's Web

"Margot. Margot!"

On hearing the echoing, metallic voice, Margot retreated from the bedsheets and arms enveloping her. Her ears snapped as though on a descending airplane, and she coughed deeply from her chest. She might've fallen from the stool she came to feel beneath her had it not been for a firm grasp on her shoulders.

"Margot, are you here?"

"'Course I'm here." Steadily, she regained her breathing, and, pressing her eyes closed, she then reopened them to electric light. Rand's reflection appeared in the bathroom mirror.

"Are you all right?" he asked.

"Yes, fine. Saw so much more this time."

"*This* time? When did you—"

"What happened?" Chloé asked from beside her.

"Hm? Um."

Margot swayed slightly, not fully emerged from her stupor.

"Perhaps your message will remind you?" Chloé knelt to pick the dream diary up from the floor, then placed it in Margot's lap, open to a page.

So then they are no more twain, but one flesh

"You wrote it with your left hand," Chloé said.

Rand yanked off the black trash bags taped to the windows against daylight. "This is inexcusable. What do you think you're doing?"

"I can help her."

"How is this help? I don't know where you took her before, but I won't have this nonsense in my house."

Chloé flared. "She asked for this!"

Freaked as she was by Chloé's insinuations, Margot had indeed broken down and offered her friend one last chance to find the answers – but on her own turf and following her own rules. Rule number one: no unsolicited contact. When they'd returned to a silent flat and seen the door to Rand's bedroom was closed, they had assumed he was still resting and set to work as quietly as possible. As it was, after his nap, he'd gone for a walk around the neighborhood himself when Margot hadn't come back yet, restless and hoping he'd run into her. The cemetery had been his first stop, but they'd long since left it.

While Rand hotly debated Chloé's methodologies, Margot rocked on her stool and recited:

"A perfect Woman, nobly planned,
To warn, to comfort, and command;
And yet a Spirit still, and bright
With something of angelic light."

On the last line, she threw her head back with a wild smile. Rand got to her before Chloé, swiftly wrapping his arms to hold her steady.

"Margot, darling, I don't understand. What have you done to her?"

"Do you have anything to drink, *s'il vous plaît*?"

In stern silence, Rand wrapped an arm beneath Margot's armpits and hooked another under her knees to hoist her upstairs to the living room. Delicately placing her on the sofa, he went to the kitchen and returned to hand both women a glass of red wine. A few sips helped to ease Margot from her catatonic state, and on seeing the way her flatmate frowned at her friend, standing beside her at the ready to show her the door, she stood and walked to them on her own power to explain.

253

"Rand, I know this sounds insane, and I have my doubts too, but we need to give her benefit of another. We have to —"

"Why the urgency with this?" Rand still looked at Chloé. "She's been making progress and needs to overcome all this in good time. It's not going to happen overnight."

"But it must," Chloé said. "*This* night." She cocked her head at him. "We lament how sometimes it seems people expire so unexpectedly. 'Before their time,' we will say. Yet when two souls are connected – living in different times, yet at the *same* time – are they born together in their separate lifetimes? Then what do you suppose happens when one of them dies? Does the other as well? Are their life spans the same, or do their years expand and contract within each other's? *I* don't know, do you?"

"Outrageous. I'll sooner have you leave than upset her with this New Age drivel."

"And close me out like Gwen?"

"What?" Rand and Margot asked in unison as their faces snapped toward her.

"I understand you have been acquainted with *la Dame Grise*, no? Lady Grey."

"Not personally, no," Rand said, his lips in a taut line.

Chloé smiled. "Are you so certain? Perhaps she is right here." She rolled her wrist toward Margot with elegance.

"What?" they again exclaimed. Margot sidestepped a few inches closer to Rand, commensurately further from Chloé.

"What have you told her about Gwen, Margot?"

"Nothing! That you were dating, but—"

"You didn't need to say anything," Chloé said. "She came to me."

Margot edged back toward the sofa. Rand's fists tightened as he glared and mechanically followed to sit beside her.

Chloé sat in the chair across the room, gripping its arms with whitened knuckles. "There was a time when I phoned you, Margot, about arranging a time to meet for our first project. You were indisposed – in the bath – and Gwen answered your mobile, you see."

"Bitch," Margot whispered. She looked at Rand. "Well, why would she do that?"

"Damned if I know," he replied. "She was probably concerned about you. I told you she was."

"Gwen didn't explain to me why, just that she was answering on your behalf. I sensed something in her voice and asked if I might quickly drop off some course materials for you. I was only ten minutes away."

And so, Gwen had allegedly given her Rand's address and met her at the main door to the building, though didn't let her past the ground-floor foyer. It had been enough of an entry for Chloé to attain a strong feeling for the space, however; she'd shivered and commented on "these musty, haunted English houses," and Gwen had been quick to pick up on it.

"How do you mean?" she'd asked, and Chloé explained she was only making conversation, a Frenchwoman teasing an English penchant.

"I then searched through my bag, realizing I had foolishly brought the wrong papers," Chloé said. "I begged her not tell you I had come, that my error would embarrass me too much, and I would instead try calling you later."

Another day when Chloé had called, Gwen answered again. Like déjà-vu, Margot was in the bathtub, so Chloé had made another excuse for dropping by. Gwen let her into the unit that time.

"She was worried about you, as was I," Chloé told Margot. "She wondered if I might know what to do. She had never met you before, so felt knocking at the door would be inappropriate."

Because answering my phone isn't.

Chloé had therefore crept toward the bathroom door herself and listened to Margot churning the waters and muttering curious things. She'd then made her way back up the hall toward Gwen, stopping at Rand's bedroom door as she did so to rest her hand on the molding and peer inside.

"She's fine," Chloé told her, though had clearly been

255

distracted by something she sensed within the room. *"We're preparing a speech for our class, and she's reciting."*

Gwen hadn't bought the flippancy. *"What was that look for?"*

"Pardon?"

"What do you see in there?"

"Rien du tout. Nothing."

"No," Gwen had said, grabbing Chloé by the wrist. *"Please tell me. Do you see something, too?"*

In this gesture, Chloé had seen what she'd been so sure she'd heard on the phone the first time: desperation. Gauging Gwen carefully, she confessed that she had felt something, always could in certain places.

Rand shook his head. "How dare you take advantage of her. She was in a real state."

Margot looked at him with a question at her lips but swallowed it.

Chloé eyed her. "You see now how it is nothing I feel I can explain to people." To Rand she said, "It was not my intention to exploit Gwen's frailty, but I had yet to gain Margot's trust, slowly. And not even I realized what value Gwen could provide, what it was that surely drew me to her in the first place. It was her terror that seemed to compel me then."

Rand narrowed one eye with a faint smirk as he nodded, though Margot couldn't decipher what he appeared to comprehend in Chloé's words. The lowered shades rustled and scraped against the open windows.

"We went for a coffee just around the block," Chloé went on, "to talk about it further. It was clear she was distressed and needed someone to listen, someone objective, who would not judge her. This is when Gwen told me what Rand saw in his bedroom."

"What Rand saw?" Margot asked. "You mean her."

"No."

Margot stared at him again. "Why does Gwen lie like that? About me, you."

He sat silently with his eyes to the floor.

256

"I mean, Rand? Can you believe this?"

"I think he can." Chloé looked to him with frozen eyes. He lifted his face to meet them, his own appearing hardened to glass.

"Rand?" Margot shoved her face into his line of sight. "Look at me."

He did. Eventually.

"Does Gwen have a problem you haven't told me about? Has she…" Margot's eyes darted around the room as conclusions came to her. "Has she been going through the same thing I have? The visions, the depression, to the point of lying to cover it—" She couldn't stomach his expression, its sorrow, its…

Humiliation?

Her mind shifted tack. "You *are* the one who saw it."

Rand's cheeks were ablaze as his eyes lowered back to the carpeting.

Chloé spoke in his silence. "I think he is embarrassed for you to know, Margot. I think he would have told you otherwise."

Margot kept shaking her head. "That's why you wanted to talk about… Well, needless to say, it was enough to scare the crap out of Gwen, wasn't it? So it really is why she wouldn't stay here anymore."

"That," Rand began, his finger seeming to excavate his broken voice from his knee, "and that I won't leave." His nail scraped more fervently, unearthing more words. "That I don't stay in spite of her but because of her."

"Who, Gwen?" Margot asked.

"Rand," Chloé said, "it isn't her. You must know that."

He sank his face into his hands as Margot marveled over the many and various 'hers' surrounding him in his life, all so dramatic in their own way and feeding on his kind heart.

If it isn't me, it's Gwen, and before either of us, it was…
"He thinks it's his sister, doesn't he?" she asked Chloé.

Rand didn't emit a sound, but Margot could see his compressed lips tremble. She laid her hand against his spine to feel his muscles shudder there as well.

Chloé merely repeated, "It isn't her."

Margot tasted the salty tang of a tear that had dripped to her lips. "Well. It isn't me either."

Tick-tick-tick... The hands regulate my heartbeat. They measure out time in unison as it also appears to stand still, if not wind back to when both our hearts allowed themselves to rest, to skip beats when also pulsing for another's touch.

Lips brush my forehead and move down the bridge of my nose in slow succession until...

"How can you be so certain?" Chloé asked. "This presence is attached to *you*, and I feel your connection to this place."

"Because Rand saw her before I even came here," Margot said. "And *I've* seen her! Through a window from another room. She's *not* attached to me." When Chloé knit her brows, Margot clapped a single note of rejoice as she said it again. "She's not attached to me!"

Rand looked up in confusion.

"It isn't *me*, Rand. It's this house. Lady Grey is *Charlotte*. She may have sent me a sign before I came here because she knew I was coming. Maybe she was trying to warn me away or something, but I did come here, and that's when the shit really hit the fan." Seeing his expression didn't break, she went on. "It's exactly what you accused Chloé of, of taking advantage of Gwen when she was vulnerable. I've never been more vulnerable in my life than this year, when I lost sight of what I want and whether I can even do anything about it." She looked at Chloé. "If there's a ghost in this house, it's tapped into my weakness and become stronger for it."

"Have you met with Gwen since?" Rand spoke up, directing his stony inquiry at Chloé.

Margot couldn't follow his thought process but imagined he might be eager for any sort of update on his estranged girlfriend, if perhaps Chloé had seen her more recently than he had.

"A couple times more, when Margot was at class," she answered. "She felt better, I think, after speaking about it all, and decided that going forward it needed to be sorted with you, Rand." Flickering a glance at Margot, she added, "Just you."

"What's that look?" Margot asked.

"She doesn't hate you, you know, for sharing Rand's attentions. She knows it's only temporary and soon you'll return home."

Margot felt herself flush. *And then what, they'll get back together? Their break is only as temporary as my visa?*

Rand remained quiet for a moment before he spoke again. "My, she confided a lot in you. Didn't she?"

"It is what women will do when pushed to a limit. It didn't take long for Margot to confide either."

The heat in Margot's cheeks and chest deepened. "You're rather charismatic. No doubt Gwen felt so, too."

Chloé's upper lip twisted into a sneer as she inspected her nails, though a tremor in her fingers betrayed her cool composure. "Eh, well. I don't suppose so, but you're kind to say it."

Margot wasn't altogether certain she'd intended it as the compliment it was taken for, but she let it go and concentrated instead on the window as a curling eye floater drifted across it.

"How does she do it, then?" she asked herself.

"Pardon?"

"How does Charlotte take possession of me like that, showing me her world through the mirror…and that day I had my eye exam…I was on the sidewalk, not even in the house, but it was like I was moving through her life in a completely alternative dimension." Her voice trailed off, but the others didn't speak. "That's what I saw. *That* is what I saw just now, in the mirror. I climbed the same staircase, and those shapes I saw in the mews, it was the bedroom furniture."

"What mews?" Rand asked Chloé. "What bedroom?"

"I don't know."

Rand laid his palm over Margot's knuckles. Feeling his thumb rub across the ripples of her fingers, she clasped his hand, then shook her head at her lap.

"Chloé, I think I understand what your concern is. I do, and I appreciate it. But I'm going to ride this thing out. Whatever happens today," she looked into Rand's eyes, "is meant to be."

"I'll stay with you tonight," Chloé said, "To look over—"

"No. You can best help me by going home." She held on to Rand more firmly.

With her pink lips down-turned and nose slightly crinkled as though she smelled expired milk, Chloé watched their hands.

"It is him, then," she said.

"Hm?" they both asked.

"Yes, it isn't you; you were quite right about that. She is him. She comes between us there, and here it will be him."

Margot's grip on Rand fossilized.

Tick-tick-tick... *The watch keeps time that I can no longer follow.*

Our lips meet, their youth preserved in their softness. Yes, soft at first, then hardening and spreading, more slippery with each contact. Together we begin to swell and ebb, lunging against our mutual provocation, and everything that has ever occurred before this all passes before my closed eyelids like a magic lantern. Dancing shadows, and nothing more.

"It is still you and I that are connected, but he—"

"Stop it," Margot said.

"But can't you feel how—"

"*Stop*. God's sake, my 'attached spirit'," she said with exaggerated finger quotations, "didn't share a cubicle with Rand's, too." Margot's laugh was a direct echo from the Catacombs. "What are the odds, Chloé?"

Chloé's eyes blazed as her voice shook. "Why is this so difficult to believe? Why any more than how we three have come together from different lands divided by seas? Until now spinning separate lives around our centers…so many seemingly independent actions and relationships, continuing on until suddenly they appear so clearly interconnected, like the threads of a spider's web glistening in the sunlight when, just at another angle, they were invisible. These are ties dictated by an order that has crossed our paths not only now, but perhaps infinite times before. And not necessarily before or even after, but side by side. Right now, in this space, in this house, in her house—"

"So it *is* Charlotte's house. Can you tell for sure?"

"It is and it isn't. There is another who—"

"The lady has asked you to stop." Rand was already at his feet walking toward the door.

"Rand," Margot refereed.

"But what if these aren't spirits that have attached to our souls but *our souls themselves*?" Chloé cried. "Reincarnated identities, from a past that is somehow wrapped around our present, maybe our future, too, and is *still happening*. The three of us together again…and now in this house. How could we *not* sense them? And if Charlotte dies tonight! If she shares her soul with—"

"I don't suppose I ever mentioned," Rand said as he opened the unit door, "how Gwen was robbed this summer."

"What does…" Margot sighed. "Chloé, it isn't that I don't believe something supernatural is happening here, but I don't understa—"

"No?" Rand continued, stepping into the doorway between the living room and foyer. "Well, it so happened that she made the acquaintance of some – 'French slag' is how I believe she endearingly phrased it, who'd seduced her into her confidences, then got her high and tried to cuckold me in an underground stable of all places!" He laughed in his silly high pitch.

Chloé's spine straightened as the muscles in her jaw clenched. So did Margot's.

"Well," he said, looking directly at Chloé, "as far as I understand, Gwen spurned the advances, but it seems the little tart didn't go away completely empty-handed. She'd nicked an antique pocket watch, the one Gwen had purchased at auction as a gift for me and was carrying that day to obtain estimates for repair. I suppose the whole incident was humiliating for her; I had to persuade her to file a police report. Never did find the culprit, though the report was detailed enough with physical features."

Chloé stared intently ahead. Margot watched her.

"She seems to want nothing more to do with this woman," he said, "even at the expense of that watch. So I wonder if things went further than she'd let on, whether she'd wanted them to or did it just to get back at me, and, in confusion or guilt, omitted some details she did know. Perhaps a surname or *actual* first name…or where the girl was enrolled in classes." He leaned exaggeratedly to look at Margot. "Or indeed any mutual acquaintances. I presume Gwen distrusted them as much by association. I see, that does make sense now. And the scoundrel probably counted on as much, figuring she could go on unrecognized." He stepped out of Margot's sight toward the unit door. She could hear the knob wobbling loosely on its screw, probably strangled in Rand's hand. "But, well, it was a good story, anyway. I apologize that I never shared that one with you."

He remained standing there, waiting for Chloé, who said nothing but collected her clutch purse and crossed the room to the sofa where Margot sat. Unless Rand leaned over again, they were both out of his line of sight. He didn't, and Chloé bent to kiss Margot on the forehead, dropping something into her lap as she did so.

While her lips lingered at Margot's hairline, her low-hanging collar exposed her small breasts, and Margot could smell a citrusy yet grassy perfume drift off them. Then, with hesitation, Chloé's lips slackened and started to travel lower, brushing down the bridge of Margot's nose in slow succession until…

Their lips met. Soft at first, then hardening and spreading, more slippery with each contact.

With a wince in her throat, Chloé detached, her taste

buds slowly filing against Margot's teeth as she withdrew. Standing up straight, she bit her lower lip, fused her gaze to Margot's, and then walked toward the open door. Margot didn't hear Rand click on the stairwell light for her before slamming the door to his property shut.

Margot flinched at the impact and raised the silver pocket watch from her lap.

"Something she stole from you?" Rand asked as he reentered the room. If he'd just heard their interaction, he didn't reveal it.

She pressed her lips, running her tongue along their inner seam to taste the sweet, nicotine-steeped saliva that had glossed them, before sighing in exasperation. "No. It's hers. Well, yours, actually."

"Ah, the taker is a giver."

"Rand." She was exhausted.

"Margot," he imitated. "She's deceived you. And to think she's been round here before without either of us knowing. Nothing but a common thief."

She fingered the wet stain left by a teardrop Chloé had also dropped onto her thigh. "With highly uncommon means, don't you think?"

"Theft, fortune-telling, and seduction are all very old practices."

"Look, I'm not defending her, all right? I have no fucking clue what went down with Gwen," *and it could've been Chloé who wrote all that weird shit in my diary while she was over here, including today*, "but that would've been one hell of an elaborate ruse just to snatch my purse."

"Or snatch your snatch."

Okay, so maybe he *had* heard. She snorted in spite of herself, unable to refute that Chloé was at ease with her physical appetite if not her psychic ability.

Staring down at the watch's frozen hands, Margot felt the impetus to move on its behalf, to go as far as packing her things and booking the next flight to Chicago. But she just sat, thinking.

"*When two souls are connected,*" Rand eventually

repeated in her silence, *"what do you suppose happens..."* He squinted. "I don't understand what, ah, you and Chloé had been…" He moved to the sofa and sat beside her, taking the watch away and setting it on the coffee table to hold her hand again. "I mean, why she wanted to watch over you. I don't know what to expect, what may or may not happen, but regardless…"

Heat radiated into Margot's hand from his palm, and she gave a gentle smirk.

"Stop stalling, Englishman," she said softly.

Rand released his grip to caress his fingertips to and fro along her forearm.

"Well, if you'd allow it, *I'd* like to stay with you tonight."

And so, acting oblivious of the fears Chloé had planted in their minds – the fears of what consequence Charlotte's death that day could possibly have on Margot's life that night – Margot and Rand shared a small mezze platter dinner and talked late into the evening.

Staying in their day clothes, they eventually moved to her bedroom, where they lay on her mattress and continued talking to exhaustion, running the gamut of ordinary topics like work, school, religion, politics, and family as they tried to stay awake. Margot tucked herself under the sheets as he, ever the gentleman, reclined above them. But after a while, he curled an arm over her, holding her peacefully, and she soon heard his sleep-deepened breathing as her memories of the day veered and collided and shattered into the speckled blackness of an emptying mind…

Until, with a jerk, his grip on her forearm tightened.

His breath seized, and she opened her eyes to seek his in the dark.

I peer through blackness and cease respiration as I behold the pale contours of her bobbing form.

Rand shuddered and gripped Margot closely, his face wet against her neck. He caught his breath so suddenly that

Margot whirled out of her half-sleep to look at him, alarmed at his rigidity and fearing he'd had a seizure.

"Sorry. I-I'm all right," he finally uttered, out of breath. "I must've, been dreaming, stopped breathing…like, I was drowning." Margot rubbed his back as he gasped against her. "Like my lungs were collapsing…and then this heaviness, on my heart…" He curled his head back down to her chest and sobbed.

Margot wrapped her arms around him tighter and stroked his hair as she pressed her cheek to the top of his head. For everything she'd experienced that summer, this was the most frightening, and she just tried to comfort them both with her embrace.

But soon she felt it, too. Not a drowning sensation, but a hybrid of emotion that penetrated her breast profoundly.

Crying out, she heaved and twisted to clutch him.

"No. No, no!" I cry, and my scream shrills through my bones. I clutch at her body and bury my face into her wet neck.

Dampened in perspiration, they panted as they clung to each other, holding fast and quivering as a single entity.

Drenched, I cling to her, vibrating into her with all my trembling, a tragic union of two bodies, with but one soul left between us.

"No!" Margot screamed as she woke with a jolt.

Rand pulled her back down and smoothed her hair, unusually calm now for the terrors that had plagued him through the night. She stretched out her limbs and rested on her back, out of breath. He wiped her eyes, and she opened them to look at him, see him softly lit from behind by the rising sun. Gently, she laid her hand on his, where it rested beside her face.

"You're here," she said. "Now."

He grinned. "So I am. So are you."

265

V

Passing stranger! you do not know how longingly I
look upon you,
You must be he I was seeking, or she I was seeking,
(it comes to me,
as of a dream,)
I have somewhere surely lived a life of joy with you,
All is recall'd as we flit by each other, fluid,
affectionate,
chaste, matured,
You grew up with me, were a boy with me, or a girl
with me,
I ate with you, and slept with you – your body has
become not yours
only, nor left my body mine only,
You give me the pleasure of your eyes, face, flesh, as
we pass, you
take of my beard, breast, hands, in return,
I am not to speak to you, I am to think of you when I
sit alone or
wake at night alone,
I am to wait, I do not doubt I am to meet you again,
I am to see to it that I do not lose you.

~ Walt Whitman (1900)

Interlude

She I Was Seeking

19th-Century London

We have begun anew. We have, haven't we?

No one need scorn, after all, for no one need know, with the exception of ourselves, who we can mutually trust will take the past year's events to our very graves, one of us already having done so…

Ah, but my story is not yet complete. To tell it full is to return to the woman of my bedside, she who strengthened what a child had tormented with premature death and a doctor bled dry…

Following my miscarriage in April of this year, Mama, in her way, did in due course seek to bring relief to my weakening state. She had therefore compelled Victor toward her conviction that a séance would be just the solution to break this dreaded curse shrouding our house. He morosely consented; I believe he did it more so to make a spectacle of my failure than because he ever really thought such an event would bring about the desired outcome. I was humiliated, but in my weak condition could do nothing but comply.

And thus we sat late evening, outside the protection of sunlight, at the oval table in our parlor as the five-shilling medium presided with his planchette. Mama had tired of table-tipping, finding its efficacy lost after the time it had unsettled her wine, so this alternative method of divination would surely perform as prescribed.

The servants were dismissed to their quarters, all but my lady's maid, my friend, whom I demanded remain. This I declared with my eyes leveled at Victor's. He remained mute on the issue thenceforth, though did his eyes speak volumes as they flickered from her to myself. Regardless, she remained, seated at my side and Mama's. For good measure (Mama would not rest until we had acquired eight participants in sum), my brother, his wife, and a woman of Mama's acquaintance were present as well. When all were settled, the gaslights were dimmed.

After a failed attempt to contact Papa, the medium availed to summon a spirit that could bring us tidings of the future, or tap directly into the malevolent being responsible for our unhappiness such that its influence could be dispelled. As the planchette swept and swerved across the table, I did not observe any details of relevance. A spirit – revealed only to us as 'M' – appeared mildly receptive to our entreaties. 'She', according to the medium, exuded an aura of sadness, uncertainty, weakness, yet gained more power the more we communicated with her... So much so, that she began to turn the tables, so to speak, in directing questions at *us*. The medium began scribbling on a slate the messages he claimed to receive directly from 'M' and could only presume were intended for me, the pathetic focus of this distasteful exhibition, who was then to compose my responses through the planchette.

The questions were posed: my age, when I was born, and when *I died*. My mood became increasingly obstinate toward this sensational exploitation of my frailty, ever more so when the same question was repeated and Victor could not contain his smug laughter.

Meeting his eyes directly across the table in the low light, I asserted, "I live!" with a pound of my fist upon the table.

"May I, Madam?" my friend asked, releasing the planchette from my hand and gallantly laying her own calloused fingers upon it in my stead. She closed her eyes as though in deep concentration, yet her hands did not move, shuddering, rather, in place, enough so to vibrate the full surface of the table. Even in the dampened light, I could see the glint of her tears. Victor snorted.

"My dear," Mama said to her. "If it is too much…"

Slowly, she opened her eyes, though kept them lowered to her lap. She turned her head gradually toward me to say just quietly, "The dilemma is, Madam, that I cannot…"

I knew it horrified her to validate what shortcomings in education we all surely expected, yet to have it floating on the air to meet our ears; ah, my poor dear. It was courageous.

I released my own fingers from wringing in my lap and returned their tips to the planchette surface, just beside hers. "Let us spell the responses together," I said and then whispered my thought into her ear.

Her eyes illuminated with inner moonlight at this, and, together, we spelled out the emblem of our friendship – the brooch of pearl and indigo stones – to communicate to this 'spirit' all that mattered to either of us anymore, regardless of what came of my condition. We did so swiftly, before any of the rest could decipher it for his or her own amusement.

"Shall we provide our signature?" I said in mockery, to which she replied:

"Let it be my name, Madam. For your protection."

Not being superstitious, I consented and, slowly through our fingers' dance, revealed to her the symbols that spelled her own identity. And so it was that we signed off in the name of Charlotte Pidgeon and sealed a private contract that we had made with one another.

I do not know whether it was the emotion of it or the closeness of the room, perfumed now with verbena and made hazy with the low-burning gases that glowed bronze and rippled the burgundy velvet surrounding us – but I began to swoon, and Charlotte caught me in her arms as I fainted.

Our bedside friendship continued to meld and purify into something precious as through wonders of alchemy, and, in the weeks to follow, nothing unsettled my mind until one morning she did not readily come to me.

Feeling stronger and already having left my bed to walk

271

about the floor several days thus, I tested my energies in ascending the stairs to the third floor, where my friend slept when not at my side.

"Charlotte?" I called weakly when I had found my strength abandon me by the fourth step. I awaited response and, receiving none, had returned to my chamber and paced before treading down the hallway to access the servants' stairwell to the rear. Nimbly, I lowered myself down step by step, a direction which I found easier, yet I did not want to descend too far and thus obligate myself to again climb by the same distance.

I was just level with the first window I reached when I paused to call my friend's name once more. Right then, through this side window that had been raised ajar for proper ventilation, I heard a muffled cry. Moving to it, I looked out and up to where the cry seemed to lift upon the air, only for my eyes to fall on the shapely form of Charlotte. My dear girl was in Victor's bedroom above, weeping at the window.

I busied my mind with what circumstances might have brought her to this state, and at that location, which fueled my ascent up the stairwell to find her where she stood. The door had been closed but not locked, and I, as Lady of the House, opened it without requesting permission.

Admittedly in trepidation that I might not find her alone, it was with a heavy sigh that I saw she was. I strode to her at once, whereupon she sank her pink, shining face into her hands and shook with greater sobs. I held her and caressed her hair, bidding her to quiet as though she were one of the darling lost daughters that would never know my arms.

"Why, Charlotte! Whatever are you doing in here, dear? What could be the matter?"

It took some time, but eventually, I drew from her what I sought.

"My darling Hazel," she pled, "please mention nothing to Master."

"Why should I? Why should he matter?"

"It is only that he reprimanded me this morning, as you

slept."

"But why?"

"He faulted me for a task in which he found me lax. However…"

"Yes?"

"Well, I believe it is fair to say Master does not approve of my attentions to you, nor yours to myself."

I raised my brow and laughed. "Ah! Is that all? Well, my dear, we need not allow him to be a bother. I shall not be having any of that, when you have done so much to aid me, to nurse me, to—"

"I believe he finds my work to exceed my station, to transcend my duties without necessity."

"Well, never you mind him," I said and assured her Victor was best left to his own delusions; he was no threat to either of us. This seemed to offer her some solace, and her tears ceased to flow.

My fatigue persisted in the coming summer months, the rising temperatures only wearying me further. Some of our servants had begun to slack in their responsibilities and became very rude in their tones indeed, and I, in my fragile state and increasingly unstable temperament, acquiesced without argument when Victor demanded that a couple of them be dismissed on suspicion of theft besides.

This placed more burden on Charlotte, unfortunately, who became more of a maid-of-all-work in assuming their foregone responsibilities. Victor began directing orders himself, his interactions with her accumulating in number and length.

Charlotte's moods darkened, as did mine in her wake, and in our limited contact we found ourselves irritable – those times when we should have been joyful in each other's company and savoring the respite from daily drudgery. I suspect she blamed me for her demotion, and, though guilty of allowing it to happen, I still could not help but resent her for showing me less attention, and showing Victor more.

I found myself taking longer to rise out of bed – unattended as I was – and lacking motivation to do anything more than sit and cry in the servant stairwell, waiting, should Charlotte cross my path or appear again in Victor's bedroom window.

I found myself intolerant of closed doors and the secrecy that could lie therein, and if ever I saw them so, I opened them at once.

I found myself alone again, losing purpose and questioning whether not to lose my life as well. It was as though by their neglect, they had signed my death sentence, and, looking to the scar of bloodletting at my wrist, I contemplated how I might be my own executioner.

He had warmed toward her; that much was evident. Once, upon entering the parlor, I observed him touching her chin as he made a light joke of an error distressing her – a joke! When before he had chastised for these frequent, clumsy mistakes... His warm frivolity made her laugh, I recall, though her sound lacked the richness that would normally lift and cradle me. Instead, her pitch was artificially high, and it echoed emptily.

I should have taken some degree of comfort in this observation, but I was cross at her energy, at her healthy pink complexion, and without thought I mechanically mimicked her silly laugh out loud before retiring upstairs, my back turning on their surprised faces. I sought the confinement of Victor's dressing room, slamming the door to wall me inside a close privacy until I could no longer bear the sight and scent of him all around me.

When Charlotte came to me that night, I chastised her for tasks she had neglected and heaped instructions upon her to coldly assert my position.

"Yes, Hazel."

"Perhaps you ought to practice addressing me as Madam once more, in the event anyone does come calling."

"Yes, Madam."

I conducted myself thus for a little more than a fortnight

when a weeping Charlotte fell at my feet one July afternoon.

"Madam, I... Oh, Hazel! What has happened to us?"

The most frigid of hearts could not have held their stinging frost at this. My own thawed at once and dripped through my eyes.

"No," she said, "do not distress yourself so. The fault is mine. You are so pale, I refuse to drain your health further."

I might have said the same of her; her pallor was not as rosy, and her eyes appeared ringed with fatigue. So when she suggested I emerge from my living tomb, as my home now felt to me, and take a turn about the garden for fresh air, I hesitated to disagree for the good it might bring her as well.

"It has been weeks, Madam. Your circulation would benefit from the exercise, and you will have me on which to lean if it proves difficult."

I nodded dumbly at first, then eventually managed to say, "Hazel. Please." Then, "Yes, a walk. But not here."

Oh! How my ailing heart leapt on walking arm and arm with my Charlotte! We strolled through Brompton Cemetery in this way, rather than on the open street – not in shame of our fondness for one another, but in protection of it.

My lungs filled, and I thrilled in the feel of once again engaging my muscles. And yet, a tickling at the back of my neck reminded me of our visibility, and my exhilaration was checked by an increasing suspicion that someone was watching the two of us, perhaps waiting for indiscretion to feed his or her gossip at teatime.

"Let us walk this way," I said as I diverted my friend onto a smaller path that led into more shade and fewer visitors, a path with which I was all too familiar. I casually looked about – scanning for leering eyes, in actuality – and my arm, interlocked with Charlotte's, grew rigid.

"My dear, it is so nice to be held close to you," she said as she laid her opposite hand onto my forearm and emitted a sigh as she squeezed it. She seemed to lean on me as much as I on her. "I have watched you, you know. As you have slept these past weeks. I have crept into your chambers as you slumber so soundly and just stood beside you, daring not touch, but permitting myself to look over you, as I always had done. The moment you stir, however, I have hastily fled, fearing discovery."

As she said it, dreams resurfaced to me, sensations I had had whilst sleeping that someone had, indeed, been near. I had only comforted myself at those times that it was my guardian angel when most desperately needed.

Charlotte proceeded to speak as she clung to me, and her pace slackened.

"At those moments when I looked upon your face, so much more at peace in sleep than I have seen of you awake, I…I would look to the lamps and ponder turning them up… but low, just low, enough that no flames would bring light but enough that their vapors would bring us both sleep, and, through that, eternal, perfect peace. Oh, how I longed to crawl in beside you such that we might sleep forever in that way." She then smiled her satisfaction at all she viewed around her. "Darling Hazel, I feel this will always be our place."

I exhaled, cupped my hand over hers, and eventually slowed her steps further.

As we stood at the foot of my infants' shared grave – indeed, where Victor and myself will lie one day – my spine shivered and sensed an unseen presence once more. Charlotte's sympathetic hands caressed my arm as I avoided looking in any other direction but the burial plot. If someone was, in fact, spying on me, they felt so very near, and I wondered if I might not even feel the pursuer's breath upon my neck…

Perhaps it was only my guardian angel again, keeping ever-close watch if I was not to be left to my own devices. Nevertheless, preferring distraction, I bent down to pluck a flower I had planted at my unborn children's resting place and recited my Wordsworth:

thou Eye among the blind,

That, deaf and silent, read'st the eternal deep,
Haunted for ever by the eternal mind,—
Mighty Prophet! Seer blest!
On whom those truths do rest,
Which we are toiling all our lives to find,
In darkness lost, the darkness of the grave…

As I concluded the stanza and twiddled the little flower in my fingers, Charlotte pulled me closer, asking if I would prefer to return home, where she would make me some tea or draw a bath if I wished to soak after the day's exertions.

I replied that I wanted to paint her.

Once home and in my bedroom, we both took liberty to forego our restrictive outer layers and corsets for lightweight muslin that allowed us to breathe. I felt buoyant, and Charlotte's ease inspired my brush. She sat so still for me – as she always had before – and adjusted herself readily to the positions I asked of her.

As the sun sank lower in the sky, so did the shadows creep across her face, altering her appearance from what I had hoped to capture. Yet she sat there, still, looking to me so sweetly; I stood holding my brush aloft, frozen as a statue, returning that gaze.

With a rustle of muslin, I stepped around the easel to approach Charlotte and run my finger down her ivory neck. I traced it back to her cheek; then, with a finger at her jaw and my thumb on her chin, I angled her face such that it would capture more of the light.

"You have the face of an angel," I said.

Charlotte uttered nothing but held me in her eyes.

Relations between us were good again from that day on. Euphoric, I might even say. My health was returning to me, and I was able to take to our stairs with more ease. Charlotte and I maintained the façade of mistress and servant whilst occupying other floors, but how my head would become dizzy and my heart flutter on ascending that penultimate flight to my bedroom, where I always knew I would find her waiting for me, no matter what work was neglected.

It was Victor's countenance that had become more forlorn as late. A transparent man, he could never conceal his smoldering eyes when looking from me to Charlotte and her to me. Not very long, then, after we had commenced our sittings for what I entitled, *Phantom of Delight* – after Wordsworth's poem and for which I dressed her in the most liquid, translucent silks – it should not have surprised me as much as it did to climb those stairs one afternoon and find Victor there waiting for me instead.

It did not take long for him to undress me after running his hand down my back in his signature seduction, the way he would settle his hot palm at the base of my spine and make my nether region yearn to yawn open. And so I allowed him to take me in body that day although I gave heart and soul to someone else.

She had heard everything from the landing.

I would later learn from the cook that a bout of sickness had delayed Charlotte's completion of duties downstairs, which now reconciles with my memory of her ill color and slouching stature as she stood there, just one flight below us. I will not forget how she turned her face to the wall as Victor stroked her cheek with a finger on his way down to depart for business matters up north at the canal. I stood there in the doorway in my robe, useless to do anything but back into the dressing room as she started up the stairs towards me.

"What have you done?" she moaned. "Why have you done this?"

"I…" I struggled to find my tongue. "He was here, and he…he is my husband."

"But is it not me that you want? Is not this, what we have, what you wanted?"

"I don't know what I want," I replied, "nor indeed ever did." *He is my husband*, reason bade me to say again, but instead I moved to close the door against sound, only for her to draw it back open.

"You did know, once," she hissed. "When it was

convenient for you, when you had everything to gain and I nothing to lose. Well, I have lost something, haven't I? I lost it to you, and now am I to lose you as well?"

"Contain your volume."

"Contain myself, indeed! I am not the one with so much to conceal!"

"Please." I seized the air for breath, cocking my head to glance anxiously beyond the doorway for what ears might intrude. "I lack the fortitude to address this now." Firming a fist beneath my bosom, I implored in a whisper, "You must know."

"Must I?" Her spiraling waves liberated themselves from the knot I had clumsily plaited for her earlier; twitching as she spoke, they accentuated the mad glare of her red-veined eyes.

"I should hope, yes, that you do."

I saw her eyes follow my hand as it dropped to just below my naval. "I should think not," she spat before throwing the door closed as she removed herself from the dressing room.

In hindsight, covering my womb with my hand during this exchange had not been deliberate; in view of my history of swift conception, it had been an automatic gesture as I realized a feasible consequence of Victor's and my actions. That would have been enough to awaken my companion's envy, and yet was not her own sudden illness and swelling as much cause for mine?

Without any regard for how grievously the previous occasion of its kind had upset me, Mama called for another séance. Same medium, same drawing room, but differing participants. Victor did not attend. Nor did Charlotte. As it was, I had seen very little of either of them.

As her friend was also otherwise engaged, "Ah! Well, five is number enough," Mama said and assumed her seat.

This time round, I brought pen and paper with which to ponder the subject of a new painting. Mama frowned upon the unneeded clutter at the table, particularly the ink that could spoil the cloth, yet acquiesced when I asserted the activity would bring me peace and only be inspired by the proceedings rather than a distraction from them. A falsehood for certain, but it satisfied her.

Lights dimmed, the medium led us in song to a discordant melody. As we chanted our last refrain and he continued to preside, I absently began to sketch on my sheet; the first contours of my pen automatically followed the line of Charlotte's jaw from memory. I dipped my pen again to scribble that out and recommence on a different portion of the page.

Ignoring the summonings of the medium, I allowed my eyes to drift instead to my reflection, visible on a black slice of window still exposed. Occupied as such by my own visage, I sought to draw it.

My features were altered in the low light, the glass appearing like the dark waters of a still pond; I sought out its depths. Lightly, I brushed my pen tip to the paper, outlining my forehead and temples and rounding out the cheeks as I would have them look, rather than sunken and angular as they actually were.

Without separating my line of sight from my own eyes' reflection, I allowed my left hand to move mechanically. I remained transfixed, no longer aware of anything around me, just that within me. I was an old woman, I was a child, a man, a blade of grass. In the quiet recesses of my mind, I began to feel infinite, that I transcended this time that caged me in a mortal coil, and I murmured what I later saw my hand had already written – a prayer from my childhood:

Now I lay me down to sleep,
I pray the Lord my soul to keep;
if I die before I wake,
I pray the Lord my soul to take.

"Yes, take it. Do more with it than I have, I beg of you…"

"Hazel, dear!"

"Stay with us, darling. And *you*, do something!"

A cough. "Er, Margaret, ah, is that you, you naughty girl? You leave her in peace at once!"

"Hazel, Hazel! Open your eyes."

I felt the pen pulled from my grip and a hand at my shoulder, shaking it gently. A red glare signaled me to open my eyes to a brighter room and my brother at my side. My sister-in-law was already holding my right hand and patting it, whilst Mama fanned herself and asked for her salts. The medium dabbed his gleaming forehead with a handkerchief and took a swift sip from a small flask he had withdrawn from his inner coat pocket.

Remembering not only where but *when* I was, I heaved a deep breath through my nose and cleared my tightened esophagus.

"I…" I choked out. "I am all right."

Massaging my throat, I then nearly strangled myself on looking down at my drawing. Behind the words of my prayer peered a woman's face, but it was not Charlotte's, and it certainly was not my own. It was not, in fact, anyone's whom I have ever had the recollection of seeing. Most prominent were the eyes; though sketched in black ink, somehow I knew their color.

"Is that Margaret?" the medium asked of me.

"Pardon?"

"Is that a rendering of her? Did you see her, or might she have drawn a self-portrait using your hand as her instrument?"

"You silly man," my brother said. He had barely exhibited patience at the previous séance, unwilling as he is to bother with much outside his own household affairs, and with the supernatural at that. "Can *you* not provide explanation for such a thing? Must you again distress my sister with these theatrics?"

"My dear sir," the medium said with fresh indignation in his voice. "The likes of 'such a thing' are something that none of us can fully explain until we ourselves depart this plane. I am only the messenger. Raise not your sword at me."

Mama had since miraculously roused from her swoon once it had become evident no one was paying her mind. "For shame, Hazel, playing this nasty trick on the people who love you, who are trying to help you. Wherever is your mind? Your decency?"

I took my drawing in hand and rose from the chair. "If you will all please excuse me. It has been amusing, but I must respectfully withdraw to retire for the evening. I do not think you will mind seeing yourselves out." And with these last words, I parted company with my guests.

One day onward, I held my own private vigil inside our church. Kneeling in my pew, I contemplated the stained glass lit by the late afternoon sun and felt just as fragmented, wishing my pieces could fit together into as lovely a whole. I inspected the details of a saint's face, but could only see hers, the one I had begun to paint on a new canvas. *Margaret*, had he said? Yes, that was it, yet even he had not been sure; the planchette had communicated a scattering of letters close to such, with the recurrence of *M* at the beginning.

Before I could think on it more, the peace was shattered by a cry and the rumble of thunder. The cacophony grew louder, so I started to my feet and shuffled as quickly as my health would allow out the door – to nearly meet my death with horror.

No sooner had I approached the street when charging horses almost trampled my path as they rounded the corner of our square. The shrieks from within the brougham in tow were like nothing I had heard, yet I imagined them as wails on winds that swept the moors. I could hardly conceive the wretched sounds to be human until I saw the driver perform a last effort at steering the beasts to keep them to the square if they could not be tugged into submission. I eventually heard his shouts over the other screams, and it was not until the horses overcame their fright and tired to a slower pace that I recognized the man was my Victor!

He guided the beasts expertly to a stop and promptly

relieved the carriage of its weeping cargo – none other than my Charlotte.

Abandoning the carriage to a concerned bystander's charge, Victor aided our traumatized servant up the street and to our door. On noticing me standing there across the way, he frowned and lowered his eyes, then turned her back and his to me as they ascended the doorsteps, arm in arm.

I stood motionless. I ought to have been concerned for the welfare of my husband and my friend, so fatal these runaway incidents can be, yet I moved not a muscle for another minute. After this duration, I pivoted round to reenter my holy sanctuary.

Night had begun to fall when I finally returned to the house; it was hushed, with the servants dismissed until morning. Victor was seated in the drawing room, buried in his evening paper in a futile effort to conceal how visibly shaken he remained. I thought a glint of gold winked at me from his vest – yes, to be sure it was the gold chain of the watch I had given him, not the silver one he had been using to spite me, and had I not noticed it before? If so, it was what I had long hoped to see, but did it bear any meaning to me still?

He looked up to meet my eyes as I paused on the landing, but he said nothing as I continued my way up the stairs.

I found Charlotte reclining on my husband's bed. At that, whatever degree of sympathy I had believed I might conjure at her fragile sight vanished behind a lens of red.

"What were you doing in that carriage? What are you doing in this room?"

"I am only resting after the afternoon's fright. I have not been well, and was too weak to climb all of the stairs again. For that same reason, Victor had offered me the ride home from market when he spied me along his route."

"Do not lie to me."

"It is the truth. And Victor wished me to lie on a bed more comfortable than my own besides." Slowly, she sat up to rise.

"He is 'Master' to you. Mind that you remember your place."

Appearing to ignore my slight, she gingerly stood and stepped toward me, taking my elbows gently into her hands as she always had done before. "Your bed would have been my preference, but for the chance it would become overly crowded when dignity again surrendered to attention."

"Take your hands from me," I seethed. "Am I really to believe you feared Victor coming to my bed now that you keep his own so warm?"

She did remove her hands, but not before she had gripped me tighter and thrust me aside – though small, toil had strengthened her – to exit his bedroom and enter my own. On recovering my balance, I rubbed my shoulder where it had bruised against the wall and joined her in time to rescue my jewelry case before she threw it into my mirror. She had proceeded to disrupt my bookshelves and the washbasin when she appeared to first notice my newest artistic endeavor, contemplating its subject with bewildered yet scalding eyes. Right then, she seized my inkwell from its stand – ah, perhaps Victor's disgust that ever I brought ink into my chamber was justified after all!

"Charlotte, no! Must we endure this again?" I shouted, but my cries fell upon deaf ears. She had commenced smearing ink over the face that had so haunted me of late, blackening those piercing eyes I had instinctively rendered the color of my name.

"Must we endure this again?" I asked once more.

She hastened to complete her artwork before replacing the ink on its stand, the latter a peculiar act of decorum.

"Ah, but there is nothing to fill you with trepidation, my dear," she goaded with false consolation. "Why, you will never be alone for as long as you have *her*." She pointed toward my canvas with blackened fingertips. "What was her name again? Was your table-tipper ever able to determine letters to follow the mysterious '*M*'?"

From the banshee cries of her day's accident to this, my evening's nightmare as she howled; it was ugly, foul. I scarcely recognized in her the woman whom I loved and scarcely recognized in me the woman capable of such love.

"You ought to refine that laughter of yours." I frowned in return with the only defense left to me. "It would be most unpleasant if you betrayed your breeding whilst enjoying one of the multitude of soirées upon which you must be so certain you shall encroach. It would be a pity indeed for some gracious benefactor to spoil your champagne when he tosses a shilling into your glass as alms."

At this, she clenched her smile into a tight line and kicked one of the easel's legs out from beneath. As it collapsed, she raised a fist and threw the object contained within it toward me; before I could observe precisely what it was, I felt it prick the forearm with which I had shielded my face. I looked down to see the brooch, which she must have had opportunity to reclaim. My knees yielded and sank me to the floor.

Charlotte stepped over me to leave, but not before saying, "Do not fool yourself that he again carries that golden trinket on your account. It is a matter of practicality, his silver one having gone missing. He informed me of such one of our nights."

As water seeped across the floorboards to soak my dress, I once again felt drowned in a circumstance beyond my control. Seeing Victor rescuing Charlotte from that carriage, our carriage… It appeared my husband had found someone more agreeable to him, someone who could pleasure him whilst paining me, and in so doing would pleasure him twofold. Threefold if she could bear him a healthy child.

Of only one thing was I certain as I fondled the blackened brooch and wept in my puddle on the floor: my options were unequivocally spent.

As a newborn cries when it exits its watery world for the one of air, so I gasped and sobbed in Victor's arms when he lifted me from the bath.

It had happened that he could not avoid hearing the pounding and shouts overhead, and he had tarried in venturing to my side only because, as soon as he had deemed his interference necessary, Charlotte had already been winding her way back downstairs, clinging to the banister with all her weight upon it. He had been alarmed to see her thus after the shock she had received earlier and started towards her to assist her back to bed. It was then he had observed the ink on her hands and flinched at the sight of a measure of blood – she must have been clenching the brooch with what strength remained before hurling it back at me, the one to whom she had originally gifted it with such opposite passion.

He had known not else what to do but wrestle her from the banister, carry her to the top floor, and force her into her own bed. Her resistance conquered, she had collapsed and allowed her eyes to close.

He had not been prepared for the ravages he next beheld in my bedroom. In a panic, he then discovered me. I had only just submerged myself into the cool waters left from the previous soak, having had the opportunity to delight in my body's airless anguish for but a few seconds.

And so, he cried with me as he wiped the hair from my eyes and kissed my scalp, rocking me as he would the infant I may never give him. Never could I have fathomed at that moment – then, when I should not have expected to escape Death's icy embrace – that in a mere day thence I would be rocking in dreadful imitation of this with another in my arms.

Tick-tick-tick… The sound creeps into my eardrums as I remember how I heard the hands of Victor's pocket watch – indeed the gold one, my gift to him – regulate my heartbeat the following evening, measuring out the time as he held me close and recited Wordsworth to me. He had earlier found the recent painting of Charlotte concealed behind the wardrobe and lauded the delicate shading and illumination that brought 'household motion' to my subject's clothes, whereas the 'angelic light' he said he beheld in me.

He stood there and traced his hand down my spine,

pressing my hips closer to his arousal; he had just returned from the canal, and I could smell his sweat and the hay of the horse stables. He then murmured Wordsworth's poem softly as his lips brushed my forehead and moved down the bridge of my nose in slow succession until there it was – I belonged to him again, and everything prior passed before my closed eyelids like the dancing shadows of a magic lantern. From then, we were "no more twain, but one flesh," as is writ in scripture, and no man nor woman would again put us asunder so long as he had anything to do with the matter.

Betwixt the ticking of his watch and the rhythm of our sighs, would there have been any way for us to notice her standing outside the door, listening when we had thought her asleep after granting her a day of seclusion and rest upstairs? Can we even now be certain she ever was?

But of course I can, when a sob that rose on the air and cut through my consciousness alerted me to the sash in time to see a stream of translucent white billow in the night wind. In that moment, the truth at last met with my recognition: it was never I who had no options. It had been Charlotte, always.

"No. No, no!" I cried when, by midnight, we finally found her in the riverbank, bobbing atop the current in her spoiled white muslin, the reeds and filth tangled in her curls.

"No!" she screamed as she woke with a jolt.

He pulled her back down and smoothed her hair. She stretched out her limbs and rested on her back, out of breath, and he wiped her eyes.

"You're here," she said. "Now."

He grinned. "So I am. So are you."

She saw the morning light peer around the window shade. Shoving her jaw into her clavicle, she looked down the length of her body. "Yes," she said.

He drew the kicked-away covers back over her. Releasing her head back, she rolled it to watch him fall quickly to sleep. She had no concept of the time.

"You're here," she whispered, counting his breaths until she faded from consciousness once more.

They lay asleep, intertwined tightly, their eyelashes resealed with tears.

Ah! The price we have paid. The price *she* paid, rather, for we both.

She shall lie buried wearing that brooch, my Charlotte. I know this because I shall bury her. We shall, Victor and I.

The mirrors have all been covered, the clocks stopped. Not even Victor's golden watch utters a tick, only points in stiff fright to that horrid midnight hour.

Perhaps we owe Charlotte nothing; perhaps we owe her everything. Perhaps we ought not ponder any longer what we owe at all.

We shall spare no expense, nevertheless, in securing our girl a proper grave and private ceremony in our cemetery. All we shall deny her is a proper formality such that our own lives can move forward without further dissection beneath a coroner's eyes. "Leave it buried in this vault," as I shall commission the stone to say.

She woke a few more times through the day to the sound of her sobs, her sweaty hair pasted across her forehead for him to wipe away and kiss time after time, just like she'd cradled his whimpers through the night.

It will never be what it could have been, or it will be what it could have only ever been…to live it over would be to live it the same.

Or perhaps it is true what some will say – whether the superstitions of our pastimes or the philosophies of all ages – that none of us ever really die, that we are all part of a much larger continuum than we can mortally comprehend.

As the sky once more dimmed into the purple haze of dusk, they still lay there stretched out on their backs, eyes on the ceiling. Staring at this blank canvas, she couldn't get over how substantially the number of floaters in her eyes had decreased since the day before.

"So," he started, breaking their long period of silence.

"Mm?"

"What happened between us, exactly?"

After mulling it over, she said, "It felt like grieving."

"It did. But then…"

"Right, there's something else now, isn't there, something stronger, like…"

He turned to murmur the rest in her ear.

"Yes," she whispered back, smiling at him.

After a little while, she propped up on her elbows and swung her feet restlessly.

"Anxious now?" he asked.

"No, just…light. I feel light. I can breathe again." When he said nothing, she asked, "Really, though, are you all right?"

"Just as sodding confused as you are. It was a release, though, wasn't it?"

"Like hitting bottom before rising again."

He returned onto his back and laid his fingers at his chest. "'When two souls are connected,'" he repeated, "'what do you suppose happens when one of them dies?'"

She rolled to her side, the fingers of one hand playing at her lips while the others tickled at the buttons on his chest. She poked at them one by one, in steady rhythm with a new sound she heard behind her.

"They still carry on, I think," she answered as she looked over at the silver pocket watch on the desk and realized it had just started ticking.

I recall from one of Mama's séances an exotic man who professed our souls not only cycle through multiple lives, but that time itself also coils in such a way that our past, present, and future existences all occur at once, side by side. Relationships repeat themselves in some form or other until all possible iterations are exhausted as the wheel spins…a parent of someone in one life, a brother, sister, friend, or lover in the next…and our impact on any one of these lives is retroactive as well as proactive, as we simultaneously influence our past and future selves every time we err and redeem.

I cannot speak to this matter, running contrary as it does to the tenets with which I was raised, yet – well, if I could live it again, but differently…

Perhaps what Charlotte and I have lost in this time might then be found in another, spared the turbulence that has occurred so needlessly here and now. Perhaps if the woman I saw in the glass – 'Margaret' – is me as much as I am she… Well, if anything worthy I have ever mustered in my life should manifest as a blessing in hers, then might she find my happiness and enjoy the fortune of falling asleep with a quiet mind at peace with the dark.

We shall begin by snuffing out the light.

Chapter Eighteen

A New Soul

21st-Century London

And in that instant, Margot had never felt so present. Looking at the silver pocket watch on the desk, she sat up to observe the regulated movement of the second hand, tried to meet its equilibrium.

"You know," she said, "a pint sounds fucking marvelous right now."

"It's not exactly as I may have described, you realize," Rand began after passing Margot a cider at the corner pub.

She'd tried calling Chloé beforehand, but she wasn't answering. Margot couldn't blame her, only hoped that ignoring her calls was the worst action her friend would take.

She saw clearly, now, the risk Chloé had taken in revealing herself to Rand and in turn revealing him to Margot. The risk of having such a gift that could make one look insane or untrustworthy, an opportunist if not a thief. A risk she'd taken only to help them all find answers, who they really were – or once had been. No matter Chloé's method, her sincerity of motive was no longer Margot's to question, and she would have to tread her remorse delicately. But in the meantime...

"What's not as you described?" she asked Rand.

They wove over to a booth tucked in the corner.

"What I've seen."

"Ah, so you're going to modify your story now, are you? I mean, besides that one critical detail of, 'Oh wait, it wasn't

Gwen who saw the ghost, it was me'!" She face-palmed herself.

"Listen, cheeky, you can imagine where I was coming from, can't you?"

He admitted that, other than the occasional blue vapor, Lady Grey wasn't so much an image that he visibly saw as something he felt within, and so often when standing near his window. What he sensed was not merely the weeping but a femininity as diffused yet distinct as a spray of perfume into the air.

"It's always felt too close to me, too visceral, to not be Sophie. And in a strange way, I'm happy to bear my sister's grief if it might mean she doesn't have to, wherever she is. Though it's more than grieving some of the time. Most of the time, actually, there's been something much stronger, the same as you and I felt today after the pain and sorrow had passed."

"Great love," Margot said, quoting his earlier whispered words.

"Which I know she was also capable of."

"Like her big bro."

"Yes, well, I've always known I'm capable. It's more a matter of… But getting back on point, you *have* actually seen the woman, you said."

She nodded. "Which does make sense if she wasn't the one attached to me but to *you*. Because the other one…in the dreams and hallucinations…she was me. I mean, I saw everything from her point of view, not her image unless vaguely in a reflection." Drawing lines in the faint condensation on her glass, she mulled over the previous night. "If Chloé were to be right that this isn't about people who are dead but still living in, like, some other dimension, I can see her concern that sort of 'living' this other person's life could've meant dying with it as well."

He screwed his mouth to the side and looked to the table.

"Today in eighteen seventy-four," Margot said, "Charlotte Pidgeon is dead. I can say that much for sure. But that's all. And I can't help but think if we were meant to know or understand any more than that it would be easier than this. For any of us."

The room fell quiet to match their silence until Duran Duran's "Ordinary World" crooned into the atmosphere. Margot's gaze slow-danced along the swirled pattern of the pub's dark velvet wallpaper as she sang along in her thoughts, taking the evocative melody of mourning and moving on as a sign. Picking up Rand's hand and intertwining their fingers, she said nothing more to contradict or affirm his beliefs, only hoped to impart, through her eyes and the way her thumb rolled over and under his, the wisdom of what he needed to do.

He pinched his lips with a small nod.

She felt the truth reverberate onto herself, and cradled it in her lowered eyelids as the must of aged and ale-dampened wood wafted to her nose. She nodded as well and thought of her impending return home.

Another hand wrapped around hers just as she was about to take it away.

"I'm sorry I never got to meet her," she said to puncture the heavy silence, wondering which of his traits Sophie had shared, if she'd had his warmth, his humor.

"Me, too."

Within the soothing heat of his palms, she weighed her next words carefully. "I think it's best I never meet *her*, though."

Rand bobbed his head at the reference to his other 'her'. After a labored pause, he said, "I care for Gwen. I do. Though I've come to wonder if that's enough when I don't seem to…that is to say, the way I have been, the way I do for…"

His mind and heart seemed at war again. Margot had no idea what she expected him to say, but it definitely wasn't what he did.

"I suppose it could have been this Charlotte haunting me. Or *being* me, as it were. Her weakness tapping into mine. Here it was her death day, and I felt *I* might have died. With you suffering beside me, through it all."

He tightened his grip on her hand and stroked her forearm as he had the night before. Slowly, just slowly, his fingertips dragged and glided, tickling at the delicate skin of her inner elbow.

"Well, I can say the same of you. This entire summer. Rand, I…" Margot cleared her throat, then swallowed, a deliberate delay to keep her voice from breaking. "It's just that I never would've gotten through all this without you. I have this amazing support system back home that I purposely left, never expecting to walk into another one here. It's like I deliberately pulled the rug out from under myself to see if I could land on my feet. I've always had everything so good; things have always come so easy, I never felt truly tested until this year."

"Life throws us enough challenges that are outside our control. Why choose to bring them on yourself? Enjoy it when things are good, easy."

Such similar words but by such a different speaker, which colored them with profoundly more meaning for her.

"Says someone who's had to deal with grief beyond my worst nightmares," she said, "and lived to tell about it. While I've just been sitting pretty and waiting to get blindsided. I'm so unprepared."

"For what? How can you prepare for the unknown?"

"I just want to know I can handle it, whatever it is. That I'm who I'm meant to be and can get on by myself if I have to, in case, I don't know…" She looked to the table and cleared her throat again, feeling her expression crumple into the emotion she'd hoped to hide. "In case everyone else leaves." Rand's light tracing along her arm became a firmer caress. "The thing is, I walk before they can. It's easier to be the one running away than the one left behind. Even when I already am."

"Who's 'they'? Who's left you behind, Margot?"

She heard her mother's voice: *"Margot, what is it? James? Your job?"* She shook her head and closed her eyes, concentrating on the warm friction on her arm as Rand's palm soothed the thoughts from her.

Yes, Mom. It's James. The job. It's you and Dad, aging every year away from me when all I really want is to be your little girl and forever feel that security. It's George growing up, getting married, and having a family of his own, playing Ghost in the Graveyard with his daughter instead of his kid sister. It's friends starting to do the same, professionals and parents displacing me in their priorities while I'm in some stunted state of adolescence. Rand and Gwen'll play house someday, too... And Derek and Chloé might still be figuring out their shit, but people like them are at least more worldly and comfortable in their skin than I've ever been... Or Sylvie, whose perpetually positive attitude makes me feel like I quit before I start...quit before the Peter Principle inevitably ties my shoes together and I trip, right? Never get fired, never get dumped if I make the preemptive strike? I was never enough for James to stay behind for and never would've been. It was only a matter of time...

Rand just sat silently as all these thoughts flooded her. He didn't stop stroking her arm, and he didn't press her to answer his question. Margot looked up and met his gaze, considering what those eyes had witnessed that summer. Her, at her absolute worst.

Yet there he was. Sitting beside her. Looking back at her with a depth in those blue eyes that said a lot of things she couldn't be certain of but calmed her all the same. She opened her mouth to speak, but instead just breathed softly through it and kept staring at him.

"You're right," he finally said, "to assume we'll never know the answers, really. But what I do know now is that I also feel light, like I can breathe again as well for the first time in years. I do think I'm ready to let Sophie go. I feel she's let go of me, at any rate."

He raised his hand to brush his fingers up Margot's cheek and tuck her hair behind her ear, his thumb lingering at her cheekbone to dust back and forth across it. He pressed his lips together and appeared to measure his next words as he searched her face.

"What I don't think I'll be ready for, is letting *you* go."

Turning the corner on their way home from the pub, they walked side by side in silence. Margot kept her eyes focused on the sidewalk, watching the play of light and shadow from the streetlamps and wrought iron fencing until something pale crept into her peripheral vision, and then just as soon streaked out of it.

A moment later, it returned. A hand, hesitantly reaching for hers. Catching it and clasping it in place. She looked up and returned Rand's shy smile.

Once they entered the square and stepped into the shadow of the church, she felt her arm lag behind the rest of her body. Rand had stopped walking, and, with Margot still in his grip, his moonlit grin beckoned her back.

Raising an eyebrow at him, she backtracked the couple of paces and let him take her into his arms. Night obscured his face, but it couldn't extinguish the sparkle in his eyes.

He cleared his throat. "I, uh…I'll need a little time," he started. "Just to sort things properly."

Dumbly, Margot nodded.

"But she already knows it's over. She's in denial of that, but she does know how I feel." When Margot furrowed her brow, he explained, "I broke up with her weeks ago. At least I tried to, but she insisted we work things out. Take a break first, if we must. So I compromised with her just to buy a little more time. Not for me, but for her, to adjust to the idea and hopefully accept it. See that it's the best for both of us."

Margot slowly tipped her head back in realization.

"But I don't want to be deceitful in all this," he said. "I need to call things off officially, and she deserves to know the full reason why."

She swallowed. "And what's that?"

He released an arm from her back to brush the hair off her face. Leaving his palm at her jaw, he again swept his thumb across the apple of her cheek.

"Well, first I'll tell you what she doesn't need to know." With his other hand at her waist, he drew her even closer. "How keen I am to kiss you, Miss Margot." He shuffled on his feet, lowering his face to hers until their foreheads touched. "How I've wanted to hold you like this for some time. And how if you ever run away again..." He tipped his chin up slightly, which touched the tip of his nose to hers. "I *will* follow you, cheeky girl. If you'll have me."

Standing there in the square, surrounded by stately Victorian columns in the still of the summer night, Margot reckoned she had just been made love to in the traditional sense. Feeling his breath dust across her lips, she lifted her chin, too, to where their mouths could meet. With eyes closed, she savored the nearness of his scent and the tickle of his eyelashes blinking against her own. Then, feather-light, his tentative lips brushed hers. Once. Twice...

They both leaned into the kiss, slowly eased into it, taking precious time exploring each other's contours and drawing energy from the magnetic charge of the connection. Rand held Margot's face as her fingertips glided along the firm curve of his back, down to the waist that pressed against hers as a modest preview of the wonderful yin and yang their bodies would make. Two beings exchanging thoughtful breath, filling each other as they surely had for lifetimes.

In the quiet space that followed the eventual separation of their lips, Rand cupped the back of her head as he brought his forehead to hers again. Nudging her face up to give him an affectionate peck, she then leaned back to focus on him and process that she wasn't dreaming he was standing there, with her, like this, in the flesh. Then she looked to the sky.

Gazing at the moon for several quiet seconds, Margot contemplated how in running away, she'd been running toward this, the entire time. She hadn't wanted to belong to anyone, not understanding until now how it felt to have someone want to belong to her, and that it wasn't really about belonging *to* each other in the end, but with.

She tightened her arms around Rand's waist and nestled her head against his chest. Listened to his heartbeat fall into step with hers. And like this, she gave up the ghost.

Postlude

Sunlight licks the leaves of late afternoon. I stride with purpose, tickling the tall grasses with my fingertips and picking a few of the blooming weeds.

I sidestep the pigeons flapping around the bounty of seeds scattered at their feet. I smile at the elderly couple seated on a bench, holding hands and pointing at a crow. I laugh with the young couple moseying behind a pram as their little girl runs squealing from an aggressive squirrel.

By light of day when graveyards are supposed to be their most dead, it is not.

Coming to a stop, I fumble with my fingers. Rather than wring out anxiety, the twisting and pinching produces a daintily bound nosegay of wildflowers.

I whisper:

"Though nothing can bring back the hour
Of splendour in the grass, of glory in the flower;
We will grieve not, rather find
Strength in what remains behind."

Stepping forward to kneel, I lay my impromptu bouquet on the grasses to kiss the twinkling grains of Charlotte Pidgeon's headstone.

"Wordsworth," I say, then glance around to ensure I'm out of earshot – not because I'm embarrassed to be seen talking to myself, but because this is a private conversation, after all. "See, I did do some research, Charlotte. I'm more of a Whitman fan myself, though. You know, free verse, liberated from convention. Though I guess all that was after your time."

I only recently found Wordsworth's ode in Rand's

anthology and recognized some of its other lines, the ones I'd fallen asleep to in the cemetery.

"At first I thought it was you, Charlotte, who recited that to me. But now I wonder if it wasn't one of the Pierces."

I look over my shoulder at the family plot I slept on that unusual Bastille Day. I ran past it earlier during my daily jog – a new regimen – and finally took a closer look at the headstone. The fact that the Victor Albert Pierce buried there matches the initials on Chloé's pocket watch wasn't lost on me. Nor was the rush of familiarity I felt on uncovering another name at the bottom:

HERE ALSO REPOSES
HAZEL PIERCE
WHO WAS MOST DEVOTED
AND AFFECTIONATE
TO THE ABOVE
"NOT LOST BUT GONE BEFORE"

Hazel. The color of my eyes. But maybe we share much more in common than that. I could consult the National Archives, really 'dig up' the Pierces' story, so to speak. See if Victor had owned Rand's house, if he's related to or employed a Charlotte Pidgeon, or if he looked at all like the man Chloé sees in her mirror. Little way to prove, though, if it was Hazel who returned to London this summer to rest her head on the same patch of grass where she's buried.

A union of two bodies with but one soul between us.

A shiver rolls down my spine at the possibility. "Maybe this *is* all meaningful coincidence, bringing us together like this," I whisper to Charlotte. "Explaining why you'd take my pin as a kid and start talking to me so many years later through that spirit board." Squinting at the grass at my feet, I contemplate what might lie below. "If you did take Grandma Grace's brooch, it's okay. I don't need it anymore. I'm finding peace in life and hope you find it in death."

I go to turn, but stop.

"And maybe you aren't dead, Charlotte," I say, "but I'm

definitely not, so it's time to break some cycles and reset others."

That was advice I did take away from Fitz, whose help was ironically the first cycle I decided to break after one more session. I like to think I was gracious about it, though, expressing my gratitude at our final meeting, then kindly asserting I'd take it from there. It really hurt when Fitz's hug mashed her enormous cowry shell necklace into my breastbone.

I also heard back from my boss – finally – who said that, unfortunately, my replacement is staying on in my old position and another won't be opening any time soon; times are tougher than were anticipated in the first quarter of the year. They could use a long-term temp, though, that could turn into a full-time role if things get better. While a huge demotion from what I left behind, it would be working with my same creative team and is mine for the taking if I want it.

With a laugh and shake of my head, I have to congratulate myself on managing to come full circle and even moonwalk back a few steps...

And yet, reluctant as I am to stare down my asshole art director again, I think I *will* take that job. At most, it's the un-easy way out I was apparently looking for in the first place, the challenge that could make me work harder for what I want.

And at the very least, I can save up starter money to open that vintage shop with Sylvie. I can't wait for her visit, when we can hash out the details, the real ones, centering on an inventory that will combine the old with the new-that-reinvents-the-old, even if it can only be sold online at first. After a productive brainstorm with Rand, the broad strokes of a business plan and website design already dance across the pages of my diary, moving one pipe dream into the pipeline. Maybe it won't happen in the short run, and maybe it won't succeed in the long one. But it's a spontaneous whimsy that can still be planned on and worked for, a beautiful opposition from my point of view.

Sylvie's clapping and squealing left a ringing in my ear after I pitched the idea via video chat.

Even Chloé is pleased to play a part. Fortunately, forgiveness has come easily to her as she attempts to give up her own ghost by reconciling to live with it…and all the others she sees. She's already planned an itinerary that will tour us three ladies through the boutiques of *her* Paris. She insists those places are the best for stylistic inspiration and for starting the store's collection. As it is, our stock is already plus one silver pocket watch, thanks to Rand's eager donation.

Only after he'd reimbursed Gwen for it, of course. It was only fair, considering…

"It's also time for *you* to make way for another soul mate," I tell Charlotte, "the one of this century who's been complicating my heart in a most inconvenient, lovely way." Yes, it means another long-distance relationship for a while, but this isn't a doomed-to-repeat-history situation. It's not about either of us trying to have our cake and eat it, too; visas, jobs, and property just aren't easy to sort. Yet I look up at the sweet face appearing before my mind's eye and smile. "We'll see. Time will tell."

Until then, I still have over a couple of months left on my student visa to exploit. When school ends, I'll stay on in London at Rand's flat until my temporary leave to remain expires.

And with his guest bedroom now available every night, I look forward to hosting two sets of visitors there in the near future: Sylvie, of course (much at the envy of Derek, who can't spare the airfare to England but did finally call his ol' pal at the end of his ego's respectable recovery period), as well as my mom and dad, who can't wait to bring all sorts of Union Jacked-out souvenirs back to George and his family. Of all the faces populating my vision in this instant, I see myself reflected in each one, multiple facets that make me whole. Reminding me that being myself doesn't mean having to be *by* myself.

Blowing a kiss to the grave, I exit to the city streets,

brimming with life in the here and now and there and then.

THE END

Fantastic Books
Great Authors

CROOKED
CAT

Meet our authors and discover our exciting range:

- Gripping Thrillers
- Cosy Mysteries
- Romantic Chick-Lit
- Fascinating Historicals
- Exciting Fantasy
- Young Adult and Children's Adventures

Visit us at:
www.crookedcatpublishing.com

Join us on facebook:
www.facebook.com/crookedcatpublishing

Made in the USA
Charleston, SC
07 September 2016